Bane of GIANTS

LEGACY OF SHADOWS

Bane of GIANTS

LEGACY OF SHADOWS

TODD FAHNESTOCK

F4 PUBLISHING

Cover Art by:
Rashed AlAkroka

Cover Design by:
Rashed AlAkroka, Sean Olsen, Melissa Gay & Quincy J. Allen

Map Design by:
Sean Stallings

Ordering Information:

Quantity sales. Special discounts are available on quantity purchases by corporations, associations, and others. For details, contact us via our website.

Bane of Giants / Todd Fahnestock — 1st ed.

ISBN: 978-1-952699-60-3

DEDICATION

For Becky Busch,
A true light in the world, now and forever.

What is Eldros Legacy?

The Eldros Legacy is a multi-author, shared-world, mega-epic fantasy project managed by four Founders who share the vision of a new, expansive, epic fantasy world. In the coming years the Founders committed themselves to creating multiple storylines where they and many others will explore and write about a world once ruled by tyrannical giants.

The Founders are working on four different primary storylines on four different continents. Over the coming years, those four storylines will merge into a single meta story where fates of all races on Eldros will be decided.

In addition, a growing list of guest authors, short story writers, and other contributors will delve into virtually every corner of each continent. It's a grand design, and the Founders have high hopes that readers will delight in exploring every nook and cranny of the Eldros Legacy.

So, please join us and explore the world of Eldros and the epic tales that will be told by great story tellers, for Here There Be Giants!

We encourage you to follow us at www.eldroslegacy.com to keep up with everything going on. If you sign up there, you'll get our newsletter and announcements of new book releases. You can also follow up on Facebook at:

facebook.com/groups/eldroslegacy.

Sincerely,

Todd, Marie, Mark, and Quincy
(The Founders)

MAPS

PROLOGUE

The group stopped running, and Davi bumped into Margery. It was far too soon to stop. They shouldn't be stopping for hours.

That could only mean the monsters had found them.

He tried to stop his panting, to hold perfectly still, to be a hole in the darkness. The hairs on the back of his neck stood on end—

"So full of fire ... So full of delicious fire ..." A voice whispered from the absolute dark before him. He knew that voice, soft and mocking. It had said those same words before slaughtering his family.

Now he had a new family, and his new family's hope had just vanished. The monsters had found them. They were going to die.

Davi and the others had been running blind forever, it seemed. Maybe weeks. He couldn't really tell anymore since the days had vanished. There were no sunrises, no sunsets, nor anything in between. There was nothing left except the long, frightening dark.

The leader of Davi's new family was called Aven, and he had a plan: to run through the endless, timeless night to the crown city of Usara.

Davi's new family was faceless. He'd never seen them before—couldn't see them now. Like the days themselves, people had vanished also. Now there were only voices, comforting hands, frightened sobs. No one was tall or short; no one was wrinkled or rosy cheeked. Every new person he met looked only how he envisioned them in his mind.

Davi imagined Aven's head like a block of wood with fierce eyes, his body tall and indestructible, with stout wooden limbs. He ordered them to hike high into the mountains. He'd come up with the idea to find the highest ground and climb the tallest tree to see where they were, because he'd known that the noktum only rose a hundred feet into the air. So in some places, the trees broke that ceiling, and a climber could see the old world, could see the sun or the stars, could see where they were going.

Aven said they were navigating their way south to the crown city of Usara. He said Queen Rhennaria could protect them. Surely she would have a plan.

Margery was another that Davi imagined in his mind. He saw her as an orange, with a wide orange smile, kindly eyes, and a big hat.

Aven was the leader, but Margery was the one Davi loved the most. She ran close to him when they traveled across the uneven ground, made sure he didn't get separated from the group. When they stopped running, she gathered him into her arms and held him until he cried himself silently to sleep. He knew how to cry silently now. He had learned that quickly. They all had.

Margery acted like Davi was her own child, and maybe now he was. This was his new family, after all. He'd never asked Margery and she had never mentioned it, but Davi was sure she'd had children. He was also sure her children had died just like Davi's family had died.

Their deaths never left his head, but he could push them down when he concentrated, or when he was running frightened. It was only when he stopped to rest, when he was exhausted, that the memories flooded back ...

The darkness slithered in through the windows of their little house. It slipped under the door, and filled the rooms with absolute, choking blindness. Then the monsters came.

Woodchip, their dog, growled and leapt out from under the bed when the monsters shattered the window. Woodchip's barking, his launching forward, and the glass breaking woke Davi with a jolt. He'd been sleeping underneath the bed with Woodchip because the dog wasn't allowed on top of his new quilt. Woodchip attacked the thing, whatever it was, scrambling out from under the bed and leaping at the window—

He died with a yip and a horrible snapping sound.

Davi's sister died next. He heard her screams from the other room as they ripped her apart.

"You're so full of fire ... So full, and we're so hungry ..." a cruel, mocking voice whispered from the dark, whispered the words that burned in Davi's mind.

Father shouted amidst the sound of breaking furniture. He growled, grunted, then gasped. Mother begged for mercy, then screamed amidst the sickening wet sound of bones breaking.

Then the whole house went horribly silent.

Davi stayed frozen, unable to speak or even breathe, under the bed. Margery would later tell him that was what had saved his life. That was why the monsters hadn't found him.

And that was where Margery and Aven had found him,, hungry and shivering, when they'd taken him in ...

Now the monsters had come again, and nothing could stop them. The monsters could see. His new family was blind. You couldn't stop a creature you couldn't see, especially a creature that could crack Human bones in their bare hands.

Davi heard Aven grunt, like a man swinging a sword, but the cruel voice chuckled.

Aven made a choking sound, like someone had grabbed his

throat. Bones snapped and Davi heard the sword fall to the dirt. Aven let out a strangled moan.

"So much fire …"

"Hold onto me, baby," Margery whispered desperately. She grabbed Davi, crushed him to her chest, and repeated the words over and over as though they could save them both. "Hold onto me … Hold onto me …"

Davi thought he felt the breath of one of the monsters on his neck, thought he heard that horrible laughter—

White light flared.

For one chaotic instant, Davi saw a flash of trees and bodies all around him, glimpsed a thin man with pointed ears holding Aven by the neck and a dozen others just like that standing so near all of them, black fingers extended.

In that one instant, he saw horror on the monster's face, saw its mouth open—

Then the light blinded Davi.

Screams erupted somewhere in front of him, but the screams weren't his new family. It was the monsters.

Blood and flesh slapped Davi's face.

I'm dead, he thought. *This is what death feels like. They have eaten me open, and I just don't feel it yet. I just don't …*

But the gore slid down his neck, down his arms, and still he felt no pain. The gore turned cold, and he realized it wasn't his flesh, wasn't his blood.

The glowing spots in Davi's eyes faded, and his sight returned for the first time since the fall of the dark.

He stood on a slanted, rocky clearing. Tall pine trees extended down the slope to his left and rose up to a ridge on his right.

Aven's group huddled in a line, hands up like they expected to be hit. Splatters of blood covered all of them. Ragged piles of bone and flesh radiated out from more than a dozen spots, all of them near Aven's people.

At the front of the line stood a man in red robes. His wavy red hair curled around his pale forehead, and he grinned.

"Well, that worked a treat," he said.

A mage! The man was a mage!

Behind the mage were more creatures, but they weren't the slender, pointed-eared people that the mage had just, apparently, exploded. These were ten foot tall, hulking creatures with crusty, stony skin and heads set low between their huge shoulders. There were three of them, and their glowing red eyes focused on the mage. One had a stone axe, the other two held what looked like small tree trunks, branches trimmed off to form crude clubs. The stony monsters lifted their weapons and started toward the mage.

They cringed at the miniature star that glowed twenty feet in the air above the mage's head, but still they came on, as though they knew if they could just kill that mage, the light would vanish.

Those were Trolls!

"Red man," one of them grunted. "Red man makes light."

"Well, we might need Khyven now," the mage said, looking to his right.

Davi glanced in that direction. There had been no one there a second ago, but now a tall woman—who looked just like the pointed-eared monsters —stood there. Her midnight hair had a single golden lock at her brow that glowed with its own inner light. She had a severe look on her angular face, and she wore a floor-length cloak. She opened it, and a big man, even taller than her, stepped out. He wore a chainmail shirt, a curved steel plate on one of his wide shoulders, and he bristled with weapons. Two swords and a dagger stuck up from his waist. A dagger was also strapped to one of his thighs. Another enormous sword hilt poked over his right shoulder. In the harsh light, Davi could see light scars across the man's tanned face, across the bridge of his nose, chin, and jaws.

"Khyven, would you mind?" the mage asked politely, like he was asking the man to pass the salt.

The mage had called that man Khyven … All the weapons. The scars. The armor. Wait …

Is that Khyven the Unkillable? Davi thought.

The Ringer smiled at the Trolls, but it was nothing like the mage's happy smile. The flash of Khyven's teeth made Davi think of sharpened steel.

The Trolls grunted, looking between the mage and Khyven, seemingly confused about which to attack.

Khyven took the choice away from them. He leapt at the closest threat. The Troll turned to meet the charge, a rope of saliva hanging from its tusky mouth, its eyes lit with excitement.

The second troll also closed with Khyven, feet stomping through Davi's new family as they scattered like mice.

The third continued lumbering toward the mage.

The first Troll flexed its boulder-sized shoulder, and the stone axe whipped up and down in a brutal, expert arc right at Khyven.

"No!" Davi shouted, thinking he was going to see Khyven die.

The axe slammed down, but it only crunched stone. Khyven wasn't there. Somehow he was *on* the axe handle. He ran up the tree-sized haft like it was a bridge, drew the giant sword over his shoulder, and swept left to right.

The Troll's eyes opened wide, and its mouth gaped. It raised one knobby arm and said, "Urk—!"

Its head toppled from its shoulders and thumped onto the ground. A moment later, its body fell backward as Khyven leapt clear.

The second Troll roared in fury, swinging its tree-trunk club in an arc that covered twenty feet of ground. There was no way Khyven could get out of the way—

But he jumped six feet straight up, clearing the club like he was jumping rope. The Troll's eyes flew wide.

Khyven lunged, point first.

The huge sword emerged from the Troll's back like a wand of blackness, trailing purple flame. The Troll vomited black blood at Khyven.

He dropped low, ripped the sword down and free, and rolled

gracefully between the Troll's stumpy legs. He spun, swinging powerfully upward into the body, continuing his cut straight through the Troll's head.

The Troll stood stunned, blood coursing down its chest and legs, then it came apart, left and right halves falling different ways.

Khyven turned toward the third and final Troll. It roared its rage, the tree-club raised over the mage. Fast as Khyven was, though, he couldn't reach the mage in time.

Two things happened then. The starlight from the mage's spell went out.

Or ... not out. It fell to a ghostly glow.

Another figure slipped from the tall, pointy-eared woman's cloak, a woman in armor. She was shorter than Khyven, dressed in full plate and chainmail, but she moved just as fast.

The club came down, and the woman threw up her sword to block it. Davi waited for her to be smashed against the ground, but her sword flared red from a huge gem at the pommel, and it sheared the tree trunk in half!

The mage ducked, protecting his head as half of the trunk fell behind him.

The armored woman snarled, showing long, pointed teeth, and she leapt onto the Troll's chest as he backpedaled.

"Not in my kingdom." Her whisper carried like a shout in the silent forest.

The Troll flailed his arms, suddenly realizing he was outmatched, and he tried to flee. The armored woman clung to him, baring those pointed teeth. She stabbed the sword into his thick body between neck and shoulder. The ruby flared like a bonfire. The woman threw her head back and gave a swift, happy cry.

The Troll fell like he'd been hit by lightning.

She landed on top of his dead chest as he slid down the slope, then leapt clear. She landed a second time on solid ground and bowed her head, shuddering, her fist gripping the hilt of the sword. She turned away, but Davi could see that she was fighting to keep from smiling, keeping her lips tight around those frightening teeth.

Khyven cleared his throat, bringing Davi's attention back. Aven's group huddled together now, Aven in the front, face tight with pain as he held his broken arm.

Khyven's steel smile softened. His eyes sparkled in the dim light, and he seemed genuinely nice.

"Sorry we're late," he said. "You're safe now."

"Relatively speaking," the mage said.

"Quiet Slayter," the pointy-eared woman said.

"I'm simply saying that safety is a relative concept at the moment. Without daylight—or even the hope of daylight—the odds of any of us surviving this ordeal is actually—"

"Enough," Khyven the Unkillable said. "They don't need to hear that."

"Oh," the mage said. "Well, yes. I suppose you're right."

"I am right."

"You're Khyven the Unkillable!" Davi blurted.

Khyven turned to face him, and his genuine smile widened. For the first time since the darkness came, Davi felt hope.

"Guilty," Khyven the Unkillable said. He extended his hand to Davi, but Davi ran straight at Khyven and wrapped his arms around the surprised man's waist. Davi hugged him hard.

"Well, that bears study," the mage said.

"Slayter—" the pointy-eared woman began.

"It does. I showed up first. I created the light. I did away with *all* the Nox—which, there were more than twenty of them. That was a far deadlier enemy by half. Khyven dances around and kills two Trolls—TWO—and he gets the hug."

"Do you want a hug?" The dark-skinned woman asked.

"No."

"Then be quiet."

"I wonder if it's a Ringer thing."

"Shhh."

Davi kept hugging Khyven tighter. He was never letting go. Never letting go ever again.

CHAPTER ONE

KHYVEN

Khyven took the giant steps at a run. The black granite walls whipped by in a blur. He passed the second landing, thighs burning, and continued upward. It was as though his mind didn't even belong to him anymore. Flashes of images, nattering thoughts. The nightmare. The Sword. The nightmare. The Sword.

His head pounded like a dagger was trying to pry open his skull.

The Sword whispered its bloody thoughts.

"Delicious, Slayer of Trolls ... A fine fight. They fell before you like sheared wheat. One more step toward our glorious purpose."

Khyven reached the third landing, turned, and shot down the hallway. He wanted to get out of sight and earshot of the refugees they had just rescued.

The Sword had gone quiet for a rare moment, clearly sated on its satisfaction at the slaughter. Apparently that had been enough blood for the next ten minutes.

So now, of course, the images of the nightmare pressed on

his mind.

Images unfurled like banners in the wind, one after the other. Lorelle—

No!

Rhenn—

No!

He shut them out with a snarl.

He'd been shutting them out for a week. The nightmare had filled his sleep, stabbing at him, jolting him awake in a cold sweat night after night until he simply stopped sleeping. He hadn't slept for three days because he didn't want to face the nightmare.

It wasn't normal. He'd never had a nightmare like this. Calling it a nightmare was a joke. It was so vivid, so real. It was real. When caught in its grips, he couldn't distinguish between the dream and his waking life.

Similar to the Sword, the nightmare seemed to have a life of its own. It fought Khyven, tried to break down his defenses so it could rush in. When he slept, he could do nothing to stop it. It seemed to have free rein once he closed his eyes. Now that he'd denied it for three days, the nightmare was trying to force its way into his waking mind.

"*Our true purpose is the Drakanoi Jai'ketakos, of course,*" the Sword started up again. "*The former keeper of the Thuros. We must find him. That one must be destroyed. As must all of his ilk. Purge them. Shall I imprint Jai'ketakos on your mind so that you may recognize him instantly?*"

Khyven pushed away the Sword's thoughts and shot toward the first room on his left. He couldn't stand it anymore. He couldn't wait for the room at the end of the hall. The Mirror Room would have to do.

He kicked the handle and slammed his shoulder against the twenty-foot-tall door. It swung wide, revealing the room with the mirrors that he, Slayter, and Vohn had discovered before Rauvelos had sent them into the Great Noktum. Aside from the dozens of mirrors, the room was empty.

"*I have tasted the blood of that one,*" the Sword nattered away.

"Forever I will feel the pulse of his fearful heart. Thump, thump, thump. Can you hear it? It infects the sublime beauty of Noksonon. I will show you where he is, Slayer of Trolls, but you must take the fight to—"

Khyven pulled the Sword from its magical sheath and hurled it across the room. The voice vanished, as it always did when he lost contact with the Sword. Unfortunately, it wasn't permanent. It had already shown him it could speak to him whether he held it in his hand or not.

The Sword flew toward one of the mirrors—

And stopped.

It hovered in the air as though bewildered. Reflections of it showed in five mirrors behind and around it, as though it had multiplied. It vanished from the higher mirrors and appeared in the lower mirrors as it descended gently to the floor. Its deadly black point clinked against the stone, and it leaned itself neatly against the lowest mirror without giving it so much as a scratch.

Khyven drew a blessed breath at the brief respite from the Sword's constant monologue—

And the nightmare struck. The images flooded over his momentarily weakened defenses and filled his mind.

He saw Lorelle screaming. Her naked, bloodied body was shadowed by her noktum cloak, and the golden lock at her brow turned black. The last remnant of her Luminent heritage vanished, and her face was twisted into a rage-filled insanity. Her black brows crouched low, the skin between her eyes wrinkled into ridges. Her mouth became a gritted snarl. Fury and desperate anguish warred on her face as she leapt upon an enemy Khyven couldn't see, stabbing them with daggers. Blood flew, but all he could see was the feral abandon as Lorelle stabbed and stabbed and stabbed …

"No!" Khyven murmured weakly as he fell to his knees, but the images were relentless. Lorelle's animal frenzy vanished, replaced by a sedate scene in a ruined temple. Gray stone faded into mist at the edge of the vision. Tall windows showed only utter blackness outside the temple.

In the center, by an altar, stood Rhenn. Her tumbling brown

hair had been pinned back from her forehead by her crown, and she was dressed in a black wedding dress frayed at one shoulder and at her hip, revealing pale flesh. Behind her lay Vohn, unmoving on the stones. A Nox bloodsucker feasted on his neck, and Rhenn didn't even look at them. She stared forward with a resolute expression, her mouth a pressed line.

At her side stood the necromancer N'ssag, smiling wide with his wormy lips. He held her hand triumphantly, hunched next to her in his unwashed clothes.

Khyven clawed at his head, trying to stop the images, but the last one forced its way through.

It centered on Slayter. As with the others, the scene faded at the edges, but Khyven could see enough. He could see too much.

The mage had been spread-eagled and suspended in the air by four silvery strands, spider webs. His bloody wrists and ankles had been pulled cruelly apart in an "X" and he was poised over a bubbling cauldron. His red robes had been slashed away from his body, stripping him naked to his waist, and his head had been cleaved open. Skin and bone peeled back to reveal his brain, and Slayter's anguished face twitched.

Giants surrounded him: a thin one, a fat one, one that looked like a person with spider legs growing out of its back, and one that stood in the middle, taller than the rest, muscular in the chest and shoulders. The tallest wore that same hateful expression of the statue in the courtyard of Castle Noktos. He glared at Slayter like the mage had betrayed him and he was finally able to take his revenge.

"Stop it!" Khyven shouted, but the vision cruelly continued on. Khyven's field of vision moved from the tortured Slayter to the Giants, viewing them closely one at a time until it dropped to view the figure to the right of the tallest Giant.

It was Khyven himself.

Khyven stood with the Giants, and his face was a nightmare parody of the reflection Khyven saw when he looked in a mirror. His eyes were larger, as though they had been magically stretched. His eyebrows angled up at the edges, and the scars on his face had widened, as though his flesh had been stretched further across his skull.

The Khyven in the vision smiled as he watched the Giants torture his friend, peeling back his flesh and poking at his brain.

"Your thoughts are invigorating, Slayer of Trolls," the Sword said, shattering the nightmare and bringing Khyven back.

"Stay out of my head!" Khyven snapped back at the thing, but its voice had banished the visions, and in this continuing hell, that was a blessing of sorts. Perhaps the only blessing Khyven could expect anymore.

He pressed his palms against the cold stones, breathing hard, and let out a shaking breath.

Once the nightmare had its way with him, it left. For a time. For several hours, the nightmare would only be a horrible memory thudding in the back of his head, rather than an attack. The pressure would slowly build, but he wouldn't have to actively fight it for a while.

As long as he didn't sleep.

"We are the perfect team," the Sword continued. *"You need me. You need me inside your thoughts."*

Khyven wanted to scream. When it wasn't the nightmare, it was the Sword. But it seemed the angrier he got with the Sword, the more he slipped into the persona the Sword wanted him to be. He longed for the violence, lusted for the blood.

Though the Sword and the nightmare fought for dominance in Khyven's mind, he was sure they were intertwined. The fiendish, nightmare version of Khyven with the stretched face and terrifying eyes looked exactly how Khyven pictured himself when he gave into the Sword's bloodlust.

And he knew in the pit of his stomach that this vision was Khyven's fate if he continued using the Sword. The nightmare was showing him the future.

He shook his head violently, banishing the thought. No. He wasn't going to become that person. He wasn't going to …

But the Sword was always there. Every time Khyven slew

another new, more dangerous creature, the Sword gave him a new name. It had started by calling him Slayer of Men. Then it had been Slayer of Nox. Now it was Slayer of Trolls.

Every direction Khyven turned, the Sword clung to him, letting him go only a little distance before pulling him back.

Khyven panted, trying to look anywhere but at the seemingly innocuous Sword leaning against the mirror across the room.

Twice already, he had been on the verge of telling Slayter to lock the thing in the deepest cell of this Senji-forsaken castle and put the strongest containment spells on the door.

But he had not done it yet. He couldn't seem to part with the Sword, and that worried him more than anything.

Already, he had begun to feel like he was missing something, like he'd forgotten something important, like he'd walked off and somehow left his right arm behind. That was the Sword.

The thrill came then, the memory of the battle. Khyven had always felt that thrill, but now it was darker, twisted. Before, he'd longed for the challenge, longed to pit his skills against a foe, reached for excellence in the spinning dance of swordplay, the dangerous art of the fight.

But now he lusted for the kill. He wanted to see the blood spurting. His body thrilled at seeing the death masks of those he slew.

He'd never wanted that before. But the Sword felt … right in his hand. It felt like putting on an old tunic that fit the form of his body perfectly, like the two of them were made for each other.

He tried to banish the rightness of it, but even as his heart fought against it, his mind made arguments *for* the damned thing. The Sword was, in fact, the perfect weapon. It was as light as a stick, able to be manipulated with deft flicks of his wrist despite the fact that it was nearly six-feet-long.

Also, the blade could cut through anything like it was paper: shields, swords, dragon scales, Troll hide, even spells. The combination of Khyven's blue wind and the Sword's magic created an unstoppable force. His blood rushed at the thought of it, of how easy it had been to cut through those Trolls.

For the first time, Khyven saw himself as the Giantkiller. He could be the savior his friends had painted him, the Greatblood Nhevalos had decreed. With the Sword, he could kill anything. He was certain of that.

But what would he lose to effect that transformation? The excitement, the bond, the lust for carnage. The Sword *wanted* him to feel these feelings, and it was getting difficult for Khyven to distinguish between what the Sword wanted and what he wanted. And if there was no difference between him and the Sword ... what did that make Khyven?

The fiendish Khyven's face rose in his mind with his terrible eyes.

He hunched there, trying to banish the image. He tried to look anywhere but at the Sword, but finally he raised his head, drawn to it.

He stood up and started toward it, its image doubled by the mirror against which it leaned. Pressing his lips into a line, Khyven stood before the Sword. He stared down at it—

A flash of light went through his mind. He shook his head, took a step back.

What was that?

He looked back at the Sword, and it still leaned there, seemingly innocuous. He would have thought it was the Sword's doing, but Khyven was intimately familiar with how the Sword affected him at this point, and this didn't feel like that.

Khyven glance up—

The fiendish Khyven, with his overlarge eyes, stared down at him from the mirror on the wall above the Sword. He smiled cruelly—

"It is time to kill again ... " the Sword said.

Khyven looked down. The Sword was in his hand. He'd picked up the blade without deciding to.

"No!" He gripped the hilt with all his strength, as though he would crush it. "I am not yours to command!"

He looked back up at the fiendish reflection of himself—

But the nightmare Khyven was gone. His true reflection stared back at him. Khyven breathed hard, staring gratefully up at his own image. He'd ... Had he pushed it back?

"Are you all right?"

He spun, whipping the blade up before him. A Nox bloodsucker!

Somehow the fiend had slunk into the castle. Somehow it had worked its way past Slayter's magical defenses. It was a female Nox, a cloak swirling back from the curves of her slender body, a cowl low over her features.

Khyven's lips peeled back from his teeth. Good. He needed a fight right now. This Nox had stumbled across the wrong victim.

He lowered his head, starting forward. He hoped he was the first of the castle's denizens that this Nox had stumbled across, though that was unlikely. If the Nox had made it this far, it had probably already done some devilish work elsewhere, killed some of the refugees, perhaps even hurt one of Khyven's friends. But whatever the thing had done already, whoever it had hurt, it wouldn't hurt anyone after this.

"Yesss ... " the Sword whispered.

"You'll never leave here alive," Khyven growled.

The Nox bloodsucker pushed back her cowl, and a blond lock at her brow glowed.

"Khyven?" she asked, her eyes narrowing.

A shiver went up Khyven's spine, and he gazed at her for a long moment, far too long before he recognized her ...

"Lorelle!" he gasped. Guilt rose like bile in his throat. He'd been about to kill her. He'd *wanted* to kill her.

He hadn't seen his beloved in the woman before him. He'd only seen an enemy!

"No ..." He clenched the hilt so hard his knuckles turned white.

He felt the Sword's disappointment, like Khyven was a fish who had slipped the hook. It wanted blood. It wanted violence. And any creature would do.

"By Senji, if you threaten her again," he growled in his mind. *"I'll bury you so deep you won't ever be found!"*

The murderous compulsion receded like a wave from the shore.

"Of course, Slayer of Trolls. Of course ..."

Khyven slammed Sword into the sheath on his back. It made a satisfying *clang* and he hoped it hurt.

"Khyven, are you—"

"I'm fine." He turned away from her, trying to get control of his emotions.

He felt her watching him with those beautiful brown eyes.

"How are the refugees?" he diverted the conversation. He walked toward the door like he had been doing that all along, like he'd raced up the stairs like a madman only to turn around and go check on those they'd rescued. He gave her a wide berth. He didn't trust himself just yet.

"Vohn is getting them situated," she said.

"Good."

"When was the last time you rested?"

"I told you, I'm fine—"

"Khyven." Her hand fell on his arm, light as a feather. He jumped, but forced himself not to look at her, afraid that he'd see her as an enemy again. He didn't want her to see the murder in his eyes.

"Khyven ..." She moved her body between him and the door, blocking him. The Sword wanted him to pick her up, slam her to the floor, dash her head against the stones ...

"Lorelle ..."

She took his face in her hands and kissed him.

It surprised him. His first notion was to pull back, but she didn't let him.

The bloodlust cracked and fell away, as though it had never been a part of him in the first place.

He made a little sound, then slowly melted into the kiss. His arms relaxed and encircled her.

In the times before her transformation, before she'd gone

into the heart of the Great Noktum, fought her personal demons, and emerged with onyx skin, midnight hair, and a marriage to the Dark, she wouldn't have instigated something like that. An inviting smile might have been the most she would do, not a body block and sudden kiss.

This new, forward side of her intoxicated him. His blood turned hot. His arms tightened around her. Her lips, her tongue, her fingers in his hair … Desire roared through him as though the Sword's bloodthirstiness could be channeled into this. Not peace, not respite, but this.

He lifted her in his arms. She was as light as a garment. He loved that about her. He loved everything about her. His heartbeat pounded throughout his body.

She tightened her grip in his hair, twisting her hands. The pain lanced through his scalp, heightened his desire. He wanted her more than ever.

She broke the kiss and slid her lips to his ear. "Khyven?" she murmured.

"Yes," he said huskily, looking desperately around the room for an appropriate place. The mirrors stared at him like invading eyes. There had to be a place. He turned. There had to be——

"How about our room?" she murmured.

Her simple common sense struck him. He hadn't thought of that. Why hadn't he thought of that?

He marched toward the open doors. They had chosen a beautiful room in what had once been servant's quarters. It was a Human-sized room in this intimidating castle of oversized everything.

It had been days since he'd visited it, but it was down one flight and to the left, down a long hallway to the very end, set apart from every other populated place.

The bulk of the refugees were housed downstairs where the raven totems had created a warm, sunlit haven in the great room, a little bastion of normalcy like Rhenn's camp where the refugees could recover.

Lorelle and Khyven had chosen a place in the dark, and he

charged there now, down the stairs, up the hallway. He kicked open the door.

Their bed, refurbished by a carpenter they'd saved that first night, was solid and wide enough for the two of them to be comfortable.

"Khyven ..." she whispered in his ear again, and he realized she'd been calling his name a few times on their way here.

"Yes?"

"How long since you've slept?"

"I'm fine."

He laid her on the bed, and she smiled up at him, inviting. She extended her arms and he fell onto her. She kissed him, fingers along his neck, in his hair again.

"We need you," she murmured.

He kissed her mouth, her cheek, her neck like it was his mission. But her phrasing stuck in his mind, and he hesitated.

"We?"

"All of us. And you're not acting like yourself. Do you know how long it's been since you slept?"

"I'm fine."

"Seven days, Khyven."

"What?"

"It's been seven days." He felt a slight prick on his neck.

He jerked back. "Lorelle ... Did you just—"

She pressed her lips hungrily to his, as though she wanted to pour her soul into him, as though she wanted to prove to him how much she loved him.

"I want you," she breathed into his ear as he felt the *somnul* take effect. "But I want the actual you."

"You tricked me ..."

"Well, I'm a little dark these days."

"Lorelle, no ..."

"I'll be here when you wake up," she promised. "I'll be here."

"No ... I can't sleep ..."

Khyven heard the Sword snarl as he fell into darkness. He

felt it detach, as though it couldn't keep a grip on his mind when he was asleep.

His eyes slid shut, and for a blessed moment, he felt like himself again, exhausted, suspended in a weightless place, and he saw clearly.

Relief and horror intertwined as he remembered the past day. He'd wanted to save the refugees from the Trolls, the bloodsuckers, but the Sword made him want to slaughter them. He'd wanted to kiss Lorelle; the Sword made him want to ravage her.

They were all his desires, but they were his desires twisted, magnified, stretched tight over a skull, expanding his scars …

Senji … he thought as the *somnul* dropped him past the Sword's reach. *What is happening to me?*

As he sank deeper, he fell past his fears, feeling weaker than he had since he was a child. His friends were depending on him. He had to be better than this, because he could feel the enemies coming for them. Not just the Sword, but everything that was promised by Nhevalos's schemes. The Giants. Tovos. Jai'ketakos. And a sense that they were only the beginning of the worst.

He could feel the very world rising up to crush his friends, and he had to stop It. He was the Giantkiller. *He* was the Giantkiller … But he had run out of strength …

Darkness fell around him as his eyes slid shut.

CHAPTER TWO

HARKANDOS

Harkandos sat on his throne, staring at the wall. A tray of uneaten food—three roast noktum hens, buttered potatoes, and a bowl of grindle stalks—sat on the stone pedestal beside the throne. Night roaches scuttled across the coagulated meat and vegetables. He paid them no mind.

He had stared at the same wall for a week. The dead bodies of Wergoi sprawled at the base of the dais against the north and south walls, testament to those who had been incautious enough to interrupt his thoughts.

Mendos himself had lost a hand.

Harkandos had a problem, and he wasn't going to move from this spot, nor be moved by another's argument, until he had resolved it.

He had returned Noksonon to the Dark again, which gave him and his allies greater power. All Noksonoi were equipped to thrive in the Dark. His next move should have been to begin the war, to sweep over the continent with vengeance for these mortals who had infested the lands. He should have covered the lands in fire, bathed them in blood.

But he had noticed something, and it gave him pause.

He'd sent his Noksonoi to different parts of the continent to scout and report about how they ought to attack. The first sign of trouble, of course, came from Usara. Orios—who had been assigned Usara—had returned with unsettling information.

The mortal kingdom that claimed the name Usara—the place where Nhevalos had squirreled away his puppets—had retreated to Castle Noktos. They'd done so immediately and efficiently. Somehow, they had the ability to see in the Dark. Somehow, they had kept the denizens of the noktum at bay. They were actually rescuing their people.

In short, they had been prepared.

And though they were clearly the most prepared, they weren't the only ones. That was when a sinking suspicion began to fill Harkandos's gut. If they were prepared, someone had prepared them. And the only someone who could have done that was Nhevalos or his pet noktum phoenix, Rauvelos.

That meant Nhevalos had known the Dark would return, that Harkandos would break the deadlock between the Lux and the Great Noktum.

The last time Nhevalos had predicted Harkandos and Harkandos had proceeded anyway, he'd ended up trapped by his own power for two millennia. So while Harkandos itched to take up arms and destroy every offending creature on Noksonon, he had paused instead to think.

The more he sat in this room, in this castle that had once belonged to the idiot weakling Tovos, the more he was convinced that a direct attack, even with the cover of the Dark, was exactly what Nhevalos wanted him to do.

At first, Harkandos boiled with rage that he'd somehow played into Nhevalos's hands again. For the first time in his adult life, he had asked for information from others. He'd demanded that Orios, Mendos, Avektos, Jai'ketakos, and Raos—such that she could even coherently speak—tell him everything they knew about this new world, this place ruled by the scuttling mortals.

In each of the exhaustive stories, Harkandos had searched for Nhevalos's handiwork.

He had discovered many things, most of which were useless. But one thing had stuck in his throat. Nhevalos had been breeding mortals. He had been taking certain mortals from certain places, taking them to other places, and mating them.

To what purpose?

That had been the question at first, and Harkandos had wanted to chase down each and every one of these mortals and slay them, but two thousand years as a statue had tempered his anger and his impetuousness. Instead, he had sent Mendos and Orios to silently abduct relatives of these unions. He did not touch the parents and he certainly did not touch Nhevalos's intended offspring. He had to assume these mortals were being watched, and he didn't want Nhevalos alerted. The rat scuttled about in secret, listening and spying, and Harkandos was determined to deny him any information if he could.

In the confusion of the restoration of the Great Noktum, a few missing mortals wouldn't be noticed, even by Nhevalos.

After peeling back the skins and the souls of the abducted mortals, after doing the same to random mortals as a comparison, Harkandos had found only one thing that had piqued his interest, just one thing they all had in common.

The relatives of the mortals Nhevalos had chosen all had a higher concentration of Eldroi blood than normal mortals. At some point in their distant past, they had mated with an Eldroi, or had been suffused with Eldroi blood. And not just Noksonoi blood. They had been instilled with all kinds. Harkandos had found traces of Daemanoi, Drakanoi, and Pyranoi as well. In some cases, all of them.

Nhevalos had pulled these mortals from all over Eldros, not just Noksonon.

Best as Harkandos could guess, the rat was increasing their magical ability. It was the only reason to enhance the Eldroi blood in a mortal. And yet, among each of these families, there was no evidence of mages. Not a single one of these parents—or their offspring—were working magic.

At least no magic Harkandos could detect.

That was impossible. If a mortal had magical ability, Harkandos would be able to see it. If they had even a moderate magical talent—even if they weren't using it—there would be a whiff that Harkandos could detect.

There was absolutely nothing.

That was initially disappointing, but after case upon case upon case, Harkandos realized he was missing the bigger picture. Nhevalos was working on something. Something big. The question was: what?

Harkandos had sat here for days already, going over the information he'd yanked from his subjects. Harkandos had the strength to overwhelm Nhevalos in a one-on-one confrontation, but only if there were no other factors coming to bear upon the battle. Of course, the rat always ensured there were. Harkandos could only imagine how long Nhevalos had taken to meticulously set his trap so long ago. Years. Centuries even.

This time, Nhevalos had had two thousand years, and Harkandos was starting with a blank slate. While every fiber of Harkandos's being demanded he jump headlong at his foe, he simply couldn't until he saw where all the potential traps lay. He had to know, without a doubt, what he was running into. He needed to understand the nature of Nhevalos's web, to cut the cords from the inside, charge through, and rip the little rat to shreds.

Then, of course, there was the opposite way of thinking. Nhevalos might simply be trying to keep Harkandos guessing. Was this meant to sap Harkandos's decisiveness? Had Nhevalos created a complex construct for Harkandos to marvel at, slowly sapping Harkandos's confidence as he wondered at the purpose of it?

Or was it a false trail, to have him looking anywhere but at Nhevalos's real threat? Were these breeding experiments simply something to distract Harkandos?

Harkandos bared his teeth.

He'd never hated anyone more than he hated Nhevalos. The rat was making him—Harkandos—swim in this watery gruel of indecision. It was intolerable. It was unbearable. It was—

Another thought came to Harkandos out of the blue.

They were shielded!

The mortals Nhevalos had bred weren't a feint. And they weren't without magic. They weren't actively using the magic, but also it had been disguised!

Harkandos sat up straight and reached into the core of himself where his magic waited like bubbling lava at the center of a volcano. He pulled some and activated the Love Magic spell he'd created, the one that connected him to each of the Eldroi who served him.

In his mind, he saw tendrils connecting him to Avektos, Mendos, Orios, Jai'ketakos, and Raos. He yanked those tendrils just enough to remind them who they served, and that he wanted them. On the receiving end, each of them would feel the yank like a fishhook in their heart.

In the real world, he raised an arm and flicked a finger, pouring a little more of his power into a quick Land Magic spell. The twenty-foot-tall stone doors on the far side of his throne room slammed open.

Mendos and Orios stood on the other side, as well as a half dozen Wergoi servants. The servants jumped, as did Mendos. Orios did not, raising an eyebrow as though she had expected the sudden opening of the door.

Well, she was a talented Lore Mage, so perhaps she had read the *kairoi* to predict when Harkandos would summon them, though that would have been a scandalous waste of her magic, and Orios did not waste magic. No. More likely, she was simply as cool a character as she seemed.

He was finding more reasons to appreciate her.

"Get in here," Harkandos commanded them, then he landed a glance on one of the Wergoi. Harkandos batted the roach-infested meal beside him. The plate flew, sending chicken legs, buttered potatoes, and roaches tumbling across the floor. "Get food. And if you bring me chicken and potatoes, I'll eat your entrails instead."

It was important to be clear with mortals. They often misunderstood commands unless carefully spelled out for them, and that could lead to their premature deaths. Harkandos took pains to be a just and lenient master. He told them what he expected to achieve success. And he always made it clear to them—usually with a few preliminary examples—what they could expect if they failed.

Orios set the pace as she entered the room. Mendos followed her, actually keeping her body between him and Harkandos. She was brave, Harkandos would give her that. Mendos was a coward, but then Harkandos had known that from the start.

Mendos still hadn't grown his hand back—testament to the weakness of his Life Magic. It was still a bony stump at the end of his arm, fingers beginning to emerge in a fist, and he held it against his chest as though Harkandos would cut it off again.

When Harkandos had raged about Nhevalos's hidden plan, breaking furniture and killing Wergoi, Mendos had had the temerity to try to use a Love Magic spell to calm him. It was so subtle just about anyone besides Harkandos wouldn't have noticed it. He might have gotten away with it.

But Harkandos wasn't someone else.

Of course, Mendos might have cast it reflexively. It was a natural action for a Noksonoi. Magic was a part of their everyday lives, and it was possible he meant no offense by it.

It was also possible Mendos was beginning a series of probes, trying to check Harkandos's defenses, see how much he might control Harkandos.

Harkandos had responded immediately and with stark clarity. He'd turned, harnessed the air, shaped it, and hardened it into a razor-sharp guillotine that sliced Mendos's hand cleanly from his arm.

Harkandos doubted Mendos missed that message: *Attempt to influence me, and you lose a body part.*

But Harkandos was a lenient master, so he'd spoken his words clearly as well. "If you try your Love Magic upon me again without my permission, I will take your arm instead of your hand, ensure that it never regenerates, and mount the rest of your body here in the throne room as an example to anyone else who wishes to influence me without my knowledge."

Quickly stifling the unseemly wails at the loss of his hand, Mendos had nodded acquiescence with wide eyes.

He had not complained since, and it was a good thing. The loss of a hand was lenient.

Mendos now watched Harkandos with a barely concealed fear, stopping well before Orios did. She stopped ten feet from the throne.

Orios's unearthly eyes seemed to look at nothing and everything at once. Stars in a black sky staring out from that calm, pale face.

"I know what he is doing," Harkandos said.

Orios's lips curved at the edges of her thin mouth. "Do you?"

"He's hiding it. The products of the rat's breeding program have a very specific magic, and he's hiding it."

"What is it?"

"That is the question, dear Orios, and you're going to find out for me. You and Mendos."

Mendos swallowed. He didn't want to be sent on a mission. He didn't want to be anywhere close to Harkandos or his plans. The coward wanted to run.

Such a disappointment.

A true Noksonoi would have taken his mild punishment and strengthened himself with it. He would have moved on. He would have understood that serving Harkandos with passion and dedication was the only possible path to a long, healthy life.

Of course, if reluctance was to be Mendos's attitude he would be far less useful. If he was always looking for an escape, he couldn't possibly properly concentrate on his tasks.

Harkandos made a mental note: If Mendos didn't show true

dedication and soon, Harkandos might have to prune him from this group.

Orios, on the other hand, responded as a true subject must. A contrast to Mendos, she appeared excited, which meant she was either a much better actor or she had concluded the truth: there was no Eldrovan anymore, no Noktos; Harkandos ruled the Noksonoi. One must serve if one wanted to keep their life, let alone have power in the new order.

And Orios hungered for knowledge and power. As long as Harkandos kept providing her with opportunities to increase her abilities and her reach, she would stay loyal to him ...

... until, of course, she chose her moment of betrayal.

And that was fine. The Eldroi, by nature, wanted to rule. They wanted to rule over the mortals, of course, but also over each other.

In the past, there were moments in history when the Eldroi had banded together. They could be useful to each other, especially when being attacked by other Eldroi. But those moments were usually brief.

At some point, Orios would make her move, would turn on him. It was inevitable. She would, of course, wait until she perceived him to be at his weakest. That was the game they now played, circling each other like Kyolars, waiting for the advantage. Harkandos knew the game, and he had the size of her. Predicting her behavior would be simple compared to predicting the behavior of Nhevalos. He planned to eliminate her before she suspected it.

Avektos arrived then, waddling into the room on his perpetually bowed legs with his prodigious belly swinging between them. His thick hands and forearms were blackened with soot and streaked with welts from the magic he had wielded. He pushed his protective glasses back on his head.

Harkandos had immediately put him to work doing what he did best: forging weapons. It was said Avektos had studied at the knee of Noktos himself when the Sword of Noksonon was made.

"At your service, my lord," Avektos said. Harkandos worried least about Avektos. While any Eldroi had the capacity for backstabbing, some were natural followers. Avektos was such a one. In order to rebel against Harkandos's rule, the smith would have to be enlisted by one of the others. And Harkandos didn't plan to give them the free time to foment a rebellion.

Raos's clicking feet reached Harkandos's ears before she crawled through the doorway upside down, spider legs clinging to the underside of the arch as she hauled her body through. She stopped just inside, perched on the wall and watching him with her bug-like eyes.

A gust of wind from the open balcony hailed the arrival of Jai'ketakos. He hovered for one brief moment before his hind claws gripped the stones of rail, then walked himself to the floor. He tucked his wings and settled himself, no doubt to illustrate, once again, his sullen reluctance at having been pressed into service. He brought his enormous head down through the archway and focused it unemotionally on Harkandos.

"Good," Harkandos said. Their arrivals had been timely, far more so than the last time. At their previous meeting, Jai'ketakos had straggled in late, and Harkandos had to burn the tips of the dragon's wings to show his displeasure.

"We have a new mission," he told them. "And you will all participate."

Avektos shrugged, sending a ripple across his round belly. Orios kept her genuine smile, like Harkandos was giving her exactly what she wanted. Jai'ketakos kept his scaled face expressionless. Mendos nodded sullenly. Raos didn't even twitch. It was like she actually *was* a spider now, waiting intently for a fly.

"As you know," Harkandos continued. "I've been collecting mortals from all over Noksonon. I've now gathered the knowledge I need. I want you to go back to these places. This time, I don't want the relatives. I don't want the parents. I want you to study the progeny. I am looking for one of them. Only one."

"You want us to bring them here," Jai'ketakos said.

Harkandos turned, burning the dragon with his glare. Jai'ketakos lowered his gaze. "If I wanted you to bring them here, I would have said so. I want you to watch them, then return with a full report. Strengths. Weaknesses."

"Strengths?" Jai'ketakos said. "In mortals?"

"I want anything unusual. Anything that might be more than normal. Something remarkable that is perhaps masked as something else." As he spoke the words, Harkandos noticed a twitch in the dragon's nostril, a veiled look in his eyes. Harkandos almost dismissed it as another petty rebellion, but something stayed his snap judgment. That wasn't a look of reluctance, hatred, or unhappiness.

It was shame.

Harkandos narrowed his eyes, and he kept talking. "Raos, you will observe the Shadowvar in Nokte Vallark. Orios, the young man from the Vellyn Isles. Avektos, the Taur-El. Mendos, the urchin in Imprevar. Jai'ketakos, the Demaijos princess."

They all nodded, except Raos who just watched him.

"Go," he said.

All of them turned to leave.

"Jai'ketakos." Harkandos stayed the dragon. He had crouched to spring into the air and paused. The others paused as well, glancing back at Harkandos. He glared at them. "Did I tell you to stop?"

Each of them snapped back around and left the room.

Harkandos crossed to the balcony. There was barely enough room for the dragon's vast bulk, but he shrank against the rail to give Harkandos space.

Harkandos walked to the rail and looked out over the ruined city of the Nox, a city that Jai'ketakos himself had burned to the ground. Harkandos imagined the dragon fancied himself the ruler of this place as he flew about killing the pathetic mortals.

"I wanted to talk to you before you go," Harkandos said.

"Of course." The dragon's voice came out steady, confident, and curious.

"I want to know more about these offspring Nhevalos is creating," Harkandos said.

"Of course, my lord. Whatever I have is yours," Jai'ketakos said.

"So, if you saw something that you think would interest me, something relevant to this search for unusual mortals, you would tell me."

"Of course, my lord." The dragon hesitated a fraction of a second. If Harkandos hadn't been looking for it, he'd have missed it.

Harkandos waited, his anger rising with every second that passed.

The dragon did not respond, as though waiting for more.

"Your tail. Your belly," Harkandos said.

Again, a pause. The dragon's face was carefully schooled. "Yes, my lord?" he said as though he didn't know, as though he couldn't conceive of the direction Harkandos was headed.

"Are they recent wounds?"

"My lord—"

"Do I need to remind you what happens to those who try to deceive me?"

"Those wounds aren't relevant to—"

"I saw the shame in your eyes, dragon. I told you what I was now looking for, and you were filled with shame. I believe that yesterday you thought those wounds were irrelevant. Today, you didn't."

"I ..."

"And you were simply going to fly away without giving me this information, the source of these strange wounds."

"My lord ..." The dragon shifted uncomfortably. Harkandos could see the thoughts frantically jumping behind his eyes. He was trying to create a story, something that would explain him withholding the information.

Harkandos bared his teeth. "If you hide information from me and I find out, it will be the end of you."

"I would be happy to tell you whatever you wish, my lord."

"I'm so glad to hear it." Harkandos's words dripped with sarcasm. "A mortal gave you those scars."

Jai'ketakos hesitated, then nodded.

"You see, this is exactly the sort of thing I'm looking for. Every scrap of information is valuable to me. It is like treasure, dragon. My treasure. And if you keep my treasure from me, I must use whatever I deem necessary to recover it. Do I make myself clear?"

"I honestly thought ... It only just occurred to me, that it might be of use. I needed to look over my memories, match them to what—"

"Excuses bore me, dragon."

Jai'ketakos glanced at the ground, and Harkandos finally saw the fear. The dragon's will was broken.

"Now ..." Harkandos said slowly. "I am going to give you a second chance. Tell me what mortal could possibly do that to a dragon."

Jai'ketakos raised his head, lips pulling back from his enormous teeth, his hatred stoked, but it was not focused on Harkandos this time. Not this hate. Jai'ketakos had been shamed by a mortal, this Nhevalos-modified creature who had nearly killed him.

Intriguing.

"It was two of them, my lord," Jai'ketakos said. "A Human Line Mage from Usara."

"A Human mage wounded you?"

"No. It was the Ringer."

"Ringer? This is another Human word for mage?"

"No."

"Explain."

"A Ringer is fighter who slays his own kind for the sport of a crowd."

Harkandos smiled. "And this Ringer humiliated you. Sliced you open. Nearly killed you."

"He ..." The dragon's scaly lips pulled back even further. "Yes."

"And what is this Ringer's name?"

"They call him Khyven the Unkillable ..."

"Khyven ..." Harkandos murmured. He knew that name. It burned before his eyes just like every memory of every person who'd had the temerity to stare at him during his imprisonment. "Khyven. And Slayter is the mage."

"I ... Yes, my lord. How did you know?"

"They live in Usara."

The slimy, underhanded cleverness of it came together in Harkandos's mind. Nhevalos had hidden them in plain sight. But then ... Of course he had.

"Shall I take you to them?" Jai'ketakos asked.

"Oh, we have met ..." Harkandos ruminated, ideas rising in his mind like weeds.

"My lord—"

"I know them. And this time, when they stand before me, their bodies will dangle from pikes."

CHAPTER THREE

HARKANDOS

Harkandos commanded the Dark to bend around himself and Orios. They walked into it. Harkandos's castle vanished and they stepped into the clearing on the largest of the Vellyn Isles near a pathetic structure the Humans called a stronghold.

Even with Amulets of Noksonon, which this cadre of Humans also mysteriously possessed, the two Noksonoi were effectively invisible. All of the Humans continued scuttling about their "stronghold," oblivious that they were being watched.

All save one.

A Human man wearing a chainmail shirt, horned helmet, and a long sword slung across his back paced the walkway along the top of the fort's wall, and he somehow sensed them. He had a dark goatee, dark eyes, and he wore an Amulet of Noksonon. He looked up, looked in their direction. His eyes did not focus on them, but he squinted like he'd heard something, though neither Orios nor Harkandos had made a sound.

Harkandos pulled magic from inside himself, creating a

barrier of silence around them.

"That is the one?" Harkandos murmured.

Orios nodded. "He sees us."

"No. He senses us, yet I detect no magic at work. Do you?"

"No."

"How did you identify him?"

"As you specified, my lord. I followed the lineage. I waited for him to do something … unusual. His father died during the restoration of the noktum, but his mother is still alive. Apparently, he led his people to this place in the chaos."

"He led them."

"They revere him as a kind of god now. They believe he can see in the Dark."

"This man is the leader of this group of Humans?"

"Of a sort. More legend than leader. He was a hunter before the noktum returned."

"Yet he saw in the Dark."

"Only after he was forced to. And apparently, he fought a number of creatures. He might have tried to fight me if I had not been on my guard. Anytime I came too close to him, he sensed me like he now senses us. I had to resort to extending my hearing."

"So Nhevalos's magic has heightened his senses. He can see in the Dark. He can hear with greater accuracy."

"I do not think so, my lord. I believe his … facility within the noktum is an ancillary effect of his power."

"And what do you think his power is?"

"I don't know. Perhaps it is … I don't know."

"Perhaps it is what?"

"Connected to something else that is greater. Elsewise it is just a greater sense of smell, or hearing."

"This is Nhevalos's army," Harkandos murmured. "This is how he plans to fight me."

"Could his plan be predicated only upon enhanced perceptions?"

That was the real question, and Harkandos didn't have the

answer. It seemed ludicrous, which meant it probably was. But it had been ludicrous to think that Nhevalos would defeat Harkandos in single combat seventeen hundred years ago.

Harkandos's lips peeled back in a snarl. His thoughts circled, chasing each other: there was power here, tremendous power—there had to be—yet it was hiding from him. Hiding in plain sight.

"Perhaps they are like the Nox Glimmerblades ... Perhaps they can commune with Noktos," Harkandos ruminated.

"Yes, my lord, but ..." She hesitated, then fell silent.

"Speak, Orios."

"How could such an army best you? So, they have a connection to the Dark ... No matter how Nhevalos imbued them, such a connection could never be greater than ours."

She was right. Simply communing with Noktos wouldn't give enough of an advantage to topple Harkandos. Moreover, such a connection would leave a mark. A mortal imbued with such power would show the magic. This man showed nothing. His talents seemed innate.

Harkandos bared his teeth again. He hated this. He hated having to study Nhevalos and his convoluted schemes, but he put his ire down. He *would* understand what the rat was doing. Killing him simply wasn't enough now. He wanted to see the schemer's plans in ruins.

"We take him," Harkandos said.

Orios unearthly eyes seemed to stare at nothing. "Nhevalos will know if you do."

"Fearing that very thing could be his plan. To make me second-guess. To make me timid." He shook his head. "No, we capture him. Quietly. And we study him. At the very least, we should get a few days before Nhevalos knows."

"And if he has laid a tracking spell across this Human?"

"Then I reverse it; I track it to its source."

"And if Nhevalos surfaces to stop us?"

"Then he is a fool, and I end him."

"Yes," she murmured.

Harkandos raised his hand. The Dark swallowed the man on the wooden wall, erasing him as though a hand had wiped him away.

"We are committed now," Orios murmured.

"We were committed the moment Nhevalos turned against his own kind," Harkandos said.

He raised his hand again, and he and Orios also vanished.

CHAPTER FOUR

HARKANDOS

T The Human from the Vellyn Isles arched his back, pulling on the chains that held his wrists and ankles. Every muscle in his forearms corded. His fists clenched. The muscles visible through the rips in his ragged tunic flexed. His entire body trembled with tension.

The man from the Vellyn Isles had only been the first. Harkandos had captured a dozen of them, brought them all here. So far, he was unimpressed.

Orios and Mendos stood by, watching Harkandos work, looking for anything he might miss about these mortal anomalies that Nhevalos had painstakingly constructed over centuries.

Thin purple lightning crackled around the prisoner's head like a miniature storm as Harkandos tried to activate whatever Nhevalos had done to these Humans. The man screamed and screamed.

The Demaijos princess had worn her voice out on the first day. And when she'd been given a sword to face Harkandos, she had died.

The Taur-El had also screamed as the lightning had torn into him. When he had stepped into the ring with Harkandos, he had also been cut down.

The Imprevaran street urchin had screamed only once before capitulating completely. She had promised him anything he wanted.

He'd put a sword in her hand. She'd come at him timidly, and he'd cut her down.

They were working on the fifth of Nhevalos's hidden daggers. The Human, a man named Ordell Tarradan—the one from the Vellyn Isles—had resisted screaming far longer than the others.

"Perhaps the lightning will not activate Nhevalos's plan," Mendos said.

"They must think they are in danger," Harkandos said. They had figured out that much after the Demaijos princess had died.

"Oh, I think he believes he's in danger. But I think maybe it is not working in this context."

"I need their powers to activate."

"He is going to die," Mendos said.

"If you have an idea, I would welcome it," Harkandos said, annoyed. Mendos liked to point out what couldn't be done, and that simply didn't have any place in Harkandos's regime.

If Harkandos hadn't been so interested in this experiment, he would have killed Mendos right then. He really would have. Perhaps he would later.

"Nhevalos believes that these mortals have—or will have—some power over me. I have yet to see it."

"Perhaps he is wrong. Perhaps he has been trying for centuries to perfect his creations, but has failed."

"No." Harkandos wasn't underestimating Nhevalos this time. "He has something. He believes in his champion. He believes in Khyven the Unkillable."

Ordell Tarradan screamed again as the pain spell activated every single nerve in his head and neck.

"Perhaps it must be activated only in a certain circumstance, a real circumstance. Perhaps it cannot be activated in a laboratory."

"This Khyven the Unkillable is clearly his favorite of these pawns. We must replicate what he can do."

It had been three days since they'd taken Ordell Tarradan, and the Human had fought. He had actually come at Harkandos, who had immediately sent a force spell at him, intending to slam him back against the wall and hold him for an initial interrogation before the long interrogation and …

Well, Ordell Tarradan had avoided it. He'd avoided a spell.

Humans couldn't do that.

It was as though he had known it was coming. He'd simply … started moving ahead of the attack, and he hadn't been there when the hard air slammed into the wall.

Orios had intervened next, stepping forward herself to engage him physically. Giants were naturally stronger than Humans, far stronger. She had swiped at him almost negligently, intending to do exactly what Harkandos had intended, except with a brutal backhand.

Ordell Tarradan had avoided that as well.

That was when Harkandos guessed what had to be happening. It was possible, he supposed—with the most outrageous good fortune—for a man to have slipped past a spell once. A one-in-a-thousand chance, but possible.

But twice? No. A counter magic was at work here.

But fascinatingly, Harkandos felt no magic at work. Absolutely none. That was when he was certain of Nhevalos's handiwork.

In that instant, Harkandos had created an invulnerability spell around himself, making him proof against any weapon a Human could craft, and he'd stepped into the fray as Orios had. He tried—he actually tried—to hit the man.

And he couldn't.

Ordell Tarradan, however, had scored several strikes on Harkandos. None had hurt him, of course. Quite the contrary, with each successful time Ordell Tarradan scored, Harkandos's excitement grew.

The impossibility of each strike confirmed for Harkandos that he had stumbled across Nhevalos's plan. He had continued to spar with the Human for an hour. Into the second hour, though, the man's mortal body had tired. Eventually, he gave out and he fell to one knee. That was when Harkandos had stepped on him, knocked him unconscious, strapped him to a proper interrogation chair, and begun studying him.

He had put the man through test after test, had tortured him with different methods. During one of these, he'd seen something flicker behind the man's shoulder.

Harkandos had immediately stopped the torture, turned the man over, then duplicated the last spell he'd sent at the man, a combination of psychological knives and actual knives cutting into his flesh.

That was when the secret had been revealed ...

The huge Line Magic scars on the man's back flickered, and then became apparent. They looked like they had been carved into him at birth, so wide and faded were they. There had been two, one overlaying the other. One had been a masterful hiding spell, something that would cover any magic that emanated from the man. The second had taken Harkandos the better part of an hour to decipher. It was complicated and utterly unique.

This was Nhevalos's master stroke. It had to be, carefully concealed as it was, and it had pointed directly at the cunning rat's plan.

Nhevalos's puppets were imbued with a highly specialized form of Lore Magic. Normal Lore Magic was about reading the *kairoi*, the twists of destiny that laced the world together. It required time, expertise, and the ability to correctly read them. It was the magical equivalent of spending time in a library.

But this ...

Ordell Tarradan didn't even know he possessed this ability. It was as though it was built into the very smallest part of body, as though his muscle strands had been soaked in it, his brain marinated in it. They reacted of their own accord. It was possible—no, it was likely—that Ordell Tarradan thought he was simply a superior swordsman, that he thought he simply had a "sense" for how to fight, when in fact it was Nhevalos's magic guiding his footsteps away from danger and toward victory.

Upon discovering this, Harkandos's first thought was to rush out and defeat each of these simpletons as he had Ordell Tarradan. To armor himself against their bee stings and wear out their mortal bodies one by one, then kill them.

But Harkandos had changed during his time in prison. He had sworn to himself that if he ever emerged, he would not only kill Nhevalos, he would destroy the rat in every way possible. He would dig up the rat's holes and warrens wherever they were. He would mangle Nhevalos's schemes, twist them into a ball, and force them down his throat.

As Ordell Tarradan's screams echoed throughout the stone room, Harkandos ruminated.

He couldn't rush out and burn Nhevalos's tapestry. Nhevalos had undoubtedly prepared for that. He *wanted* Harkandos to do that. No, Harkandos had to twist the tapestry, turn it, double it back upon itself. In the end, there must be no tapestry at all, only a frayed bundle of threads, writhing like worms at war right in front of Nhevalos's despairing face.

But how?

Each of these pawns of Nhevalos had not shown that they could defeat Harkandos. Yet Khyven the Unkillable had already defeated Tovos. He'd defeated Jai'ketakos. There was something different about the man that these inferior copies did not have …

"His screams are dying," Mendos said, bringing Harkandos's attention back to the present.

Harkandos's nostrils flared. With a flick of his fingers, he pushed together a finger's width of water inside Ordell Tarradan's mind, making it razor sharp, and slashed. The mortals' screams stopped, and he sagged in his restraints like a sack of wet meal.

Orios raised an eyebrow. Mendos looked ill, because he

knew he might be next. Harkandos almost killed the cowardly weasel right then, but he didn't. A new idea filled him instead.

"Nhevalos wants his champion to kill me because he knows he can't ..." The rat slithered through the slime, staying hidden, poking his pawns forward to do his dirty work, never revealing his face. The fearful behavior made Harkandos want to vomit. He would never do that—

Harkandos would never do that ...

And Nhevalos knew it.

He expected Harkandos to charge his pawns and personally destroy them, because that was how Harkandos was. He believed in leading from the front, not behind the curtains of deception and cowardice. Even with these experiments, he'd taken up the sword himself and fought Nhevalos's pawns.

Harkandos would have to do the opposite. *Choose* a champion. Harkandos would never do that.

Orios cocked her head curiously. "Something, my lord?"

"Oh yes. He wishes to throw his champion at us."

"Yes."

"We will take his champion. We will throw him right back ..." Harkandos began to laugh. He looked up at the mirror behind his throne, looked deeply at his own reflection and the reflection of his minions behind him.

"My lord?" Orios didn't understand. None of them understood.

"We cannot find a match for Khyven the Unkillable," Harkandos said. "So we don't ..."

Orios looked at the dead Ordell Tarradan, then back at Harkandos. She still didn't understand. He laughed again. He had done this once before. In fact, the rat Nhevalos had even been there to witness it. He'd seen it. But he wouldn't see it this time. He wouldn't see this coming.

"I will take his tapestry. I will twist it into a ball," Harkandos murmured. "And I will shove it down his throat."

CHAPTER FIVE

KHYVEN

Khyven awoke to absolute darkness. He opened his eyes, and all was pitch black.

That meant something was wrong, and he immediately closed his eyes again. Khyven and each of his friends had elements that allowed them to see in the dark. Lorelle was bonded to the noktum; she could always see. Rhenn had been reborn, and her new, supernatural body allowed her to see as well. Vohn had his ring—which they'd recovered from the rubble where Jai'ketakos had cut it from Vohn's hand. And Slayter and Khyven had Amulets of Noksonon, which allowed them to see everything in the noktum in shades of gray.

Clearly someone had removed his amulet, which meant even if Khyven opened his eyes wide, he wouldn't be able to see a thing. It also meant that any unthinking creatures of the noktum would destroy him if they were near.

Familiar fear, followed by his battle sense, seized him. In combat, there was always an edge to be had no matter the situation, if one only had the sense to stay calm and find it.

Khyven was prone, but laying down could render advantages if properly played. He was blind, but that could also be used. One of the greatest advantages in all combat was the element of surprise. If his foes thought him helpless, they were arrogant and ignorant. That could be used. He readied himself.

They would be watching him, of course, waiting for a sign he'd awoken. So he didn't move. He kept his breathing even and slow. He listened.

He heard a thump and a clack to his left, a distance away. A table. Something on a table. Someone was likely sitting at a table. Had that been a dagger?

There could be more than the one. Likely there *was* more than one, and once he started moving, they'd all attack. That would, of course, bring the blue wind, and then their advantage of sight would vanish. He'd been blind before and bested the most talented swordsman he'd ever fought. These villains might be waiting for him, but they wouldn't be ready for him. They only thought they were ready—

"Peace, my love." Lorelle's soft voice floated down to him from overhead. She laid a gentle hand on his forehead. "You are safe."

She was right next to him and he hadn't even heard her. Of course, she'd been inhumanly quiet *before* she'd bonded with the Dark.

"Why did you take my amulet?" he asked.

"Slayter."

"Slayter has his own amulet. Why is he using mine?"

"He's not using it. He's studying—Never mind. I'll get it." Her hand lifted from his forehead. Again, he heard nothing as she moved, even though he strained his ears. But a moment later, he heard her voice in the direction where the clacking sound had come from.

"Give it to me," she said.

"I was just—"

"He needs it," Lorelle said.

"But I wasn't done."

"He can't see, Slayter."

"Oh, well. Yes."

In moments, Lorelle delicately laid the chain around Khyven's neck. The room came into focus in shades of gray. Khyven's and Lorelle's bedroom. It was equipped with a bath and stall and a clever device that—Slayter had discovered—was a magical contraption that held water in a basin on the floor, sucked it up through a copper tube, and dispensed it over the head with the force of a heavy rainstorm.

He called it a "shower."

A small wardrobe tucked in against the corner of the west wall. A thin silver chain held a modest ring from the center of the room, from which multiple lanterns could be attached. Again, with a little help from Slayter, the lanterns had been induced to exude the purple glow.

The room had thin windows only as wide as Khyven's shoulders, tall as a person. These were tiny compared to the normal Giant windows and comforting for that fact.

Slayter sat at the little table, his prosthetic leg stuck out to the side. His hair was wet as though he'd recently partaken of his room's "shower," and had come here right after dressing.

On the table lay the Sword and several implements Khyven recognized as Slayter's laboratory instruments. Two sets of metal tongs of different sizes, a padded mitt, a box with a deep top that opened on hinges, revealing several clever little drawers that could be slid out.

A glowing orange ball made of pure light hovered over the sword, and several tiny, lightning-like tendrils extended down from it to the blade.

The Sword spoke in Khyven's mind, as though it had been waiting for him to awaken.

"Good, Slayer of Trolls. You are awake. We have much to do."

Khyven shut his eyes and pressed his lips together. For a moment, he'd almost felt normal. Lorelle's *somnul* had somehow kept the nightmare at bay, and he'd actually slept. But upon waking, he felt the pressure begin to build in the back of his mind. And, of course, the Sword's nattering started immediately.

Lorelle sat on the bed, took his hand, and smiled at him. It was meant to comfort, he was sure, but a hard pit formed in his stomach instead. She thought she was safe here, in this room. They all thought they were safe, at least as much as a person could be with the noktum coating the kingdom, with Nox, Trolls, and Giants wanting them dead.

But he had begun to suspect that the greatest danger to his friends was right here in this room. It was him. And the Sword.

He felt he'd only seen the barest example of what the Sword could truly do. A sword was supposed to be a tool. It was meant to be a tool, but the more time Khyven spent with this sword, the more he felt that *he* was the tool for its agenda. The Sword was devoted to killing its enemies: the Drakanoi or any invaders to Noksonon. But it was perfectly happy to kill whatever else Khyven encountered in the meantime.

And what would the sword do if Khyven ran out of things to kill? What if the war was over and Khyven was only surrounded by friends?

It wouldn't just resign itself to being put on a mantle over the fireplace. It would want something new, and he suspected it wouldn't matter what that something was. Would his friends, then, become the enemy?

"You should sleep more," Lorelle murmured.

"I don't think so."

"You've barely rested."

"How many hours?"

"Barely four."

"That's plenty."

"It's not, in fact." She pushed her hand more forcefully against his forehead and tried to push him back down. He didn't let her, and he sat up. Lorelle had her strengths, but manhandling Humans wasn't one of them. She was nearly as tall as Khyven, but he was three times her weight. Her light frame enabled amazing acrobatics and extraordinary grace, but it had its drawbacks. She could dodge Humans, outleap them, outrace them, but she could not push them around.

"Fine," she said.

"What is he doing?" He slid to the edge of the bed and realized he was naked. He stopped and gathered the sheet around himself, throwing a glare at Lorelle. She shrugged, giving him a crooked smile.

"You just decided to strip me of everything before putting me to bed?"

"Not me. Slayter."

"*Slayter* stripped me?"

"No. I did. But he told me to. He thought there might be residual magic in your clothes."

"What? Why?"

"You're funny. I'm supposed to know what he's doing? Half the time I don't think *he* knows what he's doing. How can I? He pokes around and fiddles with things and suddenly we have dragon fire-retardant cloaks, life-sucking swords, and sword-swallowing scabbards. He knows things we don't. He came in and started tinkering with the sword. He asked for your amulet. He asked for your clothes. So I gave him what he wanted. What did you want me to do?"

"Your mage is inquisitive," the Sword said in his mind. *"Did you know that intelligent blood tastes different than stupid blood?"*

"Slayter, don't touch the Sword!" Khyven wanted to jump across the room and snatch the thing up, and he cast about for his pants instead. A fresh pair was draped across a chair near the bed, though not near enough to grab.

"I'll get them." Lorelle stood up.

"Slayter!" Khyven growled. "Did you hear me?"

As usual, the mage was lost in his thoughts. Khyven picked up a pillow and threw it at him. It hit the table and slid up the Sword. Slayter looked up.

"Oh," he said. "You're awake. Good."

Lorelle tossed the pants to Khyven. He caught them and—

A fresh tunic hit him in the face. He pulled it off and glared at her. She wore an unrepentant smirk.

"I told him he should take it to his laboratory," she said.

"Oh, I quite agree," Slayter said, putting his hands on either side of the orange ball. It expanded for a moment's then contracted and vanished. The little bits of lightning went with it. "But it wouldn't let me."

"Wouldn't let you?" Lorelle asked. "The Sword?"

"Couldn't budge it."

"You touched it?" Khyven asked.

Slayter's mouth was open as though he was about to say something exciting, then he closed it and frowned at Khyven. "It's Mavric iron."

"I *know* it's Mavric iron—"

"Well if I touched it, my flesh would bubble—"

"I know what happens, Slayter. I was there!"

"If you know, and I know, then perhaps you could explain why you would ask if I—"

"Just don't touch it."

"I used gloves and tongs. Did you think I wouldn't use gloves and tongs?"

"You shouldn't even try to move it."

"Well that was the most curious thing. A Sword this size should easily weigh twenty pounds. Probably more like twenty-five. Of course, we all know it doesn't. But when I went to pick it up with the tongs, I couldn't budge it. Not even a jostle. Like it suddenly became part of the table. Like it didn't *want* to be moved."

"Just leave it alone," Khyven said.

He looked quizzically at Khyven, then at Lorelle.

"I asked him to see if he could understand more about it," Lorelle said.

"Tell me you didn't touch it," Khyven said to her this time. He didn't want Lorelle anywhere near the sword.

She arched an eyebrow.

"It's dangerous, is all," Khyven said. "And I don't know much about it except that it likes to kill. It encourages me to kill. It keeps giving me new nicknames every time I kill something new."

"Luminent blood tastes like bright light," the Sword said.

"Enough!" Khyven sent back to it, even though he knew it wouldn't matter. The Sword only listened to him when he planned to kill something.

"It's aware of you, then?" Slayter said.

"I told you that. I told you it was talking to me."

"Well, I thought it just whispered in your ear. I thought it was something like, 'kill, kill, kill.' Not a full sentience."

"Slayter, I told you …" Khyven started, and a shiver went up his back. "Yes, it is aware of me."

"This is tedious," the Sword said. *"There is a Drakanoi flying about Noksonon like it belongs here. Like it rules this place. It laughs at all of us."*

"It says it finds your experiments tedious."

Slayter's eyes glowed. "Did it really? Oh that is just … That is spectacular."

"He is persistent," the Sword said, its voice was a low whisper. It wasn't a compliment. That was a threat.

"Get away from it. Come over here," Khyven said.

Slayter looked at the Sword, then back at Khyven, then back at the Sword. His fingertips rested on the top of the table like he didn't want to lose contact with it. Reluctantly, he said, "Very well."

Lorelle watched the whole exchange, and Khyven quickly wriggled into his pants beneath the blankets. Slayter didn't take his eyes off the Sword during his short walk to the bed, like he was still doing whatever he'd been doing with the glowing sphere, but in his head.

"What exactly *were* you doing?" Khyven asked.

Not looking where he was going, Slayter knocked his metal prosthetic leg into the bedframe. He overbalanced and toppled. Khyven grabbed his arm and steadied him before he fell onto the bed. Lorelle gave a quiet chuckle.

With a bit of surprise, Slayter seemed to suddenly notice he'd reached his destination, then he sat down. "Well, I was trying to understand the Sword's properties. They're even more extensive than I originally thought. As I mentioned, there are a handful of legendary Mavric iron swords that were created thousands of years ago. I'm convinced this is one of them. The question is: which one? We simply didn't have a moment to ascertain this after its performance with the dragon, did we? Then we came back, then the world went dark, then—"

"I was there, Slayter."

"Well, Lorelle suddenly seemed to think it was important to know this now. I couldn't agree more. And I did discover something."

"And that is?"

"Simply put, that edged intelligence sitting on the table is the most powerful magical artifact I've ever studied, which is saying something considering that we're sitting in a Giant's castle with a vault full of Giant artifacts to which we've been given full access."

"All right." Khyven didn't know what was in the Vault, though both Vohn and Slayter had told him about it. He'd been too busy trying to save as many Usarans as he could.

"It's surprising because I didn't realize how much more there was to the Sword back at the palace. I lost interest."

"*You* lost interest in a magic Sword?"

"Exactly. Interesting, yes? I think it wanted me to lose interest. I think it *pretended* to be a normal Mavric iron sword. A normal Mavric iron sword." Slayter seemed amused by that concept. "An oxymoron, for sure."

"A what?" Khyven frowned, and Slayter watched him.

"A normal Mavric iron sword. Because it's Mavric iron, and nothing made with Mavric iron is ever normal—"

"No. What kind of moron?"

Slayter raised an eyebrow. "What?"

"You called the Sword a moron."

"No, I—Oh! Oh that's funny."

Khyven ground his teeth. "When I kill you, it won't be funny."

"Apologies. Oxymoron. It means contradictory terms."

"You can't just say contradictory terms?"

"But it's one word instead of two."

"When have you ever been worried about saying too many words?"

"Well, it's a *perfect* word. For this instance, anyway."

Khyven clenched his teeth, and he envisioned giving the Sword a taste of "intelligent" blood.

"Stop it," he growled in his mind to the sword.

"But you want to kill him. I just want to help you."

"I don't want to kill him! Get that through your steely head!"

"Come now, Slayer of Trolls. These mortals are holding you back," the Sword said. *"Slay them and we can continue our search for the Drakanoi."*

Khyven launched from the bed, startling Slayter and even Lorelle. He stalked to the Sword and snatched it up—

He shivered as he took it up, and he felt complete again. When he was with the Sword, it was as if everything was right.

"Yes ... " the Sword said.

"I have another idea," Khyven said through gritted teeth, putting another fist around the Sword like he was pulling Hellface's reins to make him behave. "The Sword manipulated you."

"Manipulated me?"

"Yes," Khyven said.

"Do elaborate."

"I don't need to elaborate. Shake your head, Slayter, because the Sword is blocking your better sense right now. You actually said, 'I lost interest.' You said that. When was the last time you lost interest in a magical puzzle?"

Slayter opened his mouth to speak, then closed it. He cocked his head. "Well that is fascinating."

"This is tedious," the Sword growled. It quivered in his hands. Images flashed into Khyven's mind: leaping to the bed, beheading Slayter. And after Slayter, Lorelle, and after that—

"Khyven," Lorelle's voice broke through the fantasy.

He gasped and opened his eyes. Senji's Teeth, he hadn't even realized he'd closed them.

He looked down. The Sword had punched through the stone table like it was clay. Its point poked into the floor below.

"It's controlling you, Slayter," Khyven said. "By Senji, it might be controlling all of us. I think it reached into your mind and took away your curiosity."

"Well, I ..."

"And all this time, I've been telling you about the whispers, about the power of this Sword, and you've just 'not had enough time' or you 'lost interest.' Does that even sound like you?"

Slayter got a faraway look, like he did when he was considering a problem that had many parts.

Lorelle stood there. Her playful gaze had gone serious, and she watched him with concern.

"Well, give it to me now," Slayter finally said. "Let's take it down to my laboratory and I'll do proper experiments this time."

The Sword vibrated, bidding him to pull it out and have it free in the open air. Khyven jammed it harder down, piercing the floor.

"No."

"No?"

"I find this horribly tedious, Slayer of Trolls," the Sword said in a deadly tone.

"This is one mystery you don't get to solve," Khyven said. "Let it go."

"I thought you just said to do the opposite."

"No, I wanted to point out to you how dangerous this thing is. We need to bury it. Where should we bury it?"

"Oh, well. Well, we could put it in the Vault."

"Where you or Vohn or Rhenn could get it? No." With effort, Khyven took one hand off the hilt. It was nearly impossible. His arm shook.

"Do not leave, Slayer of Trolls. We have much to do."

Khyven tried to take his second hand off the hilt, and it wouldn't come. He growled, gritting his teeth and concentrated every ounce of will on his fist.

It finally uncurled and came free.

"You are wasting time," the Sword warned.

Khyven crossed the room to the weapons rack they'd hauled up here. It held a number of weapons they'd brought from the Night Ring. A halberd he particularly liked. A steel whip. A morning star. His favorite spear. He hadn't known what this war would bring, and they'd taken everything he thought he'd might need in defense of this castle, should that moment come.

But most of all, it had his sword belt with his normal steel sword and his wooden sword, The Diplomat. He couldn't remember when he'd taken that off in favor of just wearing the Sword. But he buckled them back on now. The sheath for the Giant sword was also there, and after hesitating a moment, he put that on, too.

"You are going to rid yourself of the Sword," Slayter guessed. As usual, his leaping intellect had landed on the correct answer.

"You're damned right I am."

"I think that would be a mistake."

"Do you?" Khyven strode back toward the stone table with the Sword sticking up from it.

"Yes."

Khyven paused before the table, reluctant to take up the Sword again. "It's filling my mind with images. Would you like to know what the images are?"

"Well, based on your twitchy reactions and hasty decisions, I would guess it's telling you to kill me."

Khyven looked over at him. "And Lorelle."

"That is particularly dangerous," Slayter agreed, though he didn't sound scared. The damned mage never sounded scared.

"My point."

"But I have seen what you can do with that Sword. The Nox. The Trolls. The dragon. You cut through dragon scales like you just cut through that table."

"Yes?"

"Do you know how thick and tough and magically bound dragon scales are? Impervious. I did some research on that. There are several books on the Drakanoi in this castle. In fact, there are a wealth of books on just about every subject in this castle. You know, if I'd just come into the noktum before now, I could have learned so much about Noksonon I didn't know. Such as, that it was possible for the noktum to cover the continent again—"

"Slayter," Lorelle interrupted him. "You were talking about dragon scales."

"Oh well yes. Simply put, your normal sword would have bounced off. I'm not entirely sure it's possible for a normal weapon to pierce dragon scales. Maybe a bolt from a ballista."

"I know how powerful the Sword is," Khyven said. "I'm getting rid of it."

"Well… No," Slayter said.

"No?" Khyven headed toward the door—

It slammed shut, orange light surrounding it.

Khyven spun. Slayter held his hand up, and crumbling bits of clay fell from his glowing fingers.

"No."

CHAPTER SIX

KHYVEN

layter, what are you doing?" Khyven asked in a low tone.

"*Remove him,*" the Sword said. "*He stands in your way.*"

Khyven's arm raised of its own volition. His fingers touched the pommel. With a grunt, he lowered his hand until it slapped the pommel of The Diplomat and pulled it instead.

The Sword growled its disappointment.

"I want you to listen to me," Slayter said.

"You sound like you're stepping up to tell me I should keep the Sword."

"I think you should keep the Sword," Slayter said. "You're not thinking clearly."

"You want to know why?"

"I imagine you're going to tell me 'The Sword.'"

Khyven barked an ugly laugh. "When you closed the door, do you know what it told me?"

"To kill me, I would guess."

"Yes, it did!" Khyven growled, hating how Slayter just seemed to think he knew everything. "How do you know this isn't some work of the Giant who released the noktum? How do you know this isn't a festering sliver they've pushed into my mind? What if suddenly I'm a plant for the enemy?"

"Slayter," Lorelle finally spoke up. "He makes a good point. If Khyven turns ... I can't think of a more devastating enemy."

"He won't turn."

Khyven clenched his teeth.

"That's your burden, Khyven," Slayter said. "The Sword. It can help us fight Giants, and we need every single weapon that can fight Giants. I have a vault of artifacts. And there are surprisingly few that I think could kill a Giant, and none are as powerful as a sentient Mavric iron sword that was designed to kill Giants. We can't afford to throw away this advantage."

"It's not an advantage if it kills us all!"

"Which is why you have it. Stop it from killing us all. Guide it to where we need it most."

"Stop it? Oh, just 'stop it' eh? Great. Sure. What if I can't!"

"I think you can."

"Well good for you. Why don't *you* wield the Sword!"

"Well first, I am not a swordsman. I could be rather good with the Sword guiding my hand, I imagine, but I could never be as good as you." Slayter ticked off the reason on one finger as though it hadn't been a rhetorical question. He peeled another finger from his fist. "Second, the blue wind is the perfect—"

"Could you not be such an idiot for once?" Khyven barked.

Slayter seemed unfazed, and his eyes held an intransigent fire, which wasn't usual. "But most importantly. You are the most stubborn, willful man I've ever seen. If anyone could throw off the shackles of a magical sword, it's you."

"Slayter—"

"In short," Slayter continued. "If you can't wield that Sword, no one can. No Human, anyway. You have to hold on. You have to master it."

As he spoke, Khyven's felt compelled to draw the Sword

again. The Diplomat shook in his hand. He wanted to drop it, pull the Sword and end this conversation in blood.

He spun and grabbed the door handle, and he prayed Slayter wouldn't try to stop him again.

The door swung wide, and Khyven gasped his relief. He sprinted into the hallway, running for all he was worth.

He reached the staircase and leapt down the giant steps two at a time. Down and down and down, past the refugees at the ground level, and deep into the sub-levels of the castle. At first, he just ran without a thought, but once the polished, perfect hallways of the upper levels gave way to the rougher stone walls of the lower levels, he knew exactly where he was going.

It heartened him, that he realized he had unconsciously run toward the one place that could solve his problem. It was hope that at least in the deepest recess of his mind, his thoughts still belonged to him. If the Sword controlled him, at least it didn't control all of him.

With the Amulet of Noksonon, there wasn't a place in the world Khyven couldn't see. The rock-hewn hallways appeared in sharp relief, but not because of any light source. The amulets were tricky that way. There was no light source; the amulet made it seem like the viewer *was* the light source, and the shape of objects appeared as though with shadows behind them.

Despite the fact that he knew this to be true, it seemed to get "darker" the lower he went. Perhaps it was the knowledge that he'd gone deeper into the earth than people ever do. Perhaps it was the oppressive feeling that millions of tons of rock stacked above him in a carved and multi-layered castle.

Perhaps it was more pronounced in these deeper hallways that nothing seemed to live in this entire castle. It was as though the normal denizens found this place repellent. There were no rats, no spiders, and the sense that—aside from the marks in the dust from his friends and the odd, enormous taloned feet of the deceased Rauvelos—no feet had walked these hallways for an age.

The air was stale and heavy, and it actually seemed harder to breathe in this place. Khyven put all of that from his mind.

He went to the Vault, three stories down, which with the size of the stairs and the size of the levels made it seem like he'd descended to the center of the earth.

The Vault had tall double doors that stood out in sharp contrast to the unfinished walls. It was filled to the walls with artifacts that Khyven didn't understand. Not even Slayter understood them all, though he'd been trying to catalogue them since they'd arrived.

Vohn, in his banshee form, had brought them here and shown them what Rauvelos had left for them. He'd said he thought the giant raven had wanted to tell Vohn more, but Jai'ketakos had killed him before he could.

Khyven approached the door and cursed himself. There was a key that Vohn had passed on to Slayter, and Khyven didn't have it. Slayter said he'd discovered that the doors possessed a deterrent to those who tried to get in without the key. The first time someone took hold of the rings on the doors and pulled, they simply wouldn't open. The second time they were pulled without the key, not only wouldn't they open, but the person would be given a small lighting shock. If that didn't dissuade them, the third time they grabbed it, the lightning would be so strong it would knock them unconscious.

Khyven hadn't asked Slayter how he knew about that progression, but he was pretty sure Slayter had tested it on himself.

The Vault's magical artifacts had been safe down here for thousands of years. That might have been a sufficient resting place for the Sword in and of itself, but Khyven had thought of an even better place. A vault within the Vault.

Slayter had shown him a box called the *Ankeed Ruut*. The mage had barely been interested in the box. He'd been far more interested in weapons they might use against the Giants, not a safekeeping box. But he'd mentioned the *Ankeed Ruut* in passing because he'd been excited about the *Tolkimine*.

The *Tolkimine* was a tome that catalogued everything in the

Vault. Slayter had said it was like learning an entirely new language in a matter of moments, a language of magic and artifacts. He had gone on to mention a dozen other artifacts, none of which Khyven could remember.

The *Ankeed Ruut*, however, Khyven *had* remembered. And now it might be his salvation. According to Slayter, once something had been secured inside the *Ankeed Ruut*, the person inserting the item simply had to close the lid. As the lid clicked home, they spoke a password, and the box would remember it. If the person who had left the item was not the person to return, or if the person who had left the item forgot their password, the box would be empty when opened. Or at least it would look empty. Only the original person to secure something in the box could retrieve the thing they'd left behind.

Slayter had imagined there might be a hundred items in the box. Apparently it didn't have a stated capacity. There could be untold powerful artifacts trapped in there from millennia ago, items that would never again be retrieved because their masters were long dead.

That was the place for the Sword. Khyven could lock it in there and then, as long as he never returned to open it, no one could ever find it again.

But he'd forgotten the damned key to the Vault.

With a snarl, Khyven grabbed the giant rings—one on each door and each too thick for his hand to get around completely—and shook the damned thing while growling his frustration to the air.

He let go. It was useless. He'd have to climb all the way back up to Slayter, get the key, and then explain why he was going to get rid of the Sword to a bright-eyed mage who was going to try to talk him out of it again.

And every moment he spent here was another moment the Sword might start talking to him again. It was a miracle the thing had shut up this far. He didn't know why it had gone quiet. Perhaps there were no lifeforms around to kill, so it simply wasn't interested.

It also spoke to the notion that the Sword, at least, didn't read minds. If it had known why Khyven was headed here, it would have protested, he was sure.

He glared at the doors, and he was tempted to grab the rings again. He knew they'd shock him, but somehow he felt he deserved it at the moment.

"You want the key?" a soft voice asked from behind him.

CHAPTER SEVEN

KHYVEN

K hyven whirled, and Lorelle materialized from the wall. Normally, with the Amulet of Noksonon, it was impossible to hide in the shadows. There were no real shadows. But Lorelle's bond with the Dark seemed to follow different rules. Apparently there were nonsensical shadows within the noktum that only Lorelle could see. And use.

"You followed me."

She blinked, then said, "You're a sword fighter."

"What?"

"Oh, I thought we were stating the obvious. You going to grab those handles again and get jolted? Or do you want the key?" She produced the big, thick, golden key and held it out on one finger.

"Yes."

"I have to admit, watching you grab those handles again would have been entertaining."

"What are you doing here?"

"My mother always told me there were no dumb questions,

but ..."

"Lorelle—"

"You go running off agitated. Angry. Exhausted. And you think I'm simply going to stay in the room with Slayter while he calmly switches subjects from you to his beloved Vault catalog?" She shook her head. "No, I don't think so."

"I'm getting rid of the Sword."

"Are you." She spoke her question like a statement.

"Yes. I am."

"I don't think you should," she said

"Why not?"

"Because Slayter doesn't think you should."

"Slayter's an idiot."

"All evidence to the contrary."

"The mage is smart in a lot of ways. But when it comes to some things, he's an idiot."

"But this is a magical artifact, Khyven. Who are you going to trust more?"

"He doesn't know this artifact. I do."

She touched her chin. "Maybe."

"No. For certain."

"How many times has he been wrong?"

"What?"

"Slayter. How many times that you can remember?"

"The man stumbles around all the time! He forgets things. Doesn't pay attention to other things. He trips over his own feet."

"Yes, he does. But when he says, 'This is what we need to do.' Or 'I have an idea that may work.' How many times has he been wrong?"

"I ... I don't know."

"Zero times. It's amazing to me that he doesn't hate all of us, as dumb as we must seem to him. He sees this sword as a component to victory. Only a fool wouldn't give that serious consideration."

"Well, he's wrong. He's wrong this time."

"Hmmm ..."

"Are you going to give me the key or not?"

She flipped it to him, and he caught it.

"Don't do it."

"Don't do what? I didn't even say anything."

"Whatever you're going to do. Don't do it. You should trust him."

"I would, except neither of you know what you're talking about. I'm trying to protect you."

"I know that. Slayter knows that. You think we don't? You have our backs. That's not what is happening here."

"And what is happening?"

"You need to believe we'll have yours. Despite what it seems, Slayter doesn't just talk to talk."

"You don't know ..." Khyven clenched the key in his fist, pressed his knuckles against the metal door. "You can't hear it in your head. You don't wonder if every action you make is your own. I'm not afraid you don't have my back, Lorelle. I know you do. I'm not even afraid I won't have yours. What I'm afraid of is that it won't be me standing there at all. One minute I'll be me, and the next I'll be this ... thing. This bodiless entity who lives for blood."

"You won't let it do that," she said softly.

"You don't know that!" he shouted, clenching his teeth. He didn't want to shout at her. It felt like his blood was boiling. He kept waiting for the Sword to whisper into his mind. "I don't know if I have that strength."

"You do."

"And what if it asks me to ..." he began but clamped his mouth shut. He didn't want to say that. He didn't want to think that.

She approached him, her hand rising like she would stroke his cheek.

"Don't." He turned and warded her off with a quick gesture. "Don't touch me. I'm not ... I don't trust myself."

"Oh Khyven ..." she murmured softly. But she stopped, and

her hand slowly floated down to her side.

He thought about if he should tell her his greatest fear. He simply didn't know what was right anymore. Should he just do what he came here to do, or should he let her see the ugliest part of himself?

It cracked his heart, the notion of what she might do if he told her his fear. When she saw it … Was it safer to keep her on the outside?

He wrestled with that and Lorelle, bless her, stayed quiet.

In the end, cowardice lost. He couldn't hide from his fear. If she was going to pass judgement on him, then he would simply have to take what he had earned.

"What if it's not the Sword at all," he murmured. "What I'm the one who wants to fight, to murder, to hunt down those who have angered me and destroy them. What if I'm just that same selfish Ringer who now has more power than he ever dreamed? Enough power to murder at will—"

"You're not."

"But I am, Lorelle. Today, fighting those Nox, those Trolls, I loved it. I felt …" He remembered the rush of euphoria. "I wanted to kill them, and the only disappointing thing was that I didn't have more of them to cut down."

"Khyven," she protested. "That's not you—"

"What about Rhenn's camp? What I did to you, to Rhenn, to Vohn … I brought Vamreth down on you. Rhenn's followers … I may as well have killed all those people. Two hundred people, Lorelle. It may as well have been my hand on the hilt of those bloody weapons."

"You came to save us," she said. "You *did* save us. You fought for us like a mad Kyolar, gave Rhenn and me time to escape. And then you saved us again. You sacrificed your life to end Vamreth and return Rhenn's kingdom to her. You made up for—"

"Don't say that. Don't even think it. Nobody can make up for something like that." He shook his head. "You can't undo that kind of damage. They haunt my dreams … All those people.

All because you spurned me and I took the revenge I thought I deserved. I ran back to my old life and unleashed death upon you. I was weak, selfish, and petty for just one moment and two hundred people died. Nothing can ever change that. Nothing I can do will ever make up for that. And now I have this Sword. It's like having Vamreth's entire army right here in my sheath, and every moment stands on the edge of a knife for me. If I slip and fall ... I know I'm going to wake up and see that horror all over again. People falling to chopping blades, to burning fire, to an inhuman bloodlust. Except this time it'll be my hand on the hilt, raising and falling, chopping people to bits ..."

"You won't do that."

"You say I'll resist. But what if the Sword is just stripping away the lies?"

"What lies?"

"That I'm actually a knight, that I'm worthy to be your lover, worthy to be friends with Rhenn, Slayter, Vohn.... What if the Sword isn't forcing its agenda on me, but feeding on what is already in my heart, giving me the freedom to be what I truly am? What if the Sword only whispers the truth about a person's soul?"

He waited for her to recoil in horror, to close up like the Lorelle of old: eyes hard, lips pressed together ...

But compassion glistened in her eyes, and she whispered, "No."

That quiet, confident word swept through him like a wind. Suddenly his certainty was just a pile of leaves scattered by a warm and powerful wind.

"Lorelle—"

"No." She interrupted him, holding up a hand. "I have listened to you, Khyven. Now you listen to me. You are not that selfish Ringer. You never were. You had the heart of a hero as a child, from the moment you leapt out of that burning building. But fate—or the conspiring of Readers and Giants—took you. They bent you and shaped you and twisted you until you thought you knew what your life should be. But you bent and twisted yourself back. Don't you see? Even the machinations of these near-gods didn't stop you from reverting to your true type. That is what I see when I look at you, when I look into you. Not some selfish, murderous man seeking any opportunity to ply his bloody desires on the world, but a man who has come through his fire and bears his scars and burdens nobly. You are not what Vamreth tried to make you, nor even what Nhevalos tried to make you. You are that boy, grown into a man. You are that hero. You are Khyven the Unkillable."

He stood there, breathing hard, and he suddenly realized he was holding the Sword in his hand ... He didn't remember drawing it. In fact, he hadn't heard its whispers since he'd begun his descent into the castle.

"I can't hear the Sword," he murmured.

"I know," she said.

"You know? How do you know?"

"Because I'm blocking it."

"How can you do that?"

"I feel it in your mind, Khyven. I can't hear what it says, but I can feel it there. That's what a Luminent soul-bond is. I am inside you. Since you fled Slayter, I flooded your soul with mine. I've been trying to drown it out."

"And when you stop?"

"Khyven—"

"When you stop, what happens?"

She just watched him, a sad look on her face.

He shook his head and inserted the key. With a quick twist and a heavy *click*, the doors opened to reveal the inside of the Vault.

It was organized with wooden bins like a fish market. In addition, racks adorned the black stone walls all around, made for taller artifacts. There were scepters and jewelry boxes, swords and spears, antique chests, cubbies filled with scrolls, and ledges with sculptures. Two desks sat against the far wall, and neither of them were for writing or drafting. Slayter didn't know exactly what they did, but he was working on it.

There were three rows of those wooden bins, plus the shelves and ledges along the walls, in addition to the weapons racks. Everything was neat and orderly, with aisles wide enough to fit a giant raven. Whatever else Rauvelos had been, he'd been a tidy creature.

Slayter practically salivated when he entered this room for the first time, but Khyven had had just about enough of magical things. He ignored everything around him and strode to the last bin in the middle row. Within was a small leather box, one foot square. It had thick gilding, metal riveted to the sides with polished metal nubs at the corners and a lock on the front. The whole thing was in shades of gray and black.

Khyven didn't know why, but he imagined in the sunlight, the leather of the box would be a mottled purple, like snakeskin, and the metal gilding would be gold. He withdrew the box, took it to one of the desks, set it down on the flat surface, and opened it. Though there was a keyhole on the front of the lid, it didn't require a key, not like the Vault doors required a key. The thing simply opened up. Inside was a normal interior made of wood. He could see the grain of it. It was smooth and polished, and he imagined it would look like lacquered redwood in the light.

He drew the Sword from his back.

For the first time since he'd fled his and Lorelle's bedroom, the voice slithered into his mind. It was quieter, like it did not have the absolute dominion in his head that it usually did, like it was straining to reach him.

"What do you think you are doing?" the Sword asked.

In answer, he held it over the box and, just as Slayter had said would happen, the box changed shape. It elongated from a one-foot cube, its width stretching to seven feet long, though the rest of its dimensions stayed the same.

The box became exactly the size the Sword would need.

"The Ankeed Ruut?*"* the Sword said, as though it recognized the artifact. *"Don't be silly. You don't want to do that."*

Khyven laid the Sword in the box.

"We belong together, Slayer of Trolls. We were meant to——"

Khyven closed the lid and whispered to the keyhole, "Never again …"

The keyhole responded with a profound click, shutting away the Sword, locking it away forever.

Khyven gasped as his mind emptied. It felt like his head had been a giant cistern filled with water, and suddenly the plug had been pulled. All the water flowed out, and none of it was his. He could never have imagined how much space the Sword had taken up in his mind until it all drained away.

He staggered back from the *Ankeed Ruut* and fell to one knee. He also felt like someone had swept all the vigor from his body. Lorelle was suddenly there, holding his arm. His ears rang with that deafening silence, and his body felt gutted.

"You're all right," Lorelle murmured. "I'm here. You're all right."

The *Ankeed Ruut* slowly retracted back to its normal cube-like shape.

"It's gone …" he said. "I didn't know how … How large it had become."

"I felt it. Let's get you out of here."

"No."

"No?"

"Check it. Check the box."

"You mean open it?"

"I have to know."

She hesitated, then nodded and went to the box.

He struggled to his feet, but he had to push up on one of the wooden bins to manage it. He had no strength, as though every ounce of his exertion over the last few weeks had all come due in this one moment.

As though the Sword had been propping him up all this time.

By Senji…

Lorelle opened the box. It was empty.

"Good," Khyven said wearily. "Good."

"Shall I put it back in its bin?"

He nodded. It seemed entirely too much effort to talk, and he suddenly feared he was going to pass out. She took his arm and draped it around her neck, propped him up. Apparently, she thought the same.

They exited the Vault, locked the doors, and he gave her back the key. He didn't want it. He didn't ever want to see this room again.

"Hold onto your stomach." She unfurled her cloak.

Khyven grunted. "We're going that way, are we?"

"You think you're climbing those steps again? You're cute."

"I am. So very cute. Didn't you know?" Exhausted as he was, he felt freed. So free, he could actually manage a joke.

"I do know," she said.

The cloak curled around him like a gentle arm, and the Dark took them both.

CHAPTER EIGHT

KHYVEN

Khyven awoke in the sunshine. Buttery light filtered through the leaves overhead and dappled the ground in a blanket of almost-sensible shapes. Dark and light, dark and light, like a normal world.

Am I dreaming? he thought. The last thing he remembered was Lorelle's cloak wrapping around him.

He blinked, turned his head. Beyond the shady grass where he lay, a green meadow stretched out. The whole area looked too peaceful to exist. It had to be a dream. This was the promise of a lazy summer. A scattering of warmth in a world that had turned as cold and deadly as a dagger.

I have to be dreaming, he thought again. He sat up.

"Not bad, is it?" Lorelle's soft voice came from behind him. Khyven wrenched himself around to look at her, blinked again.

She wore the red dress, the same dress she'd worn that day in Rhenn's camp when he'd tried to tell her that he could love her. That they might be together.

The day she'd unequivocally rejected him.

Lorelle hadn't worn a dress in ... Well, he'd never seen her wear a dress since.

"If I remember, you liked this one." She gave him a half-smile.

"I *am* dreaming," he said aloud.

"You and me both. She did a good job, didn't she?"

Khyven stood up, reflexively reached for the Sword at his back—

It wasn't there. No. Of course it wasn't. He'd put it in the *Ankeed Ruut*. He'd rid himself of it.

"She ... You ... This ... Is all this going to start making more sense?" he asked.

"A holiday. So no, it doesn't make much sense in these times. But she insisted."

"She?"

"Who do you think?" Lorelle made an arc across the sky with her hand. As always, he was captivated by her grace. She was like a willow bending in the wind. She was the wind itself. There was nothing more beautiful to him than Lorelle dancing, and he simply couldn't stop looking at her when she did that.

For the first time in a long time, he smiled.

"The sunshine. The meadow. I think she's trying to recreate that place I mentioned once to you."

"Rhenn did this." Khyven finally shook loose the last of the fog. He felt like he was waking from a great sleep. He glanced around and noticed the edges of the noktum all around them, pushed back by the raven totems they had used to encircle Rhenn's rebel camp before. "Rhenn set this up."

"I think she's nesting." Lorelle wore that half-smile that was part mocking, part genuine, and one hundred percent Lorelle. "She might be testing it out on us first."

"This is *your* meadow," Khyven said, remembering the conversation in a meadow very much like this one, back in Rhenn's camp, back when he thought he knew everything he needed to know. "The one where you're safe."

"Where my friends are safe, yes. That's what I think she was thinking."

"But we aren't safe," he said. "Behind that wall of night are all the problems we left behind."

Lorelle moved toward him, seeming to float over the ground, though he could see her dark toes lightly touching the grass. Despite the urgency he felt in his bones, in his twitchy muscles, in the hair that raised on his forearms at all that needed doing, at all the battles that were coming, Khyven couldn't help but be mesmerized. She was so beautiful. He stared at the slope of her long smooth neck, the swish of her dress below her swaying hips.

Before he'd quite had his fill of looking at her body, he glanced up at her eyes, and her gaze caught him. She gracefully moved up next to him, a mere hand span away. She seemed so relaxed for their being in the midst of a world-destroying war, for them being a heartbeat away from disaster. He knew that calm, seemingly carefree look was supposed to relax him, but he couldn't relax. He just couldn't.

She took his chin in her delicate fingers and kissed him. Her lips were light, feathery and intentional, like the brush strokes of an artist. She softly broke the kiss and backed up, but only an inch.

"How long have I been asleep?" he asked.

"Long enough for you to recover. Long enough for you to rest."

"That's not an answer."

"We are safe," she murmured. "For this moment, we are safe. How's that for an answer?"

"I'm not sure it's true."

She ran a light fingertip along his jaw, then over his lips. "A little lie, perhaps. But if it nourishes us for the moment, is that so bad? Can we not steal a moment for ourselves?"

"This is your new face?" He grinned, despite himself. "Thief of time?"

She pushed her cheek against his, so smooth, and whispered in his ear. "Lay down in the warm grass, and we will steal what safety we can before the storm."

"You're not worried about mingling with this dark soul?"

"I'm sorry ..." she whispered. "Whose soul are you referring to?"

He laughed.

"I tell you what, my lord, why don't you let me show you what I think ought to be done with your soul. And your body. And we'll both leave these gloomy thoughts behind for just a moment. Lay down."

"You're not giving up on this 'living within a dream for a few minutes' idea, are you?"

"A few *minutes*? I may have to hurt you a little bit for that."

He chuckled, and he finally surrendered to her relentless seduction. "If I'm lucky."

She arched an eyebrow as though he was supposed to say something more.

"Is there something I'm missing?"

"Will you make a lady ask thrice?"

"Which 'lady' are you referring to?"

Her foot slipped behind him and with an expert twist of her hips, she swept him off his feet. He thudded heavily to the ground with a grunt and a laugh.

"*This* lady. And I asked you to lay down."

"Is this where the hurting begins?" he coughed.

"Need I ask thrice about anything else?"

"No," he said. "No, you won't."

She kissed him. He took her in his arms, and he had no intention of letting her go anytime soon.

CHAPTER NINE

SHALURE

Shalure gasped and woke. A hazy white mist drifted over her head. Breathing hard, she sat up. She was draped in white clothing, a diaphanous gown that seemed familiar. The V-neck, the folds that sloped down to her cleavage, the bare arms. Yes, she'd worn this dress before, but it had been red.

She looked down at the grass. It was also white. Lucious blades of the softest, most vibrant grass she'd ever seen … and it was white. Even her arms were paler than normal, verging on white with just a hint of the pink of her normal skin tone.

"What is happening?" she murmured, and gasped again.

Her tongue was back. She could speak! She moved it around in her mouth, touching the insides of her teeth, stunned.

"Gods!" she murmured.

"No," a voice said.

The mists parted to reveal an enormous boulder right in front of Shalure. A woman in full battle armor leaned casually against it.

"Just me," the woman said. Her ice blue eyes were as hard as diamonds, and she regarded Shalure coldly.

Shalure's first instinct was to retreat, even if it meant crab crawling away from the woman, but she kept a handle on her fear. Everything about the woman exuded power. She was seven feet tall if she was a foot, a head taller than Khyven. The white-enameled plate mail armor seemed ... frosty, like she had pulled it from a snowbank. A huge, two-handed sword hilt rose above her right shoulder. A battle axe hung from hooks at her left hip, a pair of long daggers from her right. If that wasn't enough of an arsenal, a wide-bladed spear leaned against the boulder. The spear had blood on it.

A floor-length blue cloak hung from the wide shoulder plates, and every curve of the armor seemed perfectly sculpted to the woman's body. Her white hair was pulled back from her face and woven into a braid as thick as Shalure's wrist, which wound around the woman's neck and down along her right side, ending at her waist. She wore coal black gloves and boots, the only dark color in her icy ensemble. The boots seemed to shift and flicker like mirages. Shalure couldn't look directly at them.

A sense of familiarity hit Shalure alongside the bone-deep fear. She was in the presence of a killer. Everything about the woman screamed it. But somehow ... Shalure knew this woman.

Except Shalure had never met a woman who stood seven feet tall. She'd never met anyone who wore armor like that. And there was no crest that told the woman's house.

"Shalure Chadrone," the woman stated, as though confirming something.

Shalure swallowed, still caught between the instinct to flee and the determination not to.

"You were once a lady when you were connected to your father. Then almost a lady again," the woman said, and her lip curled. "*If* you had married someone of standing. If you had attained that which you so desperately craved. Social standing. Validation. Worth. You'd have been a 'lady.' Would you feel better if I addressed you with your chosen moniker? Would you feel your value increase?"

"I …" Shalure finally had a tongue again, but she could find no words.

The woman's eyes flashed. "Lady Shalure it is."

"Wh-where am I?"

"Almost dead now," the woman said.

A spear of desperation stabbed through Shalure. "No!"

"Is it really such a shock, *Lady* Shalure? You've been almost dead for quite some time now, even before I saved your life. Moping around for the lack of a lover's attention. Would it really have mattered if Jai'ketakos had finished the job?"

"Wh-what?"

"I'm speaking of the sad existence you led. Seeking your power in the acceptance of others. Letting Vamreth paw at you for his pleasure instead of yours. Following Khyven the Unkillable like a lovesick puppy. Flopping down in a *shkazat* den."

Tears welled in Shalure's eyes. "Why are you being so cruel?"

The woman gave a throaty laugh. "Cruel? I haven't even begun, *Lady* Shalure."

Shalure got shakily to her feet. The woman was a foot and a half taller, and she looked down at Shalure.

"I *love* Khyven," Shalure protested.

The woman's icy face warmed just a shade, the corner of her mouth turning up in a smile. "He *is* delicious. I'll grant you that. Now *that* is a fighter. A woman's lust flares in the belly when she looks at those shoulders, that chest, that swagger as he swings his sword." She drew a breath like she was inhaling a glorious spring morning. "That much is true. That much I understand. But you don't love him."

"I do!"

"You follow him like a puppy, desperate for a scrap of attention, believing that he can give you your self-worth. He is a true fighter. You are not."

"Stop!"

"Look me in the eye, *Lady* Shalure."

Suddenly, all Shalure could do was stare into those enormous, icy eyes.

"You conspired with a coward to trap Khyven," the woman whispered. "You manipulated him to secure a title."

"That was before," Shalure said raggedly.

"Before what? Before you submerged your mind in *shkazat*? Before you let lesser men have whatever was left of you?"

"How do you know all this?"

"This is what I do, *Lady* Shalure. I determine who is worthy."

"Khyven a good man!"

"Oh, he is. He honors me every time he draws his sword. His curses in battle especially warm my heart. But I am not here to judge Khyven. I am here to judge you, and you only want Khyven for what he can do for *you*."

"No!"

"What is his favorite color?"

"I ..."

"What are his dreams?"

"To ... be a knight."

The woman shook her head, and her voice lowered. "You are nothing but a frightened mongrel bitch, scurrying around and hoping others won't kick you. Your desire for Khyven is only that he might take your fear away. That he might shield you from the dangers of the world. You're so afraid you've shriveled into a tiny little thing. It is repellent."

Shalure began crying. "Stop ..."

"You called my name, *Lady* Shalure. You could simply have died when Vohn pulled you into his banshee form. But as you slithered into that quasi-state, you called out to me. So here I am."

"You ..." A revelation washed over Shalure. The familiarity. The sense that she had met this woman a hundred times before. "Who are you?"

"You ... called ... me ..." the woman said slowly, like she was talking to an idiot child.

Shalure glanced at the long, white braid, at the sword, the axe, the woman's towering height …

"You're …"

The woman showed derisive teeth. "Look at how you shiver. You struggle to muster even the courage to speak. You know the truth, but you dare not utter it."

"You're Senji!"

"Yes," the goddess drew the word out. "You'll find that plain talk will serve you best here. Truth is like a river that flows through each of us. Yours has been dammed up with the stones of fear, the driftwood of lies, the debris of apathy … Believe me when I tell you, *Lady* Shalure, this is your final moment. The terrified rabbit that is you … The conniving weasel that is you … They will all die in this place."

Shalure's heart thundered; she huffed hard like she'd just run up all the steps in the palace. "I don't know what you want me to do."

Senji sneered. "Rabbit."

"I'm not … dead?"

"No. But it is coming for you. You are approaching a choice."

"What choice?"

"I would never have answered your prayer, *Lady* Shalure, if you'd called to me when Vamreth ripped out your tongue. If you'd called to me as you lay insensate in the *shkazat* den, I'd have let you die."

Shalure's shame pressed on her from all sides. She began crying again.

"But then the most unbelievable thing occurred. You found a spark of courage. Not for yourself, but for Lorelle. With borrowed wisdom, you helped her find her way again. That was not easy for you. You faced your fear to help someone who was not yourself. That caught my attention."

Shalure wiped at her tears, recalling the moment.

"And then came the dragon. Ah …" Senji turned her face up, again inhaling like she was smelling the sweetest spring breeze. She turned her gaze back to Shalure. "You took charge. You dragged Vohn backward when he had frozen up. You forced him to think, to act. You saved his life. You acted like ... a hero."

It felt like a string pulled tight in Shalure's chest, tugging on her heart. Vohn. The dragon.

"Did he ... live?"

"He did. Because of you. That's what a hero does, you see. They face their fears to help one another. That is why I am here. That ..." Senji crossed her arms over her chest. "Is why *you* are here. Tell me ... Would you have given your life for him?"

Shalure's shaking steadied. Her breathing slowed. "Yes ..."

"The truth feels different, doesn't it? It affects the entire body, gives strength. Gives you a backbone. And that is something you lack, isn't it, *Lady* Shalure?"

"What do you want from me?"

"What do you want for yourself?"

"I ... I don't know."

"That is a lie. If that were the truth, I would not be here." Senji paused, considering Shalure like she would consider a weapon she was thinking of purchasing. "You've always wanted power ... That, I can work with. But you have to stand there, *Lady* Shalure."

"I don't know what you're saying."

"Do you think I became what I am by waiting for Elren to look my way? To lend me his strong arm? To tell me I have worth?"

Shalure blinked. "Who ... Who's Elren?"

Senji gazed past Shalure for a moment, as though reminiscing, then she blinked and waved one of her callused hands. "A pretty swordsman from long ago. *My* Khyven, if you will. It doesn't matter. You want power, but you've always looked to someone else to give it to you. That is a tragedy."

"I ..."

"You paint yourself with a brush of weakness. You've connived, *Lady* Shalure. You've lied. You've manipulated.

You've let the stupid use your mind, the lustful use your body. They forced you down narrow corridors, and you ran like a mouse in a maze. And when they failed you, you threw yourself into a fog and hoped your soul would stop screaming."

"Vamreth used me—"

Senji spat on the ground. "Vamreth gave you what you asked for. You put yourself into his hands. He did not dispense the injustice. *You* did."

"I had no choice! I ..."

"You had yourself! Did you really think you would feel stronger after letting the vermin paw at you?"

"He was ... He was a king. I thought ..."

"Are you telling me, after looking into his eyes, that you did not recognize him for the viper he was? Tell me that now, *Lady* Shalure, in this place of truth. Tell me you didn't see what he would do to you in his eyes."

Shalure tried to meet the goddess's gaze, but she couldn't. She looked down at the ground.

"You couldn't believe that the strength you required, the power you craved, was inside you. That is cowardice."

"I didn't know what to do ..." she said in a small voice.

"No. You didn't. But you do now."

Shalure blinked back the tears, looked up into Senji's face. She shook her head. "What ...? I'm—"

"Stand up. Fight," Senji said through her teeth. "Fight for yourself! Or by my white braid, your road will end here."

"End ...?" Shalure's eyes went wide.

"End."

"I'm dying. Wherever my body is, I'm dying."

"I have held you in stasis because of that one flicker of courage. Because you saved Vohn's life. But if this blubbering mess is as much fight as you have in you, then yes. You're going to die. Because clearly that is what you want. It's what you've wanted for a long time."

Tears streamed down Shalure's face. "No ..."

"No what?"

"I don't want to die."

"I think you do."

"No!" Shalure clenched her fists. "I …"

Senji narrowed her eyes, then her lips twisted in disgust. "You can't even speak truth to save your life. How are you going to fight for it?" She drew a dagger, flipped it, caught it by the blade, and threw it at Shalure. It stuck into the white grass between her feet.

She looked down at it. "What … What am I supposed to do with that?"

"Grow a spine," Senji said. "Best me, and all you want is yours. I will give you what you've never had. I will give you power like you've never felt."

Shalure swallowed. "I—"

"But if I best *you*, *Lady* Shalure, this glade will be your grave. I'll leave you here, gutted. You will spend eternity looking at the ropey patterns of your blood splashed across these white grasses. And your body, back in the palace, it will wither and die in a day."

"Fight you?" She looked helplessly at the dagger in the grass, then back at the seven-foot-tall warrior woman before her, at the enormous sword and the axe strapped to her back.

"Fight me," Senji whispered, an eager gleam in her eyes. With deliberate slowness, she reached up, grasped her sword's hilt and pulled. The deadly edges of the sword glimmered as every inch of it emerged from the scabbard until it was free. Senji brought the six-foot blade around and leveled it at Shalure, point first.

"But you … You're a goddess."

"Yes I am."

"The goddess of *battle*."

"You had a chance to fight earlier fights. Easier fights. You didn't. So now you get me."

"I can't beat you!"

"Then I get to spill the entrails of another gutless girl on my sward."

"I ... I don't want this."

Senji chuckled. "Of course not. Cowards wait for their choices to get easier. Only they never do. And now you are out of choices, *Lady* Shalure. You get me. Pick it up."

Shalure looked down at the dagger again. Without knowing how, she was certain that once she touched it, Senji would attack.

"Pick it up!" Senji roared.

With an anguished cry, Shalure snatched the dagger from the ground and pointed it at the goddess of battle and death.

Senji's straight white teeth gleamed. "That's more like it."

"P-Please ..." Shalure held the dagger forward with shaking hands.

"I hate begging ..." Senji saluted with that enormous white sword. "I'm going to cut that out of you first."

Senji screamed and lunged at her.

CHAPTER TEN

SLAYTER

The magic light hovered over Slayter's new laboratory table. The polished black stone had light and decorative Line Magic inscribed into its surface, all created to enhance spell casting. All created by Giants to serve their spells right here in an authentic Giant nuraghi.

"Slayter, you need to sleep," Vohn said, hovering nearby with poorly contained agitation. He twisted the ring on his finger, the ring that Rauvelos had given him. They'd found it again amidst the rubble that Jai'ketakos had created when he'd bulled his way through the castle. Ever since Vohn had returned to corporeal form, he'd obsessed over the ring. It was firmly situated on the index finger of his right hand, but he wouldn't leave it alone. He twisted and twisted it with his other hand, as though constantly checking that it was still there. His left hand was, of course, missing its index finger, where he'd put the ring the first time.

"I did sleep. How is your ankle?" Slayter asked. He'd done his best to heal the ankle when Vohn returned to corporeal form—apparently he'd broken it in the flight from Jai'ketakos—but Vohn had limped for the first week. Bones were tricky. Flesh was easier to mend than bone.

"Don't distract me. You did not sleep."

"I did."

"When?"

"Am I supposed to remember? Who remembers when they last slept?"

"Everyone!"

"Well, I find that logic flawed. It's highly unlikely that everyone remembers when they last slept. For example, I don't. That's one. And if there is one, odds say there are more. Just consider the general inclination of large numbers and you must conclude that there are at least a dozen other people who also don't remember, and that's just in the kingdom of Usara alone. It's far more likely, in fact, that there are multiple dozens."

"Now you're arguing with me just to argue."

"I am arguing with you because you're being silly."

Slayter winced, shifted. His stump throbbed. He hadn't tended to it in a while. He really should remove the steel prosthetic he and Vohn had created together, clean it, clean his stump and let it rest for a while. He glanced down at a thin streak of blood that went from the stump cradle to the metallic ankle. A few drops dotted the floor. He was bleeding again.

He shook his head. He'd deal with that later. There were simply too many questions. He'd been trying to focus on just one moment at a time, the puzzle within each piece, but there were just so many pieces.

Slayter turned his gaze, eyes burning with fatigue, back to the table. A pile of dried *asenta* root was piled incautiously next to his left hand, and the *Tolkimine* open to his right. The *Tolkimine* was always with him now, at least when he was in the castle. It was a wealth of information.

But he really shouldn't leave the *asenta* root right out in the open. That was probably why Vohn was being a mother hen. He should squirrel it away in one of his pouches. At least Vohn understood him. If Lorelle came in and found it, she would lance him with *somnul*, take him from this place and *force* him sleep.

"I can't afford to sleep," Slayter murmured, adjusting the *Tolkimine*. Its corner didn't line up exactly with the corner of the table. It needed to line up with the corner of the table. He blinked and lined up his three scrapers exactly parallel and breathed easier afterward.

"This organizing of your table can't wait until after you sleep?"

"Nothing can," Slayter said.

"Slayter—"

"You don't seem to realize—nobody seems to realize—that we're out of time."

"We're safe for now, long enough for you to get some rest."

"Oh, that's not true. Safety of any kind is a grand illusion right now. No, we are on borrowed time. We have been for …" He trailed off. He didn't actually know. He didn't know how long they'd been on borrowed time. "Well, perhaps our entire lives."

Vohn rolled his eyes and twisted the ring on his right hand. "Then how is that different than any other day."

"Because I know that now. Because I can do something about it."

"Not if you're falling over from exhaustion. What if we find another group of people who need our help?"

"Exactly my point. I'm making a beacon."

"A what? What kind of beacon?"

"It has occurred to me for some time that we're fighting in the dark."

"That occurred to you, did it? Slayter, the entire continent—"

"Well," Slayter interrupted. "That being the issue, it should be dealt with."

"You're talking about dealing with the issue of the noktum?"

"No. With the Nox. The bloodsucking Nox. The undead, bloodsucking—"

"I know which Nox you're talking about!"

"They explode in sunlight."

"Slayter …"

"So we just make sunlight."

"You're talking about removing the noktum. *You're* going to remove the noktum."

"Yes."

"All by yourself."

"Well who else is going to help me?"

"All right." Vohn's hand closed on Slayter's wrist. "You're going to bed."

"Why?"

Vohn sighed. "First, you're practically falling over. Secondly, you're no longer making sense. Like, *really* no longer making sense rather than just your normal not making sense."

"How am I not making sense?"

"You just said you're going to remove the whole noktum."

"I did not."

"You *just* did!"

"Not the whole noktum."

Vohn gave him a flat glance.

"A beacon. Now you're just not listening. A beacon, for others to return to the castle. I can't banish the entire noktum, but with the Dilagion Core, I could make a tunnel through the dark. Anyone who walked in that tunnel would be safe. Or, well, safe from the Nox. And I daresay the Trolls don't enjoy light. So they wouldn't really be completely safe from the Trolls, but fairly safe. And of course Kyolars can come into the daylight, but they don't like it either. Like the Trolls."

"Slayter—"

"So they'd be seventy percent safe from Trolls and Kyolars. One hundred percent safe from Nox."

"That's not—"

"That's a damned sight better than how safe they are now, I think."

"I'm not saying that—"

"And the Cakistros would just walk right over them."

"Slayter!"

Slayter blinked, looked over at Vohn.

Vohn had been on edge ever since Paralos let him go. And it was a fine mystery, to be sure.

When Vohn entered the banshee state after he'd been shot in the chest with an arrow, Paralos had kept him in that state. For some reason unbeknownst to Vohn, she'd wanted him in the noktum, part of the Dark. She'd been intent on it, and only the distraction of an ancient creature called the Worldbreaker in Nokte Murosa had pulled her attention away. During that window, Slayter had extracted Vohn, brought him back to his body and healed it. And it had been a very near thing.

Since then, Vohn had assiduously avoided the noktum and any opportunity for Paralos to ensnare him again. And then Vohn had not only been forced into the noktum, but he'd been forced to fight Jai'ketakos and take on the banshee state again.

Then the inexplicable had happened. This Giant, this Paralos, who had blocked Vohn from returning to his body before had not only helped Vohn save Rhenn and Lorelle from Tovos—who was apparently now an undead Giant enslaved to N'ssag—but she had …

Let him go.

There had been no struggle. The noktum had swallowed the continent and then coughed up Vohn. He'd returned to the palace, standing right next to Slayter, right after the noktum swallowed the city. Slayter had, of course, asked him how he'd overcome Paralos, and his answer had been, "I didn't. I tried to take my corporeal form and … I did. She was there. She was right there, but she didn't stop me."

A fine mystery.

And Slayter simply couldn't let that rest. He'd had to do some research to look for a Giant named Paralos. Did they have a new ally? Or was this some kind of ploy that Slayter simply couldn't understand yet?

Since they'd become the new stewards of Castle Noktos,

Slayter had spent as much time as he could reading about the Giants. There were numerous books that went back farther than anything in the Usaran palace library. It was fascinating.

He thought—

"Slayter!" Vohn barked.

"Yes?"

"You stopped talking and then just started staring at the wall."

"Oh, yes. Well, I think I know how we beat them."

"The Giants?"

"Who else would I want to beat?"

"I don't know! I wouldn't be surprised if you suddenly started talking about ducks!"

Slayter cocked his head. "Hmm. Ducks *are* a problem."

"The Giants, Slayter. How do we beat the Giants?"

"Well, I think I know how we *did* it. Maybe not how we do it, but how we did it seventeen hundred years ago."

"And that is?"

"By working together."

"By working together? We *are* working together."

"Well, yes. I mean, such we are."

"Such that we are? What do you mean—Nevermind.

"How does that win this war?"

"Well, it's possible that the Giants have learned since then, so maybe it doesn't, but I doubt it."

"You doubt what?"

"That the Giants have learned. It's tough to unlearn something inborn. They probably don't realize they do it. Or they don't think it is a flaw. They might not even see it."

"You've lost me again."

"Insonene Vambly."

Vohn threw his hands up. "Now you're just saying sounds. That's not even a word."

"A person. A mage."

"Insonene Vambly is a mage?"

"*Was* a mage. She's been dead for centuries."

"Oh for the love of—"

"She wrote a rather dramatically titled book called *The Murderers Who Made Us*, all about the Giants."

"She wrote a book."

"More like a clutch of essays interspersed with political commentary about the mages of her time. It read like a crazy person's journal."

"Gee, I wonder what that would be like ..." Vohn muttered under his breath.

"Directly after the Human-Giant War, she absconded with a Giant's head. Just his head. And she kept it alive. Sort of. It was a fascinating combination of life magic and chemistry—not dissimilar to what N'ssag does. She asked all manner of questions of this Giant's head, this Eldroi, which is how she referred to it. Not sure if you know that term. That's what the Giants call themselves. And there were four primary tribes of Eldroi at the beginning of ... well, of the settling of Eldros: the Pyranoi, Drakanoi, Daemanoi, and Noksonoi. Before the Human-Giant War, there were a number of wars just among the Eldroi tribes. They called them the Elder Wars."

"The Giants fought each other."

"Oh all the time! That was how the Lux was made. That was how the Great Noktum was originally made. Luminents and Shadowvar. So many things were created because of them. The Eldroi almost destroyed each other several times in their fight for dominance."

"I don't understand how this relates to anything we're talking about."

"They hate each other. That's the point."

Vohn blinked, and Slayter saw the light dawn in his eyes. "You actually did have a point."

"I always have a point. They don't like to work together. They hate it, in fact."

"But *we* do ..." Vohn murmured.

"I wouldn't go that far, but we're certainly better at it than they are. Phenomenally better at it, which gives you an indication just how bad they are at it."

"They don't understand community," Vohn murmured.

"They don't understand how the sum of a group can exceed the individual abilities of the individuals. That doesn't make sense to them. Based on what I read, they only banded together in the first place because Noktos—their progenitor—encouraged, convinced, or coerced them to. In short, there is no unifying force keeping the Giants together. They were out of practice working as a community by the time the Humans formed their rebellion—or perhaps they didn't think they'd need to work together. We were only weak little mortals, after all. When the Humans rose up, the Giants couldn't form an effective unified front to repel them. And that was how we won. It's quite fascinating."

"And you're saying that's what we have to do again."

"I'm saying that's what I'm trying to do right now while you're trying to convince me to sleep."

"You're trying to form a community by yourself? That's not forming a community, Slayter. That's just running yourself into the ground trying to do more than a person can do."

"Oh, not at all. I'm doing the things that I can do, that only I can do, for the group. That's what being part of a group means."

"Being part of a group also means letting the others look out for you. Standing sentry when you need to rest."

"Well, I'll take you up on that when we have time."

"Will we ever have time?"

"No. I don't think so. I think this battle could come any day. It could come today."

Slayter moved to his right where he had laid out all of the components he would need. There were five clay patties that he'd made perfectly smooth and perfectly round, and then had drawn his symbols upon, leaving only one line in each unfinished. The clay was still smooth and malleable. Another reason to do this today. By tomorrow, they'd be dry and useless.

There were also three scratchers next to the clay patties. He would only need one, but he liked to have his choice when the moment came.

Before all of the ready-made spells sat a three-foot-tall onyx frog. Slayter put his hand upon it.

This was one of the artifacts they'd pulled from the Vault, and it had taken three days of study—in between jaunts to save refugees—for Slayter to figure out what it was.

This was the Dilagion Core.

"I don't think you should do this, Slayter."

"I need you to stay quiet now, Vohn. This is going to take a great deal of concentration."

Vohn sighed nervously and crossed his arms, and then Slayter tried not to think about him.

Slayter remembered two brief entries about Dilagion Cores. He'd unearthed them in the *Book of Xos* and the *Reeven Tome*, two ancient accounts written by Giants themselves. Dilagion Cores were receptacles, like a cistern, except instead of holding water, they held magic.

This one held Giant magic, and once Slayter explored it with the correct—and very careful—combination of spells, he'd discover just how much.

He wasn't sure why the thing had been carved to look like an enormous frog, but inside it was a vast pool of eldritch power unlike anything he'd ever experienced.

The Human body was kept alive by life-force. It was the very essence of what animated a person, pushed hot blood through the veins, gave people the spark to think and the strength to act. That life-force could be siphoned to access one of the five streams of magic. That was what mages did. They pulled from their own life-force to create the miraculous, seemingly from thin air.

Of course the downside was that it could also kill a person, if they depleted themselves too far. There were herbs and roots that could shock a person back awake, give them a bit of artificial life-force, but they were dangerous. If the body had been depleted and the herbs were the only thing keeping the mage alive, they died when the herbs wore off. There was only so much life-force to draw from before a body simply stopped working.

The Dilagion Core had the equivalent of a hundred Human life-forces. Perhaps a thousand. It was more than Slayter had been able to guess with his probing spell.

And all of this life force could, apparently, be used to access a magic stream with no apparent consequence to the caster.

For Slayter, it had been like stumbling across a feast of roasted chickens and fresh baked bread after starving to death.

He'd never known just how limited he was until he'd found the Core.

Of course, playing with Giant magic came with an inherent danger, as Khyven had discovered when he'd put on the Helm of Darkness or picked up the Mavric iron sword. But Slayter was far past being careful. People were dying. This could help them.

He selected his scratcher—the medium-sized one—and completed the final line on the first spell. Orange light flared, and he opened his mind to the Dilagion Core. The orange light flickered, then purple light enveloped Slayter's entire body, going up his hand, around his neck and shoulders, then down his other hand to the spell. The orange light changed to purple, and Slayter felt no exhaustion.

It was working!

He gently pushed the first clay disk up—it was laid into a square wooden plate with edges—and pulled the next closer to him, still keeping a hand on the Dilagion Core.

He completed the second symbol. The orange light barely had time to spark when the purple overtook it, the Core replacing his life-force with its never-ending well of power.

Slayter scooted the second spell up to a new formation above the unfinished spells—a pentagon with each spell as one of the junctures, and slid the third in front of himself. He repeated the process again, and two more times, placing each carefully in the pentagon shape.

As he finished pushing the final spell into place, completing the pentagon, the forces he'd summoned began to spin within him, outside him, through the Core, up to the roof.

"Yes ..." he murmured. By Senji, it was the most incredible feeling he'd ever had. "Yes!"

Buttery yellow light burst up from the pentagon shape, soaring up and around the room. It seemed to be exploring everything.

Vohn shielded his eyes from the blinding light.

"Slayter!"

"Isn't it magnificent?" Slayter shouted. He didn't care about the light scaring his eyes. He had to see what it did!

It finished its race around the room and shot out of the balcony.

Slayter focused his mind, keeping himself from falling into the wonder of his own spell. So much strength! The Core had so much strength!

He sent it out into the noktum, asked it to make the shapes he'd wanted. He saw the tunnel of light going straight down to the courtyard, straight through the closed and broken front gates, straight to Usara. From there, he made it fork, up along the sea following the north road, and down along the sea forming the south road.

For the first time, Slayter felt a strain on his mind, a pull from his own life force. It seemed that making the choice, altering the spell, required his own special intervention.

He leaned into it. One random tunnel of light wasn't going to help anyone. Slayter envisioned running a safe passage up all the main roads of Usara, to each of the cities and towns inside the kingdom so that each refugee still out there in the dark might see it, each refugee might find it, get inside it, and be protected. He envisioned it going up to Blanuri, north to Wheskone Keep, onward along the Dead Road and through to Turnic.

He envisioned it going south to Veste, through the Veste Forest, across the Lowlands. Then he envisioned it going west to Grau, to Aur, and around the mountains to—

A fizzle of orange flashed in Slayter's eyes, and then the blinding light vanished.

Or perhaps he did.

He thought he felt the thump of stone against his cheek. He thought he heard Vohn shout.

Everything went dark, and for a keenly disappointing split-second, Slayter thought his spell had failed and the noktum had flooded into the room again.

Then relief forked through him as he realized the truth.

That's not it at all. It's not the noktum. It's me. I've passed out—

CHAPTER ELEVEN

SLAYTER

No you don't …"

But I did, Slayter thought. *I'm sure I did. I'm rather good at magic, you know.*

"Wake up, my friend. Wake up," Vohn said to him. There were gentle pats on his cheek.

I am awake, Slayter thought. *How could I possibly have created a light beacon without being awake. That's just silly.*

"Eyes open, Slayter. Come on now."

My eyes are *open,* Slayter thought. *It's just dark. It's always dark. The noktum spilled over the entire continent, you know. It's always …*

Except everyone had Amulets of Noksonon now. The dark wasn't dark anymore, not for anyone who wore an amulet. Not only that, but he also wore a raven ring like Vohn, a stylized silver ring with Rauvelos's head carved on the top. Slayter had found a few of them in the vault, and while the amulets—except for Khyven's, apparently—needed recharging, the rings didn't.

Which meant it wasn't dark, not for Slayter. Yet … He couldn't see. That must mean—

"Open your eyes, my friend. I have your vial, but you have to drink it," Vohn said.

Slayter tried to open his eyes. He couldn't.

Well that's not right either, he thought.

He tried again, but his eyelids seemed to weigh as much as steel plates.

"I swear, Slayter, if you've killed yourself, I'm going to kill you," Vohn said.

Oh! That's what it was. He didn't have enough energy to think random thoughts and still open his mouth and talk.

"I *did* sleep," Slayter murmured.

"Oh thank Grina!" Vohn said.

"Khyven hasn't slept either, you know," Slayter said. His eyelids still weighed far too much. It was altogether too difficult to open them.

"You are *not* Khyven."

Slayter paused. His fatigue pulled at him so hard that he almost succumbed to it. But he had to get his eyes open. He had to see if he'd succeeded at his spell. He felt he had. He had to have. The Dilagion Core was simply amazing.

"Well that stung," he finally mumbled in response to Vohn's statement. "What is your point?"

"Khyven is a legendary, muscle-bound Ringer who has trained every day of his life for every physical challenge there is, including sleep deprivation. You are a Line Mage who spends most of his time indoors reading books."

"Well that's just mean."

"Open your eyes."

"Next I suppose you're going to mention my quantity of legs."

"Slayter—"

"Why are you trying to walk, Slayter?" Slayter mimicked Vohn's voice. "Have you seen Khyven? He has a pair of legs. That's what works for walking. How many pairs do you have? Zero. You have zero pairs."

"You're intolerable when you're insensate."

To Slayter's credit, he *was* trying to open his eyes. Those iron plates just wouldn't move.

"I'm going to slap you now," Vohn said.

"Slap me?"

"Wake up!" Vohn slapped Slayter sharply. The iron plates clanged, and for a second Slayter could see the room. He latched onto that success and shoved at the iron plates.

After what seemed like an eternity, he levered his eyes open.

His worktable was blinding. Bright, buttery light shot from the pentagon all the way to the roof, made a right turn like all the rules of nature had been suspended, and shot toward the balcony.

The castle's black stones glistened in the bright daylight he'd created. The Dilagion Core hummed, as though it was happy to have been given a task worthy of its potential.

"Well … That worked," Slayter said.

"Less talking, more drinking."

A clink brought Slayter's attention around. He lolled his head to the side. One of his vials of *asenta* root extract was poised at his lips, held in Vohn's hand.

"I'm going to have to open my mouth for that, aren't I?" Slayter murmured.

"Only if you want to live."

"I do. I have to see my spell. Does it go toward Usara?"

"Yes."

"How can you tell?"

"Drink the damned vial."

"I will—"

Vohn's hand stuttered, and the precious liquid dripped on Slayter's chin instead of into his mouth.

Painstakingly, Slayter tried to turn his head. It didn't work. Instead, he craned his eyes about, trying to follow Vohn's stunned gaze. The doors were all closed. No one had opened or closed them in the last few moments.

But a dark, cloaked figure now stood in the room with them.

CHAPTER TWELVE

SLAYTER

At first, Slayter thought it was Lorelle. The cloak that shrouded the newcomer's features and poured from her shoulders like liquid, pooling on the ground, was definitely a noktum cloak. But when she pushed back her cowl, it was clearly not Lorelle: a rounder, Human face, and round ears. She was at least a head shorter than Lorelle and curvy in that Human way that Lorelle wasn't. She had pale skin—Usaran skin—not Lorelle's obsidian black—blue eyes, black hair, and spectacles perched on the bridge of her nose.

The bespectacled woman regarded him with a half smile in the wake of her statement, and gave a little shake of her head. "You are something else, Slayter Wheskone."

"It's ... been said," he said.

"You created a tunnel of light through the noktum."

"More than one, actually ..." But that was all he had the energy for. His eyes slid shut again.

"Go ahead, Vohn," the woman said. "I'll wait. Best to tend to him first."

Vohn gently tipped back Slayter's head and put the vial to his lips again. The blue liquid splashed onto his tongue, and Slayter suddenly imagined his body in colors.

His body was gray, but the moment the life-giving liquid touched his lips, those lips became a bright, vibrant blue. The blue moved to his tongue, then down his throat. Dark blue color led, and where the liquid had been it faded to a light blue. Now his throat was dark blue and his lips light blue. Now his chest was dark blue and his throat light blue. Now his belly and his arms. He swallowed and swallowed until his entire body had transformed from gray to light blue.

He gasped, sucking in a hard breath that dragged on his throat like fingernails, like he hadn't used his lungs in a long time.

"All right. All right, then." Vohn sighed. He bowed his head, and Slayter sat up. The exuberance of the draught coursed through him.

The woman waited patiently. Vohn turned to her, suddenly brandishing the lightning rod Slayter had given him. He leveled it at her.

"Questions," Vohn said.

"I don't think that's entirely necessary, do you?" Slayter said.

"She has a noktum cloak, Slayter. Where did she get it? I can't think of a single good answer to that question, so I think I'll keep this pointed right at her until I do."

That was actually quite a good observation, Slayter thought. "Well, she's a Reader."

Vohn frowned, glanced sidelong at Slayter. "How do you know that?"

"The Readers are tasked with moving events. If the Giants attacking Usara isn't the most important event, it's probably fairly high up. Enough to warrant a visit, I'd wager."

"Perhaps more than that." The woman smiled.

"You're here to look after us," Slayter said.

"My name is Elegathe."

"And you're assigned to Usara?"

"It is my sole purpose to ensure that *all* of Humanity survives."

"So you haven't been assigned here."

"I am the High Master of the Readers of Noksonon. I make the assignations."

"And you're here to …"

"Help."

"With information."

"Yes."

Slayter paused, watching the woman. "You gave Lorelle the fake Plunnos, didn't you?"

Vohn's eyes went wide, then his brows crouched low. His lip curled. "You're *that* Reader?"

The woman hesitated a moment, as though she hadn't expected that question. "Yes, I did."

"She didn't like that much."

"You think I should have given her the real one."

"Yes," Vohn interrupted.

"Hmmm," Slayter said.

Vohn looked incredulously over at Slayter. "Yes, she should have!"

"She's a Lore Mage," Slayter said.

"So?"

"So if I had given your friend a real Plunnos, she would be dead."

"You don't know that!" Vohn turned to her again. "You sent her into the Great Noktum with that Nox. She could have died."

"We could all die. And the timing of when we do certain things is what determines whether we die or not," Elegathe said. "She went into the Great Noktum, yes, and there she gained the skills she needed. There, she found the Plunnos she was looking for and used it at the right time to aid the queen."

"If she'd gone earlier, Rhenn wouldn't have been transformed into a bloodsucker!" Vohn said.

"If she'd gone earlier, Lorelle would be dead. Rhenn would be dead as well."

Vohn looked back at Slayter. "I don't believe it."

There were too many variables to know for sure, but Readers did read the future. That was what they were dedicated to.

"She could be right," Slayter said.

"I don't believe it," Vohn repeated.

"But she could be right."

"I'm here to warn you," Elegathe said.

"Why didn't you warn us about the noktum swallowing the entire kingdom?" Vohn asked.

"Because you were as prepared as anyone could be."

"That's not true!"

"Really?"

"Yes, if we'd have known ahead of time, we could have prepared the rest of the kingdom!"

She shook her head. "No. If you had told everyone in the kingdom of Usara that they needed to pack up their belongings and move to Castle Noktos in the middle of a noktum, they'd have ignored you. And then the enemy would be alerted."

"Enemy," Slayter said. "You know who is coming."

"I do."

"And what is your warning?"

"That they are coming soon."

"When?" Slayter asked.

"One week."

"One week?" Vohn exclaimed.

Slayter's mind jumped to life with the possibilities—and what could be done—with one week. Knowing when the enemy was coming was a tremendous asset.

"You would do better to strengthen the defenses of the castle, Slayter Wheskone, than make tunnels of light snaking throughout the kingdom."

"Yes ..."

"You're not just going to take this at face value, Slayter," Vohn said.

"Of course not. But I am going to take it. You know who

our opponent is."

"Oh yes," Elegathe said.

"It's Harkandos, isn't it?"

Elegathe smiled. "You really are something, aren't you?"

"What can you tell me about him?"

"I can tell you everything that Humanity saw fit to record. But we should get started. A week is practically no time at all …"

CHAPTER THIRTEEN

RHENN

R henn stood on the balcony of her new meeting room. The balcony had been crafted to Giant-sized proportions. It was nearly the size of the entire foyer of the Usaran palace.

Most of her attendants and subjects who now lived in Castle Noktos opted for what had once been the servants' quarters because they were Human-sized. But Rhenn planned to use every ounce of advantage this castle possessed to save her people, and that meant making it her own. Rhenn had insisted on using the chambers the Giants themselves had used long ago. She used the throne room for audiences. She used the meeting room adjacent to her chambers with its courtyard-sized balcony. Castle Noktos belonged to her now. A monstrous castle for its monstrous queen. Because that's what she was now. A monster.

The thrill of the Troll's stolen life still thrummed through her body as she looked out over the sculpture garden far below. The thrill was a curse. One feeding was never enough, even though her body hummed with energy. It was a horrible daisy-chain that made her want to feed again and again until she was glutted.

She didn't need to feed directly anymore, didn't need to sink her teeth into a living creature and tear it apart, thanks to Slayter's sword. But the bloodlust still filled her when she used it.

And when her blood rushed, she felt like she could so easily spin out of control, felt like she could simply turn on her friends. The woman who gloried in the taste of blood wasn't her. It was what N'ssag had put into her.

She didn't want the sword. Stabbing the sword into an enemy was still taking a life to perpetuate her own.

But she had no choice. It was that or resist the bloodlust. She had tried that, and every night, a little more of her slipped away until she went charging into the woods and ripped apart a deer with her bare hands and teeth. If she didn't feed the bloodlust, it would eventually break her will. And next time, it might not just be a deer that paid the price.

She hated herself for being the thing that N'ssag had created her to be. But her self-hatred was only a fraction of what she felt for N'ssag. When she finally faced him—when she finally had him at her mercy—she would give up all restraint. She'd show him the monster he had created and tear him apart. She would look into his terrified eyes as she pulled bloody pieces from his body one at a time.

He had turned her into the opposite of what she was meant to be.

In her first life, Rhenn had embraced joy with both hands. Yes, Vamreth had killed her friends. He'd killed her brothers and sisters. He'd killed her parents. For anyone else, that would have destroyed any capacity to find joy. But Rhenn had defied it. She'd hated giving Vamreth that final victory. So she had gone in the other direction. If she had a hankering for something, she indulged it. If Rhenn wanted a mug of ale—or five—she drank them. If she wished to take a lover who had a pleasing voice and wide shoulders, she tumbled him. If she wished to recklessly attack a force two times larger than hers, she rode headlong to her fate.

She couldn't do that now. She couldn't indulge her desires anymore, because now they were a murderer's desires.

When Nhevalos took her to Daemanon, he'd taken everything. She'd left a queen who could lead her people to a prosperous age.

She'd returned as this.

At first, she had kept her pain locked tightly inside. She had borne her affliction with a tragic resolution, and she'd thought often about suicide, about the moment that Usara would be stable enough, safe enough, for her to end her own life.

But since the noktum swept over the continent, she had come to a strange realization: she was uniquely suited to leading her people through the dark.

It was like Rhenn herself was a playing card. On one side was the young and vivacious leader who had fought her way back to the palace, the perfect queen to rule in the sun, crafting a time of peace and prosperity for her people.

The other side of the card was this night-thriving, bloodsucking queen who had struggled to rule under the shine of the sun.

But now, the entire world had flipped along with the card that was Rhenn. In this kingdom at war, cloaked in eternal darkness, a queen who breathed dark and loved battle was, in fact, the perfect queen.

Her previous self would have struggled to lead her people through this benighted Usara, but her new self was an exact match for the task.

Rhenn no longer felt inept, constrained, half-fighting herself. The more she let loose her desires, the better a leader she became for her people.

What her people needed now in their queen was, in fact, a monster. So she would be that monster until they no longer needed her.

A bright light burst forth from the balcony one story down and two to the left. This wasn't unexpected—Slayter had told her what he planned to do—and Rhenn squinted as she held onto the pommel of her sword.

Another advantage Slayter had worked into the sword was a partial immunity to the devastating effects that N'ssag's creations experienced when they were subjected to sunlight. Before the sword, a light that close, that bright, would have blinded Rhenn, caused her skin to start smoking, and would surely have driven her from the balcony in a desperate attempt to get away.

Now, she watched as the enormous tunnel of light slithered out of the balcony like a mythic snake, dropped to the ground and extended across the courtyard and out the gates toward the distant city of Usara. It pulsed and throbbed with so much power Rhenn could barely conceive of it, and she was looking right at it.

Though she could barely look at it, she loved it. This would go out into the kingdom, as far as Slayter could send it, and it would bring hope and safety to any of her subjects that remained alive out there in the dark.

Slayter was a genius. He was quite possibly the most powerful mage in Noksonon—perhaps even for a millennia—and now he'd been set loose in a castle with every magical artifact he could possibly have imagined, as well as many he couldn't have. He was like her, uniquely suited to this horrible circumstance.

And perhaps that was exactly as Nhevalos had intended. Oh, she hated him. Like N'ssag, Nhevalos had destroyed her life, but unlike N'ssag, he had also saved her people.

She tried not to think of Nhevalos, tried not to think about how he might have been right to do what he did to her. But she thought of him often. To not think about Nhevalos and his schemes was to close her eyes about what might hit them next.

She wondered how long it had taken Nhevalos to concoct his schemes, and how they had begun.

She wondered what he was doing now, and which of his machinations would begin to turn events next ...

Chapter Fourteen

NHEVALOS

One thousand, seven hundred and seventy-two years ago. Before the Human-Giant War ...

Nhevalos looked out over the courtyard of Castle Noktos. The sculptures glowed with purple light. Any invading weeds had been summarily expunged. The flagstones were as pristine as the polished tiles inside the castle. Rauvelos had seen to it.

The tall, straight gates stood open in welcome, which on any other day would be ironic.

Paralos strode through, made her way across the immaculate courtyard that he'd made—or rather Rauvelos had made—immaculate just for her. They were both aware of each other, though neither had acknowledged the other. Her appearance in the courtyard at all was entirely a matter of courtesy. The Noksonoi had many efficient ways to travel through the dark. Walking was for making a statement, and her statement was: *I come in peace. See how I allow you to regard me?*

He heard the scrape of a slipper on the floor behind him, and he turned.

Paralos stood across the room, looking out the high, thin windows, perhaps mimicking his pensive stare out over his grounds. The noise of her slipper had been for his benefit. After making her way across the courtyard, letting him know her intentions, there had been no reason to climb the steps.

She was one of the taller Noksonoi at nearly fourteen and a half feet. Her sleeveless black gown showed slender, muscled arms. Her straight black hair swept back from a gentle widow's peak at her forehead, flowing down close to her scalp and then fanning out like a shining black curtain to touch her bare shoulders. She'd worn a gown. He had seen her in a gown before, of course, but then Paralos enjoyed all manner of garments and show. It only now occurred to him that she might have seen his invitation as a prelude to coupling.

The Eldroi didn't often reproduce, less than once every few hundred years. It was nothing like the way the Humans did it, or even the Luminents or Shadowvar. Mortals bred like animals, dropping to the ground to rut whenever the mood struck them.

Generally, Eldroi would rather kill each other than create a new Eldroi. One more Eldroi in the world meant one more Eldroi to hate, or at the very least strive against. But every now and then, the mood struck a pair of Eldroi, more often because of intellectual curiosity than anything else. An experiment, really.

Paralos had that look now. And frankly, had the circumstances been different, Nhevalos might have entertained the idea. Her appearance was captivating, head to toe.

But that wasn't his purpose.

She continued regarding the courtyard below, giving him her profile and a flattering view of her body. Her black dress wrapped around her neck like a choker and flowed down over her clavicle, her breasts, the slope of her belly, and the curve of her hips, hugging them. Yes, she thought he'd invited her to couple.

He was moved by her appearance, but he was more

interested in the jolts of blue lightning that subtly appeared around her elbows, hips, knees, and shoulders when she moved. Clearly a spell. He suspected it was designed to enable her to mimic a Luminent's lightness and grace, a Land Magic spell that assisted her muscles in more easily lifting her natural weight.

Compared to Luminents, the Eldroi were ungainly. Moreover, their size and bulk were often destructive in the miniature settlements of their mortal servants. Not that the average Eldroi would care. To an Eldroi, the greatest purpose a mortal like a Luminent could serve was to die for them.

Clearly Paralos had chosen to leverage this affectation in an effort to draw his eye. It worked.

Alternatively, she might have wanted to experience what it was like to move fluidly through the world, rather than powerfully, to see things the way a Luminent saw them.

Either way, it was time to confess his real reason in inviting her. The truth was: he needed her. He had gone over his plan again and again in his mind, and it simply would not work if he didn't have at least one ally among his own kind.

In a ridiculously dangerous plan, this was the most dangerous step of all. It could all end right here. What he was about to reveal to her would draw death to him like Kyolars to a downed Darklinger.

If any of the other Noksonoi knew what was inside his mind, they would destroy him.

"That is a pregnant pause, even for you," Paralos finally said, and he smiled. He loved her lively mind. A pregnant pause.

"Would you like some wine?"

"I would." She turned to him as though to state firmly without words that she'd given him plenty of time to view her.

He crossed to the cabinet of spirits, withdrew his choice, filled two glasses, and brought one to her.

She took it, swirled it, and sipped. "This is quite flavorful."

"It is Lumyn wine. Their fermentation process is quite something." Nhevalos swirled his wine and also took a sip.

He had taken to keeping Lumyn wine because it was tart,

which was … odd. Compared to the night berry spirits the Eldroi preferred, anything mortals created, including Luminent wine, was considered sour swill. The thatch-roofed huts in the Luminent work camp, which its inhabitants had taken to calling "Lumyn" had created this drink from grapes, which grew only in the sun, in the places where the Lux had destroyed the noktum. It was one of the curious things that Nhevalos had been ruminating upon for some years: that mortals could be clever and, in the case of the Lumyn wine, even ingenious. A tart alcoholic drink. Who would have considered it? And yet, Nhevalos was secretly coming to find that the wine was far better than Eldroi spirits.

Of course, for Nhevalos to even think a mortal could produce something better than the Eldroi could produce was scandalous.

"Did the wine come with the castle?" she asked.

She was toying with him, and he noted it with excitement. She could be the one. She could be the ally he needed.

This castle was Nhevalos's single point of pride among the other Noksonoi. Most considered him irrelevant, but that Noktos had bequeathed to Nhevalos this legendary castle had elevated him.

Nhevalos was a quiet Noksonoi who never did much of anything. Up to this point, the other Noksonoi never considered him at all, or if they did, it was only as an afterthought to some other, more important business. Then, to the surprise of all, the great Noktos had entrusted Castle Noktos to Nhevalos right before he vanished into his master spell after the Great Shattering.

"No. I brought it here myself," Nhevalos said.

"Hm." She took another sip and watched him. That was as much conversation as he was going to get out of her. She wanted to know why she was here, and he suspected she had, by now, realized that it wasn't for a coupling. But that she had engaged in so much social banter was, in fact, a good sign. If she'd been bored, she would simply have left.

"There is going to be a war," he said.

She raised a thin black eyebrow. She had not expected that opener. "Well then."

"They killed Vedakos," he said.

"Bedeos instigated it, I heard. Not the mortals. He used them as a tool." Paralos came to stand next to him, swirling her wine before sipping again.

"Hm," he said.

"Did you have a point?" she asked.

He loved her subtle mind. Most Eldroi didn't have subtlety. Perhaps Noktos had. Perhaps Udalos, once upon a time. Certainly not Harkandos. To a moron like Harkandos, the only currency was raw power. He had absolutely no interest in elegance. His idea of handling a problem was smashing it with a flying boulder.

Right now, Paralos was trying to piece together the thinking behind this invitation, Vedakos's death, and why it would be of special interest to her. An Eldroi death was always worth noting, of course. Eldroi did not often die. But it wasn't worth spending more than a passing moment upon when, truthfully, no one was going to miss Vedakos.

She might now be wondering if, instead of an invitation to procreate, this was actually a prelude to another attack on her. The two of them had been circling each other for some time, and they'd both interfered with each others' projects out of boredom, as many Eldroi did. He had stymied her Frozen Wyrm project to see if he could do it. She'd sabotaged his work on hay that could not catch fire, burned down his entire project, in fact by—against tremendous odds—negating his protection spells.

That had been intoxicating.

"This isn't actually an invitation to procreate," she said.

"No."

"And here I wore my dress." Her words spoke to disappointment, but her voice egged him on. "You're going to make me guess about Vedakos."

"He was killed by mortals."

"Bedeos was working through them." Eldroi throwing mortals at other Eldroi; a story older than time. "He despised Vedakos."

"We all despised Vedakos," Nhevalos said. "But that wasn't what happened."

Her mouth quirked like a parent amused at something a child says. "You're one of those who thinks the Humans are actually using the streams of magic?"

"They are."

"Are they?"

"I know they are."

"Do you?"

"How much time do you spend around mortals?"

"I like the way the Luminents move." She did a graceful courtesy. Thin streaks of blue lightning flickered over her hips, knees, and shoulders as she made the gesture as though she was as light as a feather.

"You don't see the parallel," he said.

She straightened, and her mocking smile became a shade more genuine. She was keen to follow the game. Silence reigned between them for a long moment. "No, I do not."

"They are like Noktos."

Her mouth quirked in a half-smile. "The Humans?"

"The Humans."

She narrowed her eyes, and the half-smile seemed forced. "I do not see the joke."

"It is not a joke."

Her smiled vanished, and she hardened. "You are comparing mortals to the most revered, powerful Noksonoi to ever live?"

"Yes."

"If you're trying to entice me with wild statements, it's not working."

"I am completely serious."

"In no way is a mortal like Noktos. Not a single way."

"In the most important way. Their essence."

"Nonsense."

"No. Elegance."

"How?"

"Because no one sees it. That is why it is elegant. It is right in front of our noses, yet no one will look at it for the same reason you will not."

"How?" she reiterated.

"The mortals have something we do not."

She laughed. "Yes. They have weakness. They have bodies that wither and die. They have helplessness. Shall I go on?"

"They have passion. No one seems to notice that. Moreover, they have heart. They would die for each other."

"The key point here is that they would die."

"They are a danger to the Noksonoi. That you don't see it— that you refuse to see it—is what makes them so dangerous."

"They are beasts. Harkandos alone could destroy them in a fiery blast."

Nhevalos paused, holding her indigo eyes, then said, "Not with just *one* blast."

"A hundred, then. A thousand blasts. The result would be the same. You actually think the mortals are a threat?"

"Ask Vedakos."

She watched him for a moment with those eyes the color of shadows in the Great Noktum.

He stayed quiet.

"You're either insane," she said. "Or you are more than the others think. We've all wondered, you know, since Noktos gave you his castle."

It was a quick change of speed, and he felt again that she was perfect for this. "Is that why you're here?"

"I'm here because you invited me."

"But you didn't know why."

"I prepared for the obvious. I confess I had hoped for more."

"And?"

"If you find your courage, perhaps we will see."

"My courage?"

"You've been waiting to tell me something this entire time. I'm hoping you find your spine before this intrigue slides into boredom."

"I'm working on a new project."

"That is obvious." She tensed a little. He saw it, and he interpreted it: If he's going to kill me to ensure I don't interfere with his project, now was the time. I am ready.

"While your challenges have been diverting in the past," he said. "I want to work with you on this project."

"Still so vague," she taunted

"The mortals are going to be my project."

"The mortals?"

"The Eldrovan is going to war."

"Over Vedakos? Against the Humans? I hardly think so."

"The Humans have magic."

"Again, I hardly think so."

"Then imagine it for a moment. Then view what I'm saying through that lens." He watched her for a moment. "What is the one thing the mortals have that we do not?"

"I have already enumerated these for you. Weakness, fragility, mortality, fear so thick you can smell it. Shall I go on?"

"They work together."

"This is their miraculous parallel to Noktos?"

"He brought us here. He organized us. Together, we overcame the most powerful of all Eldroi. We overcame Nirapama."

"You think their triumph in overcoming Vedakos is an equivalency to *that*? Nirapama was the most powerful Eldroi ever to walk the world. Vedakos was a fool."

"To us, yes. To them, he was a god. And they killed him. How much difference is there, really, between him and, say, Harkandos?"

She snorted. "A world of difference."

"And how many mortals would it take to overcome Harkandos? Twice as many? Ten times as many?"

"There is no number large enough. Mortals are fleas to him."

"Oh, I think you're wrong. I think there is a much smaller distance between Vedakos and Harkandos then you imagine."

She betrayed no expression, but her taunting smile had vanished.

"When the Eldrovan orders the attack on the Humans. They will fight back this time."

"And they will be crushed."

"Many of them, yes."

"They are mortals," she emphasized.

"And they have suddenly grown a spine. Enough to destroy Vedakos. That will embolden them."

"Very well, let's imagine they do have magic. They cannot fight off the Eldrovan. Harkandos is the most powerful wielder of magic since Noktos. And Xos, Bedeos, Orios as well ... It will be a slaughter."

"They don't know that."

"Because they are ignorant."

"Ignorant enough to attempt the impossible. And, with my help, succeed."

Her breath caught in her throat, and her eyes widened. She saw it then. "You ..."

This was the deadly crossroads. He watched her face so closely. At the slightest indication of the wrong emotion, things would move very fast. The *kairoi* had shown him she would do one of three things now.

First, she might attempt to kill him. If she succeeded, she'd gain standing with the Eldrovan by downing a betrayer.

Second, she might flee to regroup with the Eldrovan or, perhaps, Harkandos himself. If that was the case, he would have to kill her before she left the castle. Rauvelos was standing by with very explicit instructions to confound the magic of the noktum cloak.

Third, she might see that his plan was—

"You mean to take on not just one of our fellow Noksonoi, but all of them." She made no move to use her noktum cloak nor to flee physically through the window. But he didn't let down his guard.

"I intend to build a project so grand that my name will be known forever. As everlasting as Noktos himself."

She raised her chin, and the corners of her lips turned up at the ends, curves carved in the marble of her face.

"Brilliant." She closed her eyes like she was in ecstasy, let out a breath like he had caressed her.

He waited while she had her moment. There was nothing more satisfying to the Noksonoi than setting themselves above another Noksonoi.

"You plan to top them all," she finally said.

"Yes."

"You believe you can do it?"

"*We* can do it. I will need you."

"Yes, I believe you will."

"We will move like Sleeths through the noktum, and we will stick a dagger into every other Noksonoi. But they won't know it until we twist."

"Move like a Sleeth?"

"They will not know about us. Not until it is too late."

"I see. A new kind of warfare."

"The Noksonoi have always used mortals in their wars against each other. They throw them as a catapult throws a stone. But they have missed their true value."

"Their true value. You mean this passion you speak of, this 'will to work together.'"

"We will build the mortals into a net that will capture our fellows. We will milk the mortals' passion to throw themselves heedlessly at an enemy. Except this time, they will think they are in control. Instead of yanking them where we want them to go, we will instead appear to follow them. We will be their 'allies.' We will seem to help them go the direction they wish to go."

"Will we?"

"But it will be our direction. Our plan. Our project."

She moved closer. He waited for the dagger, for the magic paralysis spell. He had counters for both—and many more—at his fingertips. She leaned in, fingers touching his cheek, and pressed her lips to his. A kiss.

He had not expected a kiss.

She leaned back, viewing him with those purple eyes. "Harkandos thinks you are a weakling and a fool."

"By the time he realizes different, I will have him in hand."

"Yes, I think you will."

"So," he said. "Does this mean you—"

She slowly let her hand trail down his jawline, each individual finger slipping from his chin one after the other until she brought it back to her side.

"When do we begin?" she asked.

CHAPTER FIFTEEN

NHEVALOS

Nhevalos came through the Thuros into the circular room, rainbow lights flaring around him. The lowest room in Queen Rhennaria's Usaran palace was quiet, wrapped in the Dark of the restored Great Noktum. There was a tonal difference between the natural dark and the noktum, even underground where the sun never reached. Nhevalos could feel the noktum like a caress. All Noksonoi could. The Dark was pregnant with power for those who could use it. Noktos had made it that way to give the Noksonoi the advantage over invading Eldroi during the Elder Wars, long before the Human-Giant War had shaped the world for the last two thousand years.

Rhennaria's Humans had fled this place, and even without the powerful feel of the noktum, the little details would have told that story. Since her return to power, Queen Rhennaria had always kept three lanterns burning in this place. Since her abduction, Slayter had hung a number of spells around the Thuros and in the room. All were missing now.

The two gates in front of the tunnel that had led to the

noktum before everywhere on Noksonon was a noktum again—Vamreth's and the original—stood open and a pair of Kyolars lounged on the far side of the room. They had been sleeping, but they awoke the moment Nhevalos stepped through. They had come here looking for something to eat, no doubt, and possibly even found something, some foolish human who hadn't followed the queen's orders or hadn't been quick enough about it. If not that, then the Kyolars had no doubt been scouring the city for any chickens, hogs, or cattle left behind.

The Kyolars immediately leapt to their feet, raising their heads, but their interest in Nhevalos vanished instantly. He was master here, and all the creatures of his realm knew it. The two Kyolars lowered their heads and backed out of their hunter's stances. They loped into the tunnel and were gone.

Nhevalos stepped down off the dais and took a moment to consider the part this room had played in his plans. It was, after all, just one piece, but every piece was important. It was what neophyte Lore Mages didn't understand about this elusive stream of magic. Seeing and manipulating the future wasn't just about seeing what you were looking for. It was about seeing all possible futures. It required nurturing every little avenue that might lead to the goal.

Every detail mattered. Each little pebble could be the one that started the avalanche.

This room was one of those details. It had spent almost every day of the last two millennia empty, unloved, unvisited. Its mighty Thuros had remained locked and inert. But Nhevalos had known its importance all along. This was where the queen and her young Luminent friend would come after their parents had been slaughtered. One pebble. This was where they would return a decade later with Khyven and kill the usurper. Another pebble. This was where Nhevalos would take the queen to Daemanon, where she would undergo her transformation into the hero her people needed.

And then the avalanche had begun.

Rhennaria had gotten almost all of her people out of the

crown city before N'ssag had sent his bloodsuckers hunting for her. In the next several days, Harkandos would come as well, and Noksonon would face the deciding moment of the age.

Nhevalos took a deep breath and let it out.

So many years. So much effort. Every week—sometimes every day—reading the *kairoi*, guiding the mortals, placing the pebbles ... All to get to this moment. Soon, Khyven would face Harkandos, and the scales would tip toward a world where mortals made their own destiny. Forever. And Nhevalos's name would be remembered as the Noksonoi who had reshaped the continent.

He considered how satisfying it would be: the look on the faces of all of those Noksonoi who had doubted him, who had seen him as inconsequential. He would love to watch them stand in awe at what he had accomplished, understanding it all too late to do anything about it. Of course, that was a fantasy. Most of those Noksonoi had already died in Nhevalos's initial coup, the first Human-Giant War, and those who still remained would most likely die in the second. But Nhevalos would know, and that would be enough. He could imagine their dumbfounded expressions.

But it wasn't over yet, and he had learned long ago never to celebrate before the battle was done. That was how mistakes were made, and Harkandos was awake now. Nhevalos couldn't afford even one mistake.

His plan had become exponentially harder this close to the end. When the game board was clear of players, moving the pieces was easy.

But now Harkandos was awake. He was looking. He would make moves of his own, and every time he did, it might change the board.

Of course, it also might not. Harkandos was not a planner, and Nhevalos had taken his measure long ago. Never much of a thinker, Harkandos was also notoriously impatient. He believed he could make the world the way he wanted it in an instant because he had more strength than any Noksonoi in an age.

Grab it. Make it so. Kill anything that opposed him. It was the arrogance of power.

Harkandos had never needed—and therefore never learned—to patiently wait for the right timing. He could overwhelm any other spell caster like a bull stepping on a duckling, so why bother with patience? Why bother with planning?

The only time Harkandos had shown any restraint was when the Eldrovan had still been around, and before that Noktos. Noktos could have, through sheer power alone, put Harkandos in his place. And so could any three of the Noksonoi of the Eldrovan. So Harkandos had played nice …

… and threatened the other Noksonoi behind closed doors.

Bullying was Harkandos's way. It was why he'd stepped into Nhevalos's trap the first time, and it would be why he would step into Nhevalos's trap again. Except this time, the trap would not be a cage. It would be a sword through the heart. Nhevalos had no plans to simply hold the titan of magic this time. This time, Harkandos must die. There could be no long-term plan as long as Harkandos walked the continent.

Harkandos had railed against his imprisonment for nearly two thousand years, but Nhevalos had, in his own way, done the same. Half measures were dangerous, and imprisoning Harkandos had been a half measure, a stopgap because Nhevalos had not, at the time, had the power to do more. He simply hadn't had the strength.

Now, though, he did. Through a thousand *kairoi* meticulously placed, Nhevalos had spent nearly two millennia crafting his great and powerful arrow.

Even enormous beasts could be slain with a single arrow, and Nhevalos had made many, many arrows. Khyven was the best of them, and Nhevalos would now bet everything upon him.

The *kairoi* had shown the outcome a dozen different ways. Harkandos would assemble his forces, awaken the other Noksonoi he could find, beat them into submission, and then go looking for anything that was a threat.

Usara would be at the top of his list. Harkandos would see recovering Castle Noktos as absolutely necessary, for the shame Nhevalos had brought upon Noktos's stronghold. Harkandos had always felt Castle Noktos had belonged to him.

So Harkandos would bring a force with him. He would think to simply stamp out the Humans Nhevalos had assembled all at once, all in one place.

And then, on the battlefield, Khyven the Unkillable would meet him, bearing the Sword of Noksonon. Harkandos would attempt to swat the mortal away, and that would be his undoing. The *kairoi* had been very specific.

The battle would then begin in earnest. Harkandos would wake to his threat, but too late. He would bring his magic to bear, but Nhevalos's creation, the modified Lore Magic within Khyven would come to full life, and the Sword of Noksonon—having bonded with its new user—would do the rest.

The "blue wind" would anticipate, give Khyven the path to victory, and the Sword would ensure it was not wasted. No direct attack spell—fire or lightning—would be able to hit Khyven because of the Lore Magic's warning, and if Harkandos somehow managed to create an area-wide enchantment, the Sword would cut through it.

The battle—and the victory—would happen fast. There would be no fencing, no back and forth, no witty repartee. Khyven did not hesitate when threatened. He killed. Harkandos would still be fumbling to understand how Khyven had managed to evade his attack when the Sword of Noksonon pierced his chest.

After that critical moment, the *kairoi* branched out and became harder to predict. Harkandos's thugs might continue to fight. Avektos had always been a little slow to turn direction. Orios was, and always had been, thoroughly unpredictable. Mendos would almost undoubtedly flee, as would Jai'ketakos.

But the most likely future path was that all the other Noksonoi, having witnessed Khyven destroy their liege, would flee. They would go back to doing what they had been doing for the last seventeen hundred years.

And that would be the end of it.

Nhevalos crossed the room and bowed to fit through the eight-foot-tall doorway to the Human-sized spiral staircase. He was now nearly ten feet tall and gaining inches every week. He had released the spell some time ago and it was still slowly undoing itself a few inches at a time.

For an Eldroi, transforming from one form into another was relatively routine. For certain, the size and mass of a creature increased the complexity and the drain from such a spell, but it could be done quickly. The problem was, it was a magical drain the entire time an Eldroi held a foreign form. So, for short periods of time, an Eldroi could pass as Human.

But eventually, they would have to relinquish the form and take their true shape or spend enormous amounts of magic to stay in the new form. Additionally, there were Eldroi or even some Human mages who would be able to see what the transformer was doing.

For Nhevalos's purposes over the last few centuries, that simply wouldn't do.

The other way to transform was to actually change the physiological composition of his body. Permanently. That kind of spell took months, even years, to effect properly to make a reasonable facsimile without incurring physical damage to the body, or worse, the brain.

That was the kind of long-term spell that Nhevalos had used to transform him to Human size. It was the kind of spell that the Drakanoi had used to make themselves all dragons. It was also used by many Eldroi as they slid into their interests. Raos was a perfect example. She wasn't emulating any creature in particular, but simply embodying how she saw herself.

Nhevalos had used the spell to walk among Humans for centuries, but the time for subterfuge was ending, and he had reversed the spell. As a result, his body had been slowly transforming back to his true form over the last few months.

But it did make moving through Human structures more difficult.

He crouched and uncomfortably climbed up the stairs. Reading the *kairoi* was best done at the spot where he wanted to see the future. The amount of magic required to, for example, read the future of Daemanon in Noksonon was prohibitive. To read Rhenn's future, standing in that Thuros room would have done quite nicely.

But Nhevalos wanted to read the *kairoi* that would soon converge on Castle Noktos, where the battle between Khyven and Harkandos would take place.

The best place to throw the spell would be atop a tower in Castle Noktos, but it was far too dangerous for that. All the *kairoi* indicated that if Harkandos caught even a single glimpse of Nhevalos, the brute would come straight for him. Such a meeting would play into every one of Harkandos's strengths, and both of them knew it.

So Nhevalos must ensure that he stayed hidden for a little while longer. Soon, it wouldn't matter. The battle was near—it could happen today.

When it did, the last place Nhevalos could afford to be was at Castle Noktos.

He emerged into the queen's study and proceeded through the empty castle to the topmost tower room on the southwest side. He had used the room a number of times over the years, unbeknownst to Vamreth and King Laochodon before him. That it was rarely used by anyone had helped, as did the fact that it was five stories tall and had a wide archway with wooden shutters over the glass windows. He opened both the windows and the shutters and looked out over the quiet Human kingdom of Usara.

Of course, before the Human-Giant War, before the two thousand years of mortal-ruled Noksonon, this had been Nhevalos's realm. This was where the original Noksonoi had arrived from Lathranon before they split off and went to different locations on the continent. Back then the seat of power was, of course, Castle Noktos. Nhevalos's domain stretched all the way from the northeastern tip of the Claw to westernmost Imprevar and Triada in the south.

For the first time, Nhevalos felt a wash of satisfaction. Soon, this would be over. He could claim victory. The Humans would go back to building their little civilizations and he would ... what?

Begin his next project, he supposed. It did appeal to him that he might take up residence again in Castle Noktos. Except this time, perhaps he would be a small kingdom among the kingdom of the Humans. To treat with them, interact with them in the same manner as, say, the Sandrunners.

And, of course, he would undertake the project to extract Paralos from the Dark. He owed her that much, at long last.

But first, he must get past the upcoming crossroads. All his plans had come down to this.

He drew a long breath and plunged his mind into the magic deep inside himself. He envisioned a ghost of his own body pulling himself down with ethereal fingers, deep down, hand over hand along ghostly threads of power, deep to the core of himself where a vast lake of silver lava bubbled and boiled.

This was his magical power. As he plunged those ethereal fingers into the silver lava, he felt how the lake connected to a hundred rivers, the rivers to a thousand streams, and the streams to a hundred thousand events that had happened or would happen.

Magic wasn't something found only within the bodies of those who could wield it. It was everywhere. It flowed and collected in all the places of the world.

It had taken Nhevalos years of traveling the world of Eldros, sitting in a spot, and doing exactly this: connecting his magic to the land, searching the thousands of obscure possibilities to see what might happen in that place.

Nhevalos had been everywhere, from the mighty stone structures of the Pelinon Empire in Daemanon to the elder dragon caves on Drakanon to the fiery volcanos of Pyranon.

And, of course, to every square mile of Noksonon. He had searched for the one lone future that would allow the mortals to overcome Harkandos and his cohorts. It had all centered on Harkandos, of course. With him, the Eldroi could rise again; they could eliminate their mortal creations and remake the world once more.

And every time Nhevalos had invoked his Lore Magic, Harkandos's *kairoi* led to Castle Noktos.

In the few threads where Khyven slipped, where he failed— all of which had faded not long ago—Nhevalos had created fail- safes throughout the continent, mortals with strong Eldroi blood, blood that Nhevalos had bred into the most promising families.

Nhevalos had given the Blue Wind to more than a dozen mortals who might step in should Khyven fail.

The Sandrunners' Champion of the Sun, Txomin, had been such a one. And that had almost been a disaster. It had brought one of Nhevalos's greatest fears to life: that his creations would someday meet and destroy each other. Strong magic had a way of attracting its like, which was why Nhevalos had placed his creations as far apart on the continent as he could.

Still, Txomin and Khyven had found one another, and Khyven had almost been lost during that confrontation.

Nhevalos drew another long breath, pulled on the silver lava, pulled it up, up to him until his ethereal hands dripped with the silver magic.

He opened his eyes.

He flung his hands at the open window, feeling the unstoppable power surge through him. When filled with so much magic, it felt like he could command the sun and stars to spin on their axes, pull them down from the sky or shoot them off into the empty black. He felt he could flatten mountains or cause mountains to raise from a flat plain. Everything seemed within reach and completely under his command.

That euphoric invincibility was a side-effect of pulling so much magic into oneself. It was why the Eldroi, who were so filled with magic, had made so many mistakes throughout their history. They were like omnipotent gods who nevertheless stumbled and bumbled about, often falling over like children.

It was the great lie, the seductive whisper magic offered: that they were invincible. It was that lie that had likely felled Noktos himself. It had certainly felled Harkandos once, and would do so again.

So Nhevalos resisted the nearly irresistible temptation to believe he was the master of everything, no matter how large, and channeled the power into his purpose.

He plunged it into the palace, into the crown city of the Humans, into the wall that surrounded it, into the plains beyond and the forest beyond that, lighting up the land all the way to Castle Noktos.

And he teased out the *kairoi*.

The invisible threads marked the paths to the future like roads marked the route to the next city, slowly flickering and becoming apparent. They looked like roots that had grown a half dozen feet above the earth, twisting and turning in every direction, growing over or below each other. Some were as thin as filaments from a spider's web, some as thick as tree trunks. Some went off into the obscure distance beyond the field of Nhevalos's spell. Some intertwined and bound together into formidable looking cables.

The smallest filaments were tiny events, the kind of daily predictable events that anyone might experience, often in some little corner of the world where nothing much happened. The thick, intertwined *kairoi* were confluences of great power and portent.

These were the events that would change the world not just for the participants who made up those *kairoi*, but the entire region, the entire kingdom, or the entire continent.

Now, the largest, thickest *kairoi* cluster that Nhevalos had ever seen twisted about itself, leading toward Castle Noktos. Thick root after thick root overlapped and intertwined to create a fierce, shining node the size of a small silver sun.

This was the battle.

On the other side, a few smaller *kairoi* led away. The results of the confrontation, the far fewer possibilities that led away from that clash.

Within each of the *kairoi* was the portion of a possible life. The tiny threads that made up the larger roots were possibilities, and if he touched them with his mind, he could see that life as though it was actually happening now, instead of the future where it actually existed.

He had seen so many futures of Khyven's life now. Nhevalos had seen when Khyven had died from the Helm of Darkness instead of being saved by his friends. He had seen when Khyven had been killed by arrows at the edge of Nox Arvak, ripped apart by Tovos in the dragon's cave, immolated in Jai'ketakos's flames at Wheskone Keep.

Nhevalos had seen every death and every possibility that could have been Khyven's life. And he had steered the man past them all.

Soon, Khyven's usefulness would pass, and Nhevalos could let him wander on his way, to die as he chose.

Nhevalos reached into the thick cluster of *kairoi*. It was filled with Khyven's *kairoi*. There were, of course, the *kairoi* of his friends—most of whom died in that battle—as well as Harkandos's, who would certainly die in the battle.

He followed the threads. There were even more paths for Khyven in this than before, nearly twice as many, all leading to the battle where …

Nhevalos reached the node and started. It was Khyven. And Khyven. And Khyven.

But no Harkandos.

At first, the shock of not finding the battle between Harkandos and Khyven almost popped Nhevalos out of his spell casting. Nhevalos had made a point of coming back to this place every couple of weeks these last months, and casting this same spell to ensure that everything was going to plan.

But this … wasn't what it had looked like. This wasn't

even ... It was as though all of Nhevalos's careful work—his centuries of planning—had been wiped away. It was ...

It didn't even make sense.

He picked through the *kairoi*, drawing closer. Khyven and Khyven and Khyven, all possibilities drawing near, but none of Harkandos.

What was happening?

Panic began to rise in his belly. This was wrong. This was so horribly wrong. This was—

He reached the giant node, the great battle.

The fight was Khyven against Khyven.

What?

That wasn't ... It wasn't even possible. It was ...

A chill fear swept through Nhevalos, icing his insides such that he couldn't breathe. The spell began to slip from his grasp, and he desperately searched the cluster.

Khyven came to the castle. Khyven emerged from the castle to battle ... himself.

They fought, and Khyven won. And Khyven died.

Khyven walked away, leaving Khyven dead on the battlefield, a sword through his heart.

And then, after that confusing, deadly node of the future, another *kairoi* merged with the outcome.

It was, at last, Harkandos. He towered over the victorious Khyven and looked down like an approving father, smiling that wicked smile of his. He reached down and patted the surviving Khyven on the shoulder.

Frantically, Nhevalos pulled himself closer, further inside the *kairoi*, trying desperately to see the details, to search for something that could explain this.

And what he sought caught his attention.

He found it in Khyven's face. This was the Ringer's countenance, and yet ...

It wasn't.

The scars on his face were pulled wider apart. The slant of his eyebrows was higher on the outsides of his brow, giving him a demonic look. Even his eyes were larger, his eyebrows darker.

It was as though Khyven had been cast in Harkandos's image, as though a mirror image of Nhevalos's champion had been—

Nhevalos gasped and jolted out of the spell. The image of the roots, the *kairoi*, flickered, faded, and died away.

Nhevalos stared at the empty dark, eyes wide.

"No ..." he murmured aloud.

A memory came from centuries ago, a moment when Harkandos and Nhevalos had stood in a room together. Harkandos been bragging about his latest achievement. Nhevalos had watched as Harkandos had duplicated a mortal, had forced a Taur-El to stand in front of a mirror. On the other side of the room, Harkandos had set up a second mirror. And as Nhevalos watched, Harkandos had reached his muscled arm into the second mirror and pulled the essence of the Taur-El through the first. The original stayed where he had been, unaware, as a similar copy—with certain features twisted—emerged in Harkandos's fist.

That's what this was ...

Harkandos wasn't galloping blindly toward his fate as he had done last time. He had seen through Nhevalos's veil; he'd seen the truth.

Harkandos had used his mirror spell again, this time with Khyven. The powerful idiot had somehow found a way to undo Nhevalos's centuries of work. He had made a duplicate.

And that duplicate was going to kill Khyven.

CHAPTER SIXTEEN

KHYVEN

Khyven stared up at the stars, at the giant full moon as his fingers traced the line of the amulet on the ground. He'd removed it, wanted to experience the day and the night without the interference of magic.

He couldn't remember the last time he'd just considered the beauty of the sky. He'd spent nights on the road with Slayter, nights at the old man's camp before the Night Ring. He'd seen the stars plenty of times, but it had been years since he hadn't been preoccupied with staying alive. For the first time in a long time, he felt relaxed.

He smiled up at the glowing lights above. It was an incredible gift, this moment out of time, out of the noktum. Rhenn had known exactly what to give to the two of them.

Lorelle slumbered beside him, the two of them draped in a silk sheet she had brought. She'd brought blankets too, and a basket filled with fruit, butter, and fresh baked bread whose aroma had hovered around them while they made love.

But they hadn't eaten any of it yet, and that beautiful smell of warmth and safety had faded with the day. He was hungry, but he didn't want to reach over Lorelle to get the basket. He didn't want to disturb her by moving in the slightest, in fact. She was perfect. She slept like a portrait, her ebony shoulders peeking above the white sheet, so smooth. Her head was turned to the side so that he saw only her profile, her smooth cheek and pointed ears. Her midnight hair splayed out across the grass like stylized rays from a dark sun, all save the single golden ray, that single lock. It serpentined across the black like a path of hope.

And that's what she was for him. He had never wanted anything more than he wanted her, and he couldn't imagine he ever would.

"I want to stay here forever," he murmured so softly his words had no sound, just the weight of his breath. "I want to be here, with you, forever."

She didn't stir, and he continued to watch her. He wondered how long she had watched him after he'd almost died from the Helm of Darkness, after she'd given him her soul. Had she fretted for that long month, wondering if she had only given her soul to watch him die anyway.

He didn't think she was in love with him then. She had only given him her soul out of loyalty, out of repayment for saving her friend, for liberating her friend's kingdom. She'd done it because she was a good person.

He thought this because being soul-bonded to him had not been enough once he had awoken. It had taken her transformation in the Dark, a journey that he hadn't been a part of, for her to realize that she loved him.

He believed it now, though. She had shown him that she was his, and he hers, in every way. He did not doubt that anymore, but he didn't think she had started there.

In the beginning, she had been a good person, virtuous, aloof, and disciplined. And he'd been a selfish man, dangerous and violent, who would do anything to survive. They had both changed. She was reckless now, mischievous, prone to break rules, still that same good person. And he ... he was the same dangerous and violent man, but perhaps not selfish anymore. Or at least he didn't want to be. He wanted to care about others more than he cared about himself. He wanted to be a good person like she was a good person.

And maybe now, he could be. His past had been full of violence and death. He'd done it in the beginning because he'd had to, kill or be killed. But the killing soon became his job, then a doorway to fame, and finally a way to rise above his station.

He still heard the roar of the crowd, still felt approval of every screaming fan. He still felt sublime satisfaction of excellent swordplay, of building his body to be fast enough, strong enough to create a fighting prowess so powerful that it stood like a wall between him and death every day. He learned how to survive the Night Ring. He came to dominate it.

And eventually he came to love it.

Could a person spend years learning something without coming to feel that their skills were, in fact, their personality? Could they do this without coming, eventually, to love it?

He was a warrior. A Ringer. A Knight of the Dark. That was his talent ...

But in this moment, what he wouldn't give to just be a lover, a consort. This breathtaking Luminent had given herself to him, and right now all he wanted was to give to her the same—

Khyven's thoughts vanished as he saw a strange shadow against the tree ahead of him, a shadow that ought not to be shaped like that. His throat tightened like iron hands were choking him. He wanted it to be a trick of the moonlight. He wanted it to be his wild imagination, so used to seeing threats everywhere that it couldn't help itself. But it wasn't.

The Sword leaned against the trunk ten feet away from him.

He grasped desperately for the Amulet of Noksonon in the grass, put it over his head. The night clarified, and he could see everything clearly.

The six-foot blade leaned there, its edge glowing with silver light. He silently put his hand on Lorelle's arm and squeezed, probably far too hard.

Her eyes opened like she'd been faking. She didn't jump, didn't jolt. She made no sound at all, but her gaze flicked all around, to him first, where she registered his fear, then around the glade, where she settled on the Sword. She sat up slowly, and her feet slid underneath her with an inhuman grace like a string had lifted her up from the earth until she was crouching in the grass, ready to spring.

"It ... can't be," Khyven murmured, instantly feeling silly saying such a thing. Clearly it could. The Sword was here.

The presence of the thing sent the prickle of spider's feet up his spine. The last thing he'd have assumed was that he'd underestimated that bloodthirsty, eldritch weapon. But clearly he had.

It made him wonder just how *much* he had.

"You are surprised, Slayer of Trolls?" the Sword said in his mind, and Khyven's heart hurt. He'd rid himself of the thing. And for one blessed moment, he thought he was free. *"You didn't think that the* Ankeed Ruut *could hold me, did you? Dalamos was a fool, far more appreciative of his skills than anyone else was."*

"I don't know who Dalamos is," Khyven thought back, not knowing what else to think.

"I was made by Noktos himself. I was cooled in troughs filled with the blood of five Eldroi. Part of Noktos's very soul was forged into me."

"I don't know what that means."

"What it means, Slayer of Trolls, is that a trinket like the Ankeed Ruut *cannot hold me. All it can do is show me how much you don't know."*

Lorelle pulled her cloak to herself, slipping it smoothly over her shoulders.

"I don't ... want what you offer me."

"Oh, but you do."

"I don't."

"No one has ever rejected me. I am the greatest spell my master ever wrought, save one. Eldroi have killed to possess me, Slayer of Trolls."

"I don't want to be a slayer of anything."

"Death stalks you through the weeds like a serpent, and you march blithely on as though your ignorance will protect you. You are unaware. I am

not. I am your shield and sword together. I am what you lack. And you, my wielder, are what I lack. We were made for one another."

"*I don't* want *you!*" Khyven leaned to his left. His weapons were there, his normal sword and The Diplomat. A normal steel sword couldn't directly stop the Sword if it flew at them, but it might deflect the thing long enough for Lorelle to transport them.

"*Don't be foolish,*" the Sword said.

"*Leave me alone.*"

The Sword paused. "*I did not take you for a coward.*"

"*Take me for whatever you want. Just stay away from me.*"

"*Death comes for you, Khyven. It comes today. It comes now.*"

"Lorelle?" he said.

"You got it." She flared her cloak, and they both vanished into it.

They arrived in the palace, in an alcove off the great room. Khyven checked the urge to vomit, controlled his stomach, and then looked down. He was still stark naked, and just beyond the corner, people rushed past.

"Really? Here?" he said to her.

His pants and tunic hit him in the chest. He fumbled with them, juggling The Diplomat and his steel sword. Apparently she'd thought to grab their clothes. "I didn't take us here. I took us to our bedroom. Something ... shoved me."

"The Sword?"

"All I know is that it wasn't me."

Again, those spider feet ran up his back. The Sword. Could the Sword actually cast spells?

He dressed and buckled on his sword faster than he ever had. "That was the most pleasant moment of my life followed by the least pleasant, I think—"

"Khyven," Lorelle interrupted him. Her naked body was shrouded to the ground by the cloak, and she hadn't dressed yet. She clutched her little red dress in her hand, stared off at nothing, and drifted to the archway. Her gaze flicked over the people bustling by.

That wasn't just someone hurrying to a chamber pot, or some baker rushing to make sure his loaves didn't burn. That was dozens of people rushing toward the atrium.

"What's happening?" he asked.

She responded by drifting into the room and joining the rushing people. Khyven followed. The agitated crowd pressed themselves against the towering windows of the atrium and stared, dumbfounded, over the tunnel of light that went down the center of the courtyard and through the broken gate, the tunnel of light Slayter had created ...

And the army that stood beside it.

The Giants had come at last.

CHAPTER SEVENTEEN

KHYVEN

Khyven forgot about everything as he approached the windows.

The atrium was one of three on this side of the castle. Another just like it, destroyed when Jai'ketakos chased Vohn and Shalure through the castle, lay in rubble two hundred yards to the left.

The windows of this atrium rose, as narrow as a person and as tall as a house, before a stonework crosshatch broke them, then continued up another distance of tall windows, then stonework, then windows … Stone and glass alternated this way for a hundred feet before the wall curved into a dome over the expansive room.

The refugees of Usara parted for Khyven as they saw him, and the murmurs of fear quieted to whispers of hope. They knew who he was. Every one of them had seen him and Rhenn's inner circle fight the monsters of the night.

Khyven approached the spear-like windows overlooking Castle Noktos's courtyard, fallen to ruin over the centuries.

Defiant charcoal grass grew up between the stingy, tightly-fitting cobblestones. Eerily preserved statues dotted the landscape, patched with black moss. The courtyard was almost as large as the entire city of Usara, a vast and open sculpture garden that led to the broken gate and the ten-foot wall surrounding the castle.

A glowing tunnel of light spilled down from Slayter's laboratory above and snaked up to the broken and leaning gate. It stood like a golden spear of hope stabbing into the distance, toward the crown city of Usara, marking the way for stragglers to make their way to this place, marking the way home. Slayter had talked about doing something like this. Khyven shouldn't be surprised that he'd managed it. He really shouldn't be surprised about anything Slayter did anymore, but the sheer power required for something like that was astounding.

But the beacon, meant to bring back Usara's lost children had brought something else altogether.

Beside the tunnel of light, just beyond the wall, stood an army of horrors.

Khyven buckled on his sword belt, adjusted it automatically.

The wall—which had been so imposing when Khyven had first passed through it with Rhenn, Lorelle, Vohn, Gohver, and a small band of artifact raiders so long ago—suddenly seemed like a joke.

Hundreds of Nox slunk back from the fearsome vanguard, as far as they could get from Slayter's beacon.

The horde of Giants, however, stood just behind the broken gates, bathed in Slayter's light like it simply didn't matter. There were five of them, and Jai'ketakos's enormous bulk spread longwise behind them, like he had been posed there for some horrific painting. His glowing yellow eyes stared sullenly up at the Slayter's laboratory.

In front of Jai'ketakos, on the right-hand side, stood a bearded Giant. He had a flat-topped helm with a single, sharp horn protruding from the forehead. He stooped so low his shoulders rose like rounded hills behind that helmeted head. The creature's eyes couldn't be seen beneath the helm's shadow, but his body was a nightmare parody of a brawler run to fat. His belly was large and round and hung almost to the ground. His thick, solid legs bent, the knees pointed outward as though to give his belly space to swing so low. His arms hung from those stooped shoulders, one straight and almost touching the ground, the other bent and holding the haft of an axe that must have been twelve feet long. That enormous axe-head could cut through a maple tree with one swing.

Beside the fat Giant stood a tall, thin Giant, as though an intentional counterpoint. He wore black clothing and the warm breeze blew back his silver-bordered black cloak. His pale face was sharp in every way. Long, sharp nose. Cheekbones cut from marble. Even the angled bangs of his black hair looked like a wide, flat blade half sheathed over his face. He carried nothing, no weapons. A mage then, like Slayter. But then, according to Slayter, all Giants were super mages, beyond belief.

On the right side of the group, shielding itself from the light, loomed a small Cakistro, one of the enormous spiders that walked ponderously above the noktum forests.

No wait ... Not a Cakistro. There was a figure at the center of those monstrous spider legs. That was another Giant.

She stood with the others like she belonged with them. Like the other Giants, she had a mostly Human face except for bulbous, insect-like eyes. Giant spider legs had burst from the Giant's back, arcing up in abrupt angles, then downward to stab the earth and hold her atrophied body aloft. The Giant's body seemed vestigial, dangling limply from the tall legs like an afterthought, as though the only thing of consequence the body possessed were those powerful black spider legs and that bug-eyed head, looking at the castle with inhuman impassivity. The spider Giant's lank, greasy hair fell in tangles down from her face, nearly touching the ground thirty feet below.

To the spider's right was another female Giant. She stood in the full light of the beacon, and her eyes drew Khyven even at this distance. They were black and filled with stars, and seemed as though distance did not apply to them, like they could suck you in whether you were two feet or two hundred feet away. He couldn't even properly see her face at this distance, but he could see into those eyes, could feel the cold depths of the night sky.

She was the shortest of them, but she still towered over the army of Nox and Trolls behind her. She wore black robes with no ornament or piping of any kind. Another Giant without a weapon. Another Giant who would be throwing magic.

Next to her was what looked like one of the walking corpses N'ssag had resurrected in the nuraghi of Daemanon. Hideous burns had ravaged its body. One of its eyes hung from its socket like a drop of egg yolk. Charred teeth grinned from that half of its face. The other half was pale and arrogant, casting a baleful glance upon the castle. Dark black hair flowed down that side of its head, and Khyven suddenly realized he recognized the Giant.

That was Tovos! That was the Giant who had tried to make Lorelle his puppet, who had almost killed them all at the dragon's horde at the heart of the Great Noktum.

Next to him, no taller than the middle of his thigh, stood the necromancer N'ssag, slowly caressing his dirty hands like he was washing them, and smiling.

In the center, fully fifteen feet tall, stood the leader of the group, Harkandos. That was the demonic Giant Khyven had fought when Slayter had almost unleashed him from his statue prison, right here in this courtyard.

Each of the other Giants had a distinctive look, no doubt relating to their personalities. Harkandos was muscled, thick in the chest and in the shoulders like a Ringer who fought for his livelihood. He was bald, with a thick beard covering his cheeks, chin, and the top of his chest. His mouth was turned up in that same arrogant sneer he'd had as a statue. Except this time, the Giant was not stone. He was alive and he radiated power.

The other monstrosities all stood behind or around him, clearly deferring to him. Khyven could only guess what kind of creature could humble and dominate this assemblage of Giants, but Harkandos did.

The Spider Giant hung over thirty feet up in the air.

Jai'ketakos was like a monolithic backdrop, taller still, behind them all. But Harkandos held the center as if, were he to suddenly spread his arms, he'd flatten them all.

This was the entire gang of Giants from Khyven's nightmare. He swallowed.

"Where's Rhenn?" he murmured. "Where are the others?"

Without another word, Lorelle flung her cloak over him. His stomach twisted, his body compressed as though being sucked into a tube—

And they stood in the queen's meeting room.

Rhenn, Slayter, and Vohn clustered at the balcony, looking out over the horror that had arrived. All of their backs were to him and Lorelle.

"Nothing changes," Rhenn said. "We knew this was coming, and now it's here. We've prepared. We unleash our preparation."

"I don't know that we prepared for *this*," Vohn said as though his lips were numb.

"Look at her body," Slayter said. "It doesn't look like she's even using it. It's like her bug-eyed head and those spider legs are where her … life-force is."

"We fight." Rhenn ignored Slayter's commentary. Her own gaze was fixed on N'ssag, who stared back up at her. "That's what we came here to do. That's what we do."

"Cakistro legs," Slayter amended, shaking his head like he had been silly. "Cakistro legs, of course. Not spider legs."

"We need to summon Khyven and Lorelle," Rhenn said. "They're—"

"We're here," Lorelle said.

Rhenn and Vohn glanced back at them. Neither one batted an eyelash. Slayter continued staring at the army.

"Good," Rhenn said, almost turned back, then gave Lorelle a quick appraisal with a raised eyebrow.

She secured the front of her cloak with one hand. "We were rushed."

Rhenn gave a little smile, which turned sad quickly, then she faced the army at the gates.

Khyven stood in front of Lorelle as she unclasped the cloak, let it fall to the ground, and wriggled into her little red dress. She shook her head and murmured, "Every time there's an attack, I'm in a party dress. Every damned time."

"Will your new beam of light help us?" Rhenn asked Slayter.

"Really just the sheer magnitude of that transformation," Slayter murmured, though clearly it was a running commentary only for himself. "I mean, she actually looks like she started as a Cakistro and then—"

Slayter cut off his own monologue and looked over at Rhenn as though he'd just heard her question. "Oh, well, no. I don't think so. I mean, it will certainly hurt the bloodsuckers, but I don't think they are our main problem. Giants are not hurt by light. They lived in light for longer than we can imagine before the Great Noktum was cast. In fact, Giants on other continents still live in light. Just imagine the Giants are alligators and the Nox are gnats. That's about the appropriate difference in power—""

"Slayter," Rhenn interrupted.

"Yes?"

"I understand that the Giants are the more powerful enemy."

"Oh, well. Then I suppose no," Slayter finished. "The light will not help us."

"What else in the Vault might?"

"We could use the Axe of Artivos. That could cleave a Giant's head in two. Of course, we'd have to have someone to wield it. I'm thinking maybe Lorelle with the cloak. She could drop it on their heads. Of course, Tovos has control over the Dark. He invented the cloaks. So, if they expect it, which they might, they could counter simply by canceling the effects of the cloak. We might try the Syvorn Portal. I don't know where it goes, but I experimented enough with it to know that things tossed through it go somewhere else, and they don't come back. And if you close the portal when something is halfway through, it chops it cleanly in half. Doesn't matter what it is. We could try to put the Syvorn Portal over a Giant's head and then close it. That would probably work. And then of course, there's the Dragon Chain. We'd have to get them to hold still long enough to get it on their ankle. Or wrist. But that's a pretty lousy weapon for a battlefield, being as how anyone who touched them could free them. So never mind about that—"

"Slayter, I don't need a catalog. I need you to equip us. We need the best artifacts for this fight."

Slayter nodded, and he cocked his head. In all likelihood, he was going through the entire catalogue in his own mind instead.

"I don't understand," Lorelle said. "Why are they just standing there? If Giants have even half the power Slayter claims, wouldn't they attack? Just storm the castle?"

"I don't know," Rhenn said. "It smacks of theater."

Khyven had felt the same, the way Jai'ketakos had curled behind the Giants, the way they had arranged themselves, almost as though for effect. "Theater? To what purpose?"

"Is there some barrier?" Vohn offered. "Some force that the wall has created that we cannot detect?"

"There's no barrier," Slayter said. "Not magical, at any rate, if that's what you mean."

"Protocol," Khyven murmured. "What if it's some unwritten rule among the Giants? A touching of swords before the battle."

They all looked at him.

"Hmmm," Slayter murmured, surprised. "Khyven might actually be right."

"Thanks," he said drily.

"I mean, it is possible they can sense that I have twelve lightning rods pointed at that gate that will activate if any Eldroi come through. But if they can, they could also counter those spells. But actually, it's more likely what Khyven says. Some kind of tradition. For some Giants, tradition was everything. What if Harkandos is one of those?"

"Lightning rods? Good," Rhenn said. "Let's get more things pointed at that gate. That beam of yours, can we move it?"

"Move it?"

"Rake it over N'ssag and his creations. Thin down their numbers like we did in Daemanon. The Giants are our primary foes, but not having to deal with an army of Nox bloodsuckers will help."

"Yes, I ... Yes, that is doable." Slayter turned to go, as though he'd finally decided on the arsenal he wanted to use.

"I'll take you," Lorelle said.

"Wait." Rhenn held up her hand. "Something's happening."

"Trespassers of Castle Noktos!" Harkandos held up his hand in a salute. His voice boomed supernaturally loud; it seemed to come from everywhere, not just the direction of the gate.

Khyven waited for the declaration of war, a statement that would fulfill some ancient law before this army, which clearly wanted to leap past the gate and attack, poured into the courtyard.

But the declaration remained unsaid. The army stayed still.

Harkandos surveyed the castle and the courtyard like a landlord about to evict unwanted tenants, then finally turned his smoldering gaze up at the balcony where they all stood. He looked directly at Rhenn.

"Queen Rhennaria Laochodon," the Giant boomed. "We have come to bargain."

CHAPTER EIGHTEEN

KHYVEN

Did he just say bargain?" Vohn voiced everyone's confusion.

"Interesting," Slayter, who had been headed toward the door, turned and drifted back to the balcony's rail.

"Slayter, if you understand this, explain," Rhenn murmured hastily. "What's going on?"

"Well, what I've read of Harkandos—the big one, the mean looking one."

"They all look mean," Vohn said.

"Quiet Vohn." Rhenn put a hand on his shoulder.

Slayter glanced at Vohn, smiled, then continued. "Well, Harkandos is feared even among the other Eldroi—er, Giants. They think he's the most powerful mage among them. There's no legend of Harkandos ever bargaining. That's not to say he never has, I suppose, but the histories say that he never bargains and he never lies because he doesn't need to. He just takes what he wants, or others give it to him in exchange for not being destroyed, I suppose. There are notes that Rauvelos kept, or perhaps it was Nhevalos. I'm not sure whose handwriting it was. Of course, if it was Rauvelos, any handwriting at all would be a remarkable feat, being as how he has no hands—"

"Stay on Harkandos," Rhenn interrupted.

"Oh, well … Harkandos is, well, he's like a tyrant king."

"Then why bargain?"

"It is fascinating …" Slayter said.

"Is he trying to trick us?"

"I think if he wanted to kill us, he would simply trample over that gate and kill us," Slayter shrugged. "Of course, you're trying to pull from me a personality reduction from a handful of historical passages. At best, I have a twelve percent chance of being right. Perhaps even—"

"If he could just kill us," Rhenn interrupted again. "Why hasn't he?"

"I think …" Slayter began, but trailed off.

"What?"

"Well, I think you should ask him."

"Queen Rhennaria," Harkandos boomed again. "Will you come down to parlay?"

"Parlay," Slayter said, smiling. "Good word. It means—"

"I know what it means," Rhenn said.

"I will take you down there," Lorelle said.

"Don't go down there," Vohn said.

"Take me, too," Khyven said.

"Oh, and me," Slayter added.

"Everybody quiet." Rhenn's hand cut sharply down through the air. "I'm going down. Me, Lorelle, Khyven. Slayter, you prepare the defenses. Vohn, you help him."

"He can probably hear us, you know." Slayter shrugged. "I mean, if he wanted to."

"Do it," Rhenn responded.

Lorelle threw her cloak over all of them. Khyven's guts twisted, he spiraled down a dark funnel, and then they stood thirty feet from the gates, the brilliant tunnel of light glowing to their left. It truly felt like a tunnel. It didn't illuminate anything beyond its own self, as though the noktum was pressing in on it.

Harkandos glared down at them exactly as he had done when he was a statue. Angry. Superior. Khyven almost made a crack about that. The barely controlled thrill in his chest always made him want to make jokes when he was about to die. It had actually become a tactic, something that threw his opponents off their stride. He'd used it a number of times in the Night Ring, but he didn't think bravado was going to knock this Giant off balance.

"Let us put all the stones on the table," Harkandos said. The Giants behind him looked smug, except for Jai'ketakos, who looked unhappy.

"Stones?" Rhenn said.

"You have never played Eldroi Stones?" Harkandos asked.

"It's a game," Lorelle supplied. "Like chess, but simpler."

"I have not, but very well. I understand the idea," Rhenn said.

"I prefer not to dance around our issues with lies or deception," Harkandos said. "I know about Nhevalos. I know you are his chosen ones." His gaze game to rest on Khyven.

Rhenn hesitated, though her face remained strong.

"I know," Harkandos continued. "That your so-called Khyven the Unkillable possesses power, perhaps enough to kill an Eldroi. I know this because I know Nhevalos's plan."

Khyven's heart beat faster. It didn't bode well that Harkandos knew the secret of the blue wind.

Harkandos continued. "Is this enough for you? Do you believe that I have come here telling truth?"

"Our mage says you are not known as a liar."

"Deception is for the weak. Is that us, Queen Rhennaria? Or shall we treat with one another like rulers should?"

"What do you want?" Rhenn asked.

"I have come to take this castle. I've come to kill you all for desecrating a place that is holy to the Noksonoi, and for overreaching in your arrogance, for filling up these lands that belong to me and calling them your own."

"And we are here to destroy you should you attempt such a foolish thing," Rhenn shot back.

Harkandos smiled thinly. "We understand each other then. As I see it, we have two choices. The first is that you spurn my offer, my followers and I break through this gate, and we all see just how good Nhevalos's plan is. If you believe in him and his schemes, then surely that must be your choice. But Lore Magic is fickle, even in the hands of a master."

Harkandos lowered his head, his eyes smoking with glowing mist. "If you choose this and your forces do not prevail, I will slaughter each and every one of you. I will purge this castle and kill each of your subjects for your hubris." He paused to let that sink in, as though they all needed a moment to visualize it.

And Khyven hated him.

He felt the hatred rising like a fiery beast inside him, growing from cub to predator in an instant. At the same time, a cold clarity swirled like snow around the fiery beast: Khyven wanted to kill this creature, this arrogant monster who talked so casually about slaughtering innocents.

"If you do not wish to gamble the lives of your loved ones," Harkandos continued. "Then hearken unto me. I will make you a one-time offer."

Rhenn's face was a mask of determination that mirrored Khyven's anger. "I'm listening."

"I propose champions," Harkandos said. Again, he waited. Khyven's heart beat faster, but this time with hope. Was this a trick? If given the option to choose how to end this contest, Khyven would have chosen exactly this. One match. One fight, with him in the ring.

"These champions shall fight each other," Harkandos said. "And only each other. Neither of us shall interfere. I shall send my champion into this very courtyard, and you will send yours. Here, they will fight to the death, and this is where the battle will be decided. There will only be two results. If my champion wins, then I will allow your followers to serve me as they once did, as they were born and bred to do. And they will live as nature intended."

Rhenn's grip on her sword tightened.

"Should your champion win," Harkandos continued. "I will leave Castle Noktos to you and your followers. Forever. I will never return to this place. As a further concession, I shall leave the entirety of the kingdom you call Usara to you."

"If my champion wins, you withdraw and never return?"

"Yes."

Khyven noticed Rhenn wanted to turn and ask something of Slayter, but the mage was not with them. She kept her focus on Harkandos.

"And what of the rest of Noksonon?" she asked. "Imprevar and Triada. Lumyn and Nokte Shaddark. What about the rest of the people who—"

"Look to your own kind, Queen Rhennaria. Cast your stewardship over what you claim as your kingdom. The rest of Noksonon belongs to me."

"How do I know you will keep your word?"

Harkandos's eyes narrowed. "Queen Rhennaria, when I say something will happen, it happens. If I declare your lands under the direction of your sovereignty, then it is so. It will be as though the Eldroi do not exist in your kingdom. And if any of my followers break my word, they will face *my* wrath. I do not allow lesser beings to make me a liar."

Rhenn turned to Khyven and Lorelle, and the question was plain on her face.

"He can't be serious," Rhenn said in a quiet tone. "He wants a champion match. Like in the Night Ring. Why would he do that? What is the catch?"

"I don't know," Khyven said.

"It doesn't make any sense," Rhenn said.

"To a Human," Lorelle murmured.

"What?"

"Humans believe everyone thinks like they do. That alliances are situational. That romantic love rises from lust. That loyalty rises from need. That betrayal is inevitable except in the rarest of cases."

Rhenn glanced at her friend. "That's a dark look at Humanity."

Lorelle shrugged. "Luminents do not think like that. I am saying there are different ways to look at an offer like this aside from that he's trying to trick us."

"You think he's telling the truth?"

"I'm saying he comes from an inhuman culture, from a time we don't understand. Slayter has been babbling for days about the books he's read on the Eldroi. How the Eldroi treated each other. How none of them liked each other. And yet they built a society that functioned. They didn't constantly try to kill each other because they made pacts. Their society wasn't structured from emotional and personal connection like it is with Humans. The Eldroi don't experience sentiment like you do. Nothing held them together as a people except their word. They set it and lived by it, even if they sometimes hated it. That's why Nhevalos is called the Betrayer—why every other Eldroi hates him— because he lied to them all. He broke their code. So yes, I think it is possible that among the Eldroi, something like this pact would make sense."

Rhenn turned back to Harkandos. "Why?" she shouted up to him.

"Why?" he boomed back. "Why would I offer this opportunity to you?"

"Yes."

For the first time, a shadow of a smile crossed that fiendish face. "A worthy question, but I think you know the answer."

"I think I do, too, but I want you to say it."

Harkandos raised an arm, pointed a finger directly at Khyven. "Because of him."

"He knows about Nhevalos's plan," Khyven murmured to Rhenn. "He knows I'm supposed to kill him. He's worried that Nhevalos is right, that his plan will work. This is his way around it."

"You will choose Khyven the Unkillable as your champion,"

Harkandos boomed. "And I offer you this one chance to resolve everything in a single fight. The blood of your precious followers will not be spilled. If you win, you win everything."

Rhenn shouted back, "And if we lose, we lose everything."

"Not everything. You will have your lives. And Noksonon will have a return to the natural order."

"Natural order ..." Rhenn showed her teeth.

"If you believe in your champion, send him forth," Harkandos stated.

Rhenn turned around, turned her back to the Giants.

"I'll do it," Khyven said before she could speak.

"Just wait a moment."

"It's what I was made for!"

"Shut up, Khyven!" Rhenn whispered harshly. "And listen to me. Of course you want this. You want it to be like the Night Ring, all finished in a single bout. Wrapped up neatly in a place—in a manner—that you once dominated. Who wouldn't want that? But this isn't the Night Ring. He's got to be lying. He wouldn't just hand us this victory wrapped up like a present."

"We're fighting him regardless. If we say yes and he's lying, we're going to fight him. If we say no, we're going to fight him. But if he's *not* lying ... Rhenn ... I can end this right here."

"You can't know you're going to win," Rhenn argued.

"I *will* win."

"You don't—"

"He's going to choose one of those monsters," Khyven said. "He's going to sidestep Nhevalos's prophecy, and he's going send one of those Giants—one who doesn't know Nhevalos's prophecy—to face me. Don't you see? He wants to test if it's real. If it's not, then good for him. He gets your kingdom. If Nhevalos's prophecy *is* real, and I beat his champion, Harkandos saves his own life and only yields Usara. That's what he's going to do. I don't care who he chooses ... I'm going to take them apart. "

"You don't ... Nhevalos doesn't say anything! He manipulates and he lies and he twists everything. All you really know is that this *creature* almost killed you and Slayter in about two seconds when you woke him up. As the statue. Isn't that what you said?"

"Yes, but—"

"And any one of those other Giants won't be frozen as a statue first."

"I didn't know I was the Giantkiller then."

"You don't know you're a Giantkiller now!"

"I think I do," Khyven said.

Rhenn held up her hand and shook her head. "If you lose, we have to fight them anyway. Let's fight them together. All of us, together."

"I'm not going to lose."

"He's not going to lose," Lorelle said.

Rhenn clenched her fist, closed her eyes.

"This is the battle I've been preparing for my whole life," Khyven said. "Cut and dried. Let me fight it."

Rhenn let out a long breath and opened her eyes. She looked at Khyven, then at Lorelle, then back to Khyven. After an excruciating moment, she nodded.

"Very well," she said, so quietly he almost couldn't hear her.

"This was meant to happen," Khyven said.

"Fine. Do it." She glanced up at his shoulder and for the first time noticed he wasn't wearing the Sword. "Wait. Where's the sword? Where's your Mavric iron—"

"I'm not going to use the sword," he said.

"What?" she said. "No, they could send some magical monstrosity against—"

He lowered his voice. "I know what he wants to have happen in this battle, and I'm going to pull his teeth."

"What? Khyven, you can't keep secrets! What don't I know that I should know?"

"The Sword was turning me into a monstrosity," he said. "I was becoming your worst nightmare. Usara's worst nightmare. An enemy instead of a protector. I've ... seen it."

"You've seen it?"

"I think this is another reason Harkandos wants to test me. I think Harkandos knows about the Sword. I dreamed about him and this entire cohort—"

"You *dreamed* this? Khyven, I told you to tell me anything unusual that you—"

"Look, I think maybe Harkandos knows that I had the Sword. I think he knew what the Sword would do to me. I think he *wants* me to fight with that Sword. He wants it to dominate my mind, because then he'll have exactly what he wants. If the Sword makes me one of his brood, then the job's done. He doesn't have to fight me anymore. Nhevalos's prophecy is broken."

"Khyven, I don't think—"

"But he doesn't know I got rid of the Sword. If turning me was his objective, then we have the advantage now."

"Khyven—"

"I've seen what I become if I let the Sword have me. It's all the worst things about me made large. A nightmare Khyven. The only thing worse than me dying in this battle is me turning against you, becoming a tool for Harkandos."

Rhenn shook her head. Her brow creased with worry.

"I still have the blue wind," he said. "I will beat his champion."

"I saw what the Sword was doing to him," Lorelle said. "Felt it. Khyven may be right."

"Let me do this," Khyven pressed.

Rhenn bowed her head for a long moment, then nodded. "By Senji, Khyven … Are you sure?"

All the weight on Khyven's shoulders suddenly lifted. Knowing whether or not to keep enchanted swords, where best to use his skills, what to trust and what not to trust … These things were all slippery eels he could never seem to hold for more than a second. But fighting …

He understood fighting.

A smile crept across his lips. "Yes …" he said. "I'm sure."

Rhenn let out another breath and nodded again. She turned

back to Harkandos.

"We accept," she said. "Let it be decided here and now, in one-on-one combat."

Harkandos nodded. No smile. No leer of victory. Only acceptance. "Bring forth your champion."

Khyven started toward the gate, then turned around and gave Lorelle and Rhenn a crooked smile.

"Maybe I'll start off with the Diplomat," he said. "Just to scare them."

"Don't joke," Rhenn warned. "This is the fight of your life."

"You know how many times I've heard that?" He grinned wider. It all came down to a fight. It always had.

He turned back around and stared up at Harkandos as he neared the gate. The Giant looked down at him, no excitement or triumph on his face, only a deadly glare.

"I'm ready, Giant," Khyven shouted up at him. "Send your champion to face me."

Harkandos looked to his left, and Khyven waited for him to point at one of the misshapen Giants.

Instead, a cloaked, cowled figure—Human-sized—moved forward from the darkness behind the wall of Giants. He was large for a Human, with wide shoulders and an easy, athletic stride. The figure jumped gracefully up the tumbled stones, into the tunnel of light that speared through the entrance, moved through the broken gate, then came down the other side and into the dark again.

A Human champion?

The figure stopped a dozen paces away.

"I present my champion," Harkandos said. "Khyven the Unkillable."

The figure pushed back his cowl, and Khyven's blood froze.

His nightmare stood before him.

CHAPTER NINETEEN

KHYVEN

T he horrible parody before Khyven smiled crookedly at him just like Khyven had smiled at Rhenn and Lorelle, except its mouth was too wide. Its eyes were overlarge, as they had been in the nightmare. Its eyebrows slanted up at the edges of the brow and its hair looked wild, like it had slept on it but hadn't combed it … ever.

Khyven couldn't breathe. He stopped moving forward, stared at his doppelgänger as it reached the bottom of the rubble and squared up a dozen paces away. Khyven's thoughts raced as every assumption about his nightmare fell away.

Several things occurred to him at once.

First, his nightmare hadn't been warning him about himself. It had been warning him about *this* creature.

Second, Khyven had left the Sword behind because he thought it was going to turn him into this. But maybe it wasn't going to do that at all.

Third, if Khyven was destined to be a Giantkiller, not a doppelgänger killer, would anything Nhevalos had predicted now come to pass?

And finally, if this creature had Khyven's face ... Would it have Khyven's abilities? Would it have the blue wind?

He almost looked back at his friends, but stopped himself. If he spared even one glance their way—if they saw his doubt—they'd leap into action. They would undo what they'd promised, and Harkandos would attack. Everyone could die because of one glance.

He wasn't about to let that happen.

"Well you're just about the ugliest smear of dock slime I've ever seen." Khyven drew his sword. He left the Diplomat in its sheath.

The doppelgänger hummed its breaths like some eager beast. But it didn't say anything, and Khyven wondered if it was mute, perhaps just an actual animal in a man's form.

Its eyelids twitched around those crazy, overlarge eyes as the thing smiled grotesquely wide. It reached over its shoulder and drew a slim sword from the sheath on its back.

The blade was black iron, pitted and angular. It had a long, straight edge to the last handspan of the sword, where it made a sharp hook into a needle point.

And it was made of Mavric iron.

This is the fight of your life ... Rhenn's words returned to him.

Khyven knew enough to respect what Mavric iron could do, and he circled his opponent. The blue wind leapt to life.

"You're ..." the doppelgänger huffed. "... wearing my face."

"So you *can* speak," Khyven said, and the two slowly circled one another, sidestepping as they took the other's measure. "I thought maybe you were mute. Or just stupid."

The thing grinned impossibly wide, the corners of its mouth nearly touching its ears, and made that eager humming again.

Khyven shoved down his doubt. He'd faced uncertainty before. This was just another bout. Every time he'd stepped into the arena, it could have been his last. This was no different. He would walk to victory one step at a time. One step. Then the next.

The blue wind swirled, forming a lively mist at his feet, encircling the feet of his opponent, but it didn't form into any spears headed his way. It also didn't show any funnels where he should attack, which meant this creature was still sizing him up.

Or it was playing with him.

"Khyven ... the Unkillable," it breathed, and Khyven didn't know whether that was a question to him, or if it was simply saying its own name.

"Where did you come from?" Khyven asked.

The doppelgänger gave its breathy chuckle. "From youuu ..." It drew the word out, and Khyven felt a shiver up his back. The thing really was a walking nightmare. Even the way it talked. The twitchy way it moved. Like an insect.

"Giant magic, eh?" he said. Vague blue funnels began to form on the shoulder and the left leg of the doppelgänger. "They should stuff you back in your bottle."

The creature made its breathy laugh. Its eyes widened even more, which Khyven wouldn't have thought possible.

Khyven put his arms up in the air, sword high, and turned to Harkandos, giving his back to the doppelgänger. "This is what you give me to work with? This parody can barely even speak."

It was a calculated move. He was hoping to draw the creature out, to make it attack. The blue wind would alert him before the thing could reach him, and its overconfidence would tell him something.

But it didn't attack. It just gave that breathy laugh again, as though it had known Khyven would do this.

Well, that was all right. There was more than one way to precipitate an attack. If the thing wouldn't commit, Khyven would *make* it commit.

He lowered his arms from the gesture, but before he'd even lowered them completely, before he'd even begun turning back to his foe, he fell backward and launched himself—upside down—at the creature.

It was a move he'd used before when running from a crowd of six. They'd had him on the run toward the wall. He'd hit the wall and launched straight back, slicing the femoral arteries of two opponents before they even knew what had happened.

Khyven did the same now, except without the benefit of the wall, just his own balance, sure footing, and leg muscles. He came straight at the doppelgänger like an arrow, sword flashing out.

The blue wind flickered. One moment it showed a swirling funnel at the doppelgänger's leg—

The doppelgänger jumped. The funnel vanished. Khyven's sword missed the thing by an inch. A fan of blue light appeared and sliced down at Khyven. It appeared out of nowhere, but he was ready for it. If this doppelgänger had his looks and his speed, Khyven had prepared for it to have his magic too, which meant this fight wouldn't go the way the others had. Everything would move faster.

So Khyven was already leaning his head back. The doppelgänger's sword tip whistled past his throat, missing by half an inch. Khyven rolled. The doppelgänger landed.

They turned and faced each other once more.

"Seems like you should have had that one," Khyven said. "A missed opportunity?"

The doppelgänger opened its mouth and gave the breathy laugh. The creature circled him.

Khyven's heart raced, but it brought on the euphoria he'd learned in the Night Ring. He had only later come to find that the blue wind was magic. Of course, he'd always known it had been the source of his unlikely victories, but he'd thought it was his own perceptions, skills, and instincts, honed from years fighting for his life. And before Lorelle had suggested the blue wind was magic and Slayter had confirmed it, Khyven had always believed his ability to completely give himself over to the fight—to actually love it—was his invincible shield. When swords began ringing, when combatants struggled in earnest, he lost all doubt, all questions. He stopped hoping for anything except the next exchange. When Khyven had battled other men, he'd never thought of what might happen after. He'd never considered there would be another day for him, another hour, or even another second. He simply became the battle, and it filled him with joy.

It was as though, no matter what else might happen, he at least had that divine moment where he was moving, where he felt his muscles pushed to their limits, where he heard that transcendent music of physical power. His power.

He felt whole in those moments, just as he felt whole now. He needed nothing else except the joy of seeing his opponent coming for him, the joy of striving to ensure that he swung stronger, moved faster.

And because he loved it—until he discovered that the blue wind was magic—Khyven had believed that love of the fight was why he prevailed.

Now that he had effectively been stripped of the blue wind, it felt like those first times in the Night Ring, back when he didn't know about any magic, back when all he had was what he took into the Night Ring with him.

Khyven returned to that state of grace now. He grinned at his opponent.

The doppelgänger showed its own eager teeth, as though it knew what Khyven was thinking and it, too, loved the joy of the fight.

"Let's see just how good you are, shall we?" Khyven murmured.

He closed, and the doppelgänger didn't wait this time. It charged. Their swords rang, and Khyven didn't watch for the blue wind.

Instead, he watched the set of the doppelgänger's inhuman eyes. He watched the shift and movement of its feet, the precursors of its body language.

He fought as though there was no magic, and the euphoria sang through him. The flickers of blue wind came and went.

Khyven had experienced new sensations from the blue wind lately, more than just what might attack him and more of what he *should* do in any given situation, and he felt that returning. He felt the stuttering of it trying to give him advice, then abandoning it. Trying again, then abandoning it again as whatever similar power the doppelgänger possessed thwarted Khyven's own blue wind.

Clang clang clang

Swords slammed together and rebounded. Khyven spun. The doppelgänger spun. Swords came together again. Mavric iron rang against Ringer steel.

They circled, attacked, circled, attacked. Khyven didn't know how much time passed as each of them tested and attacked, neither gaining advantage. It could have been thirty seconds. It could have been an hour.

Then, finally, he teased out his opportunity.

The doppelgänger's sword point whistled past Khyven's left ear, a strike meant to skewer him through the eye, a strike he let through, a strike he had plans for.

Instead of blocking it in front, he whipped his sword around behind his head and blocked it there, a ridiculous counter. His arm shuddered. His sword shrieked. But it worked.

In the same moment, Khyven slapped the flat of the Mavric iron blade away with his palm.

And his own sword was already moving. Wound up behind his head, it whipped around with such force and speed that the doppelgänger's demonic eyes went wide in surprise for the first time. It saw it coming, but it simply didn't have time to move.

With its sword swinging violently away in the opposite direction, it had no time to block, no time to draw a dagger to counter Khyven's swing. The blade arced toward its neck.

The doppelgänger shrugged, bringing its steel shoulder plate up at the last possible second. Khyven's sword bit into it, but the swing was far too powerful to stop. It sheared through the plate and sunk into the doppelgänger's skull just below the ear.

But the plate had slowed the swing. Khyven had wanted to behead the thing, but the blade only bit half an inch into bone—

And stuck.

Khyven yanked, trying to dislodge it, but it only pulled the doppelgänger forward. With a fierce, powerful cry, the doppelgänger brought its Mavric iron blade straight up——

——and shattered Khyven's sword.

Suddenly without the anchor, Khyven lost his balance, stumbled backward. It was his turn to be surprised. No one was that tough. Khyven had cut into the man's skull. A normal person would have gone down. At the very least, it should have rattled its brain, sent it stumbling in delirium.

But with half of Khyven's sword sticking out of its head, the doppelgänger lunged. Khyven met the charge with his half sword, adjusting for its new shortened length. It wasn't much, but it was still sharp enough to kill. He parried and moved in——

The Mavric iron sword cleaved through Khyven's broken blade. Red sparks flew, and the sword blew apart.

Fiery pain burst in Khyven's chest.

He knew he'd been wounded, so he spun, tried to get away. He needed to assess the damage——

His body stopped as though on a hook.

He looked down.

The Mavric iron blade stuck up from his chest. For a moment, it didn't seem real. There was a sword through the middle of him.

There couldn't be a sword through the middle of him because if there were ...

If there were ...

Khyven let out a little sigh. He grabbed the black blade with both hands—realized he'd dropped his own sword. He had no weapon, only weak little starfishes on the ends of his wrists that fumbled dumbly with the black iron that had impaled him.

"What ...?" he said in disbelief.

The doppelgänger's face came close to his, half of Khyven's sword still stuck in its skull just above the neck. The broken shard came close enough to poke Khyven in the cheek, a tracery of pain.

"Done," the doppelgänger whispered. "Done."

The strength left Khyven's body, and he fell backward.

Somewhere in the distance, he heard a scream.

A burn rose in the center of him, radiating out from the horrible wound.

He heard the scream again. Was that him screaming? It should have been his scream. Except it wasn't.

Lorelle was screaming.

A raucous din arose all around. At first, he thought it was the ringing in his ears, but it was Harkandos's army: shouting, raging, whooping with victory.

But above it all, Lorelle's ragged shriek cut through the din.

He wanted to shout back to her, to tell her he would be all right, but he couldn't speak. He couldn't move. All he felt was that horrible shaft of cold iron through his body, pinning him to the ground. He felt the horrible cold of death closing in on the burn at the center of him, and he knew with despair that ...

... that Lorelle was feeling everything he was feeling.

The burn surged up, glowing throughout his body as though he'd always been sewn together with it, except someone had now set that thread on fire, and that fire was trying to fight the horrible cold of the Mavric iron through the center of him.

In a brutal tear, the fabric of Khyven's self ripped down the middle. The burning thread holding him together snapped apart in a hundred places. Flaming bits of thread spun like tiny, defiant suns ...

And vanished.

Lorelle shrieked a third time, a heartrending cry that attacked the heavens.

Lorelle, he thought. *I'm sorry. I'm so sorr*—

The doppelgänger put his boot on Khyven's chest and yanked the sword out. With the blade reversed in a double grip, he lifted his fists over his head and plunged it into Khyven's chest a second time.

The burn vanished. All feeling vanished.

Khyven plunged into icy blackness, and he knew no more.

CHAPTER TWENTY

RHENN

When Rhenn saw Khyven's twisted twin come up and over the rubble of the broken gate, her heart fell. All her recent doubts assailed her. This was the double-cross. This was the trick Harkandos had played that they couldn't see. Khyven wasn't going to fight a Giant, but some twisted twin of himself.

She wished she'd commanded Slayter to join them on the battlefield. This maneuver was rife with Giant magic, which Rhenn barely understood. If anyone would have an idea what to do next, it would be Slayter.

But there was no time now. The decision had been made. They were in it up to their necks, and Khyven was simply going to have to rise to the challenge.

And he did.

By Senji, the fight was … inhuman. They both moved with utter mastery of their bodies, so fast they blurred, so precise their blades never missed by more than an inch.

In combat, Khyven's mastery of the *moment* was so complete

that a person simply couldn't look away. It was why he had been the ultimate crowd favorite as a Ringer. Any veteran sword fighter could see his expertise, but Khyven naturally added a flair for the layman viewer, as he'd been trained. It was a performance, and yet somehow the performance didn't detract from his staggering skill.

If a normal swordsman tried to be flashy, he gave up opportunities. Flourishes cost time, and time could cost a fighter their life.

But somehow Khyven made the flourishes work in his favor, not against him. He turned them into surprises. It was as though the world bent itself to work for him, and every move was simply a step toward his inevitable victory.

When the fight started, Khyven opened with a ridiculously dangerous move that almost got him killed. It also almost sliced open his opponent's leg. It was not a move any swordmaster she had ever seen would dare try, not in a battle such as this. It was a desperation move for the end of a fight, but Khyven used it at the beginning. Again, that natural flair, and it surprised his opponent—almost enough to end the battle right there.

But Khyven's twin seemed to be everything Khyven was. Somehow, he dodged and they circled each other. They came at each other time and again, and Rhenn bit her lip at how close each strike came. Any other combatant—on either side—would have been dead in the first exchange, the second exchange—*any* of these exchanges.

And then came Khyven's clever move. The coup de grâce. Senji's Braid! His behind-the-head parry was absolutely stupid. It would have killed any other swordsman. But in Khyven's hands, it was brilliant, unexpected, and every inch the kind of dangerous thing he would do.

Rhenn would not have thought of something like that. It was just so … ridiculous. Especially in this, the ultimate fight. Even if Rhenn could have conceived of that block, and moreover pulled it off, she would never have had the confidence to try it. Not against a powerful opponent. It was simply too much to risk. One slip and the fight would have been over with Khyven's head rolling on the ground.

But Khyven danced with violence like it was music. By Senji, not only did the block work, but it rendered the two effects Khyven had surely wanted.

First, it stunned his opponent. Only for a quarter breath, but that was practically a lifetime between these two. It was certainly all Khyven needed to work his bloody magic. Secondly, it gave Khyven the perfect opportunity to use those finely honed muscles to bring his sword around as fast as the glimmer of light on a wave.

Even his evil twin couldn't stop that, though he tried. His last-second shrug, flipping up his shoulder plate, was brilliance, but Khyven was just too much of a beast. He was so much stronger than he looked—and he *looked* like a man who could bend a plow with his bare hands.

"Yes!" Rhenn shouted when Khyven's blade sunk into his twin's head. He'd missed the neck, but a head shot would drop a swordsman nearly every time. And even if it didn't, it would stun them long enough for Khyven finish the job.

But even as Rhenn raised on her tiptoes, her victory cry on her lips, everything changed.

The doppelgänger lunged forward. Khyven's sword shattered in a flash of black iron.

And suddenly that monstrous sword was sticking out of Khyven's back.

Rhenn's victory cry curdled on her tongue. A breath of interminable silence hovered in the air.

Lorelle shrieked.

The inhuman sound cut the air like a dagger tearing agonizingly through rusted tin. It was like Lorelle's voice became razor blades, ripping her throat out on the way up. The shriek drove into Rhenn's ears even as the reality of what had happened hit her like a gut punch.

For the first time in a long time, Rhenn froze. She didn't know what to do. A part of her still dared to hope. That part thought for sure that Khyven would pull out another miracle, that somehow the sword through his chest wouldn't stop him. He'd spin and cut his doppelgänger's head from his body.

But the creature drove Khyven to the ground, even as Lorelle shrieked again. The evil twin yanked the sword out and drove it into Khyven's chest once more.

Lorelle launched herself from Rhenn's side like an arrow. She flew thirty feet into the air toward the combatants, and her feet hit the ground in a full sprint.

Rhenn's paralysis broke then, and she leapt after her friend. Even with Rhenn's supernatural strength and speed, there was no catching the Luminent, but she kept right behind her.

One thudding thought kept pounding in her stunned mind.

They killed Khyven ... They killed Khyven ...

It didn't seem possible. It just didn't seem possible.

With another scream, Lorelle reached the doppelgänger. Her midnight hair flew like a banner behind her, unbound. Her cloak flew out even further, and her red dress rippled in the glow of Slayter's tunnel like a smear of blood.

Two daggers appeared in Lorelle's hands, and Rhenn knew she was going to be half a second too late.

Luminents were unbelievably fast, inhumanly agile. One to one, no Human could match them unless they somehow got ahold of them.

But this wasn't just any Human. This was a nightmare version of Khyven, the unbeatable warrior. And if the doppelgänger had the blue wind, even Lorelle could not beat it.

Rhenn was simply too many steps behind.

The twin turned, that broken blade still stuck in its head, and looked up at Lorelle without fear. She descended, but he was already moving.

"No!"

It was the word of Rhenn's heart, but it wasn't spoken by her.

The denial wasn't a shout of pain or rage. It was a thundering command.

It came from Harkandos, and the Giant strode forward, his fist up.

Lorelle froze in midair as though caught by an invisible hand. Harkandos flicked his wrist, and she shot away from the doppelgänger like a flicked fly.

She hit the ground next to Rhenn, throwing up turf and tumbling to a stop like a broken spider.

"Lorelle!" Rhenn skidded on the grass next to her friend. She'd hit so hard Rhenn thought she would be snapped in a dozen places. But Lorelle rolled to her feet, seemingly unharmed except for the scrapes on her face and arms. Dirt had smeared all over her. Her hair hung in her face, glowing a bright purple. The dark glow illuminated her eyes, which burned with hatred.

"Gnnnrrrrraahhhh!" she shouted.

"Is this how your honor your promise, Queen Rhennaria Laochodon?" Harkandos called as he marched up to the gates, stepping into the great spear of light. With one massive hand, he wrenched both gates from their moorings. Mortar and rocks exploded from the hinges as he threw the tangled iron behind him. He stepped over the rubble with one huge stride, reaching his horrible Khyven twin and the unmoving Khyven himself.

"Your champion has fallen," Harkandos picked up Khyven's limp body in one hand.

Lorelle launched herself at the Giant with another shriek. Rhenn followed.

But before they could reach Harkandos, he hurled Khyven's body away. It sailed over the wall, limp and twisting in the air, and landed somewhere out of view.

Lorelle leapt at Harkandos. The Giant flicked a finger and she bashed into something invisible right in front of him. She fell limply to the ground.

Rhenn screamed this time, drawing her sword. Her blood boiled, but she had been in enough fights to know she had to channel this rage, to make it useful. Khyven was dead. Lorelle might be dead now, too. Rhenn and all of her subjects would be next if she couldn't best this Giant.

She had to be smart, had to keep thinking, couldn't let her emotions cloud her judgement.

Using her supernatural speed and dexterity, she shifted directions, much like Khyven had done with his horrible twin, launching herself at Harkandos's feet.

"If you will not keep your word, then I will keep it for you," Harkandos growled. He brought his hand low, palm facing her.

The very air slowed Rhenn down. It was as though a thousand tiny hands tugged at her clothing, grabbed onto her sword. The blade became untenably heavy. She screamed to keep it upright, but it dragged her arms down.

She let it go, drawing a dagger, but now it was her very arms that were too heavy. Tiny, localized hurricanes pushed down on them, on her head and neck, on her back. With a struggling cry, she fell to her knees.

Then the wind came from the other direction, as though the ground had opened a vent, though there was none to be seen. It blasted up, flipping her in midair and slamming her back down onto the ground on her back.

Coils of rich earth rose up like snakes, wrapping around her wrists and ankles, slithering over her belly, over her neck. She surged upward, managing to break the dirt over her neck, but the rest turned solid as steel.

She struggled again, pulling until something snapped in her left arm, firing pain through her. She couldn't pull free!

Harkandos hove into view above her, narrowed eyes looking down like she was so much garbage.

"Humans do not have the capacity for honor," he said. "I was told some of you had grown this capacity over the years and I did not believe it. I see I was right."

"I'm going to kill you!" Rhenn screamed.

"No. Your followers are going to become my possession as you promised." He turned to those who had come through the gate behind him, or over the wall in the case of the Nox who had to avoid the light. "Take them."

The army streamed around Rhenn, heading toward the

castle.

No! She shouted inside her own mind, struggling against the unbreakable restraints. *No!*

She prayed that Slayter had come up with something, anything that might turn the tide, that might spirit away her people to a safer place. But she didn't know what that could possibly be. Slayter was brilliant, but what could he really do? They'd already played their ace, and they'd failed.

"And you, Rhennaria Laochodon, you are no longer a Queen of Usara ... You will return to your maker."

She glared up at him, wondering how he was going to kill her—

And then she realized what he meant. Her maker ... Not Senji, not the gods...

From behind Harkandos's leg, N'ssag shuffled into view. Thunder boomed, and rain began to fall from the dark overhead. N'ssag rubbed his hands together eagerly, turning them over and over like he was washing them.

"Oh, my queen ..." he said. "Our dance will begin again. And now all shall be as it was meant to be."

CHAPTER TWENTY-ONE

ELEGATHE

E legathe hid herself behind the curtains of Slayter's balcony, staring at the nightmare army. None of this was planned. Harkandos wasn't supposed to be here yet. And that wasn't the battle the *kairoi* promised. All of Khyven's friends should be bracing that army, not just Khyven. And also, this battle shouldn't have happened in the courtyard.

And she shouldn't be in Castle Noktos at all.

Harkandos and Khyven were headed toward one another like the ground and a stone dropped from a great height. That had always been inevitable, but this attack was a complete surprise. It shook her to her core. For a normal person, that wouldn't have been any more cause for alarm than the natural terror of Giants at the front door.

But for Elegathe, this mismatch instilled a terror unlike anything she'd felt since before she'd apprenticed to Darjhen, back when there was no explanation for the things that went bump in the night and no way to navigate them, back when there was no map for life. No *kairoi*, no Lore Mages, and no

Nhevalos. As a girl, she'd thought Humans were simply at the mercy of the fates and that there was nothing she could do about that.

Since the moment she had understood such a thing as Lore Magic and begun her slow accumulation of skill in it, she hadn't feared the unknown. She only feared those who also knew—and could do—what she did, of which there were few.

In short, she only feared the Nhevaloses of the world, the ones who could manipulate the future, shape the world to their design. And even those could be manipulated by one who possessed a subtle mind. She'd learned that even among Lore Mages—Humans and Giants alike—Nhevalos was a master.

Despite how much she sometimes hated him, he was so accomplished in his mastery that Human Lore Mages were a laughable shadow of his power. Giants working Lore Magic were like simpleton cousins. Nhevalos had orchestrated the Human-Giant War itself. Seventeen hundred years ago, Nhevalos had taken on nearly every other Giant of the age ...

And bested them.

She had come to believe that when Nhevalos said something, it would come to pass.

And he had told her that Harkandos was going to attack Castle Noktos a month from now.

So as she peered at the forces arrayed at the wall, a cold certainty crept through her: Nhevalos had not foreseen this.

She should have been terrified of the Giants, of the army of Nox bloodsuckers, of the menagerie of other horrifying creatures behind them, back and back as far as she could see. But she was more terrified of what this alternate battle, this misread future, had to mean.

If Nhevalos had been bested here, one of two things had happened: either he had lied to her and set her, Khyven, and all of his friends up to be sacrificed ...

Or he had been wrong.

She wasn't sure which was more horrifying. If Nhevalos had lied to her, then she was going to die. They were all going to die.

But if he had been wrong, if he had somehow been outwitted … It meant everything Elegathe had relied upon her entire life was false. The course of her life—of others' lives—wasn't controllable. It was just as changeable as the weather, as the random shapes of waves on the ocean, as every other unpredictable thing.

She might as well fling a prayer up to Senji as trust to Lore Magic or the conniving Giant.

She watched, entranced, as Harkandos made the challenge, as Rhenn accepted.

She watched in horror as Khyven fought the twisted, magical duplicate of himself, watched him lose. Watched him die.

That stole her breath for so long she felt faint, and she stood paralyzed. She felt like she'd suddenly become a paper person, a thin veneer wrapped around nothing but air.

Khyven was not supposed to die. He was supposed to win.

Everything she'd thought was immutable had suddenly blown away in the wind. Nothing was certain. Everyone in this castle was about to die. They were about to—

The silver cuff on her ear warmed. Its intricate designs—Line Magic crafted by Nhevalos himself—glowed and suddenly she heard his voice.

"Elegathe?" His voice was urgent, distant, a whisper.

"Nhevalos!" she said. A brief wash of relief flowed over the rotted feeling in her gut.

"Elegathe." His voice resolved into full clarity. He now sounded as though he was standing right next to her.

"I'm here. Harkandos is—"

"I know what is happening," Nhevalos cut her off. "Let us not waste time with the obvious. You have to get Khyven right now. Before it starts. You have to pull him from the fight—"

"It's over. Khyven is dead," she said. Lorelle shrieked below, the sound ripping through Elegathe's heart. The queen and the Luminent leapt at Harkandos as he ripped apart the gate, stepped over the rubble. "They've gone to fight him. They've—"

"Quiet," Nhevalos said tersely.

There was a long pause. Elegathe had never seen Nhevalos emotional. In every interaction she'd ever had with him, he'd always been composed, infuriatingly emotionless, ready with the next cold statement of what must be done.

He'd never paused like this, like he was struggling with his own emotions, like he was gnashing his teeth at his defeat.

"Get the mage," Nhevalos finally said.

"What?"

"Is Slayter still alive?"

Lorelle and Rhenn attacked Harkandos, and he put them down like he was swatting flies. The battle was over in seconds.

"Nhevalos, Harkandos is here! He's just killed Lorelle. Rhenn is bound to the ground. He's brought a half dozen other Giants, an army of bloodsuckers, and a horde of monsters besides—"

"Is the mage still alive?"

"I ..." She hadn't seen Slayter below. "He's not in the courtyard—"

"Get him. Bring him back to Imprevar."

"Everyone in this castle is going to die if we don't—"

"There is nothing we can do for them. Get Slayter."

"He won't go!" Elegathe found herself shaking her head. "He's going to try to help his friends. There's no way I'm going to be able to convince him—"

"I didn't tell you to convince him. Take him. Explain later. If you don't, we lose everything."

Fighting the despair that they already had lost, she swallowed. "And so everyone else dies? Everyone except the mage?"

"Usara is lost. It belongs to Harkandos now. There is no point in lamenting it. He has made his move. We must make ours now or lose the game."

Game? Game!?!

She had hated Nhevalos many times in the past, but never with as much passion as she hated him now.

"Get the mage." Nhevalos stated as though he could hear

her thoughts.

Will that even work? She thought. *Will it even be enough to—*

The study door opened behind her, and Slayter limp-walked to his worktable, the steel table from his own laboratory in Usara. Vials of liquid in wooden stands, urns of powder and bits of coal, curled and flattened bits of parchment and paper, and haphazardly stacked tomes littered the table. He pushed them aside as he plunked down the Dilagion Core in the cleared space. That was the artifact keeping his shaft of light alive.

Slayter noticed her then, his head shooting up like he thought she was a bloodsucker. He let out a breath of relief. "Good. Help me."

He didn't say anything about Khyven's death, though she was certain he knew. Slayter always babbled about one thing or another that had taken his interest. This was the first time she'd seen him so business-like.

"If I'm going to generate a lightning bolt capable of punching through that Giant out there, I'm going to need the Dilagion Core to do it. I'll have to release the light spell."

She approached him, moving around the table to his side.

"It's going to be a lightning bolt?" she asked.

"To start. If I'm lucky, he won't be expecting it and he won't have a defense built up against it. I might even kill him with as much power as I'm going to put into it. But I doubt it. If lightning bolts were effective at killing Giants, I would have read about it in one of the accounts of the Human-Giant War. But he probably won't be expecting one this powerful, and probably not from me. So I might singe him, maybe even wound him badly. That could be the break that we need to evacuate the city."

"And where will you go?" she asked in a sad tone, knowing the answer. There was nowhere left. The whole continent was shrouded in darkness, and every creature in Harkandos's army worked fluidly in the dark.

Humans did not.

Nhevalos was right. There was no hope for the people in this castle. They couldn't be saved.

Elegathe hated herself as much as she hated Nhevalos as she approached Slayter from behind.

"I wish I could keep the beam of light going while doing this, but I simply cannot think of a way. The beam would certainly shield the evacuees from the bloodsuckers, and possibly even ward off most of the monsters. It won't stop the Giants, though."

She closed in, and for the first time he noticed that her positioning was odd.

"Elegathe, I need you to—" He turned, his eyes focused on her, saw the expression on her face. His eyes widened in mild surprise as he recognized something.

"I'm sorry," she murmured, flicking the edge of her noktum cloak out and around him. "I'm so sorry."

"Well this is just—"

The cloak enveloped him, and Elegathe took him away.

CHAPTER TWENTY-TWO
VOHN

ohn stared at the battle, at the horrible ending, through the tall windows of the atrium. He couldn't believe his eyes.

Khyven had lost ...

When the Giants had showed up, Rhenn had left Vohn and Slayter behind to prepare a defense. Vohn had immediately deferred to Slayter, of course. The mage was an absentminded, tangled ball of indecipherable frustration most of the time, but if there was one person who could best calculate how to assist Khyven the Unkillable in stopping a host of Giants, it was Slayter.

And he had not disappointed.

He'd immediately sent Vohn down to the Vault to get two things. Vohn didn't even know what they were: a wire square containing a glass ball that in turn contained what looked like a miniature thunderstorm.

And a piece of fruit.

It was long, slender, and had a fleshy yellow peel. It couldn't possibly be fruit, though, could it? It couldn't possibly. It had to have some greater meaning, so Vohn hadn't questioned it, though if this had been any other moment, he'd have harangued Slayter for engaging in time-wasting whimsy.

Once out of the one-way tunnels that led to the Vault, there were two ways to reach the upper part of the castle. One went to the grand staircase where he and Shalure had fled Jai'ketakos. The other was a smaller servant's passage Vohn had discovered after the third time Slayter had sent him down to the Vault for something days ago.

In order to keep an eye on the parlay going on outside in the courtyard—but also because every time Vohn used that enormous main staircase, all he could see was a fire-breathing, slavering dragon coming after him—Vohn had come up the servant's entrance and by the atrium.

Now he stood, witnessing the challenge, the acceptance, and the battle between Khyven and the unholy aberration with Khyven's face. Vohn held his breath as swords flashed, as those two terrible combatants leapt at each other and leapt away.

Then the thing stabbed Khyven in the chest.

Vohn cried out. Tears sprang to his eyes and he covered his mouth with his hand.

Khyven fell. He died. He …

He *lost*.

The last realization shouldn't have been the most important. Khyven's death should have been. But that he had lost … It hit Vohn as though the moon itself had suddenly fallen to earth with a thud. It stunned him into a paralysis so deep he couldn't move as the crowd of Rhenn's subjects around him shifted uneasily, not knowing what Khyven's death meant yet.

But Vohn knew. It meant that everyone in this room was going to die.

Khyven had *lost*.

Harkandos ripped the gate away and strode into the courtyard. Lorelle and Rhenn charged him.

"No," Vohn whispered. He wanted to shout it. The denial

was a scream in his soul, but his paralysis reduced it to a whisper. Harkandos slapped Lorelle down with his magic so hard it must have killed her instantly. He batted Rhenn down far more gently and imprisoned her as N'ssag's bloodsuckers leapt on her.

That quickly, it was over. Khyven and Lorelle dead. Rhenn a prisoner.

Gasps arose from the smarter members of the crowd as they realized what that had to mean.

Harkandos's menagerie of monsters followed him through the gate, spilling through it like water through a broken dam. The undead bloodsuckers crawled over the wall like a host of ants, staying away from Slayter's tunnel of light.

Screams rose around Vohn as the Usarans finally realized that their protectors had failed them. They were the lambs, and the slaughter was coming.

They began to run, fleeing for one of the four exits from the atrium. Most went down the main hallway, but some fled down the glass hallways on either side of the atrium.

Vohn should have told them to head for the part of the palace that was cordoned off with raven totems, to make their last stand in the sunlight. He didn't think it would save them, but at least the Nox couldn't get to them there. It could buy them a little bit of time.

But he didn't say it. He didn't say anything.

Khyven had lost.

If someone had asked Vohn yesterday, "What are the things of which you're certain?" he would have told them a number of things. He'd have said that Queen Rhenn was the right leader for Usara. He'd have said he'd witnessed true love at least once in his life. He'd have said he'd met and had the pleasure of arguing with the smartest person on Noksonon. On a regular basis. He'd have said his greatest fear was his own banshee power.

These were his certainties.

But above them all was that he knew, somehow, that Khyven was going to win the day.

It was an unreasonable certainty. Laughable, some would

say. How could one Human possibly win against these unfathomably powerful beings, change the outcome of an ages-old war that had returned. That simply wasn't possible.

But Vohn had seen Khyven do the impossible four times now. With every sword in his face, with every disadvantage, Khyven had racked up impossible victories. Txomin. Vamreth. Death from overexposure to Mavric iron. An entire army of bloodsuckers in Daemanon.

Yes, Vohn knew that Khyven had magic that showed his opponents' weaknesses. Yes, he knew that Nhevalos had cleared the jungle of the future out of Khyven's way. He knew all these things, but his certainty came from more than just Khyven's advantages. Khyven had … some other quality. Something that went beyond all of the magic and Nhevalos's planning.

And Vohn had known it almost from the start.

It was why he'd left Rhenn's camp to sneak into the dungeons in the Night Ring when Vamreth had captured Khyven. He'd felt that there was something different about the man. They had all discovered that beneath the man's selfishness was a hero. But beneath the hero—beneath the magic and the training and Nhevalos's destiny—was something more.

Hope.

When Khyven walked into a room, hope came with him. He brought the possibility for anything. There was at least a chance at a brighter tomorrow when Khyven stood next to you.

The man was the second most frustrating man Vohn had ever met, but he wore hope like a billowing cloak. Vohn had been surer of that than anything else in his life. He didn't know why. He didn't know where that feeling came from. He didn't fully understand it.

But he'd been certain of it.

When Khyven fell, it felt as though there was no more hope in the world. Before, the coming of the eternal noktum was, to Vohn, just a brief sojourn into hell before they found a way out. Temporary. He was certain that Khyven would lead them out of the dark somehow. That certainty bolstered his heart.

Now it felt like his heart had been ripped out.

Numbly, he watched as the bloodsuckers unfastened Rhenn's restraints to move her. He watched her leap at them, fighting. She killed them left and right.

And still he couldn't move.

Khyven had *lost*.

Rhenn was mighty, but the Nox were many. They overwhelmed her, kicked her, punched her, broke her.

And still Vohn couldn't move.

When that battle was over, the horde started again for the castle, dozens of Nox leaping and sprinting toward him.

Remorse flooded through Vohn. He should have gone to them! He should have helped Rhenn! He should have helped Lorelle, Khyven, any of them!

The Nox were almost to the doors, and Vohn's paralysis finally snapped loose.

"Slayter," he murmured.

The crowd of Usarans still worked its way through the main entrance in a stampede. People cried out, fell, were trampled underfoot as they all tried to get out at once.

Vohn turned and sprinted for the fourth exit from the atrium, a modest little door that everyone had overlooked in favor of the larger exits. Another servant's entrance, it went up through the castle. It went to the third floor where Slayter's laboratory was.

Vohn opened the door and sprinted into the stairway. He climbed and climbed. He climbed until his lungs burned, until his legs felt heavy, useless, just sacks packed with jelly.

He forced himself up those steps faster than he ever had before, and reached the floor where Slayter's laboratory was, and burst into the hallway—

Three Nox were already on the landing. They'd already come up the main, Giant-sized stair, and were heading toward the doorway that was Slayter's laboratory.

All three of them stopped and turned. They spotted Vohn.

He froze again. He should run. But he also had to get to

Slayter's laboratory, which was beyond the three Nox. He couldn't just leave Slayter, couldn't just stand here with the two items that the mage might need to turn this nightmare around.

For a crazy instant, he thought of charging them. He almost did it.

But that was suicide. He would never make it past them. He would never make it …

Not as he was. He would never make it past them as a Shadowvar. But as a banshee, he could fly right over their heads. He could get to Slayter.

Vohn reached for the ring on his finger that kept him from transforming into his banshee self, the ring that kept Xos and Paralos from being able to hold him as part of the Dark.

His fingers closed over it, and just as he was about to yank it off, an iron hand closed over his neck and another over his wrist.

Vohn squeaked, looking up and over his shoulder. A fourth Nox! It had been behind him, behind the door.

The other three hissed and leapt forward even as the fourth Nox slammed Vohn to the ground and opened his mouth, fangs protruding below black lips.

Vohn scrabbled, trying to reach his hand, trying to get at the ring, but the Nox seemed to intrinsically sense that the ring was important. He kept Vohn's hands pinned.

Those fangs plunged into his neck—

"Stop!" a thundering voice shook the very wells.

The Nox jerked his head up, a fleck of Vohn's blood on his lips.

Eyes wide, breaths coming in gasps, Vohn turned to look at the grand staircase.

The enormous Harkandos rose into view. His head, then his bulging shoulders, then his torso, as he ascended the stairs. He drilled the Nox with his infernal glare.

"That is the Shadowvar Vohn," Harkandos said.

The Nox looked down at Vohn, then back at Harkandos.

"Go," Harkandos commanded. "I want this one."

The Nox let Vohn go and leapt after its fellows. Vohn gasped, reaching up to his neck. Blood spurted from the tear the bloodsucker had made, and he pushed against it, trying to stop the flow.

Harkandos reached the top of the stairs, towering over Vohn. His glare was horrible. Vohn could barely breathe under that glare. It was as though it had reached into his chest and let loose a kaleidoscope of terror.

Harkandos murmured, and beneath Vohn's fingers, his flesh came together, mending. The blood stopped flowing.

Vohn shouted, scrabbling backward on his one hand and two legs like a crab.

The Giant crossed the distance between them with one step, as calm as ever, as though no matter how fast Vohn crab-walked away, no matter how fast he might *run* away, it would never be fast enough.

"Come with me," Harkandos said. He walked past Vohn as though expecting Vohn to follow him. Vohn got to his feet. He could run the other way. He could slip down the servant's entrance. The Giant would never fit in there. He could—

Harkandos stopped and turned, and now that gaze was even worse.

Vohn suddenly realized that he couldn't outrun this Giant. Harkandos hadn't taken Vohn in hand because he didn't need to. If he wanted someone captured, or thrown across the hallway, he didn't need his hands. He had his magic. Vohn had seen what Harkandos had done to Lorelle.

Vohn swallowed, glancing down at his left hand at Rauvelos's ring. One quick pull, and he could become the Dark itself. He could fly away from here …

His heart beat faster yet. If he transformed into the banshee, he wouldn't be able to extract himself this time. He could escape this place, but could he return to himself after? He could find Slayter, perhaps, and Slayter might help him return like he had the first time … Or perhaps Vohn would wander the Dark for years like he had the first time he'd become the banshee. He—

"Pull that ring, and I'll cut off your hand," Harkandos said, as though reading his mind. "I have questions for you, and I would prefer to ask them without you whimpering about a missing limb."

Vohn's heart hammered, and he felt an entirely new certainty.

This Giant was the opposite of Khyven. Khyven was the personification of hope. But one look at Harkandos, and Vohn knew only despair.

Everything would happen exactly as Harkandos wanted. The Giant was certain of it. And when under that implacable gaze …

So was Vohn.

He drew a shaky breath, left the ring on his hand, and haltingly followed the Giant.

CHAPTER TWENTY-THREE

VOHN

Harkandos strode up the hall. Like he was being pulled in two, Vohn reluctantly followed, his mind racing to think of what else he could do that the Giant couldn't immediately undo. He supposed if he'd been Khyven the Unkillable, he'd have just charged and the events of the world would have swirled around him, conformed to his desires, and somehow he'd have beaten the Giant.

He supposed if he'd been Slayter, he'd have calculated every possible way out—or way through—and chosen the one that had the most unexpected result and the most likelihood for success, and then done it. With a wagonload of magic behind it.

He supposed if he'd been Rhenn the Queen, he'd have—

No.

Vohn wasn't any of his friends, and if he knew only one thing at this moment, it was that he wanted to know if Slayter was alive. He'd seen two friends die already, and Rhenn was probably being tortured right now. He had to know if Slayter had survived.

Harkandos went through Slayter's laboratory door, and Vohn followed. The Giant walked to the center of the room.

There was no one there.

Harkandos continued to the far wall, inspected the balcony, turned, and looked down at Vohn.

"The mage is gone," he said.

Vohn looked around, past the messy steel worktable, past the wooden tables overflowing with overlarge books—books made to fit a Giant's hand—that Slayter had pulled from the extensive Castle Noktos library.

"I don't ..." A flicker of hope rose in Vohn's chest. Had Slayter escaped?

"You don't know where he is?"

"I ... don't," Vohn repeated. He was going to die here. Rather than watching each of his friends die, Vohn was going to be the next to fall. Slayter had somehow escaped. That meant Vohn was next, and the only consolation he could take from that thought was that he wouldn't have to watch Slayter die also.

Harkandos nodded, as though this was expected. "Humans are like rats. Give them a test to their courage, and they will flee."

"You're wrong about that," Vohn said, his anger flaring. He half expected Harkandos to blast him out of existence with a fireball or something, but the Giant's expression did not change.

"He did not flee," Harkandos stated.

"No, he did not flee. He's regrouping in a place that even you, with all your magic, won't be able to find. He's going to figure out exactly what it will take to topple you, and then he's going to rain down destruction upon you. And you'll never see it coming."

Harkandos seemed unconvinced and thoroughly unthreatened by Vohn's dramatic statement. And now that Vohn had said it, he felt a little ridiculous. Even if Slayter had escaped, as it seemed, what were the odds that he could defeat a Giant's army?

Khyven had *lost* ...

"Khyven the Unkillable," the Giant echoed.

Vohn twitched under the Giant's relentless stare, as though he'd read Vohn's mind.

"Rhenn the Undead Queen, Lorelle of the Dark, Slayter the Mage ..." the Giant continued. "And Vohn the Banshee." He said the words like he knew each of Vohn's friends—knew Vohn—like they were intimate acquaintances.

Vohn swallowed.

"The Betrayer's puppets. The spiders at the center of the web. Two are dead. One has fled. And your false queen, well ... She is no longer in my hands. She was given as payment to an ally. If N'ssag chose not to end her, she will soon no longer be the woman you knew."

So as Vohn had assumed, she'd been given to N'ssag. His heart hurt.

"That leaves you, little Shadowvar. The afterthought. The follower who bends to the wills of the stronger members. The least of your group."

Vohn clenched his fists and raised his chin.

"But still a member of the group ..." Harkandos finished. "And I would wager you know practically everything they know. That makes you useful. Very useful."

"Where is she?" Vohn asked, and hated that his voice came out tremulous.

"Being remade, I suspect. She was broken after she fought. She tried to get to her maker, tried so hard. She killed four of N'ssag's undead puppets before they brought her down. I heard bones snap. N'ssag is obsessed with her. He will no doubt spend the time to try to heal her before he pulls the life from her and uses the Mind Harp to shape her to his will."

Vohn swallowed. If he'd been Khyven, he would have thought of a devil-may-care quip to throw in the Giant's teeth. If he'd been Slayter, he would have calculated the odds that N'ssag would fail.

But he wasn't. He didn't know what to say to that horrific vision of Rhenn's future.

"There," Harkandos said. "I have answered your question as fully and truthfully as I might. Now it is your turn."

"I … I don't know where Slayter is."

"Where is Rauvelos?" Harkandos asked instead, unexpectedly. "Where is the Betrayer's steward? I would very much like to speak with him."

Rauvelos had been the most frightening thing Vohn had ever met until a few short weeks ago. And at that time, he could never have imagined wanting to see the giant bird or talk to him ever again. But now, Vohn wished Castle Noktos's steward *was* here. He wished it more than anything. Nothing had phased the bird. Nothing had seemed to frighten it. Not the impending noktum, not the impending war of Giants, and not the dragon that came looking for him and then…

"He's dead," Vohn said.

"Is he? You see, that is what the Drakanoi told me, too. And he also said you were there."

"I was."

"And he died?"

"Yes."

"How?"

"They fought. They … battled overhead. It seemed for a while that Rauvelos was going to kill Jai'ketakos. He'd wounded him over and over, but …" Vohn trailed off, remembering the horrible battle, remembering how once Rauvelos was dead, there was no protection for him and Shalure.

That made him think of Shalure, still unconscious in the castle's makeshift infirmary. She'd never awoken since he'd hauled her into whatever altered state he went into when he became a banshee. She'd been reassembled with white sand. Even Slayter hadn't been able to pierce that mystery.

And now she would die, unconscious on her bed, as the Nox came for her and every other person in the infirmary, either to devour them or to turn them into one of their own.

"But what?" Harkandos snapped him from his reverie.

"But the dragon turned him into ash."

"He burned Rauvelos."

"It … For a moment, it seemed like Rauvelos was going to escape, that he'd be fast enough, but then the flames caught up with him. They … incinerated him. Only ashes floated down from where he'd been. And then Jai'ketakos came after us."

"I heard you tried to take someone with you into your banshee state. How did you do that?"

"I don't know."

"Surely you know a little."

"I … didn't think about it. I was terrified. I knew she'd die if I didn't make it happen somehow. And then … it happened. But … it killed her."

"Except it didn't kill her. It rendered her unconscious. And her hair turned white?"

Vohn hesitated, then said, "Yes."

How did he know this? How could he possibly know this—

Then it hit him, the first possibly useful thing that Vohn had gleaned from the conversation. He had no idea how it would be helpful without his friends, but suddenly Vohn knew something he hadn't known before.

He had a spy. Harkandos had a spy within Rhenn's kingdom.

CHAPTER TWENTY-FOUR

ELEGATHE

E legathe had become accustomed to the dwindling, squeezing, swirling mechanism of the noktum cloak. It barely even bothered her anymore. It felt to her like the shock of cold water on a hot day, something to be endured for an instant and then forgotten.

But this time as it pulled her through, she felt ill. Her heart hurt with the shock and despair of Nhevalos's lost plans, with the horrors that even now were being enacted upon Queen Rhenn's subjects. Somehow her defenses against the gut-squeezing nature of the noktum cloak fell away.

The familiar stones of Tarventin's bedroom chamber formed around her, the expansive balcony, the huge bed where she'd spent some of the happiest moments of her life, the pillars holding up the vaulted ceiling that measured the distance of the enormous living quarters of her lover.

He wasn't here, thank Senji. She would need to explain to Slayter what had happened, and what needed to happen next. She'd have to do with a heart torn in two from indecision.

Having Tarventin around would only complicate an already complicated situation. Elegathe's anchor had been ripped away, and she was following Nhevalos's advice because she didn't know what else to do.

She unfurled the cloak, releasing Slayter, and he swirled out of the black to appear before her.

The mage fell to his knees and vomited upon the stones. He held one hand up as if to say, "Just a moment. Give me just a moment."

She felt pity for him. She felt pity for every single person on Noksonon. And she didn't know what to—

In a sudden, illuminating flash, she realized he wasn't doing that at all. He wasn't holding up a hand to indicate he needed a moment to recover his stomach. His fingers tightened with purpose, clutching something.

He snapped the clay disk, and orange light flared out.

"Wait—!" she cried, but too late.

Orange bars of pure fire erupted from the disk. They arced toward her like spears and for a moment of surprised horror, she thought he was going to burn her alive.

But the arcing spears rammed into the stone floor all around her, forming a blazing birdcage.

She tried to dodge, but she was far too slow. She backed away, hissed at the heat from the fiery bars, spun and found she had nowhere to go.

"Slayter, stop—"

But in the second she'd taken to assess her prison and flinch away from the heat, he'd drawn a second disk and snapped it. Orange light flared again, but no more fire shot at her.

Instead, the clasp at her neck snapped open. The noktum cloak jumped away from her shoulders even as she reached for it. It slithered like a Sleeth through the bars and flew to Slayter's outstretched hand.

He caught it without looking up. His head was still bent over, vomit dripping from his mouth. He coughed, hacked again, and spat out the rest.

"Bleech …" he said, finally raising his head to look at her, blinking through watery eyes. "I simply must solve that problem someday."

He stood upright on shaky legs, found his balance, then looked at the cloak in his hand as though, for an instant, he didn't know where it had come from.

"Slayter," she said. "I brought you here to protect you."

"Hmmm," he said, ignoring her as he considered the cloak. With a grandiose sweep, he shook it out and tried to put it on his shoulders with a flourish. He missed. The cloak passed over his shoulders and fell to the floor in a heap.

"That would have worked for Khyven," he muttered under his breath.

With a sigh he painstakingly stooped, awkwardly managing his prosthetic leg, and picked up the cloak again. With absolutely no flair this time, he awkwardly pulled it across his back and settled it on his shoulders, then clasped the clasp around his neck.

"I'm *helping* you," Elegathe said.

Slayter finally turned his attention on her, and his usually merry eyes were hard. "Yes, well. Perhaps you actually think you are."

Unexpected fear fluttered through Elegathe's belly. Her view of Slayter Wheskone shifted. She'd always seen him, partially through Nhevalos's eyes, as an absent-minded, quirky-but-brilliant mage. She'd seen him as a piece on Nhevalos's board, an incomparable resource for the Queen of Usara, and an inquisitive inventor.

But his entire demeanor had now shifted. In a blink, he seemed like a different man. This was a mage of spectacular means, arguably the most powerful Human mage on Noksonon, and for the first time she'd ever even heard of, he looked angry. A low anger smoldering beneath the surface of his boyish face.

She had Lore Magic at her disposal, a magical cloak given to her by Nhevalos, and all the power of a king's consort. Slayter had stripped it away, all of it in an instant. It had happened so fast she still couldn't wrap her mind around it. She was alone here, and even if Tarventin walked through that door right now, how would he stop Slayter?

She was at his mercy.

Slayter studied the room, gaze flicking from the water clock to the bed, the wardrobe, the balcony, the windows on the far side of the room, Tarventin's desk, the scrolls haphazardly stacked there, and back to Elegathe.

She swallowed. She suddenly realized with another wave of fear that if he calculated he was safer—or his friends were safer—if she was dead, he *would* kill her.

Like Nhevalos.

She had to appeal to his intelligence. She had to make him understand that everyone—him and his friends included—would be better off if he let her live.

The problem was, she wasn't sure if she believed it anymore.

"You're Nhevalos's pawn," Slayter said after his inspection.

She had to fence with him, this brilliant man who was inventorying everything in Tarventin's room and cataloguing what it meant about his enemies. His advantage was undoubtedly growing with every bit of new information he absorbed.

"So are you," she returned.

A flicker of a dead smile appeared at the corners of his lips. "Yes, well … That is true, I suppose. But you chose to be. You know what he plans."

"Nobody knows what he plans."

"I am beginning to compile a decent understanding of his methods from the evidence he's left behind. He claims to be working to save the mortal races. Humans, Luminents, Shadowvar, Sandrunners, Brightlings, Taur-Els, and the Delvers. But he doesn't care about any individual. Whether they live or die. Isn't that correct?"

She hesitated. Her fear was finally calming down. She had to look at the larger picture here. She didn't just need him to free her, to *not* kill her. She needed him to listen to her.

So she let her anger for Nhevalos slip into her voice. "No. He doesn't."

"He sent you to pluck me from Castle Noktos."

"Yes."

"And thereby prevented me from helping my friends at the exact moment at which I might be of service."

"You wouldn't have succeeded."

"I recognize it would have been a slim chance."

"There would have been no chance."

"By my calculations, I'd have freed Rhenn and Lorelle to escape into the noktum, both of whom are far more facile in our new world than I am. They'd have found a way to turn this around."

"The Giants would have sensed your magic. Maybe you could have gotten off one or two spells before they burned you to the ground."

"I calculate I could have done three. Two or three, depending."

"And then they'd have killed you."

"My life isn't a prerequisite for victory."

"Except it is."

That made him pause, and he looked at her steadily. "You are a Lore Mage. Nhevalos's ... apprentice."

"Something like that."

"And how adept do you assess yourself to be?"

"One of the best Human Lore Mages there is. On Noksonon, anyway."

"And Nhevalos is Nhevalos. The master of Lore Magic."

"Yes."

Slayter's expression grew darker. His nostrils flared like he was trying to control something inside himself and barely managing it. "You didn't predict this battle. Nhevalos didn't predict this battle."

"No."

"Or you did, and you chose not to tell us."

"No. Something went wrong."

"Harkandos wielded a counterspell. He muddled your predictions. With an alternate Khyven."

"That is what I think, yes, but ... I do not know."

"And you pulled me out at that moment because—"

"I saved your life."

"For your next scheme. For Nhevalos's next scheme."

She hesitated. The fire from the magical bars made the air around her as hot as an oven. Her hair was lank with sweat, and it dribbled down her face. Her robes began to stick to her. Her glasses slipped down her nose.

She didn't know how to answer that question. If she lied to him—and lied unsuccessfully—she felt this would change from polite conversation into something frighteningly different.

"Yes," she said.

"Except your last scheme failed. Yet you felt that the best thing to do was remove me from a situation where I could've helped my friends. You took me somewhere else where you could try again. To try to fix your mistake. Come up with a better scheme."

She swallowed. "Yes."

"That is short-sighted."

"He's trying to win this war. He thinks saving you will do that."

"You have put your faith in Nhevalos, yet all he has done is lie and manipulate you. And now he has made a horrible mistake. Khyven is dead. One questions whether he is, truly, the master of Lore Magic."

"He has guided us truly this far."

"You don't know that. You don't know anything except what he has told you. This endgame was to defeat Harkandos, to use Khyven to do it. Two spectacular failures today would make a rational person believe that Nhevalos doesn't, in fact, know what he is doing. Why let him try again?"

"Because he is the best equipped to help us escape this horror."

Slayter shook his head. "One hour ago, I might have

believed that. Not now. Clearly, Nhevalos is dangerously arrogant, an inherent trait of Giants, apparently. He is certainly less knowledgeable than he wants us to believe. That combination—arrogance and ignorance—are, in my experience, a recipe for disaster. He doesn't see his ongoing mistake. And because you do not question him, neither do you."

"What mistake?"

"He doesn't care about who dies. Not Lorelle, or Rhenn, or me. Not until today, of course, when whatever plan he created was ripped to tatters and he was forced to find a backup plan. It seems that, to him, only Khyven was worth preserving, and now Khyven is gone."

"He told me saving you was of paramount importance."

"Now, you mean. Only now that I am his new Khyven. And I am to trust his judgment after witnessing what happened to his *first* Khyven?"

"I … I don't know."

"I don't think *he* knows. If this was really a mistake, and things have gone against his plan, then he certainly doesn't know. And if Khyven's death was all part of his plan …" Slayter stopped talking, and he stared past her at nothing, the corners of his mouth turned down.

"He will come up with a new plan, and it will be informed by the most powerful Lore Magic to ever—"

"You took me away from my friends," Slayter said, still not looking at her. It seemed like a hundred things were going through his mind.

"They were going to die anyway—"

"No. Though they probably have by now." He turned his gaze back to her, and there was an emptiness in his eyes now, like the loss of his friends had opened the door to something utterly cold.

She realized he was even now deciding whether or not to kill her.

"Slayter," she said desperately. "There is still hope for Humanity. For—"

"For your plan, you mean," he said in a monotone. "There is hope for what you want, but not for my friends."

"Isn't the survival of our entire people more important than your friends?" she asked.

"Debatable."

"Debatable?"

"Open to debate," he clarified.

"No, I mean. What is debatable about that? Without Humanity, everything is gone."

"Hardly."

"You don't want to save Humanity?"

"Not for your reason."

"My reason? My reason is the same as everyone's reason."

"Hardly. My reasons are comprehensive. You believe in saving Humanity because without Humanity, you would be dead."

"How is that different than why you—"

"Fear," he cut her off. "You want to save people because you're afraid. Of death."

"Slayter—"

"You talk like you have considered every angle of this situation, which I doubt. I have found that most people are not capable of considering every angle of a situation. And almost all of those who are capable of seeing all angles are disinclined to do so because of emotional reasons. You, for example, do not dare consider the notion that Giants might be a more viable form of life."

"Than Humans?"

"They were certainly more advanced than we have ever been. Perhaps the world would be better off—all of life would be better off—if the Giants retook control."

"You can't possibly believe that."

"I *could* possibly believe that, which is why I have considered it and you have not. Which is why I have considered the most important variable in this equation and you have not: the reason for living. The value of a person, of a life. You say I should have loyalty to Humanity because I am Human. But I am not driven by a fear of death, which causes people to overlook the most important thing of all."

"What is the most important thing?"

"Knowledge. Understanding."

"You can't learn if you're dead!"

"No, I can't learn if I spend all my time avoiding death. I do not seek to avoid my death in order to learn. I seek to learn. Trying to anticipate one's death, when it might happen, and what might be lost is a waste of time. Have you ever compiled any data on how often people avoid knowledge to preserve their own lives?"

"I—"

"Every day. A thousand times a day. It is more common by far than not. Every now and then, you will see a rare person who charges at fear, who sees beyond the veil that stops others. Khyven for example, and Rhenn. But it doesn't happen very often. Not often at all."

"You'd let Humanity die because of a … a pet philosophy?"

"Everything is a pet philosophy until it proves true. Your master's Lore Magic is nothing more than a thought—a pet philosophy, if you will—until it happens. Personally, I have never felt a loyalty to Humanity at large. My loyalty has been to knowledge, magic, and what the mind might create with that knowledge and magic. The accumulation of knowledge and magic will likely advance much faster under the Eldroi. In my estimation, there is only one thing Humanity does better than the Eldroi."

"What?" She was grasping at straws now.

"Connection," he said. "Humans bond together for silly reasons. Petty, fearful, dreamy reasons completely unattached to reality, but wherever the reason, those connections are one of the most powerful things I've ever seen in the world. It was why Humans defeated the Eldroi during the Human-Giant War. It is the only thing about Humanity that is … superior."

"Then fight for that!" she said.

"Oh I was …"

"Then continue to—"

"*You* severed my connection, Elegathe. I was connected to Rhenn, to Khyven, Lorelle, Vohn, and Shalure. I had determined my quest for knowledge and power would transform me into an abomination like Vamreth the Usurper unless I attached myself to a moral compass. I chose Rhenn. I chose her family. They have never led me in the wrong direction. I experienced the connection that is the superior contribution Humanity has made to the world. And you took that away." He held her with that dead-eyed stare. "So tell me, Elegathe, if you were me, what would you do? With all of my reasons for compassion stripped from me. What would you do now?"

The heat pressed in on her, sapping her strength. Her clothes clung to her, drenched in sweat. She could barely stay on her feet. "Don't do this," she whispered.

"Don't do what?" he asked. "Kill you?"

She swallowed.

"Why not?" he said.

"Because I can help you."

"You have no help that I require."

"Please …" she said, her voice quivering. "Don't …"

He shook his head. "You think you know me. Nhevalos thinks he knows my future."

"Slayter—"

"You are both wrong. And I've wasted enough time with you." He raised a new clay disk in his hand, snapped it.

"No!"

Orange light flared out. The fire bars vanished. A whoosh of wind flowed over her, cooling her slick skin, filling her mouth, her nostrils, blowing her sweaty hair back from her face.

"Khyven called this a potion," Slayter said.

A powerful lethargy took her, and she fell to her knees. She raised her head to look at him, but it felt like there was a bull sitting on her neck. She could barely see him as she tried to keep him in her field of vision.

"It's not. It's a spell," Slayter said.

"Slayter ..." she murmured as the spell flowed through her. A sleep spell.

"If you chase me," he warned. "If you interfere with me again, your worst visions of me *will* come true. I will be the killer you fear. I promise you."

She wanted to tell him to stop. She wanted to keep him from leaving. But she couldn't muster the strength to speak.

Her head thumped against the flagstones, and all she could see were his burgundy boots, one on his good foot, the other wrapped around the metal spar of his prosthetic. She saw the edge of the noktum cloak swirl over those boots.

He vanished.

The spell took her, and she lost consciousness.

CHAPTER TWENTY-FIVE

ELEGATHE

Elegathe."

Elegathe felt her name like a corkscrew bristling with short, tiny needles. It rotated up her nostrils, into her nasal cavity, and then into her brain.

She screamed and sat upright. Her sweaty hair flung out like a fistful of limp ropes, wrapping around her head and smacking her in the face.

"No!" she shouted. Her last memory was of Slayter standing there with his dead expression, a wholly different person than she had studied, than she had heard about. A killer with a boy's face. A killer who had spared her life for reasons passing understanding, but who would never spare her again if he saw her. She was sure of that. He had made her sure of that.

The intense pain from the corkscrew burned up into her brain, and she thrashed, shaky hands going to her nose as she rolled to her knees. She keened as she scuttled toward the door on her knees, the palms of her fists pushed against her cheeks on either side of her nose, trying to ease the horrible pain. She lurched upright, barely keeping her feet as she canted sideways, lunging for the door.

Her panicked mind did not assess how the door could possibly help her. She only knew she had to get away from the pain. Her foggy brain, until a half second ago completely asleep, was certain Slayter had returned. He had changed his mind about killing her. He had returned to Castle Noktos and found all of his friends dead, and he'd come back to make her pay for saving his life.

"Elegathe."

Again, her name, and for a fearful second she flinched at it. Her name had brought the pain, and in that eternal second, she'd become fearful of the very sound of it.

The pain vanished.

She gasped, and her slanted lunge for the door finally betrayed her. She crashed to her knees.

"I'm sorry ..." she murmured, sweaty hair dangling in her face. "Slayter, I'm so sorry."

"Elegathe, I need you to pay attention."

Her pain-jolted, panicked mind finally settled, and she came back to herself.

She looked down. Her sweat-stained robes were twisted sideways, her limbs tangled. Blinking, she saw the man talking to her was not, in fact, Slayter.

It was no man at all.

Nhevalos, a shocking fourteen feet tall now, stood in Tarventin's suite, glaring down at her.

Senji's Braid!

She closed her eyes, pushed firm fingers into her cheeks, which echoed over and over with the absence of that excruciating pain.

"Did you just do that to me?" she said.

"Pay attention."

"I thought I was dying!"

"It is the counter spell for Slayter's sleeping rune. The pain is an aftereffect."

"Aftereffect? I thought someone was stabbing my brain."

"That is what it's meant to do."

Through watering eyes, she looked up at him incredulously. He watched her with no expression, his enormous hands calmly at his sides. She swallowed, and a rush of freezing certainty came to her.

She should be far more afraid of Nhevalos than Slayter. He'd just put her through excruciating pain like he was stabbing a rat with a fork.

"You *hurt* me."

"That is not important, and I have come to tell you what is. Time is short."

She clenched her teeth, heat rising in her face as what had just happened came into full clarity. She *was* that rat to him. And he wasn't ever going to hesitate to use that fork.

Awkwardly, she shifted to her knees again, hissed as they touched the ground. They were scraped bloody from her unthinking flight. With a grunt, she pushed herself to her feet, but her legs were entwined in her tangled robes, which had twisted so far around her body that her shoulder and half her torso was exposed.

She shielded her half-nakedness with her back while she jerked her robes back into place. They came slowly and awkwardly, heavy with sweat.

"You should have warned me," she said as she adjusted. "You told me to take Slayter here, and he almost killed me."

"He wouldn't have."

Once her attire was, if not fashionable, at least covering everything it should, she turned and glared at him as she tightened her belt. "You didn't see his face. He'd just watched two of his friends die. He had no reason to believe his other two friends had survived, and he blamed me. He is quite ready to kill."

"Good."

"He was quite ready to kill *me!*"

"He would not have killed you."

Now that she was fully awake, not barraged by pain or addled by sleep, she remembered what Slayter had said before he had left.

And I am to trust his judgment after witnessing what happened to his first Khyven?

She had never felt entirely comfortable around Nhevalos, but she feared more for her life than ever before. She had trusted him because of two things only. That Darjhen had told her to trust him, and that he was ... well, he was a Giant. Surely he must know more than her.

Darjhen was now dead. Khyven was dead. And both, arguably, had happened because of Nhevalos as much as anything else.

At this moment, based on Nhevalos's failures, it seemed that he knew about as much as any Human. Why should she help him—why should she put her life into his hands—when he so clearly didn't care about hurting her or even killing her?

Before, those risks had seemed an acceptable price considering what was at stake. But it looked different after this crushing defeat. Darjhen had been convinced that, by following Nhevalos, the outcome was certain. Humanity would win.

It didn't look that way at all right now. Suddenly, it occurred to her: what was the advantage of following Nhevalos's lead over, for example, Slayter's?

Of course, he *was* still a Giant. He could kill her as easily as he'd just tortured her.

How did she tell him she didn't want to be part of his team anymore?

"I couldn't ... keep him here," she said. "I failed you."

"You succeeded. You plucked him from the fire. Before you did, his *kairoi* all led to death. Now he is in Usara, hatching plans. We must make sure one of them works."

She nodded. "Very well. I will stay here and brace for Harkandos's attack."

Nhevalos paused, which Elegathe had come to understand as annoyance.

"You will come with me."

"Imprevar's defenses need me here to—"

"Imprevar is irrelevant if we lose Usara. This is the battle. If Harkandos wanted Imprevar, he would take it."

"Then why did you have me prepare the kingdoms for—"

"Because once Harkandos is dead, Orios would try for dominance. And if not her, then Mendos. There would still have been a threat. We could have fought that threat, especially if Khyven had survived. But not Harkandos. All of those preparations are now irrelevant unless we can kill Harkandos."

"And how are we going to do that?"

"We are going to use Slayter."

He spoke just as clearly, just as commandingly as before, but this time Elegathe heard the truth. Every day, every year, for eleven years, it had been Khyven. Khyven had been the chosen one. Now suddenly it was Slayter. Nhevalos was grasping at straws. Worse, he was willing to inflict pain or death upon anyone to grasp at those straws.

"You want me to—"

"Where is your cloak?"

"Slayter took it."

Again, that pause. Disappointment? Frustration? She couldn't tell. She simply couldn't read him.

"Very well." He flicked out the edge of his own noktum cloak. The corner curled, extending toward her like a tentacle.

"Wait, I have to tell Tarventin—"

The cloak wrapped around her. She felt the lurching in her gut, and Tarventin's suite vanished.

CHAPTER TWENTY-SIX

LORELLE

Lorelle burned in a fire, swords sliced at her from above. She screamed, wriggling through the flames that rose from the rough rocks underneath her, so hot they were almost lava. Her flesh sizzled as she dragged herself across them.

The burning, slicing hell closed in. The swords cut into her and she screamed again. The blades cut deeper; the fire raged hotter. He body blackened and bled. Slicing … burning … slicing … burning—

Lorelle awoke with a start, her body convulsing. The awful burning and slicing shrank into a burning, bleeding knot in the center of her chest. Her soul was dying—the soul she'd bonded to Khyven. Because he was dead. She'd been ripped in half inside her body …

Her body! She *had* a body …

She suppressed the slicing and burning, opened her eyes against mud. The grit scraped against her eyeballs. She screamed into the ground, but it only served to form a bubble that popped out of one nostril. She could barely breathe for the mud packed into her mouth, her throat, and all but one of her nostrils.

One traitorous nostril.

She raised her head and the mud slid down her throat, clogging her windpipe at last. It tried to kill her, but her body reflexively coughed it back up. Black slime striped her arm and shoulder, and she sucked in a breath she didn't want.

Khyven was dead. Her beloved ... was gone. She should be dead, too.

Tears welled in her eyes, moistening the grit that blinded her, and she felt the wail rising from the depths of her ragged self. It burst from her tortured throat, roared into the pounding rain coming down on her. It sounded like anything but herself. She could have been a wounded Kyolar.

She sucked in another breath to scream again, and her battle instincts told her to stay silent. Harkandos had slammed her down hard, likely thought her dead, but he'd underestimated her Luminent durability. If she kept screaming, the noise would bring the bloodsuckers. The Giant's army would rush to finish the job—

Her vision slowly returned under her furious blinking and the deluge that poured down on her. The army did not come.

The muddy courtyard was empty. It was ... later. The battle was over.

She should have been trussed up like a festival bird, a prisoner for whatever ghastly pleasure they could conceive, but she wasn't. Her arms and legs were free. She was alone. They'd simply left her here, a body on the battlefield.

The fire of her torn soul raked her insides, wave after wave, and a low moan leaked out of her mouth, unending. Rain ran down her face in rivulets. She spotted one of her daggers just within reach, half buried in mud.

She snatched it up and put it against her throat. A quick slash and—

A distant sound stopped her. She couldn't say why it stopped her. She intended to kill herself. She had lost half her soul, lost her beloved, and she couldn't stand another second of it. Lorelle had let them kill Khyven, her sister, her friends. She should follow them all.

But the sound stopped her, and she turned her pointed ears toward it. What was it?

Through the rain, she saw the hazy bulk of Castle Noktos. The sound was coming from the castle. It was muffled by the rain, but her Luminent ears could pick up sounds at a very far distance.

Screams. Those were screams. Rhenn's subjects were screaming. The monsters were slaying. The Nox were feasting.

She kept her muddy dagger pressed tight against her throat, but she didn't pull it.

Khyven was dead. Her life was over. There was no hope. Any of the previous lives she'd lived with Rhenn, as her sister or as the advisor, all of it meant nothing now.

Only agony remained. Agony and …

Hatred.

She lowered the dagger. She still made the low wailing sound, a sound that continued independently of her own will, stopping only when she ran out of breath and gasped another.

She looked down at the dagger.

And she understood. Yes, she *should* be dead. Yes, her life was over.

But this was her new life. This dagger. This agonizing existence. The existence she deserved for her failure. There was only one thing to spend it upon, and she was obligated to do so.

She didn't get to take the easy way, a sweet and painless death.

No, her death must be paid for. She must pay for her failures. And those who'd ripped her soul from her must also pay. She would take her pain and bring it to those who had made it.

She would inflict her pain on those who had killed Khyven.

Amidst the infernal music of her low wail, she stood up. Her legs were shaky at first, but she tightened her muscles and they became solid. She accepted the pain. She accepted her grief. She used the raking fire and blades to harden her resolve.

Let her death be the slowest and most agonizing that a mortal could endure. Let her death be the quickest and most brutal that a mortal had ever seen.

But let it be done while she was killing them.

She splashed quietly through the rain toward the castle, toward the enemies that she was going to slay.

One at a time ...

CHAPTER TWENTY-SEVEN

ZAITH

Zaith stood in the hallway, cloaked by the irregular shapes of the purple shadows as only a Glimmerblade could. He wanted to hide from the world, and even the Nox who passed him—heading to the feasting room where Harkandos kept their portion of the living Humans—did not see him. He pretended that he was his own Nox during this moment of separation from his fellows …

But the weight of N'ssag's mind was like a boulder that had rolled onto him. The guts of his soul were squished all over the ground. Sometimes he felt like he was on the edge of dying, like he only had one last breath. Sometimes he felt numb, like he had once been a strong and powerful river that had been reduced to a choked trickle, that made no noise, carved no path.

Always, though, he felt trapped. Pinned beneath the boulder. Unable to stop what his body was commanded to do by …

By his master.

He flicked his attention away from the thought, because anytime he thought too hard about his master, he thought about escape. Anytime he thought about escape for too long, he returned to the room, the wooden room inside his mind. Whenever he resisted thinking the way that N'ssag wished him to think, whenever he resisted doing what N'ssag wanted him to do, his body went inert. He fell to the floor like he was dead. He could no longer perceive what was happening in the real world. Instead, he heard harp music, lilting and horrifying, and his soul floated on the music to a room in his mind with wooden walls. Inside the room, he was always bound and helpless. And N'ssag arrived, talked to him until he was again slaved to the necromancer's will.

The first time he'd heard that music, it had been like a light in the darkness. It seemed he had awoken from … nothing. Before the music, it was as though his soul had been pushed into the cold mud and forgotten. That first time, the music had lifted him up, and he'd returned to a body alive with fire. Coppery taste filled his mouth. The fire spread throughout his limbs, and its burning brought strength. So much strength.

That first time, he had opened his eyes to a room in Aravelle's destroyed palace, and before him stood nothing less than a damned Human, and not even an impressive one at that. No warrior this one, not like Lorelle's paramour Khyven. Of course Zaith despised all Humans out of hand, but Khyven could clearly fight. That, at least, could be respected.

N'ssag wasn't even some trumped up leader, given powerful titles by Human followers. Nobles, such people were called. They carried, at least, the power of their followers.

No, the shrinking little man before him had had dirty robes, stinking breath, and decaying teeth. He looked like the dregs of a Human society, the lost souls who had abandoned all control of their own destiny, languishing in the gutters and alleys of what passed for civilization in the Human lands.

"You belong to me now," the greasy little man had said.

Zaith had leapt at him, fully intent on breaking his neck and shutting his arrogant mouth forever.

That was the first time he'd gone into the wooden room

inside his mind.

That strange harp music seemed to grab hold of his soul and yank it from his body. He'd had the vague sense of his body falling, then the noktum had vanished, and he was in the room.

The room had wooden walls and sunlit windows. He was chained to one of the walls with links so thick he could never break them. N'ssag was there with him, except he wasn't little anymore. He still wore that odious robe with its dark, oily stains and frayed sleeves. His unwashed hair was still plastered to his scalp with the glistening Human slime that clung to his body. His lips still looked greasy and his teeth were a brownish color. But his body was different. It looked like he had stolen it from a Lord of the Noktum, then compressed it down. He stood over eight feet all, muscles upon muscles bulging on his shoulders, over his arms, and across his hunched back.

That first time, N'ssag had walked over and pummeled Zaith until he'd submitted.

The second time, Zaith had tried to pull the chain out of the wall. The greasy, hulking N'ssag had walked over and pummeled him again until his body was crushed and broken.

The third time, Zaith had readied himself to take all the pain and never give in. N'ssag had beaten him as before, but Zaith hadn't capitulated. Finally, as Zaith looked up through puffy, swollen eyes, N'ssag had brought Zaith's little sister in from a side door. He'd put a knife to her neck and slowly began to drag it across her throat.

Zaith had screamed at him to stop. He'd lost that confrontation, too.

He knew the vision of his sister in the wooden room wasn't real. He knew that his sister was already dead, that she'd been destroyed by Tovos and buried long before N'ssag had resurrected him. He knew that her being in that room inside his mind was a tactic, but he simply couldn't allow his sister to be killed. That had held him in thrall for a long time.

But finally Zaith had held down his gorge and bid N'ssag do his worst. He'd screamed and spat at N'ssag as he'd killed Zaith's sister. Over and over and over. At least a dozen times.

But nothing changed, even though Zaith resisted, even though he endured the torture of watching his sister die. Each time, Zaith cried out at her death, despite himself, and he crumpled in his chains.

Every time he awoke, he was still in bondage, still bound to N'ssag's bidding. It seemed that if he capitulated, N'ssag won. And if he fought, N'ssag won. No matter what Zaith did, he never awoke with command over himself.

It had been more than a week since the last time he'd tried to fight N'ssag in earnest. He'd taken to making little rebellions, to waiting for when he felt N'ssag's attention was elsewhere. When he felt the weight of N'ssag's presence ease, he would go wandering the castle in places where he'd not been commanded to go. He discovered that if he didn't turn his rebellion into a fight, only a slight deviation, he could—for at least a moment—pretend he was his own Nox.

But they were small rebellions. Lingering when told to go somewhere. Going elsewhere, but only by a small distance, then finally doing what he was told. Giving only half his effort when asked to kill a person. He had taken to doing this in every combat, and at this point he was sure that N'ssag thought him a mediocre warrior. The man didn't know anything about the Nox, about the hierarchy, about Glimmerblades. If he had, Zaith was sure N'ssag would have used him in a dozen other ways. Instead, Zaith took to hoping against hope that during each combat, he'd be cut down. He hoped his slowness, his intentional hesitation would bring a death blow, but it never worked. Humans were far too slow.

So Zaith had done as N'ssag commanded. N'ssag pointed the direction, and Zaith killed. Again and again and again. N'ssag wanted thugs, and that was what he had made of Zaith's elegant and beautiful people.

That was what he'd made of Zaith himself.

Zaith now stood in a quiet hallway within Castle Noktos. It had been two days since Khyven the Unkillable had died. Two days since the Nox had been allowed to feast on some of the remaining Humans in this place. The Lord of the Dark, Lord Harkandos, had corralled all the Humans in a room full of sunshine, but he had given a hundred of them to N'ssag to feed his army.

N'ssag, of course, had been distracted these past days. He'd been handed his paramour, the object of his affection: the queen of Usara. Lorelle's best friend. The one she'd gone searching for in the Great Noktum. Apparently Rhenn and N'ssag had a history. He had given her the undead gift, and she'd almost killed him for it. He'd not yet had the stringless harp. He'd not yet perfected his will-crushing techniques.

Zaith wished he had been made when N'ssag was still imperfect in his art. He would not have failed to kill the stinking Human if given the chance.

Zaith watched the purple shadows of the noktum—which only Glimmerblades could see and use—float nonsensically through the hallway.

By the Lords of Dark, he had wanted to live. He'd wanted to fight for his people, to make the world the way it ought to be. Ironically, that was exactly what he was doing now. But he'd been reborn into this horrible slavery. He'd always wanted to serve this purpose for the Lords, but how could this be his reward for loyalty? To be savaged by Lord Tovos? Burned by Jai'ketakos? Reanimated by a foul Human? How could this be his reward? He'd wanted to spearhead a glorious war.

Now all he wanted to do was die.

But he couldn't kill himself. He had tried. Others of his kind had also tried, but anyone who attempted self-destruction was sent straight to the wooden room inside their own minds. Zaith had seen no one actually resist N'ssag once they'd been trapped in that room.

No one except Aravelle. Amidst all those who had been brought back into this bloodthirsty life, Aravelle was conspicuously missing. Something had happened there. N'ssag would surely have tried to make her his slave. Somehow she had escaped him, and Zaith thought about it every day. If she had ...

He mulled it over how Aravelle might have done it, over and over, but he had tried everything he could think of. And sometimes, when he thought too hard about it, sometimes N'ssag would catch him at it, and he would go back to the wooden room.

This was his life now, a twisted thing, waiting in a hallway watching the purple shadows of the Dark shifting and changing. Waiting for a death that would never—

A figure moved from one irregularly shaped purple shadows, flitted across a small space, and vanished into another.

A Glimmerblade!

The act stunned Zaith. There were no other Glimmerblades who had been resurrected. Well, not like Zaith, anyway. Melureth had been pulled back into this undead life, but he was not the same Nox he'd once been. Something about the process had turned his brain to mush, and Zaith had not seen him use the purple shadows.

Without a sound, Zaith left the protection of his own shadow and followed this other Glimmerblade, this user of the Dark. He caught glimpses of the Nox, black hair flying, full-length cloak shrouding his body, moving so fast he was almost a blur as he leapt from purple shadow to purple shadow.

Who are you? Zaith thought.

Zaith had been trained to be a Glimmerblade since he was a child, and he had excelled past all his peers throughout childhood and into adulthood. He was very good at what he did, and with the new strength and speed of his resurrected self, Zaith could move without even a whisper of sound.

He stayed close to this new Glimmerblade, flitting from shadow to shadow as they were doing, and a small hope kindled inside him. If there was a Glimmerblade within N'ssag's undead army that had kept their talent hidden as Zaith had hidden his, then perhaps this unknown Nox had also found a way to throw off N'ssag's yoke.

As the figure approached the feasting room, there were two

glutted Nox, blood smeared down their faces and their fronts, standing before the half-open door. From within the room came the wails and screams of either the Humans who were currently dying under the fangs of the Nox, or those waiting their turn, squeaking with terror.

But the two in the hall just stood there, their bodies full of the coppery fire of life. They were not guards. Not alert. Not paying attention.

And why should they? The battle was over. The fighters were all imprisoned or killed. The remaining helpless Humans were either trapped in this room, awaiting their turn to be food, or they were in the lighted room surrounded by those raven totems, protected from the bloodsucking Nox until Lord Harkandos decided what to do with them.

The Glimmerblade vanished into an irregular purple shadow ten feet from where the two glutted Nox swayed on their feet as the power of the blood coursed through them. Zaith knew that feeling, knew it well.

Was the Glimmerblade here to take his fair share of the Humans? Was he here—

The Glimmerblade attacked.

Three things struck Zaith at that moment, and it paralyzed him. He watched, fascinated.

First, the Nox was female, not male. As she crossed the long distance to her targets, her cloak rippled back from her neck like a flag in full wind, revealing her grimy, dirt-smeared body beneath a short and muddy dress.

Second, there were no female Glimmerblades who had been resurrected by N'ssag. There had only been two before the dragon, and they'd been burned to bone. Neither of them had made the transition into N'ssag's army.

Third, she was attacking. Attacking! How could she …? No Nox had enough autonomy to attack anything except what N'ssag ordered them to attack.

Zaith should have rushed forward, should have tried to stop her. In his old life, he would have.

But this was Zaith's army. He didn't want N'ssag to succeed. And though he couldn't actively oppose his master, he longed to see his army crumble. In fact, maybe this Nox maid could kill N'ssag himself …

She gave him no time to consider. Long blades flashed out, and both blood-drunk Nox looked up just as she slashed their throats.

The first stumbled backward, hands flying to his neck, eyes wide with disbelief. He backpedaled until he hit the wall, trying to keep the blood from gushing out of him.

She leapt upon the second, feet on his chest, bearing him to the ground. Her knives flashed left, right, left, right, fast and methodical. The Nox hit the ground and his head rolled away.

She sprang toward the first, who sat at the base of the wall, feet kicking as he pressed his hands to his throat. Like a relentless beast, she leapt upon him with the same slashing motion of her knives.

His head rolled away as well.

So she knew how to deal with the undead. A knife through the chest would only stun N'ssag's Nox, not kill them. Only removing the head from the body—or mangling the body so much that it could not move—was sufficient.

Zaith moved from the shadow in which he hid, standing in full view. He intentionally scuffed his heel on the ground.

The Nox maid spun, spotted him instantly.

Zaith sucked in a breath.

"Lorelle!" he said.

She bared her teeth. A low whine leaked from her mouth, like a dog wanting in from the rain.

She leapt at him.

Zaith was the fastest Nox in Aravelle's army. He had trained to be a Glimmerblade and honed his combat skills to a keen sharpness. And he had been imbued with the superhuman speed and strength of all of N'ssag's creatures. He should have been able to dodge her.

But he hesitated. He didn't know if he *wanted* to stop her.

That was all the time she needed.

Her feet hit his chest. The weight of her body followed like a mallet strike. She rode him down and slammed him into the ground. Zaith's head clonked against the stones so hard he almost blacked out.

Her knives flashed up, crisscrossing at his throat.

Her low whine stopped. The knives poised there, tight enough that they cut into his flesh, but not deep. A trickle of blood went down the side of his neck.

"Zaith," she rasped.

He flashed back to their last interaction, in his other life, back before he'd become a slave to N'ssag. He recalled in vivid detail the last thing she had done before he'd died. She had killed him. Tovos had forced her to cut his throat, dominating her mind much like N'ssag currently dominated Zaith's.

He couldn't read minds, but he would have bet anything that she saw that same scene now, except as the one pulling the knife, trying so hard to resist, but pulling the knife anyway.

"Zaith," she repeated, and this time her voice sounded almost like the Lorelle he had known. The knives at his throat trembled.

"Lorelle—"

"You live," she said, and she vanished. The noktum cloak wrapped around her, and she retreated into the shadows like a black blanket folded and folded and folded again until it was gone.

Zaith lay there, joy fighting with despair.

Lorelle was alive. Lord Harkandos thought he'd killed her, but she'd somehow survived.

She could have killed Zaith, but she hadn't.

He rolled onto his belly, pressed his head to the stones between his elbows.

"You should have killed me," he murmured. "You should have …"

No one answered him.

"What am I going to do now?" he whispered so quietly he

might not have even said the words aloud.

What am I going to do now ...?

CHAPTER TWENTY-EIGHT

VOHN

Vohn stood in Harkandos's meeting room to the right of the sturdy wooden chair that had been brought in and placed on a dais. Harkandos sat in the chair two hours out of every day, and he had commanded that any questions be brought to him during that time. This was the moment his subjects could communicate with him.

There were eight primary leaders who were allowed in this room.

First, there were the five Giants: Avektos, the fat Giant with the long arms who was apparently a weaponsmith of some kind. Mendos, the tall, thin Giant who always seemed to be frowning. Jai'ketakos, who always alighted on the balcony to give his report as even the Giant-sized door inside was problematic, and who always gazed at least once at Vohn with hungry eyes. Raos, the horrific spider-Giant who made Vohn shiver every time she entered the room. Tovos, or at least an undead, mutilated version of Tovos. And lastly Orios, the one who always had that lazy smile on her chilling face and those fathomless black eyes with stars in them. Of all those in the room aside from Harkandos, Vohn feared her the most.

And of course there were the four captains of the other aspects of Harkandos's army: N'ssag, the creator and leader of the undead Nox. Ukthag, the leader of the Troll army. And Vencilan, a new addition, a Human who had risen from within the Usarans. He had convinced Harkandos that he could reshape what was left of her followers into loyal subjects and warriors for Harkandos's war. Vohn knew him. The man was a weaselly little courtier who had never had much power in Rhenn's court. But he did have a silver tongue and a knack for making himself look good by standing on the work of others.

Those were the eight who were allowed in Harkandos's audience chamber. Anyone not of those eight were summarily put to death if they entered this room during this sacrosanct time. Vohn had witnessed it twice in the last two days. One had been a Nox drunk with blood. He'd stumbled in by mistake during that two-hour audience.

Harkandos hadn't even looked at the intruder. He hadn't paused in his attention to Mendos's report. He'd merely raised a hand and the Nox burst into flame. The creature had fled, screaming as he died.

The second had been one of the surviving Usarans, a man Vohn also knew. His name was Jelkor, a nervous assistant baker who had been drafted into Harkandos's service to bring refreshments to the various chambers throughout the castle. He'd brought a tray of snacks into the audience room during a meeting by mistake. Vohn didn't know where he was supposed to deliver his goods. Probably, Vohn guessed, the young man was simply addled by fear. Certainly his hands had shaken so badly that the cups and plates rattled.

But no one would ever know why the young man had entered, what his excuse might have been, for he'd never had time to tell.

Again, without acknowledging the quivering young man or even glancing in his direction, Harkandos had raised his hand

and Jelkor had been squished to the ground as though an invisible column had fallen upon him. Only a bloody, mangled circle of flesh remained where he'd once stood.

One thing Vohn found strange was that Harkandos, though clearly of the opinion that he ruled the world and everything in it—and was more than happy to prove it at any moment—had not chosen to make the actual throne room his audience chamber.

There was a throne room in Castle Noktos. Vohn had seen it when he and Slayter had gone exploring, looking for an appropriate laboratory for the mage to set up shop.

The throne room was enormous. It made the expansive throne room at the Usaran palace look like a storage closet, and Vohn had hated the place immediately. It seemed large enough to contain the entire Usaran palace with room to spare. The vaulted ceilings were so tall they seemed like a new sky. The whole place … Well, it felt like the home of fear itself, like that room had been made to strangle the autonomy from any petitioner. Vohn had felt tiny there, and he knew the room had been designed to *make* him feel that way. The huge chamber's deafening silence seemed to hold the stifled screams of a thousand petitioners who had died there. Slayter had been fascinated. Vohn had fled.

Harkandos had not taken up that throne room, though it was clear he was king here. Or lord. Or god. Or however it was the others thought of him.

Instead of the throne room, Harkandos had chosen this large meeting room that overlooked the stone courtyard, ironically much like Queen Rhenn's meeting room had overlooked the courtyard at the Usaran palace.

Vohn fidgeted, adjusting his weight from one foot to the other beside the dais. Harkandos towered above, eyes focused on Mendos as he gave a report about the goings-on in the castle. Foodstuffs. The kitchens. Sanitation.

Vohn often caught himself thinking that where he was, what he was doing, had to be some kind of waking nightmare.

Harkandos hadn't killed him. After he'd questioned Vohn, he'd ordered food brought to him, which Vohn had barely eaten even though he was starving, and then given him a room in which to rest. The only thing Harkandos had said when he had personally escorted Vohn to the room was: "Do not try to escape. You are my guest now. You have a certain value to me. Information, let us say, and I will honor you as a valuable resource. If you should try to flee, I will find you. I will tear your head from your body and keep it in a jar with spells that will keep you alive. I will ensure all of your memories are intact so that you may still serve me as a source of information. I am giving you the choice. Serve me as you are now, or serve me as that."

Vohn had lain awake that entire night, his hand on the ring that could turn him into a banshee, but he hadn't pulled it.

In the morning, Harkandos had brought him to his audience chamber and installed Vohn at his right-hand side.

"Stand here," he had said. "I want you to hear the information that comes to me. Sometimes I will ask you questions, and I want you to answer them honestly. If you cannot answer them honestly, there will be repercussions."

How did I come to this shore? Vohn thought.

"… killings," Mendos said, and Vohn's wandering mind returned to the report.

"How many?" Harkandos asked.

"One troll. Over a dozen Nox," Mendos said.

"Someone or some thing is in the castle, killing our troops," Harkandos said emotionlessly.

"Yes."

Harkandos gave one dismissive wave with his enormous hand, and Mendos stepped back to the group that waited.

"N'ssag," Harkandos called.

The grimy little necromancer, who seemed like an ant next to the Giants behind him, stepped forward. "Yes, my lord."

"Nox are dying. The Nox belong to you. You didn't know this?"

"I ... er ... Well, I have ... I have put them in a sort of waiting thrall. They have a standing instruction to feast—only upon the Humans you have provided, my lord—and to perform sentry duties throughout the castle, as you commanded. But I ... I have not been in as close of contact with them lately. As you know, I have been exerting the best of my attentions upon my queen since the battle. I ... No. I had not noticed."

"You lost a dozen of your fighters. You did not notice?"

N'ssag fidgeted, swallowed. "No, my lord."

"Then report on Rhennaria Laochodon," Harkandos said.

"She is mending. I believe I shall ... reinvent her soon."

"When you have her in hand, bring her here. I will have questions for her."

"Of course, my lord. It will be my pleasure."

"Mendos," Harkandos said.

"Yes, my lord." Mendos stepped forward again as N'ssag slunk back.

"Apparently your incomplete knowledge is the most complete knowledge we have. Why are the Nox dying?"

Mendos waited one moment, still as a statue, saying nothing, and Vohn wondered if that was the equivalent of hesitation. It simply looked so odd, like the Giant had simply frozen. But when he spoke, his voice was full of authority. "My lord, I am unsure."

"Do you think that is an adequate answer?"

Mendos's face seemed to harden. Vohn still didn't have a grasp on how to read the Giants. They didn't respond the way a Human would, or a Shadowvar. But considering how each of these Giants—these demigods—consummately deferred to Harkandos, Vohn suspected that a hardening of the face indicated fear. Or rather, a desperate attempt to hide fear.

"We have a traitor in our midst," Mendos said. "Or an enemy that somehow penetrated our defenses and is concealing himself within the castle."

"That is a pedestrian diagnosis. Essentially you are saying there is someone in the castle who wishes to hurt us. I think we can assume that by the dead bodies. What I want to know is: *who* is it? This person is somehow concealing himself from the Nox. In a noktum. That is strong magic."

"Yes, my lord," Mendos said, inclining his head and, interestingly, keeping it that way. A submission.

"Find them. Bring them before me." Harkandos again waved for Mendos to step back.

"Yes, my lord." Mendos retreated.

Vohn's mind was alive now. An enemy in the castle? An enemy of Harkandos and his army, which meant they were an ally of Vohn's. But who could it be? Rhenn was ... wherever N'ssag had taken her. Shalure, bless her soul, had been in a deathlike sleep since he'd taken her into the banshee realm. He hadn't seen her since before the battle. In all likelihood, she had been drained by one of Nox. And Khyven and Lorelle were dead ... Which left some new player on the stage that Vohn didn't know.

Or it left Slayter.

For some reason, Vohn rebelled against the notion. It could be Slayter, he supposed. It made sense inasmuch as he had been the only one of their group who had escaped. Harkandos had questioned Vohn about Slayter first and at length.

But something about it simply didn't fit. Stealth was not Slayter's talent nor his style. It was certainly possible he might take up a rebellion against the invaders, but using his magic to hide and take out a few Nox at a time? No. Slayter didn't think that way. It simply wouldn't make sense to him. He would try for something unfathomable, bizarre, a brilliant idea that would turn the game on its head, purge the entire palace of its evil denizens while at the same time producing a field of flowers that gave the milk of healing for Humans or some such thing. *That* was Slayter.

This killer was something else. Something more ... direct. But what? And could it be somehow contacted to help with—

"Vohn," Harkandos shifted in his huge chair and looked down at him.

Vohn jumped. This was the first time Harkandos had singled him out during a meeting.

"Yes," Vohn said, then belatedly. "Lord Harkandos."

The words still felt horrible coming from his lips. Vohn struggled even faking fealty to this creature. Was the right thing to simply defy Harkandos and be destroyed? It was certainly the noble thing, and Vohn had considered it. He'd thought of nothing else as he lay awake in the bed that had been assigned him last night and the night before. Khyven would have. Lorelle would have. In fact, they both already had.

But then Vohn thought of Slayter out there, somewhere, no doubt working on a plan. The mage wouldn't give up, not even for a moment, until he had come up with a way to save whichever of his friends might still live, or he would die in the process.

For that reason alone, it seemed the best thing to do was to stay alive. And for now, by pretending to be an advisor to this monster, Vohn *could* stay alive. And perhaps, when Slayter revealed his plan, help.

All of this flashed through Vohn's mind as the Giant glanced down at him.

"This killer has magic," Harkandos continued. "Could it be your friend, Slayter?"

Vohn felt a rush of relief. He could answer that question honestly. "I was considering that, my lord. I do not think so."

"Are you lying to me, Shadowvar?"

Vohn swallowed. He had the impression that attempting to lie to Harkandos would go badly. The Giant rarely evinced any expression at all, certainly nothing to indicate when he was annoyed enough to execute someone.

"N-no, my lord."

"There is magic at play here. A mage would be a likely culprit."

"Y-yes, my lord. Unless you consider Slayter's personality."

"Explain."

"Slayter would be focused on the larger picture," Vohn said, choosing his words carefully, trying to thread at least a little misdirection into what was essentially true. Slayter himself wasn't grandiose at all, but his plans could certainly be seen that way. Slayter didn't crave recognition or seek to be impressive. He simply was impressive. He appeared grandiose because he couldn't help it. It was a small misdirection, but Vohn felt that little bits of help were all he could afford at the moment. "He wouldn't do something this small."

"Thirteen deaths in two days? That is small?"

"To Slayter it is. He wouldn't take out thirteen Nox. He'd try to take them all out. Or everyone in the castle, at once."

"Hmmm ..." The Giant's face never changed expression, and he turned forward again.

A wash of relief swept over Vohn. The Giant's scrutiny was like a nearly-unbearable weight, like mere mortals weren't meant to stare too long into the terrible gaze of a Giant. Sweat broke out on Vohn's brow, and his thoughts wandered again.

Are you actually out there, Slayter? he thought. *Or am I playing for time for no reason? And even if you are, can you actually come up with a plan to turn this around?*

It seemed impossible and yet, Vohn hoped. Hope was like that, he supposed. A ray of light in the dark. But what if it was a false ray? Was Vohn giving himself hope because there was nothing else?

"Is this why your friend hasn't yet come to rescue you?" Harkandos asked. "I've noticed Humans are illogical when it comes to valuing their fellows. He doesn't consider your rescue grandiose enough to suit his scheme?"

And that confirmed what Vohn had suspected from the beginning. Harkandos didn't just want Vohn as an advisor. Vohn was bait for Slayter.

"No he doesn't. I'm not Khyven. I can't affect the larger view. I can't win a war. Slayter would see me as irrelevant to his purpose."

"And he wouldn't try to save you just because you're his friend?"

"He wants to beat you. He probably suspects you've taken me pris—" Vohn cut himself off, amended his statement. "That you've given me a place at your side. He'll expect you're using me to bring him out."

"Well," Harkandos said. "He thinks like a Noksonoi. I like this Human mage more and more."

Vohn fell into a troubled silence. Everything he'd said was true. That might be exactly the way Slayter perceived the problem. And Vohn had an attack of conscience that he might be revealing too much about the way his friend thought and acted.

But Slayter's one predictable quality was unpredictability. Vohn had never before been able predict the way Slayter would think and act. So if he filled Harkandos's head with words that rang true, perhaps Harkandos would begin to think that Slayter would be predictable.

Vohn was only sure about two things regarding Slayter. First, he was working the problem right now. He was always working the problem. He was weighing options and calculating odds.

Second, when he finally revealed his plan, it was going to be something nobody would anticipate.

"Jai'ketakos," Harkandos said. This time he turned toward the open balcony where the dragon lay, curled up and watching Harkandos with his glowing yellow eyes. "Report."

Unlike the other Giants, Jai'ketakos's scaly face wasn't a mask of attempted indifference. It seemed obvious he loathed Harkandos, but then, perhaps that was just the way the dragon looked all the time. Vohn had a hard time looking in his direction at all. Jai'ketakos had almost killed him, had shaken this entire castle chasing him. And the dragon still wanted to devour him. Vohn was sure of it. He had no doubt that if Harkandos had not thrown his veil of protection over Vohn, he'd have been a snack for the dragon on the first day.

"Triada and Imprevar are unexpectedly prepared for the coming of the noktum," Jai'ketakos said. "They were also prepared to fight in the Dark. Both kingdoms have braced for an attack. I suspect this is Nhevalos's doing."

"Mmm." Harkandos nodded. "We will deal with them in due course."

"Yes, my lord."

Harkandos turned his attention back to the group inside the room, but Jai'ketakos cleared his throat.

"Yes?" Harkandos raised an eyebrow, which was the most emotion the Giant had evinced the entire audience. Vohn catalogued that. Was this how the Giant indicated anger? So far, the only indication of the Giant's anger had been blood splattering the wall after the brutal slaying of someone who had offended him.

"I beg your leave, my lord," Jai'ketakos said, though his posture didn't seem supplicating in the slightest. His enormous, horned head rested on his claws like he was reclining before a fire. "You are missing one of the ringleaders of this band of rebels."

"Slayter the Mage."

"Yes." Jai'ketakos's gaze shifted to Vohn, those burning eyes confirming that the dragon would like nothing more than to crunch Vohn's bones in his jaws—and that the dragon was frustrated at being denied his desire. "He is out there somewhere, and I believe I can find him."

"Do you?"

"I think he will try to rescue his friend here. Human sentimentality."

"Then why not simply wait for him to make his move, rather than chasing a shadow?"

"He is talented, my lord, for a Human. To catch him in the fledgling stages of whatever plan he means to execute is to catch him at his weakest."

"You think he poses a threat to us here?" Harkandos didn't sound convinced.

"I do, my lord."

"Really?"

"Nhevalos is still out there, my lord. You have dealt his plans a resounding blow, perhaps even a fatal one … But perhaps not. And if there is any possibility that Nhevalos can bring his plans back from the fire, I believe he will use the mage to do it. It is not just Slayter we may be fighting here. It would be Slayter with Nhevalos behind him. If I act now, we could prune this plan before it comes to full bloom."

"And you think you can find him when I have not?"

"Your attentions are occupied with greater matters, my lord. Allow me to dedicate all of my efforts to finding and bringing this mage to you."

"Not devouring him yourself?"

"If my lord wishes, I will happily make an end to the mage the moment I find him."

"No. Bring him here."

"As my lord wishes." Jai'ketakos inclined his head. "So I have your leave to find him? I know you wished me to check the defenses in Demaijos—"

"Find the mage. Demaijos after."

"Yes, my lord."

A hot prickle went up Vohn's back. He fidgeted even more than he'd been fidgeting before. He wanted to warn Slayter, wanted to rush to him.

But he couldn't. Not only didn't he know where Slayter was, but he believed Harkandos's threats about making an escape attempt. Especially right now, when it seemed Harkandos had a particular interest in Vohn.

Vohn had to come up with some way to help from here, from being in the center of Harkandos's circle. That was his only real move.

But how? How could he help Slayter without knowing what the mage was doing?

Stay ready, Vohn thought. *That is how I help. Slayter will take care of the rest. He will have already calculated this. He will figure I might be here, serving as an "advisor." When he arrives, he'll know what to do.*

If he was still alive.

Vohn felt that damning flicker of hope again. *Be careful,*

Slayter. The dragon is coming for you. Be careful.

But what were the odds that Slayter would actually be careful? He had never been careful in his life.

Vohn fervently wished he could push his thoughts into Slayter's head.

He's coming, Slayter. Be ready. Be ready for him ...

CHAPTER TWENTY-NINE

SLAYTER

Slayter was ready.

He worked in his little space, reading his intelligence, sipping from and creating the spells he would need in the days—or hours—to come.

It had been two days since Harkandos had taken Castle Noktos—since Slayter had left Elegathe unconscious in Imprevar—and he hadn't wasted a minute of it. He'd taken three trips to the Vault in Castle Noktos without Harkandos's knowledge. He'd booby-trapped his laboratory, set up shop in a hidden cove, and come up with a plan.

There were one hundred and twenty-seven possible paths Slayter could have taken when he'd returned to the crown city, including beginning a long-term vendetta against Nhevalos, or picking off Harkandos and his Giants one by one from the shadows, or fleeing to another continent entirely, or rallying the other kingdoms of Noksonon to mount a counter offensive.

Slayter had discarded all but one.

His friends came first. In the last two days, Slayter had

discovered that Vohn—and possibly Rhenn—were still alive. That brought his one hundred and twenty-seven plans down to one.

Nothing else mattered until he rescued Vohn and Rhenn …

Or they all died.

Slayter had considered an immediate rescue, charging into the castle and trying to take them back. It had the advantage of speed, but that was its only advantage, and it was a thin one. He calculated his chances of success somewhere around seven percent. Its primary flaw was that it was predictable. The Giants would expect that sort of passion-driven assault from a Human.

Slayter had to do the unexpected. So he had laid out his plan.

The first part was to secure a base of power. Slayter couldn't work without a workshop, and he couldn't use his old laboratory. It would be a target, the most dangerous place once the Giants came looking for him, which they would. He figured it would only take twelve hours before Harkandos sent minions after Slayter. He was the only one of Rhenn's inner circle to escape.

Harkandos wouldn't stand for that. He wanted complete victory, and Slayter's escape was a failure for him. The minions would come, and they'd search first in his laboratory.

And they had, almost exactly twelve hours after Elegathe had taken Slayter away.

But Slayter had been industrious in those twelve hours. He hadn't slept. He'd used the noktum cloak to make trips to Castle Noktos during the first chaotic hour when Harkandos was flush with his victory, his minions were chasing Usarans throughout the castle, and his bloodsuckers were feasting.

Slayter's first trip to Castle Noktos was to recover his catalogue of Vault items, left in his laboratory. It would be disastrous for the catalogue to fall into Harkandos's hands. Slayter suspected Harkandos didn't even know about the Vault, with its untold wealth. If that was true, the catalogue would prove such a place existed, Harkandos would go looking, and he *would* find the Vault eventually. In addition, the catalogue would tell Harkandos everything Slayter knew about the artifacts, everything useful.

Slayter's second trip had been to the Vault itself. Any offensive he might mount would require more magic than Slayter possessed by himself. The Vault could give him all he would need.

So Slayter had nabbed his catalogue and made three trips to the Vault to secure the artifacts he'd needed, all in the first hour. It had been risky. He'd vomited quite a lot.

But they hadn't found him.

He'd made only one trip since then, straight to the Vault and back, which Slayter was beginning to suspect was somehow magically shielded from those who weren't told of its location. Three of his four trips into Castle Noktos had been to the Vault, and though Slayter had calculated his odds of getting caught by Tovos, a master of the noktum cloaks, at sixty seven percent, he'd not been discovered. If Rauvelos had made a shielding spell, one that caused it to be extremely forgettable or unremarkable to the uninitiated, that would make a great deal of sense. And it would account for Slayter's extreme luck.

Aside from trips to the Vault, he'd spent most of the last two days working on his defenses in the Usaran palace. He'd set up a series of misleading clues for anyone who came looking. For an astute man, the clues would indicate Slayter had been here, but had since left. For a blithering idiot, it would seem like Slayter had never actually returned to the palace in the first place.

And, just as Slayter had predicted, Harkandos's minions had come searching for him almost exactly twelve hours after Castle Noktos had fallen.

The Nox came first, a dozen of them, slithering into Slayter's laboratory where he lay in wait. He had prepared several spells for them, though in the end they only ran afoul of two of them.

The first spell concealed Slayter. It was an illusion over a space-bending spell. Essentially, it created a space beyond the far wall of his laboratory and hid it behind an illusory replica of the original wall. It effectively carved out a temporary space for

Slayter that no one could spot unless they were a mage of some ability, and if they were looking for it.

None of the Nox fell into this category.

The second spell had been the next stage of Slayter's plan.

Each of the Nox, as they came through his laboratory door, had been marked by a soft spell. The spells were delicate, like the ephemera of a spider's web clinging to a person's hair.

The spell had coated the Nox in a thin sheen that, unless they were magic-sensitive, they would never notice. And the Giants wouldn't detect it unless they were looking for it.

The spell was simple. It focused on the ears of the Nox, transmitting whatever they heard to the Vault artifact from which the spell had been spawned. It was a little wooden box with a crank on the top. When it had information, the crank rattled. If Slayter then turned the handle, it would spit out a piece of paper with every word the Nox had heard written down as though a scribe had followed him around.

Slayter effectively had twelve spies now within Castle Noktos.

Now, within his little cove, he kept working non-stop. He gathered information—reading each piece of paper as it came out of the box—and continued preparing every spell he could imagine needing in the coming days. He was almost ready. He—

A bright light flashed in the periphery of Slayter's vision. It wasn't something anyone else would have seen, even if they'd been standing in the midst of a crowd and not safely tucked behind his illusion. The light was only apparent to the caster.

Someone had tripped one of his trespassing spells.

Another visitor. Harkandos hadn't abandoned looking for Slayter in the Usaran palace. Slayter had predicted that eventuality.

"Let's see who you are," Slayter murmured.

He turned to the tiny table he had crammed behind the illusion and quietly unrolled a thick bit of parchment. It was map sized, but there was nothing on it. Slayter supposed he could have done this straight upon the table, but the blank parchment enabled him to focus a little bit more. And a little bit more could be the difference between living and dying.

He pulled a disk from his cylinder, completed the sign with his scratcher. Orange light filled the tiny space, and four symbols appeared on the blank map, latent Line Magic generated by the spell he'd just activated. After the symbols, the blank page filled with lines, representations of the corridors and rooms in the palace. The blank piece of parchment slowly became an architect's sketch of the ground floor of the palace.

A Human-sized figure walked up one of the corridors, headed for the stairway that would descend to the basement levels, to Slayter's laboratory. The figure was a ghostly representation, sketchy and slightly disproportionate as though the artist hadn't quite mastered the Human shape.

Art had never been Slayter's strong suit.

But he could see it was a Human woman, not a Nox. He could see she was alone. She cupped her hands over her mouth and seemed to be calling out.

Well, that was dangerous. If the woman wasn't a spy, then she was being reckless. Since the noktum had swallowed the continent, shouting one's location was tantamount to suicide.

Touching one of the glowing symbols on the parchment, Slayter turned the symbol a quarter degree to the right to hear what she was shouting.

"Slayter!" a woman's voice rose from the parchment.

"Fascinating," he murmured. It now seemed highly likely she was a spy for Harkandos. Some Usaran who had turned traitor.

Of course, Slayter had been expecting one of Harkandos's minions to show up, but not a lone Human woman. Interesting.

Also, her voice seemed familiar, but her representation on the map didn't. At least, not within the rough sketch his rudimentary art skills could summon.

Slayter touched a different symbol, turned it a quarter turn to the right, and spoke.

"Who are you?"

The figure in the map spun, looking for him. Of course, he

wasn't there, just his voice. The woman was fast, and she had a fluid grace. He suddenly wondered if she was more than Human. Or a spy infused with Giant magic …

He touched a third symbol on the parchment and turned it. The woman on the map enlarged as the view tightened on her. He looked for anything he might recognize.

He couldn't easily see details because of the sketchiness of the drawing, so he touched the fourth symbol, turned it as the glow flowed up around his hand. The angle of the view pivoted, and he saw her from the left, then turned it to the right, then straight on.

There. That.

This woman wore no Amulet of Noksonon, yet she moved like she could see in the dark of the noktum.

Bloodsucker.

That was clever, he thought. *But I—*

"My name is L'elica," the woman said after scanning the direction of Slayter's voice. She kept turning, though, searching, clearly realizing it was a magical ruse. "You have to leave this place."

Interesting. L'elica. The turncloak bloodsucker who had helped Rhenn at the risk of her own life.

"Nhevalos has a message for you."

"Nhevalos can suck my butt."

She hesitated. "He … wants to help you."

"And you are his offering?"

"I … I have information."

"I'm sure you do. The question is, why would I ever take information from Nhevalos again?"

"Slayter, the dragon is coming."

Slayter was hardly going to believe what Nhevalos had to say, or follow his lead in anything.

On the other hand, he'd already calculated that the next minion Harkandos would send was Jai'ketakos. Ninety five percent chance. The dragon wanted to eat Slayter. Harkandos wanted to find Slayter. It made sense.

Also, the dragon was an Eldroi. If anyone could detect the spells Slayter had hung in the palace—if anyone could undo them—it would be Jai'ketakos. L'elica's words smacked of truth.

"When?" Slayter said to her.

"Now. Nhevalos says you have to leave."

"Why would he send you?" Slayter asked.

She hesitated, and he perceived in that moment that she didn't actually know. In that instant, Slayter decided L'elica was not a spy. She was what she claimed, a minion of Nhevalos, not Harkandos.

"It's because he has no one else, does he?" Slayter supplied.

"I don't know," she said. "He came to me. I asked how I might help Rhenn. He told me to help you."

"Where did he find you?"

"Not far from here. When the darkness fell, I made my way back to Usara. I wasn't far when he appeared to me."

"He appeared to you?"

"From a ... cloak. It was black and—"

"I know what a noktum cloak is."

"Noktum cloak?"

"Why didn't he come here himself?"

The image of her stopped in the middle of the grand foyer, only a dozen yards from the stairway that led down to Slayter's laboratory. Clearly, she didn't know any more than the information she'd been sent to deliver. A classic pawn of Nhevalos.

"I don't think we have much time, Slayter," she said. "He brought me to the edge of the city and sent me here."

"Or perhaps Harkandos sent you."

"I ... What?"

"So far as I know, you could have been sent by Harkandos."

"Slayter, I came here to help Rhenn. Nhevalos tells me that she is captured. He said the best thing I could do was help you free her."

Slayter calculated the truth of her words at ninety percent. At the very least, he believed that she believed them. Additionally, he calculated Nhevalos's plan to "help" Slayter to have a twenty-eight percent chance of actually helping with what Slayter intended to do. The Giant had an agenda, and it included allowing Slayter's friends to die.

Slayter's plan did not.

"I will free her," Slayter said. "And I'll free you as well. Go back to Nhevalos. Tell him I have this in hand."

She frowned. "You need all the help you can get."

"And I feel I've been given all the help I can afford. Go." He reached out to deactivate the map when his laboratory shuddered. Bits of dust sifted down from the archway over his head. Something had hit the castle!

Three different warning spells went off at that moment, all of them from the front of the palace.

The sketchy representation of L'elica crouched, ready for combat, as she felt the shudder as well. Slayter hastily tapped the third symbol and turned it. The image shrank as he threw it to its widest range.

A hulking form stood on the stone courtyard before the palace of Usara. It was the dragon, but Slayter couldn't tell which side was its head and which was its tail. That was simply atrocious. He really did need to employ someone with better drawing skills and update this map.

Slayter oriented on the long sketchy rope coming out of one end of the body's mass, which lashed out in the open air, and considered the long sketchy rope at the other end of the body's mass, which ducked below the archway to look inside the palace. Ah. That was the head.

Well, apparently L'elica had not been lying.

"Look what we have here ..." the dragon said.

L'elica froze like a frightened rabbit. Slayter sighed. He had hoped to discourage her and make her leave, but it was too late for that now.

Slayter already had a plan for this contingency. He had a general plan for each possible contingency, actually. He had set light burst spells for the Nox and Trolls. And Tovos.

He had magic-sucking spells for the Giants who weren't particularly physical. He had materializing, falling weights for the Giants who were.

For Jai'ketakos, though, Slayter had a very specific plan. He calculated the odds of that plan killing the dragon at fifty seven percent. He calculated it at seventy five percent to also kill Slayter himself, which he found to be interesting. Mirror numbers.

Of course, that problem required Vohn's rescue first, which Slayter had hoped to do before the dragon arrived. He would have to improvise, a posthumous homage to his friend Khyven, who had never planned anything in his life.

He had the dragon plan ready to go. Unfortunately, he hadn't calculated L'elica's appearance into that plan.

"You're one of N'ssag's," the dragon said, his voice warbling through the map.

L'elica didn't say anything, still frozen like she was terrified of the dragon. This spoke well of her. And Slayter simultaneous hated it.

It spoke well because it meant she and the dragon were not allies. He hated it because if she and the dragon were *not* allies, Slayter had to change his plan. He had to make a decision he didn't want to make.

Let her die? Or take her with him?

"Damn," he said aloud, then realized he hadn't stopped the voice projection of the map. The dragon's sketchy figure twitched.

"Slayter?" he said, raising his head.

L'elica bolted for the safety of the stairwell.

Jai'ketakos blew fire at her.

To Slayter's left, crammed into the cramped space, was a short table with seven satchels. Each one had special goodies in it, depending on which plan he'd need. He grabbed the fourth one and slung it over his shoulder even as he activated the noktum cloak.

He vanished, reappeared in the foyer just as the fire was

reaching L'elica. He wrapped her in the cloak and pictured Castle Noktos.

The twisting, funneling function of the cloak took hold. Searing heat exploded around them.

"Slayter!" the dragon shouted. *"Slayter—!"*

The cloak spun them away and the dragon vanished from view.

CHAPTER THIRTY

SLAYTER

The cloak untwisted, dumping Slayter and L'elica on the rough-hewn floor of the Vault.

Slayter staggered over and threw up in the old, banded barrel in the corner of the room. It smelled horrible. Slayter hadn't taken the time to clean it out; he'd vomited in it every time he'd visited the Vault. He had a similar container—a large vase whose plant had not survived the noktum's return—back at the palace. Thankfully, he didn't keep it in his laboratory.

L'elica staggered one step backward, looked paler than usual, then recovered herself. It was a fairness in the world that bloodsuckers could also get sick to their stomachs. Slayter felt a small vindication for that, even though L'elica didn't throw up.

Slayter had noted that most people, even Vohn, seemed to adjust to the ill effects of the noktum cloak eventually, some faster than others. Lorelle didn't even seem bothered by it anymore. But no matter how many times Slayter used the cloak, it turned his insides inside out.

He had, however, taken to carrying a flask of mint-infused

water. He uncapped it now and took a long swig, swished it around in his mouth, then spit it into the old barrel.

"Where are we?" L'elica asked, looking around at all of the magical treasures.

"The Vault. In Castle Noktos."

"The Giants are in the castle!"

"Yes."

"Isn't this exactly where we *don't* want to be?"

"No."

"I don't understand."

"You sound like Khyven."

L'elica gave him a confused look.

"The dragon is looking for me."

"And if you're here, won't he find you more easily?"

"I want him to find me."

"You *do*?"

"I plan to end him. I must be near him in order to do that."

"But ... Why here?"

Slayter really didn't have time to explain his plan.

"I need Vohn."

"Why?"

"Bait."

"For the dragon?"

"I need to steal him from Harkandos."

"That's their leader!"

"I believe Vohn is with him."

"Nhevalos said Harkandos is the most powerful magic user on the continent." L'elica said.

"Yes."

"You ... You can't ..."

"Oh, but I must. Or I must die." It really was that simple.

The bloodsucker's mouth firmed into a line. "Fine. Then take me."

"As the bait?"

"Instead of Vohn. Take me as the bait."

Slayter cocked his head as his estimation of the bloodsucker went up. L'elica had risked her life to try to save Rhenn back in Daemanon, yes. He'd known about hat. It was the only reason he'd brought her here to the Vault.

But L'elica had not only helped Rhenn by offering up her life once; she was doing it again.

"That is noble of you."

"I have a long slate of mistakes to make up for."

"Pretty as that is, you can't," Slayter said simply.

"Why not?"

"Well, because you're not Vohn. Jai'ketakos doesn't care about you. Vohn, on the other hand, escaped the dragon. He particularly doesn't like mortals who escape him."

"I just escaped him," L'elica pointed out.

Slayter raised an eyebrow. "Touché."

"So? Take me—"

Slayter thought about it, making a quick calculation, then shook his head. "It's no good. He will see that as me saving you, not as you escaping him. I think he will still not care."

"Well how did Vohn—"

"Also, my flame protection spell is imperfect against dragon fire. Vohn is going to get singed. You would surely die."

"Flame protection spell?"

"You think I'd let my friend get cooked by dragon fire?" Slayter tsked and shook his head as he rifled through his cylinder of spells. He rearranged two of them.

"Slayter—"

"Also, I need you for another job."

"You do?"

"I'm going to release you into the castle," Slayter continued. "Right now, we are deep in the sub levels. You'll have to find your way to the surface. You said you wanted to help Rhenn, and here's your chance. She will be with N'ssag. You're going to free her."

"N'ssag is *here?*"

"I calculate you have a one-in-five chance."

"One in five—What happens in the other four?"

"And that one-in-five chance depends on speed," Slayter continued.

L'elica opened her mouth, closed it, opened it again, and gave a forceful sigh.

"Where is Rhenn—"

"She's in my new laboratory," Slayter cut her off, feeling the press of time. He had to get moving before Jai'ketakos woke up to the game. "In this castle. It's on the third floor. You're going to have to find it on your own. I would take you there, but the more I use this cloak, the higher a chance I could be noticed by Tovos. There are shielding spells on the Vault, but not above. It's probably why Harkandos has not found this place, and also why Tovos has not detected my invasions into Castle Noktos. But once I snatch Vohn, they might be alerted. Even if they are not, things will move quickly, and I have to use that little time to kill the dragon. So—"

"I don't understand," she interrupted him.

He paused. Having to stop his train of thought was actually physically painful for him. Why couldn't people just understand the first time? He couldn't boil it down any further.

"I have one trip. You have to walk. Find Rhenn. Help her escape."

L'elica hesitated, then nodded.

"Remember the castle is full of N'ssag's latest creations, almost all of them are Nox. Avoid them."

"His *latest* creations? They're going to be stronger than me. Faster than me."

"And they're going to know the Dark better."

She swallowed.

Slayter cracked a smile, because you had to smile when everything was so ridiculous. Long term, strung together, each piece of this gambit—defeating all the Giants—had a ninety nine percent chance of failure.

"We're going to die," Slayter said. "But I'm going to try to burn a few of them before we do. What are *you* going to do?"

She hesitated again. There was no nod this time.

"You did your job for Nhevalos. You warned me. You can flee into the noktum if you wish. There are many ways out of this castle. I'm sure you can find one. But I have to go."

She just looked at him. It was a suicide mission, and he could see the war on her face. But he didn't have time for two wars right now. One was as much as he could manage.

"Farewell, L'elica."

He activated the cloak.

CHAPTER THIRTY-ONE

RHENN

Rhenn opened one eye to the barest slit. She did it slowly in case anyone was watching. The other was swollen shut, but with her thin view of the room, she became aware of a number of things.

She was in Slayter's laboratory, the one he'd set up in Castle Noktos. She'd been strapped to the steel table Slayter had brought from the palace at Usara. The table had been tipped up so that she was on display, facing the room. Steel manacles cut painfully into her wrists, attached to a thick chain that vanished through two of the six half circles cut into the edge of the tabletop. Her ankles had been similarly chained and linked to small boulders that had apparently been hauled up to this place expressly for the purpose of shackling her. The length of the chains wrapped around and around the boulders, fastened with a lock she probably couldn't have broken, even if her hands were free.

Her armor had been removed, and her clothing was ripped and tattered where the Nox bloodsuckers had attacked her.

They could have destroyed her right from the beginning, but they hadn't. She'd made them pay for that.

She'd tried to kill them all. She'd tried so hard. After watching Khyven fall, then Lorelle, Rhenn had found an entirely new level of supernatural strength. She'd destroyed five of N'ssag's Nox bloodsuckers. She had littered the ground with their heads, and she'd come an inch away from killing N'ssag himself, again.

Twenty of the bloodsuckers had swarmed her before she reached him. She hadn't cared; she'd thought they would destroy her for what she'd done.

Instead, they'd beaten her unconscious to take her to this place, to do …

She closed her eye and suppressed a shudder. This was the beginning of her worst nightmare. N'ssag was going to have his way with her. He was going to take away her mind. He was going to make her a slave.

And there would be no Slayter to help her think her way out of this. There would be no Lorelle to spirit her away on the wings of a noktum cloak. There would be no Khyven to step into the room and upend the odds.

Her heart began to hammer.

"Oh perfect. You're awake," N'ssag's voice came from somewhere behind her.

She yanked on her restraints suddenly, fiercely, with everything she had. The muscle she'd pulled in her left arm shot fiery agony into her shoulder and neck. She felt it tear, felt the movement beneath her skin and against her bone. Still she pulled.

This was her last chance to save herself from eternal damnation. She screamed and pulled and pulled. Her entire body tightened up from her belly to her ribs to her arms and hips, legs and feet. She twisted like a fish pulled tight with a hook in its mouth and one through its tail.

Nothing. She stayed chained tight.

"Silly, silly," N'ssag said, coming into view. "You're going to damage this beautiful body."

Tears welled in her good eye, blurring the odious man from her vision. She tried to squeeze them away. She wanted to scream. She'd been helpless in front of this man before. She couldn't fight. She couldn't bargain. And there was no begging with him. The more she begged, the hotter that unholy desire would light his eyes. She wasn't a person to him. She was only a road to his pleasure. Senji only knew what he saw when he looked at her.

This was her fate. It had been waiting in her nightmares ever since Daemanon, and now it was an ugly reality. She stopped struggling, ignoring the fire in her arm, and looked down at him.

She was going to be his slave. Forever. Soon, she wouldn't remember—or she wouldn't care—that she reviled him. He would command her to kill, and she would. He would command her to lead his undead army, and she would. He would command her to come to his bed, and she ...

She closed her one good eye.

She had failed her people. She'd failed her friends. She had come to this shore where everything she was, thought she was, or wanted to be, was going to get washed away.

Some queen. She had been twenty steps behind and pitifully unprepared for this. For everything. She had thought that the greatest thing she'd ever accomplish was to avenge her parents and re-take the reins of her kingdom. And now, with her on the throne, all of Usara would be killed or enslaved. This was her legacy.

"Are you finished?" N'ssag asked as he came to stand in front of her. She opened her eye again. It opened wider, and this time the other one opened a slit as well. She could feel her supernatural body already healing the wounds. Even her ripped muscle felt like it was trying to put itself back together.

That would have taken an infusion of fresh blood, but she hadn't fed for more than a day. She moved her top lip over her bottom, brushing. Sticky blood there. He'd fed her. This bastard had killed someone, had put their blood into her.

Or he'd put the blood of something else into her.

The table propped her up for his easy inspection, and he came close. He touched the chains that led up to her ankle, and he stroked them like a pet snake.

"I had these made, you know. Made just for you. I knew we would meet again. When Harkandos told me I would serve him in this attack, I did not disagree, and I began making my chains. They're strong enough to thwart the strength of two of my primes. Oh, and my new primes are stronger even than you, my queen. I am getting very good at what I do. There are magics here in this wonderful land that I never knew about, never had access to. And now the entire continent is covered in this glorious noktum. It is ..." He sighed. "It is ... a paradise. Don't you think?"

She glared down at him, but said nothing.

"Oh come now. Will you not answer me? With all that I gave you? I made you immortal. I made you powerful, and when I kill you for the second time, when I bring you back for the second time, you will only be more powerful. This world was made for you. You and me."

"I will never love you," she said in a flat tone. "I will never serve you. I will never be your queen. Whatever you create after you kill me will be something new. It will not be me."

"Oh, I think we both know that isn't true. You will be everything you are now. But you will be devoted to me, as you should have been from the first moment. You will be the real Rhenn. You'll be the Rhenn you were always meant to be."

He believed what he said, and she cursed herself for speaking at all. But then, she hadn't been speaking for his benefit. She'd been speaking for herself.

"They had to break your leg, did you know?" he asked. "You have healed quite well since your little scuffle. Quite well. Quite well ..."

She looked away from him, around the room. For the first time, she noticed two Nox standing in the corners. She hadn't seen them the first time, but there were things Rhenn didn't know about Nox and their manipulation of the noktum. Lorelle had said there were actually shadows within the noktum, shadows within shadows that only Nox Glimmerblades could hide behind, could move through. Those two Nox might have been there all along, and they were just now stepping into a place where she could see them.

"I was thinking I would wait until you were fully healed, but I confess ... I'm so excited to get started. So very excited," N'ssag continued.

"How long?" she asked.

"Since the fight? A full day."

"Where is Slayter?"

"Oh, you are artful, my queen. So sly. I think you *know* the answer to that false question." He chuckled. "Harkandos wants the mage. Apparently he gave offense to my master some time ago. Something about a statue. Do you know what that means?"

She pressed her lips into a line. N'ssag arched an eyebrow as though she might change her mind and tell him where Slayter was. Hope flickered inside her, just a tiny flame. They didn't know where Slayter was. That was ... Well, it was something.

"No? Aren't talking?" He shrugged. "No matter. We will get the answer out of you soon. So soon. I can hardly wait."

Even in the depths of her despair, she wondered how Slayter had escaped. Had he retreated to orchestrate some kind of attack? Was he out there right now, about to ...

About to what? Take on a half dozen Giants and an army of monsters all by himself?

No. Not by himself.

It wasn't even a guarantee that Slayter had run ... In fact, the more she thought about that ...

Her hope faltered as she realized that Slayter would *never* have run away for good. To ultimately defeat the Giants, that would have been a mistake, and Slayter was far too calculating to make that mistake. His best chance was to help his friends immediately, and he'd have known that at a glance. He'd have made his last stand here, at the battle. Whatever clever idea he'd come up with, he'd have thrown it immediately, would have tried to save Rhenn and Lorelle so that they could all work together, that they could try again as a group.

No. Slayter wouldn't have run; he would have attacked.

Which meant something had happened to him.

"I was going to wait another day ..." N'ssag pulled a horrible, sharpened steel rod from his robes, a twin to the one he'd killed E'maz with. "Let you heal up a little more, but I am weary of your tight lips. I want you to talk to me, my queen."

"Words don't matter with you."

"They do when they are words I want to hear." He moved his fingers up the chain to the manacle on her ankle, then touched her flesh.

Her skin crawled, and she flinched.

"You see. This is what I dislike. This is what I can't wait to improve. To remove. I wish to transform you into a better version of yourself." He paused. "Like I did before."

She steeled herself. His hand slid upward, cupping her calf, then further up the inside of her leg. He stopped at mid-thigh.

"It's going to be better soon," N'ssag said. "It will all be better soon."

He stabbed the rod into her side. There was no warning, and she hissed as it sank into her flesh. The red gem glowed fiercely, illuminating N'ssag's eager face in the crimson glow.

She strained again, trying to break free, but the strength drained from her limbs as the gem glowed brighter. A lassitude came over her. Her vision swam.

"Put her down," N'ssag commanded. She felt the table rock. It slammed into the ground. She tried to pull against her restraints again, but she had no strength.

"Unchain her," N'ssag said.

"She will attack," one of the Nox said.

"She won't do anything now. Get the manacles off her. I want her to come to me of her own free will."

Free ... will ... Rhenn said.

Or ... she tried to say it. Her lips had stopped working. She could barely feel the hands at her ankles, at her wrists, as they unlocked the manacles.

But somehow she felt N'ssag's revolting touch, his hand moving to the outside of her thigh, up the side of her body, and then resting on her forehead.

"This was the piece I was missing," he whispered in her ear. "I gave you so many gifts, but you were never grateful ... Never grateful ... But you will be."

From somewhere, he produced the stringless harp he'd had at the final battle in Daemanon. She hadn't noticed him carrying it. Hadn't noticed...

She was fading. She was dying. Again.

He moved his fingers across the air where the strings should have been. The room began to spin. The clank of the chains, the movements of the Nox, all of it began to fade.

But N'ssag's voice grew louder.

"This was what I needed."

The room spun, dissolved, and darkened. She could see silvery threads spinning through a black abyss in front of her. Then the threads attached to her. It seemed she was just a head now, spinning though the darkness with silver threads attaching to her like snakes.

At the end of them, N'ssag's face resolved out of the darkness. Slowly, it became clearer, came closer, growing in size.

She winced as he came so close they were nose to nose.

"The missing piece," he murmured, smiling at her.

A new room resolved around Rhenn, and she began to feel her body again. Head, neck and shoulders, arms and torso, legs and feet.

Walls appeared, but not the walls of Slayter's laboratory. These were a faded, blurry brown. Wooden walls, obscured by a silvery mist. There was a single window to her right. Sunlight shone through. She should have burst into flame, but it didn't hurt her.

Not... the real world, she thought. *I'm inside my mind. This is some spell. He has invaded my mind ...*

Her body felt like concrete. She felt the bite of the ropes that bound her and looked down at herself. She sat in a wooden chair, naked, and she was bound with rough ropes crisscrossed over her legs, her stomach and chest, her shoulders. A triple coil wrapped tightly around her neck.

She could barely breathe.

She struggled, trying to break the ropes. They were, after all, just ropes. Her supernatural strength should make short work of them.

She couldn't. But her struggles tightened the triple loop around her neck. She choked, stopped struggling. The ropes didn't ease. It was a noose, and the more she pulled, the tighter it was going to get.

She sucked a breath through a barely-open windpipe, looked up at N'ssag.

He, too, had transformed …

CHAPTER THIRTY-TWO

RHENN

N'ssag was no longer his hunched and dirty self, with his grimy robes and foul teeth. He stood twelve feet tall, and the chiseled muscles of his torso stood out in sharp relief in the bright light from the window. He wore only a loincloth and his legs were just as striated as his upper body. He looked like what Rhenn imagined Harkandos must look like if the Giant had worn such a ridiculous lack of clothing.

It was as though N'ssag viewed Harkandos as the perfect template for himself, the creature he wished to be. And in this place he could be whatever he wanted to be.

The one part of N'ssag that didn't look like Harkandos was his face. That was all N'ssag, with his glittering eyes, his disgusting smile, and the dirt smeared across his cheeks and chin. The grotesquely muscled N'ssag shuffled forward, wringing his hands together.

"Do you know where we are, my queen?" he asked. "We are in your mind. Your last line of defense. Your body has belonged to me since I gave you my gifts. But you held this back. This one part. The missing piece."

She stopped struggling, huffing hard as she watched him approach.

"Here, you're nothing. The magic of the rod gives me access. The harp gives me everything else. You're going to tell me that you will serve me. You're going to tell me that you *want* to. And the moment you do, you'll no longer need to be tied down. We'll never have to have this conversation again. Do you understand?"

"That's ..." she huffed. "Not going to happen. Not ever."

"Oh, it will," he said. "Sometimes it takes time. Sometimes a long time, like for your friend's lover. But the result is always the same."

Friend's lover? Lorelle's lover? The odd phrasing made her blink. Did he mean Khyven?

"Come now." He saw her confusion. "The Nox. The one your lithe, beautiful, dead Luminent took a shine to."

"Zaith," she murmured.

"Yes ..." He drew the word out. "Yes, Zaith. Oh, he fought me. For nearly seven days he fought me. But you see, in here seven days is however long I want it to be. Seven days is ten seconds in your mage's laboratory, where you are currently insensate on the table. So you see, we will stay here as long as we need to. I am in no rush. You can struggle for days, but in the end, you will tire. And once you tire, you will give in. It happens every time."

"Not this time," she huffed.

He chuckled. "Do you know how many of the Nox said exactly what you just said? Every one. Including your friend Zaith. Do you know how many turned? Every one. The magic of the harp gives me control in this place. That's what it does. You are helpless." He indicated her bound and naked form. "And I am ..."

He looked down at himself. His moist, wormy lips spread in a smile.

"Well, I am this." He gestured at himself with his huge, thick hand. He began walking around her, behind her. She tensed as he moved out of view. She clenched her teeth and waited for him to put his filthy hands on her again.

It isn't my flesh, she told herself. *It's just in my head.*

But he didn't touch her, just slowly walked around her and back into view like he was strolling in the woods.

She breathed hard. Everything in the room seemed more real now. In the beginning, silver mist had obscured the corners, but now everything was clear. She could see the wood grain in the walls, could see a green horizon out the open window, could feel the breeze blowing in from it, fragrant of summer flowers.

"Tell me, my queen ... Tell me just one thing that you like about me."

"I despise you. Every. Single. Part."

"I will make you a deal. You conjure just one thing that you like about me, and I will untie one of your ropes. Would you like that? You'd like to be free, yes?"

Rhenn swallowed, and a flicker of hope rose within her. In this place, in her mind, if he untied one of her ropes ... Would that free her? Even one rope? Could she find a way to loosen the rest?

No! It was a trap. It had to be. He was toying with her.

She spit at him.

The wad hit him on his chiseled stomach, but he didn't flinch or even look at it. He reached up, rubbed it in like it was a balm, and smiled wider. "Oh, this is going to be arduous for you, I can see. You realize that it is no hardship for me to stand here, to wait, to look at you ..." His gaze roved up and down her body lasciviously.

She swallowed, hating him so much she felt like she was burning with fire. And as she poured that hatred toward him, she felt herself tiring. It was as though the hate was being sucked out of her and with it, her strength. Her eyelids drooped.

No!

"Fight, my queen," N'ssag whispered, his face suddenly close to hers. "Fight me with everything you have ..."

Her vision went fuzzy and her eyelids drooped. She blinked and forced them open. What happened if she fell asleep in this place? If he drew her energy out when she projected her fury, what happened when he took it all?

Would she become an empty vessel? Was that what he wanted? Then he could shove whatever he wanted into her head?

She stopped seething, stopped reacting. She tried to keep her emotions close. Anything he said would make her furious, and she had to deny him that pleasure. So she turned her face away from him, tried to ignore his voice.

He put his hand on her shoulder. She flinched—

That draining sensation came again, and she sagged in the ropes.

He chuckled in her ear. Hopelessness rushed through her.

"It is inevitable, my queen," he whispered. His cheek brushed her cheek. His hand moved slowly down her arm, gliding over her flesh and the ropes that cut into her. "No matter what you do, it will happen. One hour. Twenty days. It doesn't matter."

He spoke again, but she forced herself to ignore it. She looked past him, focused on the wooden wall.

I will deny you, she thought. *I will deny you ...*

His voice faded into whispery gibberish.

Yes! She looked past him at the wall, focused on it like it was the most important thing in the world.

His whispery gibberish continued, cool and confident. Infinitely patient.

She didn't know how long they stayed like that, with her trying to keep her emotions calm, with him caressing her arm, murmuring to her. Perhaps minutes. Perhaps hours.

But slowly, something appeared on the wall. At first, it just looked like a silhouette, a shadow cast by someone standing in front of the window, except ...

There was no one by the window. There was only the shadow.

She focused on it, and N'ssag's whispers faded even more.

The shadow coalesced, becoming sharper, and then the hazy silver mist returned, but this time in the shape of a person. A person casting the shadow.

The figure formed, no longer made of shadow or silver mist, but appearing clearly in shades of light and dark brown. Heavy boots formed on the figure's feet, brown leather leggings, a thick brown belt. It was a man. A linen tunic draped his wide back, sleeveless, and she saw the backs of his thickly muscled arms, his carved triceps. His forearms were especially powerful, muscled and scarred by a hundred old burns.

He continued to form, and when she saw the mane of his hair, her heart stopped. He faced the wall, his back to her, but now he turned. She saw his beard, his gorgeous, kind face.

"E'maz!" she murmured.

CHAPTER THIRTY-THREE

RHENN

N'ssag's whisper droned in her ears, but the bastard seemed so very far away now. She was transfixed by E'maz's appearance. E'maz looked directly at her. His kind eyes were a little sad. They captivated her, and at first she didn't notice that he held something in his arms. She glanced down at the swaddled bundle he cradled so gently.

Her breath caught in her throat. That was a baby. He held a baby in his arms.

"Hello, my love," he said.

Terror thrilled through her. If N'ssag saw E'maz, he would ...

What?

Kill him? He'd had already done that.

"What are you doing here ...?" she asked, emotion choking her.

His kind smile filled her with warmth, as though that was answer enough.

"What are you doing here, my love?" he asked.

Rhenn winced, sure that N'ssag's head would rise up, he would charge across the room and smash E'maz. But ...

N'ssag's voice continued to drone on in the background, whispering gibberish. It was as though Rhenn had descended to a different level of her mind, and N'ssag couldn't see E'maz, couldn't hear him.

"Just going to sit there, are you?" E'maz asked.

Tears came to her eyes. They welled up and spilled over, and she didn't care. She didn't care if N'ssag saw them, didn't care if he used them against her. It was E'maz. He was here. She could see him this once, just once more before she died, before N'ssag extinguished her light forever.

She knew this was just a hallucination conjured by her desperate mind, but she didn't care about that, either. If she was going to vanish, this was how she wanted to vanish.

"I missed you," she said.

"I know."

"I ... I never got to tell you everything ... There was so much I wanted to tell you."

"You told me all I needed," he said. "But I do have one question."

"Anything," she said. "Anything you want."

"You just going to sit there, are you?"

"No, I ... I'll be gone soon," she murmured. Tears coursed down her cheeks.

"Will you, now?"

"He's going to take me, E'maz. He's going to take every single thing that's me. I'll live the rest of my life in a cage, screaming without a voice."

"That's what you want, is it?"

"Don't," she said. "This is my last moment as myself. Don't taunt me. Please ..."

"I'm asking if that's what you want?"

"What I *want?*" Why was he torturing her? "No. I want you."

"Oh, I think you want more than that."

"I don't get to want things anymore! I can't move," she said.

"He has me. He finally has what he wants."

"Does he now?"

"He took everything, E'maz. He took my clothes. He took my life. He took away my friends and my kingdom. Now he's going to take my freedom as well."

"Is he now?"

Rhenn hung her head. "I don't want to talk about this, E'maz. I don't know how long I'll have. I want you to ... I want you to talk to me like you once did. Like you did when we were in your dark little house. When we were in your bed."

"And you think I'm not."

"I don't want to talk about N'ssag. If he's won, then let him have his victory. I want this. I want you, to see and feel you one last time. Your love. This may be the last time I even remember you."

"And what about her?" he asked.

Rhenn raised her head, and her gaze went to the swaddled bundle in his arms. She saw the pink flesh of one cheek, but the rest of the baby was obscured from view.

"Our baby," she said in a monotone.

He watched her, didn't say anything.

"That's our baby," she said again.

He nodded.

She felt the ropes acutely now, cutting into her belly, probably hurting the baby.

"I'm sorry," she said.

"Is that what you are?"

"Don't," she said. "Please be kind, E'maz. I can't stand this from you. I don't want this from you."

"Yeah ..." He drew the word out. "I know. But I remember the last time you wanted to kill yourself. Said you were a monster. Said that you were going to kill me, rip out my throat. I didn't tell you what you wanted to hear then, either."

"You said that I hadn't killed you yet. You said I could have, but that I hadn't yet."

"Don't sound like a monster to me."

"Yes …" She recalled the moment, remembered him kissing her, lifting her into his arms, taking her to his bed. "Yes … That's what I want. Tell me more. When I slip away, I want to hear about that …"

"You're not slipping away yet, my love."

"I am. I can feel it."

"You're not done."

"I don't have anything left."

"That the way it is?"

"Look at me!"

"I am."

"E'maz—"

"Where do you think you are?"

"Where … I'm bound and helpless and trapped inside this hell!"

"Inside your mind."

"N'ssag's magical harp has given him control here."

"You know that?"

"Yes."

"Because he told you that?"

"Every time I resist him, every time I fear him or hate him, I grow weaker. He grows stronger."

"Because he told you he would?"

"Look at me!"

"Let me tell you what I see. I see that he convinced you you're bound and helpless. That he's huge and powerful. An' that's what you see."

She stared at him through the sweaty curls of her hair.

"You've never, not once, seen yourself this way. Bound? Helpless?" He chuckled.

"You think *I'm* doing this? He put me here!"

"We're inside your mind, my love. You think anyone else besides you makes the rules here? You say you're trapped inside this place. This hell. But…" he trailed off.

"But what?"

"You pull hope from hell, my love. You always have."

"I don't ... He's using magic to trap me here—"

"Vamreth's coup," E'maz said. "You remember?"

As he said it, it was as though she was there. E'maz didn't vanish, but he faded. Between them she saw a scene from her childhood, the night Vamreth killed her parents. She saw the bloody bodies. She saw herself leading Lorelle through the painting in her father's study, down the spiral stairs to the Thuros Room, to the room with the entrance to the noktum.

"Who decided to go down there? Who pulled both of you into the noktum?" E'maz asked.

"I did," Rhenn murmured.

"And you'd have died, likely. You were just two girls alone in the most dangerous place in the kingdom. But you didn't die. And later, who came up with the idea of creating a rebellion? Who found the first raven totem?"

"I did."

"You built that camp. You created a light in the dark. You pulled those to you who hated Vamreth also, who also wanted a light in the dark."

Rhenn saw the wonderful little camp, the place where she'd begun to feel hope again, where she'd felt joy and camaraderie. She saw herself drinking with her fellows. She saw the dancing, the happiness on the faces of her subjects who had been abused by Vamreth.

"You were outnumbered. Hopeless. But you built hope with your bare hands," he said. "And then you took that kingdom back."

Between them, she saw that basement room again, with the Thuros glowing softly without casting any light. She saw Vamreth standing there, looking smug, with the Helm of Darkness on his head. Oh, he thought he'd had them, trapped behind his new gate with Khyven dying under the relentless magic of the Mavric iron.

But Rhenn had outsmarted him. She'd placed a spy in his organization years ago, and Slayter took that moment to show his true colors. He lost a leg, but he turned the tide. He brought

Rhenn just one step closer, and that was all she'd needed to seize that victory.

"You righted the wrongs, set the world to balance," E'maz said. "And hell came for you again …"

She saw herself in the tub that N'ssag had put her in, deep in the Hepreth Nuraghi. She felt her own death, felt her rebirth. She saw the whole thing again, stabbing him through the chest. Fleeing for her life into E'maz's arms. Again, she saw E'maz kiss her, saw him pick her up and take her to his bed …

"You pulled joy from death," E'maz said.

Now she saw the final battle at the Hepreth Nuraghi in the huge throne room with the V'endannians huddled behind the extravagant, Giant-sized throne, trapped, waiting for death. She saw Khyven leap into action, pulling miracle after miracle from the violence of his sword. She saw Slayter solve the impossible problem, his brilliance lifting him beyond them like wings. She saw the undead army fall. She saw N'ssag flee.

And with the sister of her heart, they chased that villain down, missing him by inches.

"You faced your fears, every one of them," E'maz said.

Now she saw the moment when the noktum rolled over Noksonon, saw herself waiting on the balcony with her friends as the dark approached. She saw them all leaping into action, making the plans that would take them to the protection of Castle Noktos.

"You spun darkness into light," E'maz said. "You led your people when no one else could have."

The harrowing flight from the palace, from the crown city to Castle Noktos, faded. A new image hovered between them, a view of this very room, but from above, like she was looking down on herself and N'ssag from a hole in the ceiling.

She was naked and bound to a chair. N'ssag leaned over her shoulder, caressing her arm, whispering in her ear.

Behind the miniaturized image, E'maz continued speaking in that calm, rumbling voice of his. "Leader. Hope-bringer. Joy-maker. Fear-fighter. Light-bearer. All of this, you are. And you say that this man frightens you? He freezes your blood and takes your will away?"

Her breaths came short and sharp.

"Is that how you want to end it, my love?" E'maz persisted. "Or will you take the darkness and spin it into light once more. One last time."

One of her ropes snapped. It was a small one, the thinnest of the rough ropes that snaked across her waist just below her belly button.

"You are not what he sees," E'maz said. "You are what *you* see. This is not his hell. This is your mind, your will, your cathedral. See it, my love. See it."

"My mind ..." she murmured.

"Don't let him convince you he is the powerful one. You have everything you need. You just have to see it."

She looked down at herself. Bare skin. Flesh cruelly pushed inward by the ropes. Except there was one that had snapped. One. And N'ssag had not done that; it had been E'maz.

Or it had been her.

See it ... E'maz's words echoed in her mind. *Spin it into light.*

Somewhere behind her, she could still hear N'ssag's distant whispers. She pushed them further away and focused on her body.

For a breathless instant, nothing happened. All she could feel was the pain of the ropes. But then a space above her clavicle puckered, then swelled like a welt.

She let out a gasp. She had done that!

She focused again, and her naked flesh began to change. The puckered spot turned into a metal scale. Then the space next to it, overlapping the first. Then the space next to that, and all around it at once.

Scale mail raced over her body like wildfire. It coated her breasts, her belly, her legs and arms. Plate mail shot up from her shoulder, creating shoulder plates like Khyven's armor.

The armor grew beneath the ropes, expanding, pushing outward, and one by one they began to snap.

In seconds, she was fully clothed, armor over her entire body, and a red cape flowed back from her shoulders. N'ssag's murmuring stopped.

The ropes burst. One by one they snapped and flew aside, slapping the floor like whips. Rhenn stood up and kicked the chair back into N'ssag's hulking form. He flinched.

She felt the reassuring weight of her crown settle on her brow. Her sword glimmered, appeared, and gleamed in her hand, a yellow fire along its edge from the light of the window.

The N'ssag monster's eyes widened, and his confidence vanished.

"Sit down!" He pointed his grimy, gnarled, overlarge finger at the upended chair. Except now, he didn't seem as big as he had been before. He almost seemed the same height as her.

"You are my queen," he snarled. "You are my victory!"

With a scream of pure rage, she charged him. He held up one huge hand, intent on grabbing her, the other swinging to bash her to the ground.

But he was a pitiful fighter. She spun, elbowing his clumsy grab out of the way, and then she was inside his guard. She thrust her sword into his chest, just under the rib cage, into his heart.

N'ssag's monstrous eyes bulged. He sucked in a breath, looking down at her in shock and horror.

He gurgled, blood erupting from his mouth, splashing on his chin. "I own you! I own you! I am your king!"

"You're nothing," she growled, twisting the sword.

N'ssag screamed, pain and rage and frustration mingling together on his face. He began to fade, turning into silver mist. Then he was gone.

She turned. The bare wooden room, the chair, the frayed and fallen ropes. Everything faded away.

E'maz, too, was fading. For one excruciating moment, she wanted to stay here. She wanted to stay here with him, where he was still alive.

But he shook his head as though he knew exactly what she

was thinking. The baby faded into silver mist, and E'maz had nothing between her and him. Just his wide, muscled chest in that sleeveless linen tunic.

He smiled again, and this time it wasn't sad. It was warm and wonderful.

"Go, my love. Bring justice," he said.

And then he was gone. Silver mist swirled where he had been.

The room slipped away, whirling around and around, turning to darkness like it had when she'd been brought here. The vertigo took her—

She slammed back into her body. Her real body.

Rhenn opened her eyes.

She was back in Slayter's laboratory, and there was no sunlight. There was no light at all. The noktum ruled again, and only her supernatural sight allowed her to see her enemies.

The two Nox stood close to the table as though they hadn't really believed Rhenn would be docile, despite what their master said.

N'ssag's head was close to hers, his sour breath drifting over her. One of his hands gripped her thigh, the other clenched the stringless harp.

Barely any time had passed here, just like N'ssag had said. Maybe a second. Maybe two.

N'ssag hadn't opened his eyes yet.

The two Nox who stood by the table didn't realize she was awake and alert. She tested one arm, moving it just a little.

The paralysis was gone. She could move.

N'ssag's eyes snapped opened, wide, horrified.

He opened his lips to say the word "No!"

But Rhenn moved faster than he could speak, faster than his bodyguards could react. They were two feet away. They might as well have been at the Usaran palace.

Rhenn lunged upward with all the supernatural speed N'ssag had given her. He turned his head to flee, but he moved like a turtle. His turn succeeded only in baring his neck.

She bit his throat. Her top teeth plunged into his artery, her bottom teeth hooked around his windpipe.

He squeaked in terror.

She chomped down and ripped his throat out. Blood sprayed. N'ssag screamed, but only a gurgling cry rasped out of his open throat. He twitched, half pulling and half falling away from her.

She followed him off the table, bearing him to the ground, one hand curling around his damned harp and the other into his filthy robe. Her feet landed on his soft belly like she was a Kyolar.

The Nox leapt up and over the table and in the last split second before they reached her, she raised her hand and smashed the harp against the ground with every ounce of strength she possessed.

The metal horseshoe snapped, shooting silver sparks and a flare of silver light.

The Nox went limp, one of them so close to her he hit her like a sack of wet flour. It slammed her off the top of N'ssag and sent her tumbling across the flagstones.

She rolled to her feet, ready to fight. She had delivered a killing blow to N'ssag, but that wasn't enough for her. She had delivered a killing blow to him before, and she wasn't going to wait. She wanted to see his eyes glassy and dead before she left this room. She wanted to tear the head from his body, and if that meant fighting these two Nox, then …

But the Nox that had hit her slid limply to the floor and didn't move. The other one, who had leapt atop the table to get to her, slumped to his side and toppled to the floor. He did not rise.

N'ssag's harp sparked and spat silver fire, but it was growing smaller, quieter.

N'ssag howled through his open throat, half crawling, half dragging his body away from her. He grappled with the steel legs of the table and pulled himself along.

There was no one else in the room. Just her, N'ssag, and the two limp Nox.

Rhenn rose to her feet. The coppery fire of N'ssag's vile blood thrummed through her, and she walked slowly toward him.

He gurgled and howled as she stalked him.

She stomped on his ankle, snapping it.

He howled again, rolled onto his back. His eyes shot open so wide it seemed as though they were going to pop out of his head. He held up his hands in a pacifying gesture even as his life's blood pumped onto the floor.

Animal noises burst from him in bubbly gasps. Perhaps he was trying to say her name. Perhaps he was trying to beg for his life.

She showed him her bloody teeth and leapt on him again.

He screamed, a ragged sound scraped up from his soul as she landed on him, pinned him with her feet once more. She plunged her teeth into his neck and ripped out another full mouth of flesh. She slammed her fingers into his head, snapped his neck one way and then the other. Then she tore his head from his body and threw it across the room with a scream.

It hit the wall with a bloody smack and fell to the floor.

Breathing hard, Rhenn looked at the head, eyes glassy and covered in gore.

"I *am* your queen." She spat his blood onto the floor. "And this is your wedding night, you bastard."

CHAPTER THIRTY-FOUR

RHENN

henn looked around the room, and both of the Nox were shaking their heads. She bared her teeth and waited for them to attack.

They didn't.

They blinked, and their eyes took on a series of emotions: bewilderment, shock, then horror.

Rhenn looked down at the broken harp at her feet, then back at the Nox. She had come to think of them as the enemy, but were they any more of an enemy than she would have been if N'ssag had infected her with that harp?

"He used you," she said.

They both looked at her as though seeing her for the first time.

"He made you into slaves. His master, Harkandos, is going to want exactly that all over again. There will be no room for what you wish. Only what he demands."

"Harkandos ... is a Lord of the Dark."

Rhenn nodded. "Yes. He is. And he is going to enslave you."

They looked at each other.

"If that is what you want, then come for me."

They watched her intently, looked at each other, then back at her.

"But Lorelle told me what happened to you," she continued. "One of your Lords of the Dark, Tovos, yoked you and betrayed you. He killed your Glimmerblade Zaith and unleashed a dragon on every last one of your people. A true leader rewards fealty with protection and glory, not betrayal and death. He doesn't crush you under heel."

"The Nox serve the Lords of the Dark," one of them said.

"And how many of them will you serve? How many before you finally see what they are? How many more Nox will die before you stop throwing your lives under their boot heels?"

They said nothing.

She held out her hand. "Come with me. Fight for me, and you'll see what glory and honor really feels like."

They hesitated.

"Throw off their yoke," she whispered. "This is the moment. Now. There will not be another."

They looked at each other again, then both bowed their heads.

"Yes," the first said.

"We will fight," said the second.

"Good," she said. "We will make an end to Harkandos and any other Lords of the Dark who would throw away the lives of Nox or Usarans."

"The others will be confused," the first Nox said. "The harp was … heavy on our minds. They will not know what to do."

Rhenn spotted her sword, its red ruby at its pommel glowing softly, in the corner of the room. N'ssag had unsheathed it and leaned it against the wall, point down on a wooden table like some kind of trophy. The sheath lay on the table beside it.

She crossed to it, picked up the sword, and slashed it in the air before herself once … twice, then smiled. "Let's go give them guidance."

"They will be at the feasting room," the first said.

Rhenn turned and led them to the doorway—

And saw the figure just as she entered the hallway. It moved quickly behind a sculpture.

It was too small to be a Giant, and it wasn't a Nox. That person had light hair. It had to be a Usaran. How had they made their way up here?

"You are safe," Rhenn said softly. "I won't harm you."

The figure stepped from the cover of the sculpture.

"L'elica!"

She wore a small smile and was shaking her head. "Your mage is something else," she said.

"You've seen Slayter?"

"He's ... planning something."

Rhenn felt like grinning. For the first time since Khyven had died, she felt a ray of hope. If Slayter was planning, then almost anything was possible.

"He does that," Rhenn said.

"He told me to find you," L'elica said. "I ... thought he was insane. I thought there was no way I'd find you up here, alive."

"He has a knack for that as well."

"I was supposed to free you."

"You may have to settle for assisting me."

"I was more looking forward to that."

"Let's stick a thorn in Harkandos's side," Rhenn said.

L'elica nodded. "N'ssag?"

Rhenn's smiled faded. "He won't be bothering you or anyone else ever again."

"He is dead?"

Rhenn nodded.

L'elica looked toward the room, as though she wanted to go see for herself, then turned back to Rhenn.

"Let's help Slayter by wreaking havoc," Rhenn said. "Whatever he's planning, I'm sure it could benefit from a little mayhem. Want to start a revolution?"

"Lead the way," L'elica said, and then, "My queen."

Rhenn raised her head, surprised, and met L'elica's gaze. Rhenn nodded solemnly. "Follow me."

They flitted from corner to corner, statue to statue, staying to servant's entrances and corridors as they made their way. Rhenn had memorized the castle by the third day they'd relocated here. She had known war was coming, perhaps not this fast, but coming. Knowing the battlefield had been her top priority.

She chose the way that would be the least likely to run into a Giant or a Troll.

She did not avoid the areas where she might run into Nox, though, and by the time they reached the feasting room, her little following had picked up more than a dozen Nox.

Rhenn had convinced Teleth—one of the two original Nox from Slayter's laboratory—to run quietly through the castle and find any other Nox, and bring them to the edge of the raven totem hall, which was where she was headed next.

In the feasting hall it was, surprisingly, less difficult than she thought to turn the Nox away from killing the Humans. She had worried that pulling them away from their feast would mean a fight, but they were just as befuddled, shocked, and horrified as the rest had been. When they awoke to what they were doing, they weren't exactly repentant—after all, what was the life of a Human to a Nox?—but they were particularly interested in getting revenge.

It was harder convincing the Humans to join the newly made Nox army. She explained to them that the Nox had been mind controlled, but that did nothing to convince her people. They'd just seen the Nox drink the blood of their loved ones, killing and feasting. The feasting room was littered with corpses the Nox had left on the ground—some of who Rhenn recognized. It was hard not to think of revenge on the Nox, rather than on some Giant who had put them up to it.

Rhenn tried a different tack.

She stepped up on a wooden barrel that stood close to the center of the room.

"You have had to endure a horror so foul it bends the mind. It seems insanity is the only path forward. Perhaps what you see is only despair, rage, revenge, that there is nothing that can possibly make this right again." She bowed her head, paused for two heartbeats, then looked up again. "And you are correct. Nothing ever can. But I ask you to look at this carnage. Look at all of the dead bodies. These were people you knew. Some of whom you loved."

She waited a moment for their shocked expressions to turn to her. Then she spoke.

"But you may have a loved one who is *not* in this room. Perhaps you have a family member that had the luck to be in the other room where Harkandos is keeping our people. The safe room. For now, at least. Now look at them again." She gestured to the bodies. "Imagine this is everyone. Not just those in this room, but all those in the safe room."

Again she paused.

"Usara stands on a knife's edge. If you do not fight now— *right* now—there will *be* no Usara. There will be no Human civilization anywhere on Noksonon. Everyone you love— everyone that any Human has *ever* loved—will be dead. Or they will be in shackles so heavy they will never take a free breath again. Neither will their children. Or their children's children. Or any Human who will come after."

Silence fell throughout the room.

"Now," she said. "If you can walk, come with me now. If you can pick up a sword, a knife, a stick, a stone, or just ball up your fists, come with me now. We have only the slimmest chance to turn this battle around, and I will need each and every one of you. Come with me now and let's show this Giant that he is not our master."

Rhenn leapt off the barrel and strode to the door.

Every single person followed.

CHAPTER THIRTY-FIVE

VOHN

The other Giants and captains of Harkandos's court filed out of the meeting room. Harkandos stood, towering over Vohn, three times his height.

"Go back to your room, Vohn Fenlux. You may sleep. You may eat. The Nox will escort you," Harkandos said.

"Where are you going?"

"And remember ..." Harkandos ignored the question. "If you remove that ring, I will grab you back from the Dark. It will cost you your hand, and you'll be right back here again." He moved through the door, and was gone.

Vohn hesitated, his body cold from the threat, then started after—

There was a slight sound behind him, the whisper of a breeze in the open curtains—

Then a vomiting sound.

Vohn spun. Slayter, with his hands on his knees and bile dripping from his mouth, stood in the room. He raised his head up, looking ill, and motioned with one hand.

Vohn was so gobsmacked he almost hesitated, then he lunged toward Slayter. In his other hand, Slayter held a clay disk. It was already glowing. He snapped it neatly in half and tossed the pieces onto the floor.

Wild orange and red lights flared. Noise burst from it like the blaring of trumpets. Vohn averted his eyes. A wall of popping, colorful fire danced between them and the door.

Slayter awkwardly wrapped his arms around Vohn. The cloak followed—

Suddenly they were constricting, sliding down tunnels that were far too small for them.

Vohn felt like his insides were being squeezed out.

Then they were standing in a field. Charcoal gray grass stretched out before them for hundreds of yards before stopping at the edge of the forest. Vohn staggered, and his stomach flip-flopped.

Slayter dry heaved behind him.

Vohn managed to get his nausea under control, but he leaned over, hands on knees, just in case. Through watery eyes, he looked up at his surroundings.

He knew this place. This was the field between Castle Noktos and the tunnel that led into the Night Ring.

He spun around. Castle Noktos loomed behind them.

They were only a hundred feet from the wall!

"This is where you bring us?" Vohn demanded. "That cloak could have taken us all the way to Demaijos, and you bring us here? What kind of a rescue is this?"

Slayter held up a hand as he took a drink from a wineskin. He swished the liquid, then spat it on the ground.

"Not a rescue," he finally said. "We're going to fight Jai'ketakos."

"We're *what*?"

"More to the point, we're going to kill him. This is where he dies."

Vohn looked around, but there was no dragon. "Slayter, Harkandos is going to chase me. He's going to find me. He swore he would."

Slayter shook his head. "Nope. We lost him."

"You can't know that—"

"I felt him reach for us. He missed. Flash-crack."

"Flash-crack? Is that what you set off in the meeting room?"

"It's loud. It's drenched in magic. He sensed the cloak, but when he reached for us, he grabbed the flash-crack. Much larger, much louder, much meatier usage of magic. Tiring, but worth it."

Now that Slayter mentioned it, Vohn looked closely at his friend. He was dead on his feet.

"And now you're going to fight Jai'ketakos?"

Slayter shook his head. "I've done the calculations. I can't beat him."

"Didn't you already beat him twice?"

"Oh, the verbal game? Yes. But that was only once."

"But at Wheskone Keep—"

"Khyven beat him. Khyven and the Sword of Noksonon. We don't have that this time. And Jai'ketakos will not permit another battle of words. I caught him off guard that first time. I won't catch him twice. But he won't be ready for you."

"Me?"

"Nhevalos left breadcrumbs for himself to follow. Except if I look hard enough, I can see them."

"Breadcrumbs …? Wait, where are we? What is this place?" Vohn asked. There was nothing here but exposed dirt, charcoal grass, and a pile of what looked like more dirt ten feet to their left. Some giant ant hill.

"I put this together yesterday." Slayter turned, looking at Vohn with those lighted eyes that meant he was feeling particularly excited about his idea. He beckoned, holding out a hand, then turned back to the dark ant hill.

"Tell. Me. What. Is. Happening," Vohn stated, trying to keep the ire out of his voice and failing.

"Yes. Of course. It's …" He paused, raised his head and looked at the horizon behind Vohn, as though seeing something playing out. "No. Actually, no. It would be better if … Yes. If you didn't … Yes, exactly."

Vohn wanted to smack him upside the head. He hated it when Slayter only spoke in half sentences.

"Slayter—"

"There isn't time." He turned and reached for Vohn's hand, then realized Vohn wasn't standing next to him like he'd beckoned him to do. He beckoned again.

Grinding the inside of his cheek with his teeth, Vohn stomped forward.

"You stand here," Slayter said, pointing to the big ant hill.

"Why?"

Slayter grabbed his hands, held them, and looked Vohn in the eyes. "Do you trust me?"

Do I trust you, Vohn thought. *Do I trust you …?*

Vohn leaned forward and pressed his forehead to Slayter's. He did it long enough so that Slayer would understand the full impact of his reply to that silly question. Vohn turned his head and kissed Slayter on the cheek.

"Forever," Vohn murmured.

He half-expected Slayter to pull back from the contact. The mage had never seemed wholly comfortable with other people touching him. But as always, he did not respond the way another person might. If there was one consistent thing about Slayter, it was that he rarely responded to expectation.

Instead of withdrawing, Slayter paused, head cocked. He reached up and touched Vohn's cheek softly, contemplatively, then smiled.

"Well …" He blinked. "That is something we shall have to devote a moment's attention to."

"Is it?" Vohn said, his smile widening.

"Well, I was going to tell you to answer my question quickly, as we don't have a moment to spare. To your credit, that was a quick answer. But in the wake of it—"

"We can talk later," Vohn said.

"Yes." Slayter hesitated. "Yes … Well, yes. That would be

good, I think."

"Tell me what to do, Slayter."

"Stand here. When the dragon comes, stand in front of that pile."

"Why?"

"If I tell you, this may not work. In fact, I'm almost positive it won't. Jai'ketakos will guess."

Vohn's annoyance flared again. "So I'm supposed to just stand here. And then I'm supposed to die?"

"No. He's going to die."

"I stand here, get flamed, and *he's* going to die."

"Most likely."

"Most *likely*?"

"Well, you should probably talk to him."

"And say what?"

"Delay him."

"How?"

"Just …" Slayter pondered a moment. "Oh! Ask him about a crossroads."

"What?"

"That will trigger his narrative. I think he'll practically be forced to give you a choice."

"And what do I choose?"

"It doesn't matter. His narrative is just a mechanism to give him permission to kill you."

"Oh fantastic," Vohn drawled.

"Or to hurt you. He likes dealing pain more than killing. Death is simply an adequate substitute."

"Slayter—"

"But it won't get that far."

"No?"

"I'm almost positive it won't get that far."

"Almost?"

He glanced down at a red stone, bordered in intricate gold filagree, in his hand. Vohn thought he'd seen Slayter playing with that stone before the Giant war had come to their gates. The red stone was glowing like a coal. It looked hot, but Slayter held it in a bare palm. "I have to run now, or none of this works. If he sees me, we both die. And everyone else will die. And—"

"I get the point."

"I'll be right behind the wall."

"Why won't he head straight for the castle?"

"You'll fire the lightning rod at him."

"You didn't say that."

"Didn't I? Fire the lightning rod at him."

"You were going to run off without telling me that?"

"I forgot."

"Is there anything else you're forgetting?"

"No." He began limping toward the wall.

"You're sure?" he called after him.

"No."

"Slayter!"

"Ask about the crossroads!" he shouted over his shoulder. "And don't be so loud!"

Vohn turned back to where Slayter had been staring at the horizon. His heart hammered in his chest.

Slayter awkwardly bear-walked up the slope through the twisted wrought-iron and disappeared behind the wall.

"This is how I die," Vohn murmured to himself. "This is how I finally die."

He looked to the skies. Left. Right. Behind him. In front of—

A black form dropped down, suddenly appearing against the dark ceiling of the noktum a hundred feet away. A huge, black-winged form.

Slayter was right. Jai'ketakos had come.

CHAPTER THIRTY-SIX

VOHN

T he dragon swooped low, gaining speed as he headed toward the castle.

"This is the dumbest thing I've ever done," Vohn muttered under his breath. He held up the lightning rod Slayter had given him and triggered it.

But Jai'ketakos's head turned the moment Vohn muttered as though, despite being a hundred feet in the air and moving at the speed of a catapult stone, the dragon could hear a quiet voice from the ground.

The crackling spear of lightning shot out, lancing through the dark toward the dragon, tendrils of light jaggedly arcing around the main stream like it was fighting itself.

Fire shot from the dragon's mouth as he reared.

The lightning missed by inches, shooting into the ceiling of the noktum and vanishing. The dragon dropped low, completing a spiral around the deadly lightning.

The bright light vanished. The dragon shot past Vohn, its dark black body made it impossible to see against the eternal night.

The after image of the lightning pulsed in Vohn's vision. He blinked furiously, peering up, trying to see. He caught a glimpse of a tail whipping, and he focused on that spot. He caught the dragon wheeling in the sky, turning back toward him.

You better be right, Slayter. By Senji, you'd better be—

Jai'ketakos swelled to enormous size as he approached. Terror gripped Vohn. He suddenly relived the panicked flight through the castle with Shalure. No nightmare could have been as scary, and now Vohn was standing in the open with nothing to protect him except Slayter's words.

At the last second, Vohn remembered what Slayter had said.

Wherever the dragon comes from, stand in front of the pile ...

He reluctantly ran toward the dragon—who ran *toward* a dragon?—and placed himself between the mysterious pile and his oncoming death. What was it, anyway? It looked like dirt. Was it some undiscovered magic in the dirt of the noktum plain?

Black wings flared. Red fire glowed in the dragon's mouth, and it plopped down right in front of Vohn. Its great body rose three stories in the air, culminating in the sinuous neck and that enormous horned head.

"Well, well, well," Jai'ketakos said. "It appears as though you have nowhere to hide this time, little Shadowvar. No tunnels to run down."

"I-I'm not running from you this time," Vohn said, hating the stammer in his voice. He realized that he wasn't quite in front of the pile, and he shifted.

He was so bad at this. What was he even doing here? This was Khyven's job! This was what people like Khyven and Rhenn did. Vohn was supposed to be in a library poring over books, damn it. This was simply ridiculous!

"Where is your friend? Where is Slayter the Mage?" the dragon asked, his yellow gaze flicking left and right. "The stink of his magic wafts from you. That little toy ... And the paltry protection spell around you."

Protection spell?

"He went to face a greater threat," Vohn said, making it up on the spot.

Jai'ketakos's eyes went flat, but he gave a smoky chuckle. "A greater threat …."

"He sent me instead."

"Then I'll send you along to hell." Jai'ketakos drew a deep breath.

"Wait!" Vohn said. "You and I have come to a—"

The dragon's head dropped low and fire burst from his mouth. Vohn spun away as it engulfed him. He screamed and—

It didn't hurt!

… paltry protection spell around you …

Vohn uncoiled from his full-body flinch and opened his eyes. Fire raged all around him, but it felt like a cool breeze over his arms and face.

The fire lessened and then stopped as the dragon reached the end of his breath. Vohn patted himself. He was still alive!

Slayter!

"Well, well, well…" Jai'ketakos said. "The mage has been advancing his skills. That is better than his last fire protection spell. But it will only be a matter of time." He drew another breath.

"We are at a crossroads!" Vohn shouted.

The dragon paused, then exhaled, but no fire came with it this time. Vohn could see the war on the dragon's face. The raised chin. The narrowed eyes. The flared nostrils.

"He thinks to mock me," the dragon murmured to himself, and he shook his horned head. "He thinks to trick me again."

"A crossroads!" Vohn said, but it didn't seem to be working. Internally, he cursed Slayter and his "I can't tell you" plan.

Jai'ketakos breathed deep and spat fire again.

It engulfed Vohn and, despite himself, he threw his arms up again and crouched. He still didn't die, but the wind that flowed around him wasn't cool this time. This time it felt like a warm spring breeze.

"When one stands at a crossroads," Vohn shouted. "One

must make a choice—"

"This crossroads is for me, morsel. And I've made my choice." Jai'ketakos blew fire again.

Vohn turned away, and this time, it was a hot summer breeze. The spell was fading. By Grina, Slayter, *do* something!

The supposedly important pile behind him had been blown over, scattered, and Vohn realized abruptly that it wasn't dirt after all, but ash. Slayter's big magic dirt was nothing but a pile of ash, and now it had been blown over the field again. The heat of the fire must be terrible outside of Slayter's spell. The charcoal grass had been incinerated, the ground blasted clean. Even the ashes were glowing.

"One more," Jai'ketakos said as Vohn turned back, looking with wide eyes up at the monster. "Perhaps two. Are you going to run this time, Vohn the morsel? You see now, I think. Your friend sent you to die. And I will find him after. I can smell him on you. He is close, I think ..."

The dragon drew another breath, and Vohn knew that this time, the heat would be more than he could stand. Slayter's plan, whatever it was, had failed.

Jai'ketakos stopped, and his head retreated, neck curling like a question mark as he reared up. His eyes widened at Vohn in fear.

"No ..."

Vohn glanced down at his hands, as though something might have appeared in them to make the dragon recoil, then he noticed a purplish glow, but it wasn't coming from his hands. It wasn't coming from him at all.

Vohn spun—

And gaped.

The glowing ashes had pushed together into a pile again, except they had ... grown. They rose up ... up ... into the shape of something massive. Vohn's jaw dropped open as the glowing purple ashes lifted, attaching to themselves like drifting autumn leaves that were falling upward. They touched, stuck to each other, and formed into the shape of ...

An enormous raven.

CHAPTER THIRTY-SEVEN

VOHN

G rina's Quill ..." Vohn murmured.

The giant raven's head formed as though emerging from an oily pool. His sharp beak, his glistening black eyes, his midnight black wings all came forth from the dark. The transformation swept down from his head, and the raven had changed. He was no longer entirely black. The raven had never been anything but inky black like the noktum itself; he'd never possessed even a dark gray feather.

But as the transformation of ash-to-living body slid down his neck to his shoulders, colors began to emerge. A light lavender started at the tips of his feathers at the shoulder. His body remained the deepest black, but that lavender transformed his wings to mauve and then dark purple as it reached the tips of his feathers. And those colors were noktum flame, as though the oranges and reds of a real fire could never be born in this place.

"Rauvelos!" Jai'ketakos said.

"You were saying?" Rauvelos said as though he'd been part of this conversation from the beginning, as though he'd never died and come back to life.

Rauvelos's body shivered as the transformation finished at his black, steel-like talons, but his implacable glare remained focused on the dragon.

"What?" Jai'ketakos blurted.

"Your crossroads. Your decision," Rauvelos clarified.

"The crossroads ... It's for ... This isn't about you," Jai'ketakos said. "Not ... about us. Harkandos has returned!"

"And his return is supposed to instill fear? Loyalty? Perhaps a feeling that the continent's destiny has arrived?"

"It *has* arrived!"

"Oh, I know this more than you could possibly comprehend, Little Prisoner. Harkandos returned because *you* freed him. You freed him because I led you by the nose to it, by your sniveling little nose."

Jai'ketakos recoiled, his head pulling back on its long neck. "No ..."

"I know what side I'm on, Little Prisoner. I've always known. You, on the other wing, are running scared. And it is delicious to hear the fear in your voice, to hear how Nhevalos's mastery now grips you."

Jai'ketakos lowered his head, flame flickering in his nostrils.

"And the Human Slayter as well. He has set you up again? That makes thrice, I think."

"I killed you once, bird. I'll do it again. And I will make sure there are no ashes to resurrect you this time."

"Except you didn't really kill me, did you? I just let you *believe* you did. You blundered along in the shadow of your betters without ever realizing that they towered over you."

"Are you going to talk me to death?" Jai'ketakos snarled.

"Oh, I would be delighted to lash you with a recitation of your moronic choices. Is it joyous working with Harkandos? Is he the soft-handed master you craved? Did he free you of your prison for good? Or do you begin to see why Nhevalos dungeon-whipped him into submission in the first place."

"He will kill you for saying that. You're—"

"I do not fear your master, lackey. And I don't fear death." Rauvelos lowered his head, his deadly beak pointing directly at the ground. His alien eyes seemed to pin the dragon like a butterfly to a board. "But you ... You stink of fear, Little Prisoner."

"This is all wrong." Jai'ketakos's wings shifted on his back. His feet shuffled to the side. "You and I ... We should be working together. Very well. You are correct about Harkandos. He is thoroughly mad. And if he succeeds in taking Noksonon, we will all suffer. We will all live under his fist."

"Ah ... Now we come to it. Betrayal is the last refuge of the coward. You shall find no ally here, dragon. Make your move."

"I don't want to fight you."

The edges of the raven's beak turned upward and he spoke softly. "I wouldn't want to fight me either."

Vohn didn't see what happened next. Both behemoths moved so fast twin gusts of wind blew Vohn upward, forward, then backward, spinning him about like he was caught in a miniature tornado, and then dropping him onto his belly.

The impact stole his breath and for a second he just lay there on his face until his lungs started working again. He sucked in a life-giving gasp and rolled over onto his back.

Purple and orange-red flames blasted across the sky. It was like a repeat of that first cataclysmic battle between these two, but this time, it was Jai'ketakos who fled. He was trying to wing his way to the horizon, and it was Rauvelos who kept cutting him off.

The dragon was overmatched in maneuverability, just as he'd been in the first fight, but this time he wasn't the attacker, and that made all the difference.

Jai'ketakos climbed toward the ceiling of the noktum, desperately trying to get beyond its reach. Jai'ketakos was at ease in the Dark, but the noktum was Rauvelos's realm. He was master here.

Rauvelos climbed faster, rose overhead, then dove down on the dragon. His sword-like beak speared Jai'ketakos in the shoulder, and the great beast jolted and plummeted as his wing folded. He recovered somewhat, frantically trying to stop his fall, but he recovered only just before he hit the ground. A rage of fire erupted from his mouth as his wings flared, saving him from the crash. The flames blasted the ground, roiling out toward Vohn.

"Oh hell ..." Vohn suddenly realized that he was in a very bad place to be a spectator. Those flames were going to incinerate him. Frantically, he scrambled backward on his butt like a crab—

A hand gripped his shoulder and orange light crackled past his head, forming a shield in front of his scrabbling feet.

The raging flames ripped past, and Vohn didn't die.

"Slayter!" He looked up at the white chin of his friend. Slayter's eyes were narrow in concentration and crumbles of a clay disk fell from his glowing orange fist.

"Well ..." Slayter grunted. "*That* worked."

Ahead of them, Jai'ketakos skimmed the ground, already hundreds of feet away.

Rauvelos dropped from the sky like a stone and stabbed his beak into the dragon's back. The raven's great talons raked next, sending blood and scales flying into the sky.

"Gods!" Vohn winced at the brutality.

Jai'ketakos screamed, spinning upside down. He was so close to the ground that he scraped the giant raven off.

Rauvelos shrieked, tumbled across the charcoal grass, wings flailing.

Jai'ketakos flapped hard, rising up over the tangled bird. He opened his mouth and his killing flame erupted again, immolating Rauvelos just as it had done before.

The flames rushed toward Vohn's and Slayter's direction again.

"Well, yes. That worked quite well," Slayter continued. "But this is my last of these."

He pulled another clay disk from his cylinder, held it up. It glowed orange and he snapped it just as the flames reached them.

Vohn shouted as the searing fire hit—

And turned cool.

"I don't think we should stay here," Slayter said, sweat dripping down his face.

"That's the first thing you've said that makes any damned sense!" Vohn shouted, clambering to his feet. Together, he and Slayter ran toward the wall and the mangled gates.

Slayter hobbled, hampered not only by his prosthetic leg, but also by the fact that he kept looking over his shoulder. They reached the rubble and the gates, and Slayter stopped, breathing hard.

"I have to look," he said. "We will never see anything like this again."

"Slayter!" Vohn shouted.

The incinerating red storm around Rauvelos died down. Vohn expected to see the raven's corpse reduced to a pile of ash again.

But Rauvelos rose from the conflagration. Orange and red flames flickered and faded away, and purple flames rose to take their place. The giant raven's wings were now made of noktum fire, dark purples all the way to his torso and halfway up his head.

Rauvelos laughed.

Jai'ketakos shot flame again, even more than the last time. It engulfed the raven again.

Vohn winced, turned to start up the pile of debris to get behind the wall, but Slayter put a hand on his arm.

"No wait. We're far enough away now. It's all right."

Vohn hesitated, then was caught by the spectacle like Slayter.

The flames died away, and Rauvelos still stood, a burning pillar of purple fire. It seemed that all the rage and power that the dragon had put into its flame had turned into power for the raven.

"Nhevalos has seen you for centuries, Little Prisoner," Rauvelos said. "What you thought was your own free will was but a script given to you by my master. And you moved with perfect ignorance. I am the noktum phoenix, born again from the very power that destroys me."

"Die, bird!" The dragon shot flames again. Again, Rauvelos absorbed them.

"Your flames brought me back to life," he continued as the orange flames swirled and flared into purple flames. "Your fire is a part of me now. That is how I work. That is the gift of the noktum phoenix. Your greatest weapon is now my greatest weapon."

Jai'ketakos flapped furiously backward.

Rauvelos cawed and leapt after the dragon.

"No!" Jai'ketakos said. "We should work together. I can help you defeat Harkandos!"

"You were not chosen to defeat Harkandos. You were chosen to die here."

"Fool! I can add my power to yours. Let me help you!"

"You have nothing I need." Rauvelos smiled. "Not anymore."

The noktum phoenix flapped high again, outdistancing the dragon, then dove, pointing his flaming wingtips directly at Jai'ketakos. Purple fire shot forth, striking the dragon between his wings, and Jai'ketakos screamed.

He spiraled toward the ground again. He did not pull up in time, and he slammed into the trees. Trunks and bones snapped.

Thrashing in rage and throwing fire, Jai'ketakos slithered out of the flaming trees. The scales of his chest smoked from Rauvelos's blast, but the dragon seemed ferocious despite it all.

He roared up at Rauvelos. "Come for me, bird! Come for me, then!"

Rauvelos dove, talons extended. Jai'ketakos jumped to meet him, then twisted out of the way. One of Rauvelos's talons caught the dragon's wing, but both of the dragon's claws sank into the phoenix's body. Jai'ketakos spun around and slammed Rauvelos into the ground.

"No!" Vohn said as he saw the bird's body crumple. Slayter's hand gripped Vohn's shoulder. Vohn glanced back quickly. "If he kills Rauvelos, he'll come for us."

"Yes," Slayter said.

"Well, he'll kill us!"

"That is true."

"Then why are you calm about it!" Vohn practically shouted.

"You shouldn't shout. Someone might come."

"Like a dragon, you mean?" Vohn shouted.

"Would it help to panic?"

"We can't afford for Rauvelos to lose!"

"No."

"Slayter—"

"Rauvelos knows what he is doing."

"He does?"

"If anyone does, he does."

"If anyone ... That doesn't mean anything! He's getting slammed and broken. I don't think that's part of his plan!"

"Watch."

Vohn turned back to the battle. Jai'ketakos pounced on Rauvelos. Clearly, the sky was Rauvelos's territory, not the earth, and Vohn now saw that the dragon had lured him down where greater size and weight were the advantages.

At this distance, it was difficult to see the carnage, but the dragon seemed to have pinned Rauvelos down. Jai'ketakos's head rose and fell as he ravaged the bird.

Purple flame exploded, and Vohn winced at the brightness, shielding his eyes. By the time he blinked through the dark spots in his vision, he saw Jai'ketakos on his back, his entire body smoking. The dragon rolled to his feet again, slowly this time.

Rauvelos emerged from the burning purple. The feathers at the side of his neck had been yanked out, revealing a bleeding wound made by dragon's teeth.

"If that was your best," Rauvelos said. "I suggest you run."

"F-Fool ..." Jai'ketakos said.

Rauvelos lifted his wings and began running at Jai'ketakos, talons stepping high in an awkward bird stride as he picked up speed.

Jai'ketakos leapt into the air, wings flapping. Rauvelos murmured something, and the dragon's left wing snapped. The dragon screamed and fell heavily back to the earth.

"You wanted to be on the ground," Rauvelos said. His run was now almost comical, his thin legs almost a blur. "Let's stay on the ground."

Jai'ketakos clenched one claw, and the earth shuddered, rippling like a wave beneath Rauvelos.

"Such raw power," Slayter marveled.

Rauvelos leapt high, fanning out one wing. It caught the air and spun him in a circle like a spiral seed. It was just enough to get him past the wave of earth.

He landed in front of Jai'ketakos and dove beak-first. The dragon's serpentine head coiled around the attack, and the beak missed.

The dragon screamed.

No, wait. The strike hadn't missed. Rauvelos hadn't been aiming for the dragon's head.

Rauvelos jerked his head free, his bloody beak sliding out of the hip joint between Jai'ketakos's leg and his body. The dragon scrabbled backward, but his back left leg dragged, useless. Rauvelos jumped again.

The dead leg threw the dragon's timing off, and though he tried to meet the raven's charge, he was too slow. His jaws snapped tail feathers as Rauvelos speared the dragon again, this time in the belly.

Blood spurted all over Rauvelos's head, and he pulled his sword-like beak out a second time. Desperate, the dragon clawed at the phoenix's neck, but clearly Rauvelos's skin was not normal skin. Had it been a regular bird, those claws would have shredded him.

Rauvelos grunted, brought his good wing around and jammed it in the wound he'd made in Jai'ketakos's belly.

"No! I can help you!"

"This is how you help me, Little Prisoner."

Purple flames erupted from Rauvelos's wing. Jai'ketakos screamed, but it was lost in the roar of the terrible fire.

Vohn had to shield his eyes from the blast, and when he could finally look again, there was only purple smoke in a fifty-foot radius around the two combatants.

"Senji's Braid …" Slayter murmured.

"What? What happened?" Vohn asked.

Slayter limped down the rubble and started toward the smoke.

"We shouldn't go over there," Vohn said.

"I have to see," Slayter murmured, his hand ruffling through his disks, coming up with a blank one. His metal scraper appeared in his other hand.

"This is foolhardy," Vohn protested. "What if Jai'ketakos won?"

But Slayter didn't listen. He limp-jogged toward the combatants. Whatever had happened, whoever had won, it was over. No more crashes or roars or explosions issued forth from the smoke.

As they neared, the smoke drifted away, revealing the hazy silhouette of the victor.

Rauvelos stood over the mangled corpse of the dragon as smoke clung to him like thin purple banners in a breeze.

Slayter scratched hastily on the disk, nearly tripping as he rushed to reach the noktum phoenix and finish his spell at the same time. Vohn trailed him helplessly, feeling once again as though everyone was insane but him.

Slayter finally stopped at the edge of the carnage, at the remains of the great black dragon. Clawed limbs, tattered leathery wings, and strips of scaly flesh lay in every direction, as though the dragon had erupted from the inside out. Blood splattered everywhere.

The air smelled like hot copper and burnt steak. Vohn wrinkled his nose.

Slayter scraped the last line on his spell, drew a deep breath and held it aloft. Orange light glowed from the sigil, and he snapped it in two. The orange light shot outward like festive streamers, lacing throughout the smoke, touching the corpse lightly, spinning around the immobile Rauvelos.

"Yes, yes ..." Slayter nodded as though he was reading a book that had illuminated some obscure concept. "Yes, I see."

The noktum phoenix shifted and turned. Purple flames licked up his wings, and his beak—bloody red right up to his eyes—swiveled around to point at them.

"Ah," he said. "Well done, mage."

"Jai'ketakos was primarily a Land Mage, wasn't he?" Slayter blurted, rubbing his fingers together as though that would help him absorb the knowledge of whatever spell he'd just cast. "I didn't see him use anything else. Was he using other paths of magic and I just couldn't detect it? Why not try a Love Magic spell? Or try to sap your strength with Life Magic? It was almost all fire, except right at the end there. Do Giants have certain magic streams they prefer?"

"You ... never stop, mage." Rauvelos huffed. "You will need that ... in the moments to come."

"I thought it might be a weakness of the Giants that we could exploit." Slayter paused, raised his index finger. "No offense."

"Indeed."

"Of course." Slayter cocked his head. "The level of power you both used ... With five streams or one, I hardly think we could match it unless we were to use the—"

"Slayter," Vohn interrupted, holding up a hand to silence Slayter's babble. Rauvelos wasn't doing well, and as usual Slayter hadn't noticed. Vohn watched their savior. Large wounds had been rent down his chest. The bite on his neck was more grisly than Vohn had originally thought, and the phoenix's head leaned to the side as though he couldn't fully hold it upright. Rauvelos wheezed like he couldn't get enough breath.

"Rauvelos ..." Vohn said. "Are you—"

"I am victorious," Rauvelos said.

"I can heal you," Slayter said, rifling through his cylinder.

Rauvelos whipped out a wing. The enormous thing looked like it was going to slap Slayter to the moon, but it only created a small gust that drove Slayter's hand away from his cylinder of spells.

"Save your magic, mage." He nodded at the mutilated body of the dragon. "This sad soul gave me plenty enough to use."

Purple fire flared around the noktum phoenix, starting at his wings and swirling around his entire body. The terrible wounds he'd sustained glowed dark purple. The tornado of lavender and purple fire surrounded him—

Then winked out.

Rauvelos stood before them. His wounds were healed. Even his feathers seemed perfectly ordered as though he had just preened.

The purple light bordering his feathers and his wings dimmed, though.

"Much better," Rauvelos said.

"Wow," Slayter said.

Vohn glanced nervously back at the castle, which was eerily quiet. "There's no way Harkandos didn't notice this fight. He'll be coming." Vohn half expected to see a Nox army boiling out of the front gates.

"The Shadowvar is right," Rauvelos said.

"That is a good point," Slayter said, also looking back at the castle. "A very good point. Why hasn't he?"

"We have entered the endgame, my mortal friends," Rauvelos said. "Very little is predictable now."

"Did he say mortal or morsel?" Vohn murmured to Slayter under his breath.

The noktum phoenix angled his eye toward Vohn, and the corners of his beak turned up.

"We must take the field one last time. For better or worse, the final act is upon us …"

CHAPTER THIRTY-EIGHT
NHEVALOS

Nhevalos emerged from the noktum cloak. He flicked it open, and Elegathe spun out, stumbling into the nearest stone pillar and throwing her hands up to catch her balance. A bit of dust sifted down from where she slapped them against the stone.

No one had lived in this ancient nuraghi in more than a millennia. There were a number of similar old structures all over Usara, all over Noksonon, remnants of an age when the Eldroi ruled, remnants of the order that Nhevalos had shattered.

His great accomplishment was supposed to have come full circle today. Its completion was supposed to have ended with Khyven, but Harkandos had slipped the noose by doing the one thing Nhevalos hadn't expected: by using his brain.

Nhevalos now remembered the spell Harkandos had invented. It had been so long ago that Nhevalos had forgotten completely about it. Harkandos had created a broken, mirror image of a mortal. He'd only tried three times, because each result had been so imperfect, so flawed, that it hadn't been worth the time or magical power required to do it. If Harkandos wanted another species, it was far more efficient to simply adjust an existing species—modify a Human, Luminent, Shadowvar or any of the races—and let them procreate if he wanted more mortals. And that was what Harkandos, in fact, did. He'd abandoned that project.

Back then, Nhevalos hadn't imagined there would come a time where recreating one specific mortal would be so important. That had been short sighted.

He hadn't been prepared for it, hadn't been looking for it. And the *kairoi* had indicated nothing. That in itself was unsettling, to say the least. It had shaken Nhevalos. A thousand years of certainties had been dashed on the rocks. He had studied the *kairoi*, come to rely on them, then suddenly they were wrong. All of them, wrong.

"We must move fast," he said to Elegathe, who glared at him, clinging to the pillar as though he'd pushed her into it. "Once again, I will need you as my Human agent."

"To do what?"

"To support Slayter."

"What *kairoi* shows that he can win against Harkandos?"

"That is what we must find out." Nhevalos had hastily set up this place to be his workshop.

"Where are we?"

"Tepsen Nuraghi," he said.

"Not Usara?"

"Slayter fled to the Usaran palace. Harkandos will come looking for him there. I suspect Slayter wants him to."

"And you came here because you don't want to be there when Harkandos comes looking."

There was accusation in her voice, and Nhevalos paused for a moment in his preparation. Frustration flickered in the back of his mind. Normally he would have ignored the pique of this Human, of any Human, but it stung more now that he had lost his footing.

In the end, he decided he could not afford to indulge in her petulance. He said nothing.

"Why don't you go help Slayter directly?" she asked.

He stopped what he was doing and turned. "Do you know why Harkandos is in Castle Noktos?"

"Because he killed Khyven," she said, and Nhevalos narrowed his eyes. It was entirely possible that she was no longer with him. That she no longer believed they could save her kind. That was inconvenient. It would go smoother if she believed, rather than having to be convinced or coerced. But if he needed to, he would.

"You mentioned the defense of Imprevar. I told you Harkandos was not coming west yet. If he is, as you say, at Castle Noktos because he killed Khyven, what does he have to fear from Imprevar? There are none who can stand against him, despite what you hope. Why not continue his conquest?"

She didn't say anything.

"Since you do not know, allow me to tell you. He awaits me. He hopes that I will, as you suggest, come to the rescue of my chosen. That is all he wants, that is all he lacks before he covers the world with his will. I am the only thing he perceives to be standing in his way."

She continued glaring at him, defiant.

"Now tell me, Reader, do you think it is wise for me to give him exactly what he wants?"

"So you're going to send Slayter instead."

"I'm going to defeat Harkandos."

She didn't say anything.

"And you ..." Nhevalos said. "Do you plan to help me or to hinder me?"

"Help you," she said.

"Good."

He turned back to the wide, cleared expanse of the long room. It was once a feasting hall for Lord Eyalos, long ago. Tall arches created galleries on either side of the main room, places where Human servants had once brought food and drink. Many of the wooden tables and chairs in the main hall had been burned during the war. Those that remained were little more than misshapen debris. Nhevalos had cleared it out during the few hours that had passed since Khyven's death. If Harkandos went searching for Nhevalos, it would be some time before he would think to look in this place.

This nuraghi, like so many houses of the Eldroi from the old days, would shield magic use. It was as safe a place as any to read the *kairoi*.

Nhevalos prepared his mind—

"On one condition," Elegathe interrupted.

Nhevalos paused. Again that frustration flickered in the back of his mind. She was very close to being a burden rather than an assistance. For one brief moment, he considered simply doing away with her, sending her back to Imprevar or even killing her. But he was dangerously short on allies at the moment.

"What ..." He turned back to her. "Is your condition?"

"You are going to illuminate the *kairoi*."

"Among other things."

"Then let me watch the *kairoi* with you. That is my condition."

He gestured at the expanse of Eyalos's feasting room. "Does it appear as though I plan to conceal it?"

"I want your permission. I want to see along with you."

"You have my permission."

She nodded. "All right."

Nhevalos turned again, and he pushed all thoughts of the increasingly annoying Human from his mind. It was time to contact Paralos. She would be angry with him—it had been a very long time—but it was time for her to fulfill all the reasons she'd gone into the Dark in the first place. She had no doubt been keeping an eye on the attack at Castle Noktos, though she was surely keeping her distance as well. If Harkandos sensed her, he could fill her life with pain, even if he might not be able to kill her.

Nhevalos produced a silver mirror from the satchel at his side and stilled his breath. Once, there had been three such mirrors. One had been destroyed during the Human-Giant War, and one had been lost for centuries. Nhevalos had thought that mirror also destroyed, but it had recently been unearthed by a talented group of treasure hunters trying to curry favor with Slayter. He now had it. Nhevalos had considered taking it from him. Then the noktum had covered the continent, and Slayter had focused on a hundred other things. By the time he got around to studying the mirror, let alone using it, Nhevalos figured it would no longer have the potential to interfere with his plans.

Nhevalos raised the mirror and touched the inner frame, right against the perfect, untarnished reflection. He circled it with a finger, just as with an Amulet of Noksonon.

The handle of the mirror shivered, like a creature waking from a long, cold slumber. Suddenly, it no longer showed Nhevalos's face. Instead, a dark blue mist—so dark it was almost black—swirled across it. The mirror now looked more like a head-sized portal, leading down to some otherworldly place.

A low humming emanated from it.

"Mmmmmm …"

"Paralos?" Nhevalos said softly.

"Mmmm," the humming became a voice, distant. But even though the voice sounded far away, like it was coming down the long tunnel of an underground mine, he could hear the sarcasm in the words when she finally spoke them. "My beloved."

"I need your help," he said.

Distant, bitter laughter. "Do you?"

"Events have changed."

"So you found the mirror. It only took one thousand seven hundred years. One would think that perhaps you weren't particularly eager to find it."

"You are still dedicated to the project."

For a moment, there was no reply, then the blue-black mist formed into Paralos's face. It was hazy around the edges, but that was her straight nose, her straight hair, all wrought in dark blue mist. When she spoke, the mouth moved like it was actually her. The eyes blinked as though she was simply in the mist, when the truth was she had sacrificed her body long ago to become one with the Dark. She was a voice of the Dark, one of three.

When they had first begun this project together—a pact to outstrip the accomplishments of their fellow Noksonoi by joining the side of mortals and giving them the continent— neither one of them could have predicted exactly what would be needed down that road, even with Lore Magic.

Then suddenly the moment was there. Xos was going into the noktum, sacrificing himself to change the balance of the war. He would become one with that sweeping, powerful spell, just as their progenitor Noktos had done when he'd created it, and in doing so, overwhelm the Lux and bring back the darkness.

It was thought at the time that if the noktum could be restored, the Humans would be thrown into chaos. Their war would be disrupted. The Dark would negate the advantage of their passion and numbers, and the Noksonoi could regain control.

Clearly Noktos's lifelong fight against the Lux had created a stalemate, leaving the continent half steeped in the Dark, half open to the light of the sun.

The idea of the Eldrovan was simple. If Noktos's life force was not enough to overcome Nirapama's master spell of the Lux, then surely two more Noksonoi lives, striving to bolster the power of the Dark with their life-force and their driving agenda, would finally overwhelm the Lux.

Nhevalos remembered thinking the plan would work which was, of course, why it had to be stopped. Back then, the Eldrovan had begun to suspect Nhevalos of acting strangely. But then, they'd suspected several Noksonoi of acting strangely. In the final days of the war, they had become paranoid, and it flew in multiple directions.

The Noksonoi had never been dealt such a defeat from mere mortals. Up until the rebellion gained momentum and several Noksonoi were killed, no one had *wanted* to believe it. A Human should not have had the ability to kill a Noksonoi. At first, most Noksonoi could not conceive of how that was possible because most Noksonoi could not conceive of a Human wielding magic.

In their arrogance, they jumped quickly to the notion that, if Humans could wield magic, someone had to have taught them.

Someone. A Noksonoi. A traitor.

Of course, the truth was that Humans had learned how to tap into the streams of magic by themselves. The Noksonoi couldn't bear to contemplate that truth, so they didn't.

But some Noksonoi floated the notion that there was a traitor in their midst. They'd first thought it was Lekalos, the sharp-tongued hermit who lived in the wild places and took on the appearance of whatever mortal beast had taken her fancy that decade. They had assumed she had, at some point, taken on the form of a Human and taught them magic.

The Council had sought her out, held her down, and killed her as she screamed vituperations. They thought they'd solved the problem, or at the very least revenged themselves upon the instrument of their downfall.

They'd been far from the truth, but the notion of the traitor in their midst grew, and many began to search for another possible traitor, which made it much more difficult for Nhevalos to move about. There were some who immediately suspected him, but then there were some that immediately suspected Harkandos and a half-dozen other Noksonoi, as well. The Noksonoi slammed doors to communication amongst themselves. Lekalos's summary execution spooked them all, and had been condemned by many. The resulting distrust and chaos provided just enough cover to protect Nhevalos.

It was shortly after Lekalos's execution that the Humans and their mortal allies had broken the backs of the Noksonoi defense at the Battle of Dezreneth. The Noksonoi were expected to crush that little pocket of resistance easily. They'd sent six Noksonoi and an army of three hundred mortal beasts, as well as Wergoi and the Taur-Els that were still on their side. Dezreneth had been an out-of-the-way outpost with barely a hundred defenders, but a hero had arisen there, a warrior woman named Senji.

The battle had been a disaster for the Noksonoi. Senji had set traps and fought with the fury of a hundred Kyolars. Three Noksonoi were killed in that battle, their forces routed, and the remaining three Noksonoi fled.

That had turned the tide of the war, and the Eldrovan became desperate. Three dead Noksonoi at one battle was unbelievable, yet there it was.

Senji and her growing army had not rested on their laurels. The woman was furious and strategic. She immediately began a march on Noksonoi strongholds, killing another half-dozen Noksonoi. Humans from the region flocked to her banner. In a stunning turnabout, the Humans were only days—weeks at most—from total victory.

That was when the plan to bring back the noktum became the Eldrovan's full focus.

Nhevalos and Paralos calculated that they only needed to disrupt Xos's desperate plan for two months, enough time for a Human victory and perhaps a month more of clean up, and then they could reverse the spell and bring whichever one of them had joined with the Dark back out of the Dark.

It was, of course, obvious to Nhevalos which one of them must go. The recent suspicion cast upon him froze any plan that involved him being chosen to join with the Dark, to be the champion of the Noksonoi against the Humans. They would never let him any more than they would have let Harkandos, or the half-dozen others suspected of being the traitor, to join the Dark.

But Paralos had been, at the time, above suspicion. None knew about the secret pact she'd made with Nhevalos.

When the plan of the Council came together, when they sought a second to bolster Xos's magnificent sacrifice, Paralos had volunteered.

She had been gratefully approved by the Council. She and Xos had been sent.

But of course Paralos's goal wasn't to help Xos. It was to block him, supporting the power of the Lux instead of the power of the Great Noktum for just long enough for the Humans to prevail.

Nhevalos had promised to reconstruct her a month after the war was done. They'd planned it out beforehand. The two of them had built a powerful artifact from both of their own life forces, had crafted the reversal spell together. It would go smoothly.

But it had not gone smoothly. Xos had discovered Paralos's agenda the moment they had both become the Dark. Neither Nhevalos nor Paralos had realized that becoming one with the Dark would make Xos's and Paralos's thoughts apparent to each other. They shared a common mind. Their eternal battle began instantly, and Xos warned the Council, revealing Nhevalos.

He was forced to flee. Paralos was forced to fight Xos for dominion of the Dark. The Humans took full advantage of the chaos and swept over more Noksonoi strongholds, shattering their tenuous organization.

The Noksonoi died in greater numbers than they ever had, even in the Elder Wars among all the Eldroi. Their morale was crushed, and soon the survivors fled in every direction, using their magic to vanish, to hide from the Humans.

In a matter of days, the Human-Giant War, as the Humans called it, was over.

But in Nhevalos's sudden need to flee, he had left the extraction artifact behind, and the Eldrovan had viciously destroyed it. It had been created by Nhevalos and Paralos together, an intertwining of their life-forces: it could not be recreated without her.

She was trapped in the Dark, in an eternal struggle with the furious Xos, who had given his life for nothing.

The sudden end of war had been jagged and unclean. The original plan had been to wipe away all the powerful Noksonoi that might challenge Nhevalos and Paralos, might reignite the war against the Humans. But too many had escaped, Harkandos among them. Too many were now hidden and knew what Nhevalos had done. He was forced to hide and create defenses.

Even if Nhevalos had the artifact, he would have hesitated to pull Paralos from the Dark at that point. Once he did, the noktum would once again cover the continent, and those remaining Noksonoi who had run from the screaming Humans like frightened rabbits would find their courage again.

He told her she must continue the fight until they could purge the continent.

She had hated him for that. She hated him still. He had her trapped, and she could do nothing but help him. Nhevalos had considered that she might switch sides, help Xos, but Xos would never allow it. Once he viewed Paralos as a traitor, he would never allow her to leave the Dark alive. She was stuck.

Now, of course, Nhevalos had another reason to keep Paralos in the Dark. If she ever escaped, she would kill him. Oh, she would say anything to be extracted, but once she was, Nhevalos would have another enemy in the world, an enemy that knew more about him than any other.

The reverie of their broken history flashed through Nhevalos's head in an instant as Paralos paused.

"Your man, Khyven the Unkillable, is dead. Your plan has failed," she said. "Again."

"All plans are fluid," he said.

"Where have I heard those words before?" she asked.

"Paralos—"

"And so I am useful to you again."

"We must cobble together what we have," Nhevalos said.

Distant, bitter laughter. "Exactly what a lover wishes to hear."

"We were never lovers. We were partners."

"Oh yes we were."

Nhevalos paused at her sting. He waited for her to cool her displeasure, then began again.

"With the mirror, with your life-force, we could recreate the extraction box."

"Ah, now you work with the carrot. I wonder, what will the stick look like?"

"Another two thousand years dancing with Xos."

Silence. The face in the mirror lost its clarity, puffing into dark blue smoke. Nhevalos waited and, a moment later, her face returned, forming into sharp clarity.

"I am still dedicated to the project," she said. "I have been helping your chosen where I can."

That surprised him.

"Good. That is good."

"And what will you do now?"

"First, I wanted to contact you. We may need to move more than the containing of the noktum."

"There was nothing I could do about that, Nhevalos," she said. "Harkandos brought something entirely different to the equation. They are ... Lighteaters. I couldn't influence them from the noktum. They simply sucked the light of the Lux into themselves."

"I expected this. I knew what Harkandos was working on when I imprisoned him."

"But you did not expect he would kill your primary tool?"

Nhevalos paused. "I did not."

"Has he gotten the better of you then, *beloved*?" she asked.

"He has won a battle. We are going to change that."

"You are sure?"

"I am going to read the *kairoi* now. If there is a way, we will find it."

"If."

"There is always a way."

"Hmmm."

"And you will need to play your part, when we find it."

"More than I already am?"

"Yes."

"Will I need to sacrifice myself again? I wonder what else I can give ..."

"Every piece is in play. Every piece."

"Including yourself, Nhevalos?"

"I am the piece that moves the others."

"But if the *kairoi* insists that you face Harkandos, will you?"

"If I die, you are trapped forever."

"I am trapped forever now."

"Paralos—"

"I understand what you are saying," she interrupted him. "And I stand at the ready."

"Good. I will leave the mirror open while I cast the *kairoi*."

"I will stay as long as I can. Xos is always hunting."

Nhevalos turned from her to the long, empty hall. He settled his mind and opened himself to his own magic, to the silver lava that flowed through him.

When he had pulled the magic to him, he thought of the threads—thick and thin—that shot throughout every populated city and every barren wasteland of Noksonon and beyond. He imagined his consciousness enveloping them, making them part of his body so that he might read them, these clusters of threads that mapped out every possibility in existence, from the smallest exchange between Humans—a slap or a kind touch—to the greatest of events—the rise and fall of kingdoms—upon which the survival of entire races relied. He pulled the threads into himself.

Once he had pulled them in, he twisted, pulling back his arms and hands like he was holding a sphere, then he cast his hands—and in his mind the *kairoi*—into the room before him.

That unstoppable power surge flowed through him, as well as the belief that he was the only one who could guide the world to its ultimate peak. He alone. Everything was within reach and under his influence.

The *kairoi*, like a silver garden of vines, flickered and became apparent, lining themselves out across the hall.

Lore Magic was known for predicting what was to come. It showed the possibilities of the future, but it also showed the footprints of the past. If one wished, one could look back at the threads of the past, see what had gone before and then focus on what was to come. But most Lore Mages—Eldroi included—didn't look backward. It was a phenomenal amount of effort, lifeforce, and magic to spend simply on a history lesson.

But Nhevalos couldn't help himself now. Too many things had gone awry, and he was curious about the details. Turning from the hovering, twining, slowly slithering *kairoi* before him, he looked behind himself.

The silver threads behind were far fewer. A mere dozen instead of thousands. Also, the *kairoi* behind him did not move. Frozen in time and space, they etched out only what had come to pass, that which could never be manipulated again.

Nhevalos had only done this once or twice in his long life. He had rarely wanted to look back. He had walked those roads. He knew what he wanted to know from them.

But this time, he had to see it. He had to see where he'd gone wrong, and he stared at the genesis of the duplicate Khyven. It was, he saw now, shrouded in powerful magics. Magics so complicated and potent that anyone looking at them would think they were something other—anything other—than what they actually were. The spells played upon the suspicions of those who looked at them, offering the vision of what they expected to see. It was brilliant. It was the oldest trick of manipulators and leaders. People believed what they wanted to see, and if you offered that personal assurance to them, they flowed in the direction you led. And so had Nhevalos flowed in the direction Harkandos had wanted.

What Nhevalos had wanted to see was: Yes, of *course* Harkandos was creating powerful magics. Nhevalos knew that was going to happen. They wouldn't have any effect upon Nhevalos's plans, though, because Nhevalos was smarter, meticulous, and patient. Whatever juggernaut Harkandos created, Nhevalos believed his plan would prevail in the end because Nhevalos was more subtle, more clever. His plan would always be the well-placed arrow that would hit the bullseye.

Nhevalos had thought all these things, wanted to see these things, had believed these things, and so he hadn't looked closer.

And Harkandos had exploited that.

Never again, Nhevalos thought. As he was about to turn away from the past, his gaze fell upon the *kairoi* that showed the real Khyven's path, not the duplicate's. It wove through the thickest and most important events of the time, touching those of his friends, intertwining with Rhenn's, Vohn's, Slayter's, and of course his lover Lorelle's. Nhevalos's gaze flicked over it as it weaved its way to intersect with the *kairoi* of his duplicate ...

And stopped there.

It simply ended, a torn and ragged severing, little red filaments hanging off it, like someone had shorn through a rough dock rope with a rusty knife.

Thus ends Khyven the Unkillable, Nhevalos thought. He closed his eyes. *I was sure. I was so sure ...*

It was a hard reminder that nothing was ever set until it moved from the present into the past. No matter what the *kairoi* showed him, they were only indications of the possible. Nothing was sure until the moment came down to it, and Nhevalos had been careless. He had not thought Harkandos capable of the subtlety required to undo Nhevalos's hundreds of years of planning. He had thought this was his moment of triumph.

It was a hard lesson to take at such a late date.

Still, there was time. He turned away from the frozen *kairoi* behind him to the slow-moving snake pit of *kairoi* before him, stretched out across the open floor of the feasting hall.

He was aware of Elegathe, of her stunned silence at the panorama of *kairoi*. She was a Lore Mage, but she'd never seen anything like this before. When Humans used their meager magical ability, they saw maybe a few of these threads, only the ones upon which they concentrated, maybe half a dozen. No more than a dozen. Humans were, after all, severely limited in what they could cast.

No doubt to her, this was a staggering display of Eldroi power. Thousands of threads, large and small, lay displayed before them.

"May I speak as you work?" Elegathe asked softly, as though

such a small distraction would upset the spell. Again, a Human foible. True, it required a vast amount of concentration to call the *kairoi* and hold them here for study and, sometimes, manipulation, but concentration was something the Eldroi had in abundance. The attention span and willpower of a Human was like that of a gnat compared to an Eldroi.

"Of course," Nhevalos said. He found Slayter's glowing orange *kairoi*, intertwined and slithering against several current events, weaving over the mundane events of day-to-day life and growing toward a confluence of a number of powerful threads.

"What is that one?" Elegathe indicated a thread that was just about to touch Slayter's. It was a sallow yellow color. "Do you know?"

Of course Nhevalos knew. After Khyven had died, during the first moment he'd come to this nuraghi, he'd searched the *kairoi* for an alternative. He had set that little yellow *kairoi* in motion and had, in fact, diverted it toward Slayter.

"An assistant for Slayter," he said. "He is going to require help now that his friends are beyond help." The mage was exceedingly useful, but he was better when surrounded by others. There were many things he could do, but he was horribly vulnerable without physical protection.

Elegathe studied the *kairoi*. "I know that one. That's L'elica. The bloodsucker from Daemanon."

"Yes."

"That's his assistant? She'll drain him."

"No, she won't. I have spoken with her."

"You ..."

"I can work another with Khyven's abilities into position. It is why I created others like him, but it will take days, possibly weeks. In the meantime, L'elica can stand in his place, at least as far as protection for the mage."

"Why not simply shift your entire plan to one of the others with Khyven's powers and utilize his friends? Why continue to use Slayter?"

"There are no mages on the continent like Slayter. There are no friends of the others that can do what he does. That is why he is irreplaceable. I made fail-safes for Khyven. I have none for Slayter."

"So we are protecting Slayter until one of the others can be brought up from ... where?"

Nhevalos had never revealed where his backups to Khyven were, not to Elegathe or anyone else. He wasn't about to start now. He ignored her question.

"If Slayter needs help, L'elica will serve for now. If he needs ... guidance, she has the power to move him even against his will, if necessary."

"She just accepted your authority?"

"She was N'ssag's right-hand enforcer. She is accustomed to accepting authority."

"My beloved is quite fond of enforcing his authority," Paralos said from the mirror, which Nhevalos had propped up on one of the old tables, giving her a view of the hall and the *kairoi*.

"I do what must be done—"

A gold-white light flickered across the *kairoi*. All of the *kairoi*. It glimmered on the silver threads like someone had opened a curtain to the sun for one moment, then shut it.

Nhevalos froze, his gaze flicking over the threads. Gold-white light? He had never seen that. His frustration flickered again. Nhevalos was just about done with surprises.

"What was that?" Elegathe echoed his thoughts.

He ignored her. He knelt in the midst of the ethereal *kairoi*, looking down their lengths to see if he could catch that glimmer again, that barest sheen of gold and white light.

"Nhevalos—"

"Quiet Elegathe. School is over. I have to discover what that was. It could be Harkandos with something new." The gold-white glimmer returned and coated all of the *kairoi* before him. They flickered, showing their present positions, then jumping to different positions, then back to their original positions. The gold-white light faded.

"Nhevalos—"

"Enough." He held up a hand in her direction. "Quiet your mouth or I will make you quiet."

"She's trying to warn you, beloved," Paralos said from the mirror. "You're looking the wrong direction."

Nhevalos turned. Elegathe was looking behind him to where the events—and people—of the past were locked in place. History now, instead of possibility.

Elegathe pointed at the cluster of *kairoi* Nhevalos had scrutinized before, pointed at Khyven's severed life line.

The white-gold light rippled over Khyven's *kairoi*. It touched none of the others, only the one that governed his fate. Nhevalos desperately wished he could back up, look at the past and future possibilities together, but the casting of the *kairoi* meant all the threads ran through the caster. If he moved, the center between past and future would move with him.

He turned again, snapping his gaze from Khyven's severed thread to the future. Again, all the *kairoi* flickered, jumping to different positions, then back, as though it couldn't decide which was the real selection of possibilities.

"What is this …?" he murmured aloud.

"You've never seen this?" Elegathe asked.

Nhevalos shook his head, and he wondered if they were somehow under attack. A spell that, perhaps, interfered with any Lore Magic on the continent of Noksonon?

That would be impossible, even for someone like Harkandos. The amount of power it would require to cast such a spell … Not with a hundred Harkandoses could it be done. How could—?

The gold-white light came again, as though it was painting over Khyven's *kairoi* in the past, and this time when it rippled over the future *kairoi*, they changed positions again and stayed.

The golden glow flared, blinding, and a squealing noise filled the hall. Elegathe shouted and clapped her hands to her ears. Nhevalos flinched.

For a phantom second—so quick that Nhevalos doubted

he'd even seen it—a duplicate of all the *kairoi* appeared beneath the now golden glowing threads, except the duplicate—the old *kairoi* pathways—were gray and dying, withered and curling up below the new, glowing gold-white threads that had replaced them.

It was there and gone. A ghostly image of what had been, shriveling away. And then nothing except the glowing threads, except now the gold-white glow was fading.

The squeal died away with the glow, and Nhevalos felt a foreboding, like something had just died. Something irreplaceable.

And he had no clue what it was.

"Nhevalos …" Elegathe breathed.

This time, he didn't tell her to be quiet. He looked where she pointed.

Behind him, the gold-white glow had also faded, except it had left something behind.

Khyven's once-severed thread continued forward again, into the array of newly formed *kairoi* that showed the possible futures.

Khyven's life thread had been restored.

CHAPTER THIRTY-NINE

KHYVEN

Everything was white. White sky. White ... There was nothing aside from a single bright light that came from everywhere. There was nothing but white. Except ...

Elements began to take shape in his mind. It wasn't possible to be in a place made entirely of light, was it? No, there had to be ... an order of sorts. An up and a down. A horizon, a place to put his feet.

Somehow Khyven could "feel" that horizon. He could feel nearby trees. He could feel two figures standing over him. He could feel a ground beneath him.

But all he could see was white.

The white resolved, and there were shades of darker white, almost gray. It was like the inverse of seeing in the noktum with an amulet. Instead of everything standing out in shades of gray and black, Khyven's surrounding resolved into shades of light gray and white.

He felt more at peace than he'd ever felt in his life, as though this place in its gorgeous, bright white was the place he'd always wanted to reach, though he'd never known it had existed. He felt he could just lay here forever.

"I've got you," a familiar voice whispered. "I've got you."

A gentle sensation of comfort rippled through him, like fingertips caressing his cheek, a mother's caress.

The horizon became clearer, a brushing of light gray along the edges of mountains, the tops of trees, the bright shining of light beyond that horizon.

"The decision will be quick," the familiar voice said. "And eternity follows. You will have a choice. You—"

The familiar voice stopped and he had the sense that it—the familiar voice—that she had been chastised and had backed away.

She.

The familiar voice was a she. He knew her. He knew this woman.

His mind seemed to continue grabbing ahold of the light, shaping it to what should be, to what he should see. The ground became lush grass, all white and light gray. The figures resolved into women. Two women by the shape of them. Armored. One short. One tall. The voice was …

It wasn't Lorelle's. Wasn't Rhenn's. Was it the new woman? The Reader? Elegathe?

No. It was none of them. Except he knew that voice. He knew it intimately …

Shalure. That was Shalure's voice! Except Shalure was in a coma in Rhenn's infirmary, and everything about her from her skin to her hair had turned …

"White," he murmured, and in that moment, he had a voice. For the first time, he began to see himself as well. He was lying on the white grass, and his perspective of the two women shifted. He wasn't just there with them. He was lying on the ground before them, and they were looking down at him.

"Shalure," he said, and the short woman came into sharper focus. He saw the plates of her armor sticking out from her shoulders, saw the plates of white-enameled metal on her shins, her thighs, her upper arms and forearms. The breastplate that conformed to her curves was intricately wrought with pictures of battles. A woman with flying hair attacking single opponents and groups.

As her familiar face formed before him, so did her hair, which tumbled down to her shoulders like a white river.

Khyven blinked. Shalure. Not Rhenn. Not Lorelle. But Shalure—

Lorelle …

Her scream returned, as though it was happening all over again. Everything came back to him. The vicious sword punching through his chest, through his heart. The relentless cold invading his body. The burning thread trying vainly to fight back.

And Lorelle's heart-rending scream.

"Lorelle!" Khyven sat up—

Except he didn't quite sit up. It was as though he was tearing his body from the very stuff of the grass, as though he hadn't been fully formed until he needed to move, as though until his moment of need, he had only been part of the earth.

He felt and heard a ripping sound as he surged upright. His head and back pulled free of the grass like roots yanked from the mud.

He pulled his legs and feet free as well, and Khyven stood unsteadily upright.

The tall woman laughed. It was the deep-throated chuckle of approval, like she was watching a Night Ring bout and Khyven had drawn his wooden sword instead of his steel one.

"Where is Lorelle?!" He wobbled like a newborn colt, barely caught his balance. The indistinct horizon became more detailed, as did the forest behind them, the rolling hills to the right, and the two figures.

He suddenly realized that Shalure wasn't so much short as the other woman was enormous. A Giant? She had to be at least seven feet tall.

"Calm down, Khyven." Shalure held up her hands. Her body

language told him that she wanted to come to him, that she wanted to catch him and steady him but didn't dare cross some unseen line.

Khyven's attention turned to the tall woman. The body language between them clearly illustrated that this woman had Shalure in some kind of thrall.

He reached for his sword ...

But he had no weapons. Not the Diplomat nor his steel sword. And not the Mavric iron sword, either.

The tall woman chuckled again.

In fact, Khyven had no belt, no ...

Slowly, as he stared at his hip—as white and gray as everything else—he realized he now *did* have a belt, as well as pants and boots. He touched his chest. For a moment, it seemed he was touching bare skin, then there was a linen tunic there. He suddenly wondered if he'd had any of this clothing a moment ago. It made him dizzy.

"What is this?" he said, glaring at the tall woman. "What's going on? Some kind of enchantment?"

"To say the least," the tall woman said.

"Who are you? Are you holding Shalure prisoner?"

"To say the least," she repeated.

"I won't ask you again." He balled up a fist. "Who are you?"

"No, Khyven—" Shalure warned, but the tall woman held out a hand, and Shalure shut up as though she'd been slapped. The tall woman was laughing, and it seemed like her voice came from a long distance away. It was like the hills themselves, or the white sky, was laughing.

The details of the tall woman came into sharp focus. She had bare legs and bare, muscled arms. The arms of a warrior. The arms of a woman who knew how to handle a blade.

She wore a long loincloth of silver wolf fur. Silver wolf furs also rode her shoulders like armor plates. Her boots were made of the same fur, as was the top that bound her breasts and ended at her ribs, baring her flat, pale midriff.

A giant battle-axe poked above her left shoulder and a

longsword above her right. Double leather belts were strapped just below her navel, wrapping her waist, and a thorn bush of daggers bristled from them. Her blue eyes were the color of ice glinting in the sunshine, and her long white hair was bound back in an intricate braid.

"You came awake ready for a fight," the woman said.

"Only if you don't start explaining," he said.

"Far be it from me to stop you." Her laughter had changed to a cold smile, but her eyes glittered with mirth.

"Just tell me—"

"This is what you want, I believe." She inclined her head to her right.

He looked, and it seemed that whatever he looked at resolved into greater detail when his gaze brushed it, and now he could see a sword. It stuck up from the white grass, its hilt gleaming in the bright light. It hadn't been there a second before, Khyven would swear.

He almost snatched it up and leapt at the woman, but he paused.

It was exactly what she seemed to want him to do, and if there was one thing Khyven had learned, it was that the greatest advantage a fighter had was surprise. If she expected it, he had to be unexpected.

"He wants to fight. He always wants to fight," the tall woman said with breathy satisfaction, like Khyven was kissing her neck.

It seemed the statement had been directed at Shalure, but she simply watched Khyven with apprehension, like she was worried what he would do.

"Not always," he said.

The tall woman raised an eyebrow. "Oh?"

"Where am I?"

"That is not the question you want to ask."

"Where am I? Who are you? What is going on?" Khyven elaborated. "Those *are* the questions I want to ask."

"No. Not those, either."

Khyven was still trying to get his bearings, and the tall woman ... she was clearly a threat, but she wasn't threatening him. And these surroundings. The strange light. The ethereal—yet confounding concreteness—of everything ...

He tried to remember where he'd been just before this.

"I was ... I was fighting ..." he said. The doppelgänger. Harkandos. He'd been fighting ... "I was ... I was wounded. The doppelgänger stabbed me. Lorelle screamed." He clenched his fist and looked at the ground. "She screamed like ..."

He glanced up at the woman's icy eyes.

"She screamed like I had ... Senji's Teeth, no ..."

The tall woman grinned wide, showing slightly crooked teeth. One of her incisors slightly overlapped the other, just a bit. Her canine teeth were sharp, prominent, giving her a wolfish look.

"I ... I was stabbed. I ... Where am I?"

"Still not the question."

"Did I die?"

"Better," she said.

"Better?" he growled, and again he wanted to snatch up that sword and unleash his rage. "How is it *better*?"

"I meant it was a better question."

"Stop with the games!"

"Khyven!" Shalure warned.

"So reckless," the tall woman breathed. "So intrepid. You heart is a wild and warlike thing."

"Who are you?" he shouted.

"I do like wild and warlike things."

"Why won't you answer my question?"

"Because you know the answer. You know the answer to every question you've asked, and I don't give obvious answers."

When he'd asked if he was dead, neither this ... this jailor woman nor Shalure had told him he was wrong.

"I died," Khyven said, and his heart hurt. "I ... I failed."

Lorelle's scream echoed in his head. It was the scream of a Luminent whose soul had been ripped in half. When Khyven had died, a part of Lorelle had also died.

He clenched his teeth.

He'd failed them. He'd failed them all. He'd gone into that fight, but Harkandos had outmaneuvered him. The Giant had beaten him. Somehow, he'd duplicated the one thing Khyven couldn't fight against: himself. His own unique power set.

He fell to his knees, pressed his palms against his head, and he screamed his rage. When he'd shouted his throat raw, he hung his head.

"I'm dead. And you ..." He looked up at her. She stood very near him now, towering over him. Shalure stood rigid in the background, looking at Khyven with those same concerned eyes. He ignored her and focused on the tall woman, and suddenly he couldn't believe he hadn't seen it before. The long white braid. The silver wolf's fur. The boots. The great axe and the long sword.

"Senji," he breathed. "You're Senji ..."

"You see," she said. "If you had only a limited number of questions to ask, you certainly don't want to make that one of them."

"I've gone ... wherever dead souls go. And you're Senji the Warrior Goddess."

She didn't say anything, just stared down her nose at him. Now it seemed like she was looking for something. Behind that distantly amused expression, that half-smile on her lips, was something deadly serious, and she searched for that something within him.

"Damn it ..." He slammed his fist into the ground. "I left them. And now he's going to kill everyone in Usara, isn't he?"

"Or enslave them. He is doing that very thing right now," she said.

"And you ..." he began, and his heart lodged in his throat. "You're a goddess. Why aren't you fighting him? Why didn't you stop him?"

She raised an eyebrow, and her icy eyes glittered. "Still not the question."

Khyven leapt to his feet. "And what is the question? You want to dance around it. Why don't you just tell me?" He realized he had grabbed the sword and held it ready in his hand.

She began to laugh softly again. "Do you even know what a goddess is, Khyven the Unkillable?"

"Just answer me!"

She reached up and slowly drew her sword from its sheath. The blade seemed to just keep coming and coming as that blue sword slid out of the scabbard. Steel scraped against steel, ringing. It filled the air like music, and in it he heard voices: the cries of the dying, the screams of the bloodthirsty, the shouts of the victorious.

After what seemed an eternity, the sword came free and the music stopped.

She brought her fist down with that eternal blade between her and Khyven. It went up and up, so tall it seemed to touch the white sky above.

"Oh, I will do you one better," she said. "I will show you. You do not know what a goddess is, but you will learn."

This time, he showed his teeth. His free hand floated out to his side, ready.

"The question you should ask isn't who I am or where you are. It isn't what is going on or how I, a goddess, can help you. The question is: what can *you* do?"

"What can *I* do?" he repeated incredulously.

"Fight," she whispered, answering him as though he'd actually been asking that question, not just parroting her. "You can fight."

Blood pounded in his head. The deaths of his friends lay across his mind like bleeding wounds. And the goddess was taunting him.

Khyven lost all reason. She wanted a fight? She would get a fight. He would show this so-called goddess the fight of her life.

With a cry, he leapt at her.

CHAPTER FORTY

KHYVEN

Khyven didn't know how long he fought Senji. It felt like years.

Their swords clashed and clanged, and the strength of her blows shivered his arms. Even the Trolls hadn't sent such powerful tremors into his muscles, his bones, like her blows did. But despite their thunderous impact, Khyven never dropped his sword. His arms never failed. Despite how heavy they felt, despite how much they burned, he could always raise them to block the next attack.

They fought and fought and fought.

The day never seemed to wane. Or maybe it was the night that didn't wane.

This place was like the noktum. In the noktum, he could never tell whether it was daytime or nighttime. Everything stood out in contrast to everything else, all of it in dark shades of gray.

That was the way it was here, except everything was in light shades of gray, leaning toward white. There was no sun overhead. There was no sky at all, really. Just a hazy white mist everywhere, and if the illuminating light had a source at all, it would have to be the mist itself. Thousands of tiny moons drifting all around him.

Clang clang clang

Realizations filtered into Khyven's awareness like water soaking into sand. He and Senji were fighting. He knew that much, but that seemed to be all he knew. He could barely remember anything before the fight.

Clang, grind ... Clang!

Had he been fighting forever? Could a person fight forever?

He tried to remember something before this, before the dexterous dodge and spin, before the elegant parry and riposte, before the fervent deflect and cut. He tried to remember anything else besides the sport of fighting.

Sport ...

Khyven didn't fight for sport, did he? That seemed horribly wrong somehow.

No, wait. He did. He ... had. Khyven used to fight for sport. He'd been a ...

He'd been a ...

Someone of importance. People had shouted his name, cheered for him.

A Ringer. He'd been a Ringer. He'd been Khyven the Unkillable.

Clang clang clang

Senji grinned and brought that sword of never-ending light down on him again. He blocked it, slid inside her guard, punched at her stomach. He had no dagger, otherwise he'd have stabbed at her.

She moved, and his fist grazed her naked belly. She brought her sword around. He blocked it. Her grin never faltered, and he knew she felt the same thing he felt. The euphoria of combat. He was grinning, too.

Feint, recover, dodge, block.

But there was more. He was ... missing something. He was just a fighter here. Nothing more than a fighter, lost in the sublime world of combat as though there was nothing else.

Except there was something else, wasn't there?

Why couldn't he remember it?

Clang, stab … clang!

More realizations filtered into him. Things out of place. Things that seemed perfectly normal when he was immersed in combat, but that … weren't.

He was fighting her. She was a master. He was a master. Yet neither of them were wounded. Surely someone must have scored by now. Surely some blood would have flown. Something. A nick to the head. A gash on the arm, the leg. They'd been fighting for….

He didn't know. For a very long time, he thought, but he didn't know.

Yet Senji was unmarked. There were scars on her forearms and upper arms, on her naked thighs where blades had touched her before …

But none were fresh.

And Khyven was unmarked. He had taken no wounds. And Senji wasn't just a master. She was the goddess of combat. She was the goddess of heroes.

If anyone was a better swordsman than him, it had to be the goddess of all combat.

Clang clang clang

A flash of memory joined the filtering realizations. He remembered the start of the fight, remembered leaping at her. She had swept that immense sword at him, which seemed like a ray of sunlight stretching to the horizon.

He'd blocked it. After the block, he'd corkscrewed his sword in a maneuver designed to cripple—but not kill—an opponent. It was a lightning-fast riposte designed to slice the thigh muscle, and he'd executed it flawlessly.

She'd blocked it.

The euphoria had taken him then. He had never met anyone who had so effectively countered that move. He'd begun grinning, trying to find a way through her defenses. That was when the battle had truly begun. That was when …

… he couldn't remember anything that came after.

From that moment forward, the battle had looked … well, much like what they were now doing. And it had continued …

Forever, as far as he knew. They could have been fighting for days now. Months. Even years.

And he wasn't tired.

If they had been fighting for days, why wasn't he tired? He was a superlative swordsman, but even he had limitations. That was another anomaly. A sign that something was amiss

Clang, thrust, clang!

Senji pressed him harder, as though she sensed he was thinking rogue thoughts.

Clang, clang, clang!

"No …" Khyven whispered.

She came at him faster.

Clang, clang, clang!

"No," he said louder.

She lunged so fast he barely had time to block it. He spun, and she was there again. He blocked again.

That gorgeous euphoria flowed through him once more, and his thoughts flitted away.

Clang clang clang

"No," his mouth murmured as though independent of his mind.

She pressed him again, but this time Khyven leapt backward. It hurt to disengage. It was like being attached to the most comforting, fulfilling, achingly beautiful thing there was, and then leaving it behind.

But he did it. He bounded backward, disengaging.

She did not chase him. With a low, glittering gaze, she held her sword up, inviting him.

He lowered his.

"No," he said.

Her smile grew smaller, but it didn't go away.

He threw his sword onto the grass. "This is a farce."

She chuckled, leaned her sword on her shoulder and sauntered toward him. She didn't sheathe her weapon, though, and when she reached sword range, her eyes glowed. She towered over him, nearly a foot taller, and for a moment, he thought she'd strike him down.

"Not a farce, my fierce warrior. Payment."

"Payment?"

"Oh yes."

He tried to remember something, any kind of context for what she was saying.

To his surprise, she crouched down, then fell onto her back with a laugh. He jerked, thinking at first that it was some clever attack. It was a thoroughly odd, surreal action from this seven-foot-tall warrior woman. It was almost … childlike.

She stretched out on the white grass, put her hands behind her head and stared up at the sky as though there was a sky to stare up at. She crossed her legs, furred boot lapping over furred boot, and sighed contentedly.

She glanced over at him then, as though surprised to see him still standing. As though she'd expected, after fighting each other so strenuously, that they would flop down in the grass like old friends.

"Won't you join me?" she asked.

"I thought I was trying to kill you."

"And it was … intoxicating. But lay down now. You've proven all you need to prove. Truth be known, you proved it long before you came here. But I am a selfish bitch sometimes."

"Proven?"

"Lay down next to me, Khyven the Unkillable. It is, unfortunately, time for words. Battle brings out the best in us. It defines us. We make wisdom in the swing of a sword, you and I. We muster courage through the drive toward our choices. But then we must rest, too. We must absorb that wisdom, contemplate the courage. Violence cannot be virtuous without peace on the other side."

He didn't know what she was talking about, but he slowly

crouched, then lay down next to her. Without knowing exactly why, he mimicked her gesture and put his hands behind his head. It felt far too vulnerable. After fighting all-out against this woman, his longtime battle experience told him the last thing he should do was simply lay down next to her.

But somehow, it also felt perfectly right.

"I could fight for a century with one such as you," she murmured. "So many others are disappointments, but you ... Ah ..."

"How long did we fight?"

"Mmm?"

"It seemed ... a very long time."

"Five years," she said. "A bare blink in the turning of the—"

"Five years!?"

"What your mortal mind would equate as five years, yes." She sighed contentedly. "It is the best exercise I've had in a milennia."

The impossible notion that he'd been fighting for five straight years sent panic through him.

"I like the number five," she continued. "It's ... appropriate, if you look at the grand scheme of things."

"I can't be here for ..." he said. "I can't stay here for five years."

"Oh? And why not?"

"I ..." But he didn't know why. He only felt a bone-deep fear at the notion. He only knew that his body longed to leap to its feet and challenge Senji to another sword fight if for no other reason than to ...

Than to ...

He didn't know.

"You wish to leave this place," Senji said.

Yes! That's what it was. He had to get out of here, but ... he couldn't remember why.

"I will tell you the secret, Khyven the Unkillable," she said, again seeming to read his mind. "That is my gift to you."

Gift? "What secret?"

"The secret is this: if you do not remember why you must leave this place, you must stay here forever."

Fear blossomed in his chest.

"Lorelle ..." he murmured. The name came to his lips unbidden. As he said it, a beautiful Luminent formed in his mind's eye. Golden hair tumbling down to her shoulders. Pale, sharp ears cleaved through that golden river, pointing toward the sky. Then the hair became midnight black, and her pale skin did the same.

"Yes," Senji said, a little ruefully.

"Lorelle," he said more firmly.

"She was your lover," Senji said. "That is my second gift to you."

The images of Lorelle returned in a flood, as though they had been waiting for just that acknowledgement. He saw the fluid grace of her, moving across a room, leaping to a rooftop. He felt the kindness of her, touching his cheek, standing over his sickbed. He felt her unrelenting drive, searching for ... for someone. Her best friend. He saw the smooth slope of her neck, felt the desire to kiss it. He saw a bright and green meadow where they had made love, where they'd taken refuge in each other before ...

Before ...

Something horrible had happened, and he felt that it had happened to her, though he didn't know what it was.

"I have to get back to her!" He leapt to his feet, looking around for a door. A path. Something that led away from this place, back to where ... to where he could find Lorelle.

But there was nothing. Only white mist hung close—closer than before—in every direction.

"Loves are born and die every day," Senji said casually. "Many of them are tragic. Love isn't enough."

"Isn't enough for what?"

"Khyven ... You need to remember why you're here."

"I'm here because you ... Because you drew your sword on me ..." It was all so hazy.

"No."

"I'm here because ...."

She waited patiently, the mirth gone from her eyes.

"I'm here because I ..."

She narrowed her eyes. "Yes?"

In his memory, steel flashed. He'd been fighting, but not in white mist. He'd been fighting in a vast and dark land with horizons and castles.

Burning, ripping, up through his chest. A horrible scream. A life-ending scream.

Lorelle's scream.

He remembered his own face, twisted and grinning with clenched teeth. Overlarge eyes, slanted eyebrows.

"I ... died."

"You died."

He looked down at his hands. They looked the same as ever. He looked at his chest where the horrible burning had happened, where the ... sword had torn through him.

"Do you know what a goddess is, Khyven?"

"Send me back," he murmured, patting his chest. "Send me back!"

She smiled again, but it was rueful this time. She nodded as though she had known exactly what he was going to say.

"Do you know what a goddess is?"

"What?"

"A goddess, Khyven. Do you know what it is?"

"You're ... A goddess is an omnipotent being who looks after ... their chosen people. Like you look after Humans."

"Yes, that is what most Humans think." She nodded, as though he'd given her the answer she expected, but not the answer she wanted. "But it isn't true. Almost all goddesses and gods were once mortals. I was once mortal, like you."

Khyven clung to the tattered memories he'd recovered, for they felt like they would slip away if he didn't. He didn't know what to say to Senji's confession.

"We rise, these deities that the mortals of Noksonon pray to.

Lotura rose through the power of integrity, of pacts, of stating a word and keeping it. In his life, he was a man who never broke his word. He was a father who nurtured his children, a husband who kept faith with his wife. He was revered for this.

"Grina did the opposite, but was revered in her own way. She was a lascivious thief who stole any riches and teased forth all pleasures she could put her fingers to. She was revered for her passion, for inspiring the rush of life and absence of rule.

"Likewise with Libur. He had a single-minded drive for knowledge, and was revered for it. Asper had a massive physicality and unprecedented capacity for building and nurturing the riches of the earth. They were heroes, Khyven, each in their own way. They rose because they represented something to chase, something to believe in, something to strive for, and those around them did as they did, followed them. They believed in these heroes. They adored them, put them on a pedestal in their minds and often in the actual world as well. And then at some undetermined point, that adoration became something more. These paragons became ... more. The adoration transformed into power, and mortals became gods."

"You ... It was combat for you," Khyven said.

"It was combat for me." She agreed. "I made my legend during the original Human-Giant war. I led our armies. I fought impossible battles. I rose because the mortals of Usara needed me to rise. And I have given heart to those with courage since then. I have channeled that life, that verve, that worship. I have passed it on to the great warriors of every age. I have made them better, just as I have made you better from time to time."

Khyven had flickers of memory. His fights in the Night Ring.

"Oh, not as much as you might imagine. Just a nudge here and there. You can only receive the blessing of a goddess if you have already unlocked your own blessings. You, my dear warrior, have been a joy to watch. And the people need a hero now more than ever. I was sad to see you fall. You were not ... meant to fall."

"I died," he said.

"And mortals do not return from that. It is why they are mortals."

"You can't send me back? You can't make me whole again?"

She didn't answer, just stared up at the white mist as though she could see something in it.

"Senji—"

"I can," she said.

"Then do it! Send me back. Please!"

She drew a deep breath and let it out. "It is not so simple."

"What must I do?"

"It is not what you must do, Khyven. It is what I must do, and the consequences that follow such an act. To bring back to life something that has expired is to twist the natural order of things."

"Natural order? You're a goddess!"

She smiled ruefully. "The Giants believe they are the masters of the world. The mortals think the gods are masters of the world. But in truth, the world moves as it has always moved. The sun rises because that is what the sun does. The oceans withdraw and surge forward because that is what they do. We do not govern this and neither do the Giants. There is an order that was before any of us were here and will be long after we are all forgotten. It flows like well-ordered chaos, unfathomable. It does not like to be bent, and it despises being broken. Whenever such a bending has been attempted, there is always a backlash, and the only way to stop that backlash is to balance the scales from the start."

"There is a cost ..." he murmured.

"There is a cost." She nodded.

"I will pay it."

A smile crossed her lips, like a cloud passing in front of the sun, there and gone. "It is not a cost you can pay."

"What does that mean? Who ..." He trailed off.

"This is why I asked you if you know what a goddess is. Mortals believe gods are all powerful, that they can do anything.

That gods create and destroy as they please. That we are the source of power in the world. But it is the opposite of that. Gods and goddesses are created by mortals. We only have the power that is given to us by those who believe."

"What does this have to do with the cost?"

"Tell me you didn't feel it when you were a Ringer. Tell me that you didn't feel a rush when the crowd shouted your name, when they loved you with brutal fierceness, when they screamed as you killed others for their pleasure."

Khyven knew exactly what she meant. The shouting of the crowd was something he had learned to heighten. He couldn't have said why he'd done that at the time. Or rather, he would have said it was because that was what was expected of him. Playing to the crowd was what Vex the Victorious had done. Giving the people and the king what they wanted. If Khyven had any chance of escaping the Night Ring, he had to do what the people and the king wanted …

But when she put it this way, he wondered if their very attention hadn't been a key component to his victory. He *had* felt more powerful, larger than life. He *had* been unkillable as long as the crowd was screaming his name. It had felt like an ocean of noise carrying him on its back, pushing him toward victory.

"Yes," he said, and guilt came along with the admission, though he couldn't say why.

"Most people never experience that, you know," she said. "They live their lives with a scrap of attention here and there, never a feast. But imagine this, Khyven, imagine that it isn't just an arena with orchestrated battles, where the intent is to entertain. Imagine you are a warrior whose only intent is to save her people. Imagine you know that if you fail, all comes to ruin. The entire world. Every person you've ever loved and every person they have ever loved … Imagine how hard you would fight. Now imagine the adoration of not just those who knew you, but everyone who knows your name. Imagine your legend growing such that everyone in the world knows you, loves you, thinks about you every day. It is ten thousand times what you felt in the Night Ring."

He watched her. "Is that …?"

"That is how a goddess is made, Khyven. It elevated me. It made me immortal. Made me invincible, after a fashion. It took me here."

"Where are we?"

She shook her head. "Now is not the time to answer that question, if ever there will be."

"Why not?"

"Because you are realigning with your mortal sensibilities. Our timeless time is almost at an end."

"Timeless?"

"Khyven, I do not have power over life and death. I have … mechanisms of cheating, if you will. I can fold the paper of life and skip over certain necessities. But that is all. The sun will still rise because that is what the sun does. The ocean will still crash and recede because that is what the ocean does. All I may do is pass on what was given to me by the mortals of my time. I have tried to do this judiciously throughout the centuries, and goodness knows I have not always succeeded. We are here, after all. We are here again, at the war of wars. And we need the greatest warrior of the age to fight for us. And we need him to win."

"I'm supposed to fight Harkandos."

"You *were* supposed to fight Harkandos, but that thread was broken. I can … mend it. Maybe."

"I thought you said you couldn't bring people back to life."

"I never have, but perhaps … Perhaps I can do it once. I can give to you what was given to me two thousand years ago. I can give you the lifeforce of those who lifted me up."

"I'm going to become … a god?"

She smiled. "No. Only mortals can make a god. Gods rise from the needs of their people. I am no god maker, Khyven. I am tied to that which created me: A need for courage. A drive for excellence. A call to arms, not just to fight, but to win. A way through times of violence to times of peace. That is why I am here. That is the only reason I am here. And whereas once I was the tool of freedom for my people, now you are. I believe this is why you were born. And I believe this moment—this single moment—is the real reason I was made a goddess."

"The cost ... What are you saying?"

"I can bring you back. It will only require everything that I am."

"No ..." He was stunned. She was saying ...

"Rest your mind, Khyven. I cannot serve my people any better than this, and I would never consider this lightly. If you believe that each of us was brought here for a purpose, then surely this is mine. But there is only one question that needs answering before I make my sacrifice."

She paused then, leaning back on the cradle of her elbows, tilting her head back luxuriantly, like she was in a bath. She looked up at the misty white overhead with satisfaction, as though she actually could see something he couldn't see, something beyond the white mist. She took a deep breath, then rolled over onto her hands and knees and looked at him.

"Senji ..."

She stood up, all seven feet of magnificent fighter that she was. "Here is my question to you, Khyven the Unkillable: You have now heard what I am willing to sacrifice. My life, such that it is. The goddess that many still pray to. What are you willing to sacrifice for those you love? For your people? For the world?"

"Everything," he said without hesitation.

"And so you must," she said softly. "That promise will be put to the test. I beg you to believe me when I say that it will be put to the test, because if you don't, you will surely fail. You must give everything you are, just as I am prepared to do. Everything. It is the only way you will win."

"I swear I will."

"Then let us hesitate no longer. Fate calls. The world is in need, and we may answer. Let us save our people, Khyven the Unkillable. Let us do it together."

She drew her sword, and its light extended into the misty

white overhead. "Draw."

He had thrown his sword away, but when he went to look for it, it was in the sheath at his hip. He hesitated only a moment, then pulled it from its scabbard.

"Cross swords with me, Khyven." She smiled that same rueful smile. "One last time."

He touched his blade to hers, and the gold-white light that extended from the tip of her sword seemed to retreat from the heavens, to come back and surround her weapon, and then his. The white light then ran down the blade to the hilt, and into his hands. He felt it go into his body, felt the yelling of the crowd, felt the adoration flowing from thousands of lives from another time.

"*Sen-ji! Sen-ji! Sen-ji!*"

It flowed into him, and he gasped as he grew large. So large! He felt as if he was as tall as a mountain.

But when he looked over at Senji, she was still as she had been. She still looked down at him from her intimidating height. But she was ... lighter, transparent.

The light continued to flow into him, filling him. His memories flooded back, all of them, not just the snippets of Lorelle's face, but everything. The noktum covering all of Noksonon. The battle. His loss. The doppelgänger. Harkandos. Humanity on the brink of destruction.

"You have made me proud, Khyven," Senji said. "The path behind you has not been easy. The path before you will be harder. Face it like a warrior. That is all I ask. Make me proud again."

She was almost gone now, so transparent she might have been a mirage. She reached down and touched his brow with her thumb.

"Make me proud ..."

White-gold light flashed.

CHAPTER FORTY-ONE

KHYVEN

Khyven jerked awake. He was back in the noktum, staring up at the eternal darkness and grayness above. He was back in his body, his real body. Spasmodically, his hands flew to his chest, feeling for the wounds that had killed him.

They were gone.

The only thing he felt was smooth skin, sticky blood, and the reassuring bulk of the Amulet of Noksonon. His tunic was a tattered mess, as though something had chewed it apart.

His head rang, a pounding inside that seemed to be retreating. It was as though all the pain from his body that he should have felt when he died coalesced into his head, and then drained out the back somehow. Even as he thought it, the headache vanished.

He sat up—

And almost jumped. Three Kyolars stood barely an arm's length away, their muzzles low, covered in blood.

His blood.

They'd been feeding on him. His tunic was tattered because they had torn it apart and had ...

He felt his torso again, only barely able to imagine what he had looked like a moment before ... before Senji had healed him.

Overhead, a small pack of Sleeths circled, waiting until the Kyolars had had their fill.

The Kyolars themselves had clearly been startled by Senji's magic and his restoration. They were now rethinking it. Both lowered their heads.

Khyven rolled to a crouch. In the distance stood Castle Noktos, and before him a furrow in the dirt leading up to him, like something had hit with fantastic force. All around him were dark splashes of blood, and he realized that the thing that had hit with fantastic force had been his own body. Someone had flung him here.

Someone. Harkandos.

He could only imagine what his body had looked like when it had slid to a stop. A meat meal for these supernatural cats. And suddenly he was whole again. He shuddered.

The cats crept forward, jaws low.

It occurred to him that the Amulet of Noksonon should have kept them at bay. Anyone wearing such an amulet—a sign of favor from Nhevalos—were protected from the noktum's denizens.

But these cats had already had a taste of him and hadn't been burned. Perhaps they weren't feeling the force of the amulets like they once might. Or perhaps the wearer had to be alive for the enchantment to work.

Khyven's hand slipped down to his waist. The Diplomat was still in its sheath, though it had been twisted around from his side to his back from the fall. Miraculously, the thing had not snapped. The force with which Khyven had hit would snap bones; it must have been the sheerest stroke of luck that the Diplomat was intact. Tough sword.

His steel sword was, of course, gone, shattered in the battle with his doppelgänger.

"Not exactly the reunion I was hoping for," Khyven said to the cats as he crouched, trying to keep them both in view. But they weren't about to let him. One of the great cats circled. They were on the hunt now. They weren't going to give him any chances.

Well, it wasn't as if Khyven hadn't fought two opponents before, and even as the cats moved, and he turned with them, the blue wind rippled out from him.

A strange calm flowed through him, a relief. Up until that moment, he hadn't been sure that his resurrection would also bring the return of his magic.

But clearly Senji had taken the trouble to put his body back together, to hold his soul … wherever she had held it. She'd done all that because she knew that Humanity stood on the brink. She wouldn't have sent him back without his most powerful weapon.

"Well I haven't got all day," Khyven said to the cats. "How about we get about this—"

The cats flinched, crouching like some loud noise had gone off over their heads. But there was no noise.

Both of them turned and fled. Khyven glanced up. The Sleeths did exactly the same, flowing in a swirl and making a beeline for the trees.

Khyven could have spent a moment wondering what had spooked them, but he wasn't a novice. Whatever could scare a flock of Sleeths and a pair of Kyolars wasn't likely to be a good thing for Khyven.

He spun, looking for his new foe. He was ready. Whatever came this time, Khyven wasn't going to waste a moment. He wasn't going to consider this or that. He'd returned to fight. To win. He'd returned to give everything he had, everything he was. He'd returned to—

He froze and his gaze locked on the reason the Kyolars had fled.

It wasn't another monster, something larger and more

dominant than the Kyolars.

The Sword sat planted in the grass behind him.

CHAPTER FORTY-TWO

KHYVEN

I *was right about you,"* the Sword said in Khyven's mind.

If it had been anything else—anything in the world—from a Giant to a Cakistro to a horde of Nox bloodsuckers, Khyven would have been ready. If his heart rate had raised, it would have only been in anticipation of a glorious battle.

But his heart quickened for an entirely different reason now.

The Sword was the only thing Khyven truly feared. He wasn't afraid of Harkandos, not anymore. He wasn't afraid of the damned doppelgänger—by Senji he longed for a rematch with that thing.

In either case, he'd either prevail or he'd die for real. And he was willing to give his life no matter what. He could only imagine what that damned army had done to his friends—he had to assume they were all dead now—and if that was the case, Khyven didn't want to survive after. His only purpose was to destroy those who would take over Noksonon. And it all started with those who had killed his friends.

He longed for either of those confrontations, or any other fights that came in-between.

But he hadn't wanted to see the Sword. This fight wasn't about pitting his prowess against another person. The Sword pitted Khyven against himself.

"You are a singular destiny in and of yourself, Slayer of Trolls," the Sword said.

"You're going to just keep showing up, aren't you?"

"We are intertwined, you and I."

"I know that's how you want it to be, but I get the feeling it isn't entirely true," Khyven said aloud.

"Oh, but it is."

"If we were so thoroughly intertwined, why do you keep following me around like a puppy? If we were so joined as you say, I think we'd be joined."

The Sword stayed sullenly silent, a mannerism that Khyven had come to recognize. He'd won that point.

Khyven had gone through death and five years of combat with a goddess to return to this shore. This time, he was going to do it right. This time, he wasn't going to let a maniacal Sword control his emotions.

"I don't need you. I don't want you. You are ..." he trailed off.

He felt the Sword seething in his mind. He felt its anger.

But Khyven stopped himself. He didn't care about the Sword's anger, but he suddenly realized something else.

He saw the doppelgänger in his mind's eye, saw that twisted face, heard that breathy laugh. He saw the Mavric iron sword in its hand ...

Breaking Khyven's sword.

If Khyven had been holding a Mavric iron sword at that moment, it wouldn't have shattered. The Sword would have held. Not only that, but when Khyven had sheared into the doppelgänger's head, its sentience would have driven the blade at least half an inch deeper. The Sword would have made sure if it. The doppelgänger wouldn't have walked away from that.

In short, if he'd had the Sword, Khyven would have won the day. The war for Usara would have been over.

He swallowed, hearing the goddess's voice in his mind.

"What are you willing to do? What are you willing to sacrifice?"

"Everything," he had said.

He realized that if he turned away from the Sword, from this offer of power, he was not giving himself the best opportunity to win. He needed the Sword.

"What are you willing to sacrifice?"

Suddenly, he knew Senji had foreseen this choice. This was what she had meant. Khyven had a chance to save his race, to save all of Noksonon from the yoke of the Giants.

But he might have to sacrifice his soul to the Sword in order to do it.

"If that is what you wish," the Sword said in a lethal tone. *"If that is what you—"*

"Wait," Khyven said softly, holding up a hand. "Wait a moment."

The Sword went silent.

Khyven stood in that horrible indecision for a long time. *If I do this ...* he thought. *If I do this, then ...*

He would have to make sure that, at the end of ends, he finished the job. He couldn't allow the Sword to turn him into a villain. At least ... not past the death of Harkandos and the breaking of the Giant's army. After that ...

"I accept," Khyven said.

"That is excellent," the Sword said with genuine excitement. The foreboding tone was utterly gone. *"You and I, Slayer of Trolls, we shall right the world again. We shall make Noksonon as it was meant to be. There shall be none who can stand against—"*

"On the condition that you answer one question."

"Of course, Slayer of Trolls. I shall answer every question. I remember everything from the moment my creator brought me to life through the fire of his magic, hammered and tempered me with his own hands and quenched me in the blood of five Eldroi. I will—"

"Who do you really serve?"

"*I serve you, Slayer of Trolls,*" the Sword answered without hesitation. It was so swift and so certain that Khyven almost believed. Which meant one of two things: either the Sword was telling the truth, or it was a liar and deceiver to rival Nhevalos himself.

The Sword babbled on, talking about the exultant euphoria of the blood of the Drakanoi that woke up its mind, then the nearly-as-delicious Pyranoi that followed, the tart but serviceable Daemanoi after that, and penultimately the exotic flavor of the Lathranoi, one of the last of an Eldroi race that was now extinct. And then, in a subdued tone, the Sword mentioned the sad necessity of including a Noksonoi to balance the power of the magic.

Khyven barely listened, and a third possibility occurred to him.

The Sword might be every bit as evil as he thought, a creature designed to overtake and subvert the mind ...

But it might not know it.

The thing was the ultimate tool, even by its own admission. It seemed direct—bloodthirstily direct—about everything. But what if its master had created it to channel a purpose hidden even from the Sword.

What if the Sword itself didn't know just how dangerous it was to its wielder. Clearly it had never had the same wielder for long. And it seemed to prefer mortals, though it had told Khyven stories of the occasional Eldroi who had hefted it.

Khyven grew even more convinced when he realized that even Nhevalos, who certainly could have benefited from this powerful artifact—and who would have known its uses and every aspect of what it could accomplish far better than Khyven—had opted instead to bury it for a dozen centuries.

"You serve me," Khyven said.

"*Yes, Slayer of Trolls. I shall serve you until you are a Slayer of Dragons.*"

"I want you to serve me until I am a Slayer of Harkandos."

The Sword paused. "*I see ...*" it said after a time.

"You have a problem with that?"

"Harkandos ... He is one of the great Noksonoi. Even my master said so."

"But Harkandos is not your master."

"No ... But he is a Noksonoi."

Khyven waited.

"You have a conflict with this great Noksonoi."

"He wants to destroy my people."

"He has offended you," the Sword echoed as though it hadn't even heard Khyven's words, like the Human race didn't really matter. Nothing mattered to the Sword, apparently, except one's core purpose. And in its steely little mind, all purposes flowed into vengeance and violence.

"He has deeply offended me," Khyven said.

"Hmmm ..." the Sword said, as though thinking. *"You have righteous cause against this Noksonoi?"*

"I do," Khyven said. "He must be killed."

"Sliced from neck to groin?" The Sword asked, excited.

"I want his head."

"Decapitation ..." The Sword sighed with pleasure.

"Yes."

"Very well, Khyven Slayer of Trolls. Together, we will slay this Harkandos, but you must assure me that Jai'ketakos, the vile Drakanoi, will also die."

"That will not be a problem," Khyven said. "But I am going after Harkandos first. If Jai'ketakos stands between me and him, then he dies first. If he doesn't, then I promise you I will hunt the dragon down with any life that remains in my body."

"Yeeessss," the Sword said.

"Then we have a deal?"

"Oh yes, Khyven Slayer of Trolls. They will remember your name. We will make you immortal."

Khyven reached out and grasped the hilt of the Sword. He felt the rush of joining with it again, but this time, he had no hesitation. If his friends were still alive, he would find them and separate them from their tormentors. If they were dead, he would avenge them.

Either way, Khyven would kill what needed killing. There would be no hesitation this time. As the Sword desired, blood would flow, and Khyven would not stop until he reached the end of the road, until Harkandos, the doppelgänger, and all of those other Giants lay at his feet, or until Khyven returned to the misty white land of the dead.

Like the Sword itself, Khyven knew his sole purpose now. It wasn't to luxuriate or to love, to discover simple pleasures or simple wisdoms from a life well lived. It wasn't to lead an army or to help Rhenn rebuild a kingdom.

It was to clear the field for all the others who wished to do such beautiful and Human things.

It was to kill the enemy.

The rush of the Sword's power filled him, and Khyven turned his gaze upon Castle Noktos again. He didn't look for the Kyolars or the Sleeths. Like the most dangerous predator in any forest, he assumed they had turned tail and fled.

And he was right.

He began his march toward the castle.

CHAPTER FORTY-THREE

KHYVEN

Khyven jogged quietly toward the broken gate. Harkandos had thrown him a quarter of a mile, it seemed. The thought of the Giant's physical strength was unfathomable. Khyven weighed two hundred and twenty-five pounds. Even with his own blue wind magic and the Sword's spell-cutting magic, he was going to have to fight something that could pitch him like a pebble.

He had never thought much of assassins, people who slunk through the night and knifed their victims from behind, but he felt that in this situation, he'd make an exception. He was warming to the idea. After all, he was better equipped than usual to fit the task. He didn't have his normal complement of armor. He'd removed it in the meadow with Lorelle and hadn't had time to put it on before the Giants' attack. Also, he had two daggers in his belt that he hadn't used in the doppelgänger fight. Two daggers. Just like Lorelle.

He jogged up to the wall and paused behind its cover. The question now was: just how arrogant was Harkandos? He had just walked up to Castle Noktos, made his demands, killed anyone who stood in his way, and took what he wanted. He'd defeated Usara's entire population in a matter of hours. Harkandos seemed like the type who was born arrogant, but would his easy conquest make him overconfident as well?

Usara was the only kingdom on this arm of Noksonon, which meant there would be no cavalry coming to rescue them. So the question was ...

Would Harkandos post a guard? Could Khyven just walk up to the front gate without fear of detection?

Or was Harkandos a careful one, despite his clear dominance? Would he complement his victory with smart thinking?

As these thoughts ran through Khyven's mind, he slowly realized that it actually didn't matter. Whether Harkandos was careful or not, Khyven had to be. There could be no mistakes this time. He planned to look at this fight like a battle in the Night Ring. It was simple. His job was to kill, and if he succeeded, to kill again. He'd keep going until all the Giants were dead, or he was.

"Yes ..." the Sword said, picking up on Khyven's emotions.

"I don't suppose you've got a stealth spell in your array of magics," Khyven thought to the Sword.

"I have all the magics you need, Slayer of Trolls. I will cut through anything that gets in your way."

"That would be the opposite of stealth." It occurred to Khyven that the Sword itself suffered from overconfidence.

"You mean hide?"

"Hide. Sneak. Attack from the shadows."

"The glory comes from facing a greater opponent, Slayer of Trolls. And then carving them to pieces until the blood rains down like a storm of victory."

"So that's a no."

"They will write you into legend, Slayer of Trolls."

"If Harkandos finds me before I'm ready, they will write me onto a tombstone."

"That is humor. I recognize humor," the Sword said.

"Outstanding." Khyven leapt up the rubble where the broken gate used to stand.

Once over the rubble, he ran to the first sculpture, which stood over twenty feet tall. The base was seven feet wide, and he crouched behind it, looked over the mostly barren courtyard. It was at least thirty feet between him and the next sculpture, and that was a relatively close one. The stone courtyard was enormous and mostly empty. Even a half-asleep sentry posted at one of the many balconies facing this way, not to mention the three glass atriums, could see him coming.

But the blue wind remained quiet, and Khyven's keen eyes told him that no one was looking.

Overconfidence is the word of the day, I suppose, he thought.

He was about to start around the corner of the statue when the blue wind suddenly appeared like someone had thrown a ball of powder at the ground at his feet. It burst up, billowing to knee-level, then flattened against the ground.

A warning.

Khyven didn't know where the danger was coming from, but he suddenly felt a strong impulse to remain behind the cover of the statue's base.

He crouched, resting the Sword on his shoulder, and scanned the balconies. He felt out through the blue wind, felt to see if he could sense anything coming.

A huge shadow moved along the roofline on the lefthand side of the castle. It started as a simple mound that shifted. Then it grew. The head-sized silhouette rose, and beneath it came shoulders and a bulky body.

Wings flexed, reaching outward, and a great horned head extended on its long neck, breaking the line of the roof so that there was no doubt who and what the creature was.

Jai'ketakos.

"The Drakanoi ..." the Sword whispered eagerly in Khyven's mind.

"No. Harkandos first," Khyven thought back to it.

He felt the Sword resist, felt it want to make its case, but it didn't.

The dragon shifted, claws gripping the peak of the roof as it surveyed the land. Khyven stayed perfectly still. He'd fight the dragon if he had to, but once that battle began, it would alert everyone within that castle. The chance for stealth would end, and the courtyard is where the fight would commence. The fight for everything.

Khyven's instincts told him it shouldn't start here. Wrong time. Wrong place. Wrong opponent. He wanted Harkandos. If Khyven could take the battle straight to the Giant—if he could cut the head from the snake—the Giant's army may well fall apart.

So he stayed absolutely still. He even beseeched the blue wind to draw in around his body, to go quiescent. He'd never commanded the blue wind to do something like that before.

But it obeyed with surprising swiftness. The blue mist that had seemed to cover the ground around him drew back, massing around his ankles and knees like it was waiting, coiling quietly for a later attack.

Jai'ketakos launched from the rooftop. Khyven heard the distant cracking noise from a few of the roof tiles, heard them slide and fall from the edge and shatter on the courtyard.

The dragon winged hard upward. His great shadow whipped over Khyven's hiding place, followed quickly by a gust of wind from the powerful wings.

Then the dragon was past, an ugly blot on the gray sky overhead. Then smaller. Then just a moving dark spot above the horizon. He was headed toward Usara. Khyven didn't know why—Usara had been evacuated—but he had a sick feeling about it.

No. He couldn't be distracted. The dragon's destination was not Khyven's.

He turned back to look at the castle—

And heard a breathy laugh behind him.

"You ..." the breathy voice said. "You ... cheated."

The blue wind went crazy.

CHAPTER FORTY-FOUR

KHYVEN

The doppelgänger attacked. He feinted with an overhead strike, pulled it down short, amazingly fast, and turned it into a deadly thrust.

Khyven let it come. He had the Sword up, on his shoulder. He turned with it, naturally making it a defense. Blade crashed into blade, and Khyven trapped the doppelgänger's sword against the statue's base. Sparks exploded as metal struck stone.

Continuing the same turning motion, Khyven pulled a dagger and snapped a sidekick at the doppelgänger's knee.

But the fiend went low, saving himself from a broken leg. It didn't work perfectly for him. He presented, instead, his chest.

The full force of Khyven's kick hit the doppelgänger like a battering ram. The thing flew backward.

Khyven tried to keep the bastard's blade, tried to trap it against the stone, but the doppelgänger held on. He was phenomenally strong, and he just yanked it back with him as he went. The tip scraped and sparked, going wide as it reached the edge of the base.

The doppelgänger sailed backward, landed on his back. Khyven pursued, a hair's breadth behind.

Blue lines flew everywhere, but Khyven ignored them. This was his fight. He wasn't giving it over to the magic or anything else. He wanted to kill this fiend himself. This time the fight would be different.

This time Khyven didn't have anything to lose.

He didn't care that the doppelgänger had Khyven's style of mismatched armor while Khyven wore only breeches, boots, and a Kyolar-chewed tunic. He didn't care if his friends might get hurt, or a kingdom might fall. He didn't care about anything except killing this thing.

The doppelgänger rolled gracefully backward, somersaulted to his feet, and thrust his sword at Khyven's charge like a sharpened siege stick.

Khyven didn't slow.

He twisted his shoulders sideways, and the blade missed him by exactly half an inch. The Sword moved with him like it was part of his arm, knocking the doppelgänger's weapon aside. Then Khyven whipped around in a pirouette, again holding the doppelgänger's sword away with his own.

The doppelgänger drew a dagger and tried to stick Khyven with his other hand, but Khyven drew one of his own and blocked it as he spun. With his arms crossed close to his chest, he caught the blade as he moved, let go of the Sword with his right hand, and released all of his momentum into an elbow strike.

It slammed into the doppelgänger's temple, making a noise like a mallet striking wood.

The Sword hovered in place where Khyven had left it, not falling to the ground like a normal sword would have, and Khyven grabbed the hilt again like he'd left it leaning against a weapon's rack.

The doppelgänger's head slammed to the side, but he was already moving, backpedaling, knowing he had to put distance between himself and Khyven or that would be the end of this fight.

Khyven followed and snapped another kick at the man's gut. The doppelgänger went low again, and the foot hit him in the chest again. He flew backward.

Khyven pursued like a sprinting Kyolar.

The thing was tough. Was this what it was like for an opponent facing Khyven? Even hammered in the temple, kicked backward, the fiend recovered from both while still on the move. Somehow, he sheathed his dagger, held onto his sword, and did a one-handed cartwheel to come back to his feet before Khyven could attack.

Khyven's follow up thrust almost took him in the chest, but somehow the fiend blocked it.

"You're going to die," Khyven said.

"That is what you thought last time," the thing breathed, and it had the audacity to smile. It cut sideways at Khyven, and he bashed the blade away.

But the fiend was as innovative as Khyven himself. It took the rebound and then, with tremendous strength of arm and shoulder, reversed the rebound and sent the blade back in exactly the same strike, but much harder.

It was meant to catch Khyven in the side as he used the rebound from the clash to come around from the other side. The sudden double strike was meant to bust Khyven's rib, perhaps even cut straight through to his heart. And it would have succeeded. Khyven wasn't wearing any armor that could turn it aside.

But both the Sword and Khyven sensed the attack at the last instant. It seemed the moment Khyven reversed his strike, the Sword added even more momentum to it.

"Destroy it," Khyven thought to the Sword. *"Break that blade!"*

"Yesss ..."

The blades came together an inch from Khyven's head, hitting with cataclysmic force.

Sparks flew, and a purple light flashed.

The doppelgänger's blade did not break. Khyven felt the

Sword's disappointment in his head.

Teeth showing, Khyven leapt high, whipping the Sword around in an overhand strike. It opened up his left side, and the doppelgänger took the bait. He chopped a third time at Khyven's ribs—

Khyven caught the blade with an angled dagger, took the brunt, let the blade taste his flesh. It cut his rib, but it was right where Khyven wanted it.

He brought the Sword down with all his might, edge on flat, while holding the doppelgänger's Mavric iron sword hooked on his dagger.

At the last instant, the fiend saw it and tried to pull the weapon away.

Too late. The Sword crashed down, and purple light flared again, writhing like fingers of lighting.

The doppelgänger's sword shattered, blowing in half. Shards flew everywhere, and the fiend stumbled back, eyes wide in surprise.

The shock of the explosion drove Khyven's dagger hand down, but he instantly brought it back up in an underhanded throw.

The dagger took the doppelgänger in the throat. He brought his sword up to block it, but hadn't compensated for its new shortened length. He choked, his overlarge eyes growing to comical proportions.

Khyven didn't let up. He wasn't going to let up ever again. He charged and thrust the Sword into the doppelgänger's chest. The thing tried to block, swung down, hit the Sword with his broken blade. It clanged pitifully; there was no power in the swing, and the Sword was already deep in the doppelgänger's chest.

The doppelgänger sighed, still looking entirely mystified, then fell backward. The Sword slid out of his chest like his body was made of butter.

Still alert for a last minute, desperate attack, Khyven followed and chopped the thing's head from its body. The head rolled away, hitting the base of another statue.

Khyven wiped the blood from the Sword, but he did not sheathe it.

"Good," he said.

"Yessss," the Sword responded.

Khyven spat on the doppelgänger's headless body. "Your master is next."

CHAPTER FORTY-FIVE

RHENN

It was almost too easy, and that made Rhenn nervous.

After she'd talked with Teleth, he'd shown her where they had stockpiled the Usaran weapons after their users had been killed or captured. The Nox had piled them all in the broken atrium, along with most of the Amulets of Noksonon. The amulets had been left on those in the feasting room, but according to Teleth, the amulets had been taken away from the Humans kept in the great hall—which was lined with raven totems—a deterrent for them to try to escape. Without the amulets, they would be blind once they entered the noktum.

Rhenn visited the atrium next, for the amulets and also the weapons. They couldn't face any kind of opposition with just bare fists and sticks, despite what she'd said in the Nox feasting room.

Of course, her current army wasn't an elite team of Knights of the Sun, to say the least. The enslaved Nox had feasted upon the Knights of the Steel and the Knights of the Dark first. Only three Knights of the Steel remained.

Most of her army—the ones who were not Nox—were civilians who had been so traumatized that they would likely be more of a hindrance than an asset in battle, but this wasn't a battle. This was *the* battle. The last battle. Either they prevailed or they were all going to die.

They armed up, and everyone who could carry more than just their own weapons strapped them to their body so they could bring weapons to those confined in the raven totem hall.

They wended their way through the hallway, and for group so large, they were relatively quiet. But more than a hundred people could never be completely quiet. There were clinks of weapons. There were coughs and whispers. In the previously silent hallways, they might as well have been banging pots and pans.

But no one stopped them, and Rhenn's unease grew as they neared their destination.

The few straggling defenders she encountered on the way to the great hall were all Nox still befuddled by the sudden loss of N'ssag's control. Upon seeing the Human and Nox army, every one of them joined up.

Except Harkandos's army wasn't just made up of Nox, and the further they traveled through the castle without any resistance, without any alarm going up, the more the hairs on the back of Rhenn's neck stood up. It was as though the Trolls had been sent elsewhere, as though the beasts had been banished from the castle. And, of course, they hadn't seen any of the Giants. There simply wasn't a single enemy in sight.

So where were they?

Even though she began to feel as though eyes were watching their every move, she proceeded to the raven totem room. She considered taking her force out of the castle, bivouacking in the forest, and drawing up a plan that she was more certain wasn't simply playing into the enemy's hands, but …

What would that plan be? She had no base of power. There would be no resources in those woods, and it was territory that surely Harkandos's beasts knew better than she did.

And she simply couldn't stomach leaving half of her people behind to either be killed or held hostage. There was really only one thing she could do. She had to get her people as fast as she could and retake this castle.

Not for the first time, she wished she had her friends with her: Lorelle at her side, Khyven striding next to her, exuding that crazy confidence he inspired. She wished she had Vohn here with his sensible counsel. She wished Slayter was babbling about the odds of success, coming up with miraculous ideas at the last minute. He would have given her a reason why the castle was calm.

Finally, they reached the doors of the great hall. Each of the three double-doors had been chained and locked except for one.

Just the one.

It was the furthest up the hall, on the left. That door had brackets that had been installed by an engineer—or by magic—and a bar on the outside. It was clearly something easier to remove and replace than the chains. It had to be the guards' entrance.

And it had no guards.

"Were the Nox guarding this room?" She asked Teleth.

He shook his head. "Trolls."

"Then where are they?" she murmured. "Stay alert. None of this seems right."

"I agree," L'elica said.

They crept up to the guards' door. The hallway outside the great hall was enormous, Giant sized, a grand foyer for waiting guests. Rhenn guessed that the great hall was once used for feasting and celebrations. Nearly her entire army could cluster into the hall.

She lifted the thick wooden bar and beckoned Elcaran, one of the remaining Knights of the Steel, and Meliken, who had been a baker in his previous life. Both had survived the feasting room.

"Go inside, rally them, and pass out amulets," Rhenn said. "Then topple the raven totems. They go inert if they are lying on their sides. Once you've done that, we can all enter the room.

Elcaran gave a baleful glance at the Nox, who he had witnessed kill many of his fellows. She could practically read his thoughts. Let the bloodsuckers burst in to flame.

"Elcaran," she said. "I know how you feel, but this is the army we have, the only strength we have. If we don't work together, this tiny slice of hope shatters, and your fate will be as bad as before. You will not be safe simply because that room has sunlight."

He looked back at her, and nodded tersely. "Yes, my queen."

"Topple the totems."

"Yes, my queen."

Rhenn motioned the Nox back, but they didn't need to be told. They knew very well what was on the other side of the door. As N'ssag had purified his process, the sunlight had become even more deadly to his creations. Without Slayter's sword, Rhenn would last about a minute in full sunlight. These new Nox bloodsuckers blew apart within thirty seconds, reduced nearly instantly to sizzling bones and gobbets of frying meat.

She drew her sword and gripped it tightly as Elcaran approached the door—

"Did you really think your little rebellion would work?" A deep, chilling voice came from the end of the hall.

Rhenn snapped her gaze up. Beyond the door, the empty hallway shimmered like a mirage, vanished, and Harkandos stood there.

He nearly filled the hallway, and some of his Giants stood behind him. Harkandos wore a thick metal belt made of rounded pieces of Mavric iron, baggy pants in the style of the Sandrunners, and no tunic on his chiseled, thickly muscled torso. His heavy beard extended midway to his belly, as did a chain that was draped over his neck like a scarf, with two metal disks at their ends, each resting on either side of his chest.

"I was going to allow some of your followers to live," Harkandos said. "No longer. Clearly they have rebellion in their hearts, and that is not useful to me. I will strip your kingdom down to the bone. The only evidence your culture ever existed will be your ruined, empty cities. You will become an object lesson for any who defy me. Usarans, the people who failed to obey. The people who ended the day their foolish queen did not take what she was offered and fall to her knees in gratitude."

"I would rather die here," she said. "Than put my people into your hands."

"So I see."

Rhenn showed her teeth. "I will see your head cut from your body, Giant."

"Bold words," he said. "But bold words are all you have, Human who was once a queen. The plans of your mortal mind are obvious to me. You've come for your people, and you're sending in one of your Humans because your traitorous Nox allies will die if touched by sunlight. Look at them, huddled at the far end of the corridor for fear of that door."

Rhenn felt a horrible tingle at the base of her skull. The corridor was solid stone. Vaulted ceilings. No windows or doors on the right-hand side. All the doors on the left-hand side went into the killing sunlight.

"This is what we call a killing chute." Harkandos seemed to read her mind. He raised his hand. "Let's thin out your numbers."

"Get out!" Rhenn spun and shouted at the Nox, but it was too late. Far too late.

The entire left-hand wall, doors and all, dissolved. Solid stone and thick wood turned to sand.

Sunlight exploded into the hall.

CHAPTER FORTY-SIX

RHENN

"No!" Rhenn shouted as sunlight flooded into the corridor.

The Nox burst into flame, screaming. They tried to flee, flinging their arms up to block the sun that tore into them. Their flaming bodies leapt about, arms flailing. Horrible howls turned the entire hallway into the scene from nightmare.

Some leapt thirty feet straight over the heads of the dumbfounded Humans, but there was nowhere to go.

At the far end of the corridor, where they'd entered, the spider Giant, Raos, and a horde of Trolls blocked the way. The Nox scrambled toward them, out of their minds with pain, and fell to the axes and hammers of the Trolls. Raos watched the slaughter from her perch high on the side of the right-hand wall.

Some Nox leapt toward Harkandos in desperation, but with a flick of his finger, he swatted them down like flies, just as he had Lorelle.

Rhenn felt the sunlight like she would have felt a hundred and ten degree day. It hurt, but it was bearable.

She spun, looking for an answer. She had to do something, had to turn this disaster around. More than half her army—the most competent part—was going to be charred meat in twenty seconds. She had to—

"Stop!" Someone said from the center of the brightly lit grand hall. Rhenn squinted into the blinding light and made out a thin man in robes with a dark cloak flared behind him.

"Slayter!" she shouted in relief.

His noktum cloak unfurled to reveal Vohn at his side. Slayter held his fist high, and orange light flared.

A hurricane wind whipped around the room. One by one, the raven totems fell from their pedestals to the floor.

The great hall plunged into darkness as the noktum flooded back in.

Slayter put shaky hands on his knees and vomited on the floor.

Chaos erupted.

Raos hissed. The Trolls roared. The Humans in the raven totem hall screamed at going blind.

"The mage!" Harkandos boomed in his thunderous voice.

"Into the room!" Rhenn shouted. "Fight!"

To her great relief, she saw most of the Nox leap, run, or limp for the room. Her cadre of armed Humans charged right behind them. Some of Nox, though, those who had caught the brunt of the sunlight, curled into themselves, smoking and shuddering with the horrific pain. Some crawled.

The Trolls crashed down on them, smashing the stragglers with hammers and axes.

The great hall was almost entirely swallowed by the noktum, but two of the totems had fallen right-side up. Spears of sunlight came down to them from the windows overhead like foot-thick columns of blinding white.

But there was enough blessed dark that most of her army had been saved, and there were doors on the other side of the expansive room. That was their escape, until they could rally, until they could find some way to fight effectively. Undoubtedly every door was locked from the outside, but that could be dealt with. Slayter could dissolve one of them just as Harkandos had done with the entire wall.

But she needed to run interference for him.

"Slayter! The doors!"

The mage raised his head, wiping his chin with his sleeve. He nodded haggardly and began limp-running toward the far side of the room.

"You are talented, mage." Harkandos raised his hand. "But you'll never make the door—"

At the last second, Harkandos jerked his head up in pain. He threw something invisible at Slayter. A gust of wind blew past him, barely missing and knocked down a dozen people to his right. Slayter ducked his head and kept running.

Rhenn turned back to the Giant. He snarled and reached up to his head. Dark flickered there, then a flash of pale white metal. There was a cloaked and slender figure perched on the Giant's shoulder, stabbing him. Its cowl fell back, revealing a grimy face twisted in rage, a head of tangled, matted hair with one glowing blond lock hanging over her eye.

Lorelle!

Rhenn's heart lifted with joy and wrenched the sorrow at the same time. Lorelle was alive, but it wasn't the Lorelle that Rhenn knew. She keened as she stabbed the Giant. She had become something twisted and wild.

"Fight!" Rhenn reluctantly turned her attention back to her bedraggled and wounded army. "Fight for your lives! Kill them all!"

Rhenn's cobbled-together army leapt into action as best they could. The reality of the situation had finally sunk in. There was no way out. They were going to fight or they were going to die. With screams of fear and anger and desperation, they set upon the Trolls.

Thankfully, some of those who had brought amulets and weapons for the Humans stuck in the great hall had kept their heads, passing out amulets and swords as quickly as they could.

Everyone who now had a weapon, and many who didn't, charged Harkandos. Rhenn led the way, screaming a battle cry. She had never been more proud of her people than she was at that moment. Some were charging the Giant with bare fists. The Nox, some with their ears burned off and charred flesh all over their bodies, leapt forward to meet the charge of the Trolls and Raos the spider Giant.

Two of Harkandos's other Giants, Orios and Mendos entered behind the Trolls.

Harkandos roared, reaching up to pluck Lorelle from his shoulder, but she vanished into the noktum cloak and his hand only slapped the wound she had just made. She landed on his other shoulder, screaming gibberish. She stabbed at him again.

"Enough!" He roared, clenching his fists and pressing his arms into his sides. An explosion of air blew out from him, sending Lorelle flying across the room like a doll. Rhenn, who was almost to the Giant, was also blown back, along with fifty other wild, amateur fighters behind her.

Still screaming unintelligibly as she streaked toward the wall like a comet, Lorelle vanished into the darkness of the cloak just before she hit.

Rhenn heard the glass ceiling of the great hall shatter even as Harkandos roared.

"Kill them. Kill them all!"

Mendos raised his hands. Fire spurted from them, fanning out. The Nox flinched away instinctively, and Rhenn cried out.

The flames leapt up like a wave, then descended on the hapless army of Nox and Humans as they all threw up their arms, shielding themselves—

The flames stopped short of Rhenn's army, rolled into themselves like a crashing wave before it rotated into a cylinder and spun, flicking off bits of fire.

"What?" Rhenn gasped.

Shards of glass fell onto the ground all around, and she remembered hearing it smash a second ago.

She looked up.

A black, winged shape trailing purple fire dropped from overhead, blotting out the broken skylight.

"Rauvelos!"

The giant raven slammed into the floor, talons cracking stone and shaking the entire room. He rose to his full height before Mendos.

"If you like fire," Rauvelos said. "I'll happily oblige you."

Mendos's spinning fire cylinder flickered, shrank, and died. Mendos's face twisted into a snarl and he raised his hands again.

Rauvelos leapt into the air. His wings beat backward as his talons whipped forward and sank into Mendos's chest.

The Giant screamed.

Rauvelos beat skyward, lifting the struggling Giant up like he weighed nothing. The raven burst through another pane of the skylight. More glass shattered and fell.

Rauvelos and Mendos were gone.

"Fight!" Rhenn shouted, rushing Harkandos again. The Giant had taken the reprieve to magically heal the wounds inflicted by Lorelle, but he flicked his gaze back up to Rhenn and her army.

"You are *all* going to die!" Harkandos growled.

As if in answer, Lorelle appeared out of the dark at his side, slashed his calf—

But her cloak suddenly twisted around her neck like a noose. She struggled, legs kicking as it hoisted her into the air. Her feral scream turned into a choke as he grabbed her around the neck. She glared daggers at him.

"No!" Rhenn shouted, and she finally reached the damned Giant. She swung at his knee, but he blocked it with a hand. It was as if her sword hit stone, sparking and doing nothing. He kicked her in the gut. She felt her ribs break, and she flew backward, crashing into a half dozen people behind her.

She rolled to a stop, facing the other way. She heard Humans and Nox dying all around her, crushed by hammers, by axes, burned by spells, smashed by wind as solid as stone. And she heard the whistling scream of her friend dying as she choked.

Her gaze fell on Slayter, who had been heading for the middle door on the far side of the hall to open it, to give them an escape. But he hadn't made it yet. Something held him, cast by Orios or perhaps by Avektos, who had now entered the fray. Slayter was trapped in a glowing purple box that was slowly shrinking, pushing him down. He snapped disk after disk in his hands and orange light flared, which was probably the only reason he wasn't dead yet, but the invisible force was slowly winning. He was already bent double. If the box kept shrinking, his bones would break.

She looked at the doors. They needed to flee, to regroup. The Giants were too powerful, and they were prepared. Rhenn's army needed to get away for just a moment, turn this fight around somehow. They needed—

The middle door exploded outward as though struck by a great force.

"Slayter!" she cried gratefully. He had done it! Even in his prison, the selfless mage had fought to give them an escape—

But a figure stepped through the doorway. A six-foot sword glowed purple in his fist, and she realized Slayter hadn't opened the door. The man on the other side had blown it open with his giant, Mavric iron sword. The steel plate on his shoulder, the chain mail on his torso, and that Ringer's swagger gave him away.

Rhenn's heart sank. Their salvation had turned to ruin. It was Khyven's twin, blocking their only exit.

"No ..." she murmured, forcing herself up to her hands and knees.

The fiendish twin came into the room, and Rhenn wanted to scream in frustration.

The dust cleared from the blasted door, and a chill ran up her back. The twin had no exaggerated scars. No overlarge eyes or slanted eyebrows.

"Harkandos!" Khyven the Unkillable roared. "It is time for you to die!"

CHAPTER FORTY-SEVEN

KHYVEN

Khyven!" Rhenn shouted.

Khyven heard her shout his name in triumph, and it brought a conflicted rush of happiness and fear. He'd thought she was dead; he'd thought they were all dead, and he was overjoyed that she, Lorelle, Slayter, and Vohn were all here, all living.

But this was not the scene he was hoping for. This was not the fight he'd prepared for. He had hoped to enter the castle undetected and brace Harkandos alone, one-on-one. And everything had gone to plan. Not a single sentry heard his battle with the doppelgänger. There had been no one guarding the servant's entrance, and there had been no one in the halls.

He had felt like he was sailing under Senji's protection.

But this scene was a nightmare. Fear and uncertainty assailed him. Lorelle was choking. Rhenn was on the floor, possibly broken. People all around were burned. Slayter was being crushed. All of his friends alive but ... all about to die.

Khyven had seen himself as a spear in flight with only one

purpose. Now he had half a dozen things he must do. He had to save his friends. He couldn't just focus on the fight with Harkandos. He had to manage this nightmare.

That reality caused him to hesitate for a moment, standing in the dust of the destroyed door. Khyven unleashed the blue wind, and it flowed toward possible courses of action.

His hesitation vanished, and he knew exactly what he had to do.

Khyven heaved the Sword overhand at Slayter, then charged after. The Mavric iron blade spun end over end and struck the purple cage around Slayter, shattering it.

The Giantess with the shimmering black robes shuddered, and her starry sky eyes widened. Apparently that had been her spell.

Khyven reached Slayter only a second after his cage shattered. The Sword stopped its spin, slowed, then hovered in place.

"Need your help," Khyven drew two long daggers he'd taken off the doppelgänger. He'd also been able to don the creature's armor. One advantage of having a duplicate: the armor fit perfectly.

"Yes!" Slayter sucked in a breath, his flushed face alight with an eager smile.

"Help Lorelle." Khyven called over his shoulder, then turned his focus on Harkandos. He had to keep his eye on the prize. Harkandos was all that mattered right now. Everything flowed from that one goal.

Khyven hurled one dagger and, a second after that, the second. Both unerringly spun toward the Giant, a staggered attack. That method had worked wonders a number of times in the Night Ring. Throw one dagger, and an opponent might deflect it. Throw two at the same time, and a talented swordsman could swat them both away as a single attack.

But stagger them just a little, not so quickly that they came as one, but not so far apart that the enemy had time to reorient, and it threw off just about any rhythm.

A flare of fire erupted around Harkandos's wrist, the one controlling the spell that had turned Lorelle's cloak against her. The cloak went limp and Lorelle dropped toward the floor.

Harkandos growled and put the fire out.

That's when Khyven's daggers arrived. Harkandos swatted the first away with a hasty protection spell, but the second slipped past, sunk into his shoulder.

He roared.

Lorelle vanished into her cloak before it hit the ground.

"Yeah!" Khyven held his hand out behind himself.

The Sword's hilt slapped into Khyven's palm at the moment he reached Harkandos. Khyven hadn't even been absolutely sure it could do that—fly across the room and then return to his hand—but the blue wind had guided him to throw the Sword, free Slayter, and throw the daggers.

Khyven had promised Senji he would do anything, use everything that he could to win this battle. He didn't second guess, didn't think. The Sword had flown back to his hand. Of course it had.

The blue wind spun in a corkscrew and Khyven threw himself sideways. Harkandos's fist whipped out, just missing him. Khyven locked his stance and swung to take out the Giant's knee—

A Nox half-dead from burns flew in front of Khyven's sword. Khyven pulled the strike at the last second, but the Sword bit deep into the Nox's shoulder.

"What are you doing?" The Sword asked. *"I could have gone through that Nox and still hit Harkandos's knee."*

"I'm not killing an innocent!"

"You're not ..." The Sword said incredulously. *"Well, I don't even know where to start, Khyven Slayer of Trolls. That is poor strategy. You cannot hope to win against an opponent like this without innocent deaths. You have just shouted your weakness to Harkandos. He will throw innocents against you endlessly—"*

"Shut up!"

Three blue spears rushed at Khyven, two so dark blue they

were almost black, and one—fatter and larger—was lighter. He dodged the first two but couldn't get out of the way of the third.

Harkandos kicked out, and his boot glanced off Khyven's shoulder plate. There was so much force in it that the glancing blow lifted Khyven off the ground and flung him like a doll.

Nox and Humans arrived, and they attacked Harkandos with the verve of those who had no idea how outclassed they were.

"No!" Khyven grunted. "Leave him to me!"

Harkandos clenched his fist and a blast of fire shot out in every direction, incinerating the two Nox and three Humans who had dared attack.

The Sword jerked, rising up and taking Khyven's fist with it. It cut through the magical fire. Flames blasted on either side of Khyven, and the walls on either side of him melted.

He, however, was unharmed.

"Pay attention, Khyven Slayer of Trolls."

"Stop calling me that!"

"If I am the only one looking out for your welfare, Harkandos the Great will kill you—"

"Shut up! Every time you pop into my head it breaks my concentration."

"Ah." The Sword went silent.

There were no opponents between Harkandos and Khyven now. The other attackers had been completely incinerated. The Giant narrowed his eyes when he saw that Khyven had survived.

"I saw you die," Harkandos said. "Yet here you are. That blast should have killed you, and yet you stand ..."

Khyven leapt to his feet. At the behest of the blue wind, he circled the Giant.

"That sword ..." Harkandos said. "That is not the Mavric iron sword I gave to your mirror."

"No. But it has your name on it." Khyven ached to attack again, but the blue wind was not showing any blue funnels on the Giant, and that made him uneasy. He kept circling.

"That is the Sword of Noksonon!" Harkandos snarled.

"I just call it the Sword."

"That is the creation of the father. That is Noktos's own blade! You profane his memory by touching it."

"Well, tell that to the Sword. I tried to get rid of it. It won't go."

"Blasphemer!"

"I suppose you would be a better wielder of the Sword?"

The Giant showed his teeth. "Any Giant would be better than you."

"Then come take it," Khyven said in a low voice. He was frustrated by the absolute lack of blue funnels. He wanted in there! But he stayed patient.

"I am going to make you scream before you die," Harkandos said.

"For an omnipotent demigod, you spout a lot of big talk." There it was! A blue funnel just above the Giant's hip. Khyven feinted right and then spun left.

Harkandos's body flickered, then became solid again.

The blue funnel vanished, but Khyven followed through on the strike. He was only half a breath from—

His sword passed through Harkandos's side like there was nothing there, like he was a phantom.

Khyven lost his balance. He'd put so much strength into that strike that the absolute lack of resistance stole his equilibrium. He careened past, then regained his footing.

An illusion! That's what the flicker had been. Harkandos had put an illusion where he'd been, and then he had moved to a different location and was ...

Invisible.

Khyven backed slowly into the corridor. When he had fought Txomin the Sandrunner, Khyven had been blind. During that fight, he had relied on the blue wind to guide him.

But something was wrong with the blue wind. It had denied him an option while he circled Harkandos—practically a lifetime in a fight—and when it finally had shown him a way, it had failed. The blue wind had been as flummoxed by the illusion as Khyven had.

The blue wind had been uncertain when Khyven had faced his doppelgänger, and Harkandos had created the doppelgänger. What if Harkandos had a spell that could interfere with Khyven's magic?

If he's invisible and the blue wind isn't working, Khyven thought. *He could be anywhere.*

Khyven kept the Sword in front of himself. The Harkandos he'd tried to cut—the illusion—remained where it had been. The hulking, bearded Giant simply stood there as though waiting for Khyven to charge again.

"Your faith in Nhevalos is misplaced," Harkandos said from behind.

Khyven spun, slashing out with the Sword—

It whistled through empty air.

"He imbued you with his own breed of Lore Magic," Harkandos said again, right behind Khyven again.

Khyven spun, swung again. Again, the Sword whistled through nothing.

"What are you doing?" the Sword asked.

"An aberrant concoction, and he made you believe because of this, you were destined. Chosen." The voice came from Khyven's left this time. Khyven speared the air again.

"He lied," Harkandos whispered.

Khyven turned, pointing the Sword in front of himself. He put his back against the wall. He could see the entire battle before him. Rhenn led her Nox and Humans against the Trolls, and the conflict seemed evenly matched for the moment. Rhenn's army was three times the size of the Troll army, but the Trolls were larger, stronger, and fully equipped for battle. The members of Rhenn's army were haggard. Many of the Nox had been badly burned. The Humans were inexperienced, fatigued from their captivity, and poorly armed.

Slayter slung spells as fast as he could, but Orios flicked them away like flies. She seemed amused, like she enjoyed toying with this upstart mage.

Lorelle had reentered the fray. She also attacked Orios,

appearing and vanishing with the noktum cloak, trying to slash her. But the Giant batted her away with spell after spell, equally amused.

Raos clung to the ceiling with her spider legs, watching as though she wasn't even part of the fight.

The final Giant, Avektos, stood at the edge of the battlefield, just inside the hall. He held a great mace in his hand, taller than Khyven was, but he didn't engage in the fight either. The mace's head rested against the ground and he watched Khyven struggle, waiting for something.

We're losing, Khyven thought.

He had failed to take out Harkandos in the initial attack. That had been their chance. Khyven knew fighting, could feel the ebbs and flows of a conflict, the turning points, and they were at the turning point now. The Trolls fought all-out, but the Giants were toying with them. In control. Unworried.

Rhenn and her allies were out matched.

Khyven had to do something. He had to find Harkandos, pinpoint his location, and finish this—

"You thought you were chosen," Harkandos said from behind Khyven, from the wall itself. "But nothing is as it seems."

The wall wrapped around Khyven, and he cried out. He tried to duck and roll forward, but he was already caught. The wall had sprouted two huge, stone appendages. They encircled Khyven and pinned his arms. The wall rose up, legs emerging as it stood. Khyven saw the emerging Giant's head, which looked like it was made of the same stone blocks as the wall.

The illusion slid away like oil from a hot pan and Harkandos's bearded face emerged from the stones. His meaty fist closed over Khyven's forearm, huge thumb and forefinger pinching his wrist ...

Khyven gasped.

"He is trying to separate you from me," the Sword noted clinically.

"I ... can see ... that ..." Khyven grunted in his own mind. The pain was excruciating, and he felt his bones snap.

But they didn't.

The pain roared through him, but no break. The Giant should have been able to snap Khyven's wrist, but the Giant mashed and pinched to no avail.

Khyven noticed purple lighting crackled around Khyven's forearm. Slayter?

No, the mage was completely consumed in his battle with Orios.

"I cannot allow him to do that," the Sword said in his mind.

The Sword! The Sword was protecting him!

Not for the first time, Khyven marveled at the versatility of the weapon. Somehow, it had sent its magic into Khyven's arm and made it unbreakable. Just exactly what were the Sword's limits?

With a growl of frustration, Harkandos let go of Khyven's body, spun and whipped him by the arm, letting him go at the last second. Khyven flew up the hall, and as he did, he felt claws rake at his forearm, though no blood flew from the wounds. He felt a powerful pull on the Sword, trying to rip it from his grasp, but Khyven held on. He put all of his effort into holding on to the Sword.

He paid no attention to where was flying. The blue wind suddenly came to life again, and a huge blue spear arced toward him.

"Spin, Khyven Slayer of Trolls!"

The claws and the hold on the Sword ripped and fell away, and Khyven heard Harkandos utter another growl of frustration.

Khyven spun.

Avektos's enormous mace swung toward him. Khyven brought the Sword up to meet it.

Purple sparks flew, and the Sword sheared through the haft of the mace. The killing head of the mace, a three-foot wide spiral of sharp flanges, spun around Khyven, just missing him.

He slammed into Avektos's chest and the Giant stumbled backward.

"Hold him!" Harkandos snarled. "We have to separate

Noktos's blade from him!"

Avektos wrapped his arms around Khyven just as Harkandos had done, pinning him. Khyven tried to whip the Sword down to cut something, or up to cut something, but he didn't have the angle. He could have probably impaled the Giant's foot if he threw the Sword …

But that was exactly what they wanted. To separate him from it. What he had to do was—

Khyven looked up to see Harkandos charging. Crackling black light danced around his forearm, and a sword of pure dark energy elongated from his fist.

"Hold him still." Harkandos grabbed the energy sword's hilt with both hands and brought it up to stab.

Khyven had nowhere to go.

CHAPTER FORTY-EIGHT

VOHN

Vohn felt practically useless in battle. It was like the time with the Nox hunters in the Great Noktum. Khyven, Rhenn, and Lorelle were in their element here. Slayter seemed practically euphoric.

As usual, Vohn was just along for the ride. He was an advisor, not a warrior. The clanging of metal, roars of rage, and death cries echoed throughout the chamber. Vohn was no mage, but he could feel the magic in the air like the smell after a lightning strike. A thickness that made the hair on the back of his neck stand up.

He hesitated on the edge of the room, and likely because of his inherent Shadowvar abilities—or perhaps because he was the small fish to fry in this feast—no one had threatened him.

He clasped a dagger to his chest—it had been passed to him by Mavil Baetrey, one of the chambermaids from the Usaran palace—but he hadn't used it yet. He had considered several things he might do so far.

Rush out and stab a Troll in the calf.

Stand shoulder to hip with Rhenn and Lorelle and give his life that way.

But each time he thought of anything like that, he envisioned what would likely happen. He would charge out. He would strike, probably miss, and then he would die.

Useless.

He didn't want to simply throw his life away, but every second he hesitated, looking for something he could do that would actually help his friends, he felt more and more the coward. How his friends could actually enjoy this stark and vicious brutality was an insanity Vohn simply didn't understand.

So he stayed, frozen, willing himself to have the courage to throw his life on the fire, or the brilliance to come up with the idea that would turn the tide.

So lost was he in his thoughts, so paralyzed by indecision, that he didn't at first notice the white light that began to glow to his left. By the time he did, he gasped and turned, pointing the dagger.

An enormous figure—at first Vohn though it was another Giant, strangely shaped like the spider Giant Raos—appeared in an incandescent glow. It had wings, stood eight feet tall and had more legs than a person. The light was so bright that, at first, he had no idea what it was.

Then the glow receded and he saw it was a rider on a winged horse! The horse was all white, and its rider wore white-enameled armor. A long sword hilt protruded from a sheath on her back, and her single white braid poked beneath her full helm, which had a T-shaped slit in the front through which she could see. Her green eyes flashed as she turned and looked down at him, and he thought he saw a smile.

"Sometimes it is hard to find courage," she signed with her right hand.

"Shalure!?" he blurted.

"Yes," she said, this time aloud, and there was no impediment to her speech.

"What ...? How ...? What is this?"

"A phantom, if you will." He couldn't see her face, nothing except the green eyes, but her voice sounded wistful. "And a temporary one at that."

"We left you ... You're in ..."

"The infirmary, I know. My body is there still."

"What is happening?"

"Blame Senji."

"What?"

"I could explain, or I could help you make your choice. You once told me to find my purpose, and I have. Will you let me help you?" She extended her hand.

He hesitated, then grasped it. She lifted him effortlessly up and behind her. He straddled the horse awkwardly and grasped her waist, feeling the solidness of her, the warmth. Phantom? What kind of phantom was this?

"Now hold on tight," she said needlessly, and the winged horse leapt into the air. He pressed his face into the hard, white-enameled metal of her back as they climbed. Pump, pause, pump, pause, pump.

They soared over the battle. No one seemed to have seen them take off. No one seemed to be watching them now.

"Can they see us?" Vohn asked, wondering if he'd been slain and didn't know it. Was he a ghost now, too? Was that why he could touch her? Was that why she felt solid, because he was also insubstantial?

"Those who are looking, yes. But to most we will simply be a half-remembered mirage, a thing they think they saw, but aren't sure."

"Shalure, I didn't mean to hurt you. I didn't mean to ... I thought I was just taking you with me. I hoped that I could bring you away from the dragon—"

She twisted in her saddle. The winged horse hovered gently. Time seemed to slow, and Shalure reached out a gentle hand. She put it on his cheek. It was soft and comforting, despite the fact that she wore a full battle gauntlet.

"I know, gentle Vohn. You're the best of us, and I know you

would never willingly hurt me, or your friends, or really anyone if you didn't have to."

Vohn swallowed.

"But now is the time to fight. And you have to find your courage. Just as you showed me how to find mine, you must find yours now."

She turned back around, and time reasserted itself. She dove over the battle, toward the Giants Avektos and Orios. Avektos held a struggling Khyven. Harkandos charged them both, a crackling black sword pointed straight at Khyven's chest.

"Only you can help him now," she said. "Only you."

"How?"

"You know how. You didn't mean to hurt me, I know that. But you must mean it this time."

Vohn's mind froze as they dove. Again time slowed, but now it was not gentle. It was a decision balanced on the edge of a frosty knife.

The idea filled Vohn with dread. It could kill him. He could get lost again. And worst of all, he had no idea if it would work.

"Find your courage," Shalure whispered. "This is your purpose."

Then she and the horse were gone.

Vohn was falling.

CHAPTER FORTY-NINE

KHYVEN

Khyven stared his death in the face. He'd come. He'd defeated the doppelgänger, and he had done everything he could to defeat Harkandos. If it was over, then it was over.

But he wasn't about to just sit still.

He hadn't been able to break free. He hadn't been able to strike with his blade, but Khyven had assessed where the fat Giant's balls ought to be. And perhaps, just perhaps, Giants felt the same way about their balls that Humans did.

Khyven kicked viciously backward. His thigh and knee curled around the Giant's gut, and his heel nailed the flabby Giant between the legs. Avektos groaned, sagged, and his arms softened a little.

But he didn't let go.

Khyven thrashed, but it simply wasn't enough. He was out of time.

Harkandos loomed.

Eat this, Khyven thought. With one hand, he raised the

Sword of Noksonon and pointed it at his enemy. It was barely half the length of the enormous energy sword that Harkandos wielded. There was no way he'd stab Harkandos before dying himself. But maybe the bastard would trip and get a face full of Mavric iron.

Khyven screamed his fury. Harkandos screamed it back and—

Movement caught Khyven's attention. Something fell from above. He flicked a glance that direction, thinking he was being attacked by one of Harkandos's beasts ...

But it wasn't a beast at all ...

Vohn fell from the open air.

He landed awkwardly on Avektos's shoulder. A small ring spun past Khyven's face, glowing with purple light, and it hit the floor with a clink. Vohn shouted, wrapped his arms around Avektos's head and grabbed hold of his ears, like he was trying to pull them off.

What the—?!?

Avektos roared in pain ... and then in panic.

There was a great whooshing sound, like wind sucking air up a tunnel. The Giant's arms turned into translucent purple smoke ...

And he and Vohn were gone.

Khyven fell. Harkandos's energy blade shot forward at his chest.

"Twist!" the Sword shouted in his mind, but Khyven was already twisting. He brought the Sword edge to edge with Harkandos's magical blade and braced for the weight of it to knock him backward, but the Sword deflected the Giant's blade like it was a river reed.

Purple energy crackled and popped.

Harkandos stumbled past. The clashing of the two blades spun Khyven even faster, but he craned his neck to keep Harkandos in view. Khyven wrenched his arm backward and flung the Sword with all his might at the blue funnel that had just appeared.

The Sword flew as straight and as fast as an arrow. Purple energy crackled like a miniature lightning storm. Whatever protection the Giant had thrown about himself sparked and failed.

The blade punched through the Giant's huge, meaty calf like paper, cleaved through the bone, burst out the other side, and embedded itself into the stone. Only the hilt stuck out of the back of the Giant's leg.

"I can cut through anything!" the Sword shouted in Khyven's mind.

"Hurt him!" Khyven shouted back.

Harkandos roared, now pinned to the floor. He fell awkwardly to one knee. The Giant's energy sword spat purple flame and vanished.

Gritting his huge, white teeth, Harkandos whipped his bearded face around to Khyven. His eyes blazed with fury.

One of the doppelgänger's long daggers lay on the stones between them, and Khyven snatched it up.

Khyven's unexpected throwing of the Sword had damaged Harkandos more than anything so far, but Khyven had given away his only advantage. He had to get the Sword back.

Harkandos's fist lit up with magical purple fire. He seethed at Khyven and pointed his fist.

"You die now!"

The purple fireball burst toward Khyven. He held the long dagger up, but he knew it would do no good. The only weapon that could cleave a Giant's fire in half was currently stuck through a Giant's leg.

The fire reached Khyven—

And burst upon an invisible wall a foot in front of his face. He felt the tremendous heat above and on either side of him, but it flowed around like a diverted river.

"Urgh!" Slayter huffed, limping toward him. Orange light glowed around his fist, crumbles of clay drifting down. The mage looked haggard, eyes sunken, skin flushed as if with fever, arms shaking.

But he stood there, using perhaps the last of his magic to save Khyven's life ... He stood there, far too close to the deadly Giant.

"Rrraaagh!" Harkandos leaned heavily, falling onto his side and cracking the cobblestones with one elbow while he swung his huge fist at Slayter.

"No!" Khyven leapt forward, but he was simply too far away.

The fist whistled past Slayter, missing by an inch. The mage's hair ruffled in the breeze, and he blinked. He took out another disk and snapped it. Orange light flared.

Harkandos roared and reached back to his calf. If he hadn't been stuck to the ground, he'd have had the mage, and now he clearly planned to pull the Sword out and use it himself.

Khyven leapt for the hilt as the Giant reached, but it was no contest. Khyven was half a heartbeat too slow.

Orange light crackled around the Giant's arm, slowing it. Slayter's spell!

Rhenn appeared then, bounding atop Harkandos's shoulder.

"I told you I'd have your head!" Rhenn had somehow lost her sword, but she sank her teeth into his neck, ripping flesh, muscle, and tendons out like roots. Blood sprayed across her face and Harkandos roared in pain. Just like with Avektos, Khyven heard panic this time.

Rhenn shoved her head into the fountain of blood, gulping and tearing with her fingers and teeth. Harkandos stopped reaching for the Sword, and reached up to grab the queen.

Darkness unfurled on the back of the Giant's reaching hand, and Lorelle appeared, dark and grimy and stabbing like mad. She keened as her knives flashed up and down, up and down, lopping off his pinky finger, cutting his index finger to the bone, chopping into his wrist.

Khyven's hand curled around the hilt of the Sword.

"Ah!" the Sword said, satisfied. *"I missed you, Slayer of Giants."*

"Of Giants? Not yet."

"A prediction. My own form of Lore Magic," the Sword said. *"It is*

humor, yes?"

Harkandos had struggled against the blade pinning him to the ground, and it hadn't budged. But when Khyven touched it, it slid free like he was pulling it out of water.

Harkandos howled. Slayter slowed his movements. Rhenn chewed into his neck. Lorelle sawed at his fingers. Khyven sidestepped, cocking back the Sword, but over the melee, he saw Orios looking right at them, no more than two dozen paces away.

She was the last of Harkandos's Giants. The rest were dead or disappeared. Her starry gaze took in the tableau at a glance.

Harkandos saw her, too.

"Orios!" he called to her. "Help me!"

Ever before, she had worn an amused grin, but not now. Her face was impassive. She blinked once, lazily. Her robes folded in upon themselves, and she vanished into the dark.

"Noooo!" Harkandos roared.

"Fulfill my humor!" the Sword urged Khyven. *"Make me funny!"*

In the Night Ring, Khyven had heard many bloodthirsty chants from the crowd, urging him to violence, spurring him to victory. The Sword's was by far the most bizarre.

Harkandos tried to bring his arms down, tried to defend himself, but they simply moved too slowly. Blood poured from his neck and his mutilated left hand, and his right hand barely blocked at all.

Khyven shoved it away with his left elbow, spun closer.

He whipped the Sword of Noksonon up, locked his stance and shoulder …

And thrust with all his might.

The point punched through the center of Harkandos's chest, sliding up to the hilt.

Harkandos's eyes bulged.

Khyven yanked the blade out. Blood gushed from the wound, and Khyven stabbed him again.

Blood bubbled from Harkandos's mouth.

Rhenn leapt away from the Giant's neck as though she knew

what was coming next.

The Giant feebly tried to grab at Khyven, but he stepped on the Giant's arm and leapt high.

"I ..." Harkandos gurgled. "I ..."

"Shut up!" Khyven said through his teeth.

He chopped the Giant's head from his body.

CHAPTER FIFTY

KHYVEN

Khyven, Rhenn, Lorelle, and Slayter all stood over the corpse of Harkandos. Khyven stayed ready, the Sword poised in his hand. He fully expected the Giant to suddenly lurch to his feet and reach for one of them. He expected Harkandos to sit up and fling magic at them, burn them or freeze them where they stood.

But Harkandos's dead eyes stayed dead, one lid half down, the other wide open. His tongue lolled from his mouth, sticking between his enormous teeth. The pool of blood beneath his head, his severed neck, and below his ravaged hand stopped flowing.

Beyond them, the tide of the battle had turned. Fighting still raged, but the Trolls were backing up. The Humans had begun using the raven totems to drive them. Someone had had the brilliant idea to pick up the fallen totems and create a wall on one side of the Trolls, like a forest of light spears. The Humans would charge through, then retreat, forcing the Trolls back. And on the other side, steeped in the Dark, the Nox decimated the

Trolls' numbers.

Working together, the two distinct teams forced the Trolls back into the corridor, killing and killing. Without the Giants, the Trolls were outnumbered. They finally seemed to realize this and, one by one, fled with the Nox in hot pursuit. Khyven didn't give the Trolls good odds of making it out of the castle.

Khyven stood, dazed, and looked back at Harkandos's bloody and decapitated body, then at his friends. Rhenn seemed dazed as well, like a predator at the end of the hunt. Giant's blood bathed her chin and soaked the front of her torn clothing. She stared at the corpse, eyes ablaze. She looked like she wanted to leap upon the Giant and keep tearing at him, then she shook her head, resisting. Her breathing slowed, and her whole body shook this time, like a dog coming in from the rain. She blinked, and her eyes finally cleared.

"Rhenn?" Khyven asked.

"I'm fine. I just ... It's hard to come back, when I do that. I'm ... I'm fine."

He heard a noise, and he turned, bringing the Sword to bear.

Lorelle crouched atop Harkandos's hip like a feral fox, her knives dripping. Her noktum cloak was sodden with blood, and it hung low on either side of her. A continuous whine seeped from her lips.

"Lorelle?" Khyven said.

"Lorelle, it's all right," Rhenn said.

"What happened to her?" Khyven asked. He moved toward her.

She bared her teeth. Her low whine turned into a hiss.

Khyven stopped.

"The sword, Khyven. Put it away," Rhenn said.

Khyven lowered the Sword. "I would never hurt her. She knows that. I would never—"

"I'm not sure she knows who you are right now."

"What happened?" he demanded.

"You died," Rhenn said softly.

"But I didn't. I'm ... here now."

"Khyven, your soul bond. I don't know what paths you've walked, but you were dead. The soul bond was torn asunder. She's ..." Rhenn trailed off. Clearly, she didn't have the rest of that sentence.

"Let her be," a voice came from the direction of the retreating battle. Another Nox, a male, moved toward them with that same litheness that all Nox and Luminents possessed.

Khyven narrowed his eyes, recognizing the Nox, and the urge to raise the Sword was strong.

"Zaith," he said through his teeth.

Lorelle turned her gaze from Khyven to the Nox.

Slayter snapped his fingers. "From Nox Arvak! The one with the slashed neck—"

"Slayter!" Rhenn held up a hand, then turned to the Nox. "Thank you for your assistance, Zaith. Without you, we ... Well, thank you."

"It was an honor. Thank you for ... freeing us."

"And yet you're telling me to leave my lover alone," Khyven said. "That seems like bad advice. Or advice with an agenda."

"An agenda ..." Zaith said. "Are you asking if I plan to steal the lovely Lorelle from you? Make a bid for her affections?"

"Not asking you anything, really. Warning you."

The Nox smiled a hard smile. He bowed low, then straightened and looked into Khyven's eyes.

"You have great prowess as a fighter among Humans. This renown armors you and elevates you to a height where wisdom dissipates into thin air."

Khyven glanced sidelong at Slayter. "I think he just called me stupid."

Slayter's eyes were aglow as he watched the Nox. "Well, there are many different levels of stupid. You are quite high-functioning ..."

Khyven rolled his eyes and turned back to the Nox. "I have no wisdom, is that it?"

The Nox smiled as though Khyven and he had just shared a secret.

"Here's some wisdom for *you*," Khyven said. "I'm deciding whether to shake your hand or kill you."

"Which would be," Zaith said. "An improvement in Nox and Human relations, I think. But let us put our banter aside for a moment and speak truth. Your queen freed me and my kind. That good turn deserves another."

Khyven hesitated, then nodded. "I'm listening."

"Lorelle does recognize you. And also, you should let her be."

Lorelle watched them from atop the Giant, eyes squinted as though she was striving to understand their words. She gripped both her daggers tightly.

"She doesn't recognize me," Khyven said. "If she did, she would—"

"She recognized me," Zaith said. "She certainly recognizes you."

Khyven turned back to Lorelle. "If she recognizes me, why won't she—"

She hissed and leapt from the corpse, landed on the far side. All he could see now was her matted, grimy hair and her eyes.

"Lorelle—"

Her cloak folded up the darkness around her, and she was gone.

Zaith looked contemplatively at the space where she'd been. "I told you to let her be. You didn't."

"Maybe next I won't let *you* be."

Zaith did not act threatened. His face was sad, and it seemed that with every moment that passed, his shoulders seemed to slump a little more. He looked at the dead Giant, at the bodies strewn around the great hall, both Human and Nox. He looked at the blood that covered the floor in puddles.

"Much has transpired here, Khyven the Unkillable," Zaith finally said. "And I expect there may be no one who knows, or ever will know, the true extent of it. But I do believe that those of my kind who are left, even as undead bloodsuckers, owe what remains of their lives to you. And if not to you, certainly to your friends. No, Khyven the Unkillable. I am not your enemy, nor even your competition. Even if the lovely Lorelle would consider me a viable suitor, which I assure you she does not, I would no longer pursue her. To take from one who has given me my life, well ... Among the Nox, we consider that to be extremely bad manners. Instead, I shall bow gracefully before you. I hope you believe me, for I am in earnest. I wish only to help you and her, together."

"Then why tell me to stay away from her?"

"She will come to herself. Or she will not. And there is nothing you can do to aid this. When she does come to herself, then she will come to you." He turned and started up the corridor.

"Zaith!" Khyven called after him. "What will you do?"

Zaith paused, and turned his head, offering his profile. "Tend to my people. You're not the only ones who have been ravaged, Khyven the Unkillable." He turned the corner and was gone.

"Well, that was insightful," Slayter said.

Rhenn stared after the Nox thoughtfully.

"I think he's wrong," Khyven said, and he fully intended to go after Lorelle as soon as he could.

"And he thought you'd think that," Slayter said cheerfully. "See? Oh, I like him."

"You don't know anything about him except that he planned to turn Lorelle into a Nox."

"Not true, we learned that ..." Slayter blinked, and Khyven looked at the mage. He was pale as a sheet. His eyes were sunken, and his arms shook like leaves in a breeze. He looked down at his legs, which wobbled. "Oh, well that's so inconvenient—"

His eyes rolled up into his head and he fell over.

Khyven caught him before he hit the ground.

CHAPTER FIFTY-ONE

SLAYTER

Slayter waited on the balcony of his laboratory. Castle Noktos had been purged of Harkandos's army. All the Giants were either dead or fled. The Trolls who had survived—of which there were not many—had run deep into the noktum.

And the Nox were now, apparently, on their side, though Slayter didn't imagine that would last long. They were bloodsuckers, after all. They'd get hungry. He liked the idea of integrating them into Usaran society—anything new and unusual was far more fascinating than what had been done before—but he calculated it would take more than a year for Slayter to make artifacts for them like the sword he'd made for Rhenn. In the meantime, they'd want to feed and, according to Rhenn herself, bloodsuckers preferred Human blood—or sentient blood, anyway—to the blood of animals.

So he suspected the Nox would either leave, go back to their own hunting grounds in what had once been the Great Noktum or they would start breaking the as-yet unspoken covenant: don't eat your hosts.

Rhenn was organizing everyone who had survived the war. The woman was tireless. Of course, she *was* superhuman. Tirelessness came along her current state, he supposed. Well, as long as she kept feeding.

Slayter himself was *not* tireless, and he'd collapsed after the battle. He'd awoken in his bedroom, a place where he hadn't spent much time before the battle and where he hadn't spent much time after he'd awoken. They'd left him with a competent nurse—probably the most competent nurse left in the kingdom being as how there weren't many nurses left at all—but he had refused her ministrations, taken some of his *asenta* root extract, and gotten back to work.

There were things to do in the wake of their victory. It had been a very near thing. More than fifty percent of the people in Usara were either missing or had been slain. That was a hard hit to a culture. Slayter had read numerous history books. There had been three kingdoms he'd read about which had faced wars that had taken such a substantial part of their population.

None had survived.

They'd either been subsumed by the culture or kingdom that had attacked them, slowly fractured and died away, or they had become smaller tribal societies like the Sandrunners.

Based on his knowledge of previous kingdoms that had gone this way, Slayter calculated the odds of Usara's recovery to be less than thirty percent.

But then, those other societies had not had Rhenn as a queen. They'd not had Khyven the Unkillable. In short, Usara had the five of them: Rhenn, Khyven, Lorelle, Vohn, and Slayter.

Or the kingdom would have them, once they were all recovered. Lorelle had vanished in her insanity. Slayter needed to study up on Luminent soul bonds and what happened when they were broken. He already knew what most people knew. A Luminent soul bond was a sacred thing that was intertwined with the very fabric of a Luminent. They tore their soul in half, gave half to their lover and received half *from* their lover to make the bond. To then have that half ripped away when the lover died was immediately—or eventually—a death sentence. If it didn't precipitate immediate suicide, the Luminent descended into depression, a slide into the dregs of society, reduced to a shadow of their previous self, burning lower and lower until their light snuffed out altogether.

Lorelle was even more complicated, being as how she hadn't bonded with another Luminent. She'd attempted the bond with a Human, but Human souls weren't as expansive, apparently, as Luminent souls. Only part of her soul had bonded with Khyven, and the rest had bonded with the sentient force she called the Dark.

That could be good and bad, he supposed. The Dark might sustain her, keep her from that ugly precipice that destroyed other Luminents whose partners had died. But then, Lorelle had loved Khyven. Like Humans loved. Sharp and passionate and impetuous. It hadn't just been a Luminent soul bond. It had been … something new. That could change the entire landscape in a way Slayter might not be able to predict.

Khyven, for his part, had thrown every ounce of his time and effort into trying to lure her back. He helped Rhenn and Slayter when asked, but otherwise he wasn't focused on anything except Lorelle.

And Vohn had not reappeared yet either.

In short, while Rhenn was seeing to the needs of her subjects, Slayter once again had to look at the big picture because there was no one else. Rhenn had to care for the ordinary of her kingdom; Slayter had to care for those who were their only chance to beat the odds they now faced. They needed not just Rhenn, not just Khyven. They needed Lorelle too.

And they needed Vohn.

Vohn had vanished into his banshee mode, taking the Giant Avektos with him. Slayter had seen the whole thing. Something shimmering and white had dropped him. Slayter had no idea what that something had been, and it was driving him crazy.

There had been some other magic at work in that room, a magic that favored them, and Slayter didn't know where it had come from.

That was certainly going to be the second most pressing question Slayter was going to ask Vohn. What—or who—had helped him?

Unanswerable questions like that burned in Slayter's mind. It was like an itch in the middle of his back that he couldn't reach. Magic. Right under his nose. And he had no idea what it was nor where it came from.

He took a deep breath. He wanted to get to work. He'd laid out all the components he would need, plus a few to improve the process, but he hadn't begun his spell yet. His body was weak, and no amount of *asenta* root extract could actually replenish the body's life force. It simply gave it a jolt, a temporary boost to continue on. He had to be careful. Mages who went past their limits while taking *asenta* root extract often died once it wore off. Many histories documented the fall of many mages this way.

He drew another intentional breath, felt it in his lungs, and willed his body to be stronger.

It didn't work. Or, at least, it didn't work much. He did like the fresh air, and that was invigorating.

If he'd been Khyven, that probably *would* have worked. The man seemed to will his own body to ridiculous heights when he needed to.

Oh, I need to jump this building, I'll just grunt and jump this building.

He really was unfair, that one. He was—

"Slayter!"

Slayter started and turned. Khyven stood in the doorway like Slayter had summoned him. Boom! Just like that. Perhaps Slayter was becoming *unconsciously* magical. Perhaps he'd crossed the veil between intentional magic and unconscious magic. Wouldn't that be wonderful?

I think something, and something arrives.

That would be the most—

"Slayter?" Khyven asked, entering the room. He still had that magnificent Mavric iron sword strapped across his back. The Sword of Noksonon, arguably the most powerful magical artifact ever made and, of course, it had found its way to Khyven. It was things like that. Unfair. Just unfair.

Slayter shook his head ruefully.

"Slayter," Khyven said a third time, moving across the room to stand just before the balcony. He seemed cautious now, like Slayter was a skittish deer who might flee.

"Did I summon you?" Slayter asked.

Confusion wrinkled Khyven's brow. "Summon me? No, I … No, Rhenn told me to come look for you. You're supposed to be in bed."

"Maybe I summoned you and you don't know it."

Khyven's confusion vanished into a barely-tolerant look. "We don't have time for games."

"Perhaps we don't get to choose if we're in a game or not. Perhaps our lives are one giant game, and we simply don't know it. And there's no way to escape it."

"Stop it," Khyven repeated.

"I was merely pointing out that if I had unconsciously summoned you, you might not know it anymore than I would know it. What we should be focusing on is that it is possible that I have discovered of an entirely new stream of magic."

"Is it possible for you to make sense?"

"I make sense all of the time. I don't think it's possible for you to understand me more than sixty-two percent of the time, though."

Khyven sighed and crossed his muscular arms over his muscular chest. "I'll tell you what's possible … No, what is certain: You're going to walk back to your bed or I'm going to carry you there."

Slayter squinted his eyes and made a jumbled gesture with one hand.

"What …" Khyven let out a slow, exasperated breath. "Is that?"

"I'm banishing you. I summoned you, so I'm banishing you."

"Slayter, you barely have the strength to stand. What's the point of helping Rhenn if you die in the process?"

"What's the point of you saving Noksonon if you die in the process?"

"I didn't die."

"Except you did. I think by all the criteria of dying, you did. You just think you're special."

"This isn't about me. This is about you."

"I calculate my odds of recovering Vohn and *not* dying at about eighty-eight percent. I calculated the odds of you defeating Harkandos and not dying at about five percent."

"Wow." Khyven shook his head in disbelief.

"I know."

"Get back into bed."

"Those were steep odds."

"I had help."

"I factored that in."

"Get back in bed!"

"I will, after I do what I can to increase the odds of our survival. Vohn is part of that."

"I ... What? Is there another army coming?"

"Armies are not the only threats to Rhenn and her kingdom."

Khyven had been standing tall and straight, his shoulders back. He always was, like he was taller than everyone else— which, actually, he was, except for Giants and Gods, it seemed.

At Slayter's words, though, Khyven somehow straightened more, like a dog hearing a noise, and he gave a nearly imperceptible shrug to his shoulders. If Slayter hadn't been looking straight at the man, he'd have missed it. And Slayter actually *didn't* see Khyven's hands move, but suddenly both were near weapons. Khyven flicked a glance about the laboratory, lingering last and longest on the open expanse of the balcony behind Slayer.

Half a second ago, Khyven had been a big, angry mother hen. Now he was ready for combat. Now, he was Khyven the Unkillable.

"Not only threat? What's the other threat?" he asked.

"Instability," the Slayter said.

"Instability?"

"When something is not stable."

"I *know* what instability means!"

"Well, instability is just as dangerous."

Khyven looked like he was about to spit more threats, but he paused, thought about that, and seemed to actually understand what Slayter was saying. The big man nodded. "Oh ..."

"So it's worth the risk," Slayter said.

"Rhenn is working on the stability of the kingdom."

"Do you know what the odds are against—"

"I don't want to hear the odds. You risk yourself too often. Rhenn's words. Not mine." He paused, seemed flustered. "Except they are my words. Also. You risk yourself too often."

"I risk myself exactly the amount I can afford."

"Like with Harkandos?"

That piqued Slayter's interest. "What do you mean?"

"What you did with Harkandos, when you were helping me. It was stupid and unnecessary. You ran right up on him. I'm no mage, but it seems you mages can do things from a distance. There was no reason to get that close. It was blind luck he didn't smash you into jelly."

"Luck?"

Khyven shook his head. "Tell me you saw that enormous fist almost take your head off. Please tell me you saw it, Slayter."

"Of course I saw it. How does one miss a Giant's fist passing in front of one's nose? That's axiomatic. Or ... it's not. But it *should* be axiomatic." He paused, then affected Vohn's voice. "'That's as obvious as a Giant's fist whipping in front of your face.' See? It should be a saying."

"That isn't ... I'm not ... It was an unnecessary risk. You got *really* close to him."

"I got exactly as close as I could. I would have come closer, but I knew the danger. I picked my range based on his size and the likelihood of saving you from his spell, which I calculated would be fire. When panicked, people revert to the familiar. Harkandos is a Land Mage. I mean, he's all of them: Land Mage, Life Mage, Lore Mage, Love Mage, and Line Mage. He has access to all five streams, but I've noticed that every Giant leans into one stream over the others. So with Harkandos starting to panic, I knew he was going to fling one of the elements."

"I don't care about that. I'm saying you got too close to him!"

"If I could just finish my explanation—"

"You can get into bed, is what you can do."

"Earth." Slayter said, narrowing his eyes. "Using earth might have done the trick, but dirt and stone is slow to manipulate, heavy. That would have given you a chance to dodge. And water? No. There was no body of water around, which increases the difficulty of that. By about three times. Air? Similarly difficult. There's plenty of it, but to make air into a killing density takes, again, roughly three times the effort of just making a breeze blow. No, the most immediate element was fire. It feeds on air, of which there was plenty, and its natural state is deadly to Humans. So I assumed he'd try that."

"This isn't an explanation; it's a lecture. He could have crushed you."

"No."

"No?"

"He was immobilized, he only had the range of his arms. Harkandos stands around fifteen and a half feet tall. Quite impressive, really. Most Eldroi are between twelve and fourteen feet tall. Kind of a Giant's Giant, if you will. I mean, it is mentioned in several histories that he is tall, but Harkandos looks every inch of his impressive height and more, don't you think? I confirmed his height after having had the good fortune to observe him twice. So I could put together a plausible formula."

"Formula?"

"Well, he's relatively proportional."

"That's not a formula."

Slayter paused a moment. Sometimes Khyven appeared to act dense on purpose. Like a joke. Like one of those social bonding activities that made no logical sense but somehow drew people closer. But it was difficult to tell between those times and the times when Khyven actually *was* dense.

"Just about everyone's arm-span is about the same distance as their height, which would give Harkandos an arm-span of just over fifteen feet," Slayter continued. "That's the formula. Knowing that, and knowing that he was only reaching at me with one arm—and that his chest is about five feet across—I calculated I had a safe distance of ten feet, give or take half a foot. So I gave myself ten-and-a-half feet."

"You calculated it? When? Before the battle?"

"Before the—" Slayter cocked his head. "How would I know how he would be situated *before* the battle? Pinned to the floor like that? How would I know that?"

"How do you know *anything* you know?"

"I try to tell you all the time—"

"*Nobody* understands you!"

"I did the calculations while I was running."

"You did all those calculations while running toward Harkandos?"

"Hobbling, really, if you want to be entirely accurate—"

"Slayter!"

"It's math."

Khyven darkened. "All right, that's enough talking," he said in his no-nonsense voice, that voice that usually preceded violence. "I was told to come get you. Are you coming? Or am I carrying you?"

Something else Slayter had noticed: when Slayter got it wrong and Khyven wasn't *playing* dumb and was actually *being* dumb, the Ringer didn't like it to be pointed out.

"I have to get Vohn," Slayter said.

"You …" Khyven trailed off.

"He's out there. I'm going to get him."

A sadness passed over Khyven's face like a cloud in front of the sun, and Slayter surmised he was thinking about Vohn, but also about Lorelle, who had vanished right after the battle and whom Khyven had not yet pursued, though clearly he wanted to.

"Oh," Khyven said softly. "How?"

"Like last time. And the sooner the better. There are sentiences in the Dark. A Giant called Paralos. A Giant called Xos. And it is highly likely that Noktos is in there, too."

"How do you know all this?"

"Remember those treasure hunters that came to the palace months ago?"

"No."

"You remember. They were quite a memorable bunch."

"They were trying to work you over for money," Khyven said.

"Yes, well, they delivered a mirror that was the primary communication device for this Paralos. Apparently there were originally three mirrors. One for—"

"Cut to the point, Slayter."

"Well, you asked how I know all this."

"I'm more interested in getting Vohn."

"Yes, well, I think Paralos is a … favorable force for us. I mean, she's a Giant, so that isn't a given. And Giants will do what they do, regardless of how it hurts or helps Humans, generally speaking. But she has assisted Vohn at least twice now that we know of. But Xos is not well disposed to us, and he's in there too. My point is that Paralos might be able to protect Vohn while he is part of the Dark, or she might not. The sooner we can pull him out, the more likely we will get him back."

Khyven shook his head. "Are you sure you're up to it?"

"I calculate my odds of success without dying to be seventy two percent."

"That doesn't sound great."

"I calculate the odds of Rhenn's effort to reestablish the

kingdom of Usara without all of us—you, me, Rhenn, Lorelle, and Vohn—at about five percent."

"Well … clearly that's worse," Khyven stated the painfully obvious. "You're talking about the stability thing."

Khyven's woefully inaccurate description made Slayter feel like he was sucking on a piece of metal. He made a face. "Yes. The 'stability thing.'"

Khyven sighed and his enormous shoulders slumped. "Then I'll help you. Come on." And the man actually walked toward the table that had the components neatly laid out.

Slayter hobbled over to join him. With all the running around he'd done lately, his stump was raw in three places. His prosthetic needed an adjustment, and he simply hadn't had the time with everything going on. He was really going to have to address that soon. He could easily get an infection.

Khyven shook his head again, as though he was having a conversation inside his head and one of the voices was telling him he was doing the wrong thing. "Let's do this before Rhenn comes looking. How can I help?"

"Well, how are you feeling?"

"How am *I* feeling?"

"Yes. Robust? Exhausted?"

"I … Um, normal I guess."

Normal. Of course he was normal. When Slayter exhausted himself, it took days to recover. When Khyven had been stabbed through the heart and killed, he bounced right back. Of course, he'd also met a goddess, was resurrected, then fought several Giants at once. Now he was normal.

"Then you can help me by giving me some of your life-force."

Khyven's eyebrows raised. "Really?"

"If you want to help, yes."

"Well … Of course."

Of course he said of course. *Yes, I'm superhuman. What's a little life-force here and there. I have as much life-force as dirt has brown.*

"Good. Put this on." Slayter picked up a metal wrist band

with a sharp hook, like a scorpion's stinger, on one side of it.

"What is it?"

"Something I was working on before the noktum devoured the continent. It's based on information I gleaned from the necromancer N'ssag."

"You're going to turn me into a bloodsucker?"

Slayter stopped, frowned. "No. It's ... You think I would turn you into a bloodsucker?"

"Rhenn became one of N'ssag's ... You know ... You said N'ssag! I thought bloodsucker. You said this thing is going to suck my life-force and it's based on N'ssag's magic ... What am I supposed to think?"

"N'ssag is a Life Mage. There are about twenty thousand different things one can do with Life Magic. Turning corpses into non-corpses is only one of those things."

Khyven snapped the bracelet around his wrist and fixed the catch without Slayter's direction. If the question had something to do with physical movement, Khyven instinctively knew how to do it. But if Slayter tried to explain the most simple magic, his head became a stone.

"And I just stand here?" Khyven asked.

"There's a spring-loaded button on the top of the bracelet," Slayter said, adjusting the implements a little. "When I tell you, press it. The stinger will stab you. And you'll feel a little ... weak."

"Perfect," Khyven murmured.

Slayter had two clay disks on the table. He pulled another from his cylinder, examined it, then glanced at Khyven. "Ready?"

"Ready."

Slayter took a deep breath and centered himself. He felt his own life-force as a thin and reedy thing, but it was still enough. He figured he'd probably have enough by himself, but he'd have help in a moment. He completed the line on the first disk, and the orange glow leapt out from it. It pulled from him, and he breathed deep, feeling the power drain from himself.

"Do it," he murmured to Khyven as the Life Magic spell hovered around him like a misty orange cloud.

Khyven pressed the catch. The stinger snapped forward, stabbing him on the inside of his forearm. He frowned, but that was his only concession to the pain.

The orange glow formed a funnel to Khyven's arm, pulling life-force from him to bolster Slayter's own. It rushed into him, and he sucked in a vigorous breath.

"Yes, well ..." he murmured.

Khyven grimly leaned on the table, seemingly otherwise unaffected though Slayter had just siphoned away at least twenty percent of his vitality.

Slayter picked up the second disk, which would enable him to locate Vohn's essence in the Dark within fifty miles of Castle Noktos. If Vohn was further than that, he'd have to try a larger spell.

He completed it. Magic flowed into it. Orange light flared.

Slayter suddenly saw an orange map in his mind. It was as though he stood a thousand feet above the castle and could see all the way to the Usaran palace, twenty-five miles into the noktum in every direction.

And there Vohn was, swirling around the castle, no more than a hundred feet away.

Distantly, Slayter felt his own body, his hand questing on the table for the third disk. He found it, reached over with his other hand and, rather than *seeing* the design on its top, he felt it through the flows of his magic. He felt how the lines looped and intersected. He felt which one was missing, intentionally missing to hold the magic of the spell at bay until Slayter was ready to complete the design.

Carefully, using this extra sensory perception of the magic rather than his eyes, he finished the line.

A rush of magic flowed through him. Inside his own mind, within the map where he had located Vohn, the spell appeared like a glowing orange net. With a gentle flick, he cast it over Vohn, who seemed surprised, struggled for a moment, then calmed as he recognized the feel of the magic surrounding him, the feel of Slayter himself.

Slayter whispered to him, but wasn't actually sure if the words would reach Vohn. They might. Or they might not.

Slayter hauled in the net, not too quickly, not too slowly. Just hand over hand over hand until the net pulled closer, shrinking.

He breathed deeply and pulled his consciousness away from the map in his mind—it felt a little like sliding backward down a funnel—and back into his physical body. He brought the net along with him ...

Then Slayter was back in his body. Orange light glowed on the table. At first it was just an orange blob of light. Then it became a glowing orange body. Then it became Vohn's body.

The orange glow vanished, and Vohn lay on the table, dressed as he'd been when he'd grabbed Avektos.

Vohn breathed softly, unconscious, curled into himself.

Slayter felt like he was going to collapse again. He thought about pulling a little more vitality from Khyven, but it was the first time he'd used that spell. And now that Vohn was back, now that he was safe, Khyven was more useful to have around than Slayter was.

"Good," Slayter murmured. He pushed Vohn's dark curls back from his face, then took his hand. Withdrawing Vohn's ring from his pocket, the one he'd dropped on the battlefield right before he'd vanished with Avektos, Slayter slid it onto Vohn's left-hand ring finger—the one that hadn't been burned off by a dragon. He leaned over and kissed Vohn on the brow, then let out a deep breath. "Thank you, Khyven."

Khyven smiled gently, then gathered Vohn into his arms. "Let's get you both to bed. Come on."

"Yes," Slayter said. "Yes, that would be nice."

He hobbled around the table, stumbled, and held himself up by pressing a palm flat on its surface. Khyven shifted Vohn to a one-handed hold, cradling him like a toddler, Vohn's head resting against Khyven's neck. He put his free arm around Slayter's waist and lifted most of his weight. "I've got you, friend. I've got you."

Together, they made for the door.

CHAPTER FIFTY-TWO

RHENN

Rhenn stood in the meeting room she'd chosen. In the days since the final, bloody battle at Castle Noktos, she'd thrown out every trace of the Giants and their short rule. According to Vohn, this had been Harkandos's audience chamber. He'd chosen Rhenn's previous meeting room as his center of power. An attempt, she knew, to send a signal: Everything the Humans once ruled now belonged to him.

After the war, she could have moved her meeting room. There were plenty of other rooms in this castle, practically no end of rooms. Even when Usara's entire refugee population had come to this place, they'd only occupied a quarter of the castle grounds; it was simply immense. And now that Usara's population had been reduced by half again, they occupied an even smaller portion of the castle.

But this had been her meeting room before Harkandos, and she'd be damned if she was giving it up just because he'd squatted here for a week.

The enormous chair Harkandos had installed in here, the

tables he'd had set up for food, even the carpets that his captains had stood on while he gave audience, she had them all taken out of the room and burned.

She'd refurnished the meeting room with new tables, new chairs, and now she stood at the balcony as her inner circle gathered.

Khyven lounged in a chair, his boots on the table, legs crossed. Vohn sat at the foot of the table, and Slayter had two dozen of his clay disks arrayed out before him. He rearranged them like playing cards, deep in thought. Occasionally he'd slide a disk with his finger and put it in front of another disk.

Lorelle, of course, was still missing. It had only been two days, but the fact that Rhenn's best friend was out there, lost, insane, was almost more than Rhenn could take. When Nhevalos had taken Rhenn to Daemanon, Lorelle had gone into the very heart of the Great Noktum to find her.

But Rhenn could not do the same, at least not right now. She had hundreds of people who relied on her, not just one, and she needed to stay here to make sure that they were cared for, that their vulnerability could not be exploited by some other force that came along. The coming of the noktum, the marauding bands of Nox and Trolls, and finally the Giants had taken such a toll on the refugees of Usara—they were so battle-shocked— that even an unorganized pride of Kyolars could take this castle.

They would die without her; she was sure of that. She couldn't even release Khyven to go after Lorelle. Rhenn relied on him to hold the peace together as much as she relied on herself. Yes, she was their queen. They looked to her for leadership.

But Khyven was their hero.

They had all seen him charge into the great hall. They'd seen him sprint at Harkandos; they'd seen him chop the tyrant's head off. The legends about Khyven grew with every day that passed.

So now, it was Khyven, Slayter, Vohn, and herself holding together the scraps of Usara, exiled to this alien stronghold, cut to the bone, and vulnerable. The people in this room had to come up with a plan for the survival of her people. They had to, or it was over.

"We need to leave this place," Rhenn said reluctantly. "We can't stay here."

"Yes," Vohn agreed. Khyven nodded. Slayter kept arranging his disks.

"Likewise, we are too weak to leave," Rhenn said. "We came here because Castle Noktos is defensible, far more than Usara in a continent-wide noktum. Yes, too many horrors happened here, but too many horrors await us out there. I fear if we return to the crown city, a city that was not designed to defend itself in the noktum, we would be opening our population up to even greater dangers."

She let the statement hang for a moment. Nobody disagreed.

"So what do we do?" She prompted. "I am out of ideas. We turned Harkandos aside, but there are other dangers that live inside the noktum, perhaps even other Giants who would seek to take Harkandos's place. We may not even know they exist, but they likely know about Castle Noktos. Word will spread about what has happened here."

Even the undead Nox who had helped them with the battle against Harkandos were a mounting dilemma. In fact, if it wasn't for Zaith, who had become an unexpected ally to them, the remaining Nox horde might have already turned on them. Rhenn had been taking short hunting jaunts with the Nox outside the castle. She wanted to integrate the Nox into the kingdom, and Zaith seemed amenable to the idea, but they were both working against cultural prejudices and bloodsucker hunger. Many of the Nox still looked at Rhenn's subjects as food that had been denied them. Every day, this castle walked a razor's edge. Lambs with predators in their midst. And the lambs were outnumbered.

"We need to bring the sunlight back," Vohn said simply.

Slayter stopped arranging his disks and raised his head.

Khyven sat up. "Can we do that?"

"When I was in the Dark, I was visited by Paralos," Vohn

said.

"Who's Paralos?" Khyven asked.

"I told you," Slayter said.

"Pretend I never understand anything you say," Khyven said.

"She's one of the living Giants that became one with the Dark," Vohn continued. "Became one with the great spell cast by Noktos that covered the continent in darkness."

"All right." Khyven glanced at Slayter. "Yes. You did tell me that."

The mage raised an eyebrow.

"She told me what Harkandos had done to extinguish the Lux, and that it might be undone," Vohn said.

"How?" Rhenn's heart beat faster. If they could undo the damage Harkandos had done, if they could purge the noktum from Noksonon, everything would change. Her people would have a fighting chance. The constant darkness killed hope, it bred despair …

"They are called Lighteaters. They're supernatural creatures Harkandos created. They … eat light."

"Let's kill them," Khyven said.

"Maybe we should just kill *everything*." Slayter frowned at the Ringer.

Khyven returned a withering stare. "I don't want to kill everything. Just these things."

"I calculate a seventy four percent chance that you have killed more people you've met than not," Slayter said.

"How many people would that be?" Khyven asked.

Slayter cocked his head, and Rhenn knew he was actually doing the math.

Khyven glanced at Rhenn, winked, as though to say, "See? I *can* shut him up."

"We can't just kill them," Vohn said. "They're guarded."

"By?"

"Xos."

"That's the other one you mentioned, isn't it?" Khyven said to Slayter. "The noktum sentience."

Slayter came back from his reverie, mildly annoyed, as though he hadn't been able to exactly calculate how many people Khyven had killed in such a short time. "Xos. Yes. I suppose you'll want to kill him, too."

"You can't just hit him with a sword," Vohn said.

"I have a pretty good sword," Khyven said.

"If we simply go charging in there swinging, we're going to lose. Xos owns the noktum, *especially* the area around the Lux. Noktos himself is there, too, and both of them want Noksonon covered in darkness," Vohn said. "But Noktos, so far as I can tell—perhaps so far as Paralos can tell—is only dedicated to overcoming the Lux. His sentience is ... vague. Unfocused. Not like Paralos's or Xos's. They are every bit as intelligent and cunning as Harkandos; they just don't have bodies. Xos and Paralos have been in a struggle for two centuries; they hate each other. And Xos has recently made his place of greatest power at the Lux, where the Lighteaters are. Harkandos gave him what he has craved for two thousand years, and he's not about to give it up. What we need is someone who can weaken him. If we can weaken him enough, Paralos might be able to hold him while we ... well ..."

"Kill the Lighteaters," Khyven said.

"Yes."

"How do we weaken him?"

"There may be someone I know," Vohn said. "Lorelle and I met her. She needed our help when I was a banshee the first time, and we were able to assist her with defeating a creature called the Worldbreaker. I think she'd help us if we asked her."

"Who?"

"Her name is Ksara Sajra; she's Demaijos royalty."

"Oooo. I've never met Demaijos royalty before," Slayter said.

"Why can she hurt Xos and we can't?" Khyven asked.

"She has a very specific magical talent, a Life Magic that connects her to the Dark specifically through the sentients who reside there. And the sentient she has the most experience with is Xos."

"Oh that is delightful!" Slayter said. "Life Magic that controls the Dark."

"So she's a part of him?" Khyven asked. "Why would she want to hurt him?"

"She's part of him like we were part of Harkandos's army when he took over Castle Noktos. It is not a willing thing. He tried to dominate her, to make her his agent in the world of sunlight. But now that he has what he wants—an end to the Lux—he doesn't need her anymore. However, *she* might still have hooks in *him*. It's worth investigating at least."

"Fascinating," Slayter said. "I should very much like to meet her."

"We'll need to find her first," Vohn said. "She's the leader of a ... well, a pirate crew, for lack of a better term. They steal things. When I helped her, she was near Nokte Murosa. Where she would be now, I do not know."

"I can find her," Slayter said. "You'll retain a psychic residue from your meeting, and if I combine that with a little psylene powder—you'd have to snort it of course—there might be enough of a trace that—"

A knock interrupted Slayter, and Rhenn turned, surprised. It was almost as though they were back in the palace at Usara. Except Rhenn hadn't gotten around to appointing pages just yet. The only runner who would come visit them would be someone sent by the gate guard to report an attack.

Khyven stood up, as did Vohn.

"Come in," Rhenn said.

Aldon, the runner, entered, out of breath. He'd been stationed at the castle's front doors; he'd have had to climb two of those Giant staircases to get here.

"Visitors at the doors, Your Majesty."

"Visitors?"

"They say they come in peace," Aldon said. "They're a motley crew, Your Majesty. Two Demaijos. Dark skin, different colored eyes. A pirate who looks like, well, a Sandrunner of all things, an Imprevaran cavalry captain, and a Usaran who looks like Senji with red hair. Northern Islander, by the looks of her."

Vohn's eyes widened. "Two Demaijos?"

"Yes, my lord. A man and a woman."

"The name. What's the woman's name?"

"Ksara Sajra."

"That's her!" Vohn exclaimed. "She's here!"

Rhenn felt a chill. The whole thing felt too timely. Orchestrated.

"Yes, my lord. She told me to bring a message directly to you, if I could."

"What did she say?"

The runner paused, as though checking his memory to ensure he delivered the message exactly as it was spoken.

"She said, 'Tell Vohn I think I can bring the sun back.'"

CHAPTER FIFTY-THREE

KHYVEN

Khyven leaned against the wall when Aldon escorted the pirates into Queen Rhenn's meeting room. Remarkably, two of Rhenn's Knights of the Steel had been spared in the feasting room, survived the battle, and they now stood guard outside the meeting room, newly elevated to Knights of the Sun. They had both wanted to come into the room at the arrival of the five strangers, but Rhenn assured them she would be fine. The knights had reluctantly agreed, but insisted on stripping the visitors of their many weapons, one by one, as they entered.

The procession came one at a time, but they moved like a group. Clearly, they had seen battle together. They reminded Khyven of Rhenn's inner circle, actually.

The one called Ksara entered first. She was of medium height with her hair worked into finger-width braids so intertwined and weather-beaten they looked like thick, single strands of hair. He would guess she'd never undone those braids since they'd been made. She had the dark skin of the sun-drenched lands of Demaijos as well as their dichromatic eyes, one blue and one brown.

Clearly, she was the leader. All the others looked to her. At a glance, even Khyven could see that they loved her, believed in her. It struck him like a gentle pat to the face.

This was a tight crew. They lived—and would gladly die—for each other.

Her brother came next. He looked like a Ringer in royal, mismatched clothes, like he adorned himself in the finest clothes he found along his journey. They were all relatively new except a silken green vest with embroidery that looked like something he'd seen on one of Lorelle's rare dresses; her mother's dress, the only one that had survived Vamreth's coup. That piece of the Demaijos's clothing was old, worn at the edges, but well-loved. Khyven got the impression the man would cheerfully sell and replace anything he was wearing except that vest.

When the Knights of the Sun asked for his weapons, he cheerfully surrendered them as though he didn't care, and they pulled a veritable arsenal from him.

He had two long swords, two short swords, three daggers of different lengths, a bolo, and a chunk of metal with finger holes, meant to clench in the hand and punch. Four spikes protruded from where the knuckles would be. A man striking with that would leave four holes in his opponent's skull. The Demaijos, Ulric, grinned as he passed weapon after weapon to the Knights of the Sun.

Next came the Sandrunner. She had the tanned skin and dark hair of her people, but that was where the resemblance ended. In Khyven's experience, the Sandrunners were a serious lot, fierce and religious about their rules. This woman walked in with the swagger of a …

Well, a pirate.

Sandrunners wore light, baggy clothes that cooled—and hid—the body. This woman wore a flamboyant, wide-brimmed hat, a low-cut swordsman's blouse with a tantalizing flash of cleavage, tight leather pants, and tall black boots. She made her way into the room one hip at a time, like she was used to the ground swaying beneath her. And if the ground wasn't going to sway, then by the gods she would.

A little creature rode her shoulder. Khyven would have thought a pirate would own a bird of some kind, but this was a cat. Or … not quite a cat. Its tail was like a bottle brush. Its face was foxlike with teeth that were larger than a fox's, and its horns looked somewhat like Vohn's. They followed the curve of the little creature's skull, but instead of white, they were black and shiny.

The pirate woman lifted her sword out of its sheath with two fingers, held it up for the knight … She also held forth a dagger.

Khyven flicked a glance to her hip and the empty sheath there, then to the dagger in her hand, which been empty a second ago. He'd been watching for the draw, and he'd missed it. That *never* happened.

She glanced over at him and winked as though she'd intended to impress him, and was gratified to see she had.

Khyven did a double-take as he took his eyes off the sultry pirate and looked to the next of the crew. For a moment, he thought it was Senji herself, except with red hair. Clearly of northern Usara, the woman stood near to seven feet tall, towering over her fellows. She had the wide-shouldered, muscled body of the goddess and wore similar furs. Her breasts were bound close to her body, and three wide leather belts slung lazily from her hips, holding up not only her weapons and pouches, but her fur and plated battle skirt. Her midriff and thighs were bare, and he could see the play of muscle beneath her pale skin.

She unhooked a pair of hand axes from her belt, clinked them together in one hand, and gave them to the knights. She looked at Rhenn, at Vohn and then Slayter, but her gaze passed over them, searching …

Until it fell on Khyven, then it didn't leave.

Her gaze was the opposite of the Sandrunner's. Intense, scrutinizing, and without an ounce of flirtation. It was as though Khyven had something she wanted, and she was going to pull it from him with that gaze. She didn't look anywhere but at his eyes.

He could have continued looking into that northern blue-gray gaze for a long time, wondering about that thing that she seemed to want so desperately, but the final member of Ksara's team, an Imprevaran, pulled his attention away.

"You have enough of our weapons," he told the knights.

Both knights instinctively blocked the man. Khyven remained calm, still leaned against the wall like he hadn't a care in the world, but he was positioned exactly where he needed to be. Fights were won most often by the fighter who could surprise his opponent, and Khyven had long ago learned that most people underestimated how fast he could cross a room. If he looked uninterested and, most importantly, too far away to do anything should someone make an aggressive move, he found that he could surprise them every time.

So while he pivoted his focus to this Imprevaran, he knew exactly how close the other four were to Rhenn, Vohn, and Slayter. He knew how fast he could interpose himself between any of them and the queen. He knew the Demaijos Ringer was a strong hand-to-hand fighter. He knew that the pirate woman almost certainly had a weapon concealed on her that the knights had missed. He knew that if Ksara attacked, it would be magical and not physical, and that the Sword would put more of a cramp in her style than she could possibly guess.

This group was made of veteran fighters, but they were not insurmountable. Certainly not so fierce as five Giants. If they wanted to hurt his friends, it would not go their way.

"I am not here to hurt your queen. I have sworn it," the man was saying. His breastplate had the Imprevaran royal insignia, as well as the horse crests that indicated he was royal cavalry.

A northern wild woman, a Sandrunner who lived on the ocean, a pair of Demaijos from halfway around the world, and an Imprevaran cavalryman. Khyven suddenly felt like Slayter, who simply went out of his mind when such an interesting mystery stood before him. What was their story?

"If I might," Ksara spoke up. "We have all surrendered our weapons. If he stands in the corner, could you see clear to allow Atlas to keep his? I promise upon the life of my brother and the honor of my house that he'll behave."

"Or he could just give up his sword," Vohn said.

"That's the thing," Ksara said. "I ... I don't think he will."

"Then he's going to wait in the hall," Vohn said. "We're not letting him near our queen armed."

"My brother could hurt your queen much more, I think, than Atlas," Ksara responded. "He has the ability to make light bursts."

Slayter perked up at this.

"So you know what I am?" Rhenn asked.

"We do, Your Majesty, and my comment was not meant to threaten you, only to let you know that Atlas will behave if I tell him to."

"But he won't surrender his weapon if you tell him to," Rhenn asked.

Ksara's lips firmed into a line that indicated this particular rebellion was ongoing. "No, Your Majesty. But I assure you, we've come to help. You and my friends have common purpose. Atlas is just ... Well, he's Atlas."

"If he draws that sword, he's not only going to have to fight two knights, but also Khyven." Vohn said. "You know who he is, right?"

Ksara smiled like a woman who hadn't slept for a week. "Do I know who Khyven the Unkillable is? Vohn, we knew who Khyven was when he was still a Ringer, before he was a Giant slayer and world saver. Coronata named her kapicat after him."

"Excuse me?" Khyven asked, looking over at the pirate. She had her chin up, giving him a sly glance and a good look at her long neck as she petted the bright-eyed creature on her shoulder.

"He's Khyven the kapicat. I've been a fan of yours for ..." She sighed luxuriantly with exactly the kind of sultry voice he'd imagined. "Oh, for a very long time. They say a person should never meet her heroes. Generally, I would agree. But by Grina's libido, you do not disappoint, do you?" She looked him up and down, her gaze dramatically pausing at specific parts of his body.

Khyven felt heat rising up his neck.

"I'll watch Atlas," Khyven said. "Let him keep his sword."

"Thank you," Ksara said, and he heard true gratitude in her voice. "He would have fought you."

"He would have lost," Vohn said.

"Yes," Ksara said. "That is, I think, part of the draw for him."

Rhenn's knights, at a nod from the queen, gave an affirming glance at Khyven, then reluctantly withdrew. Atlas shrugged as though to replace his lost dignity, then moved toward Ksara's group.

The pirate woman pointed back at the corner. "No, you have to stand over there."

"Coronata—"

"If you're going to be a pain in the ass, you suffer the consequences. On your own. Give them your sword, or go stand in the corner."

Atlas narrowed his eyes and moved stiffly to the corner, turned his back to it, and glared at everyone.

"That is Atlas." Ksara gestured at the Imprevaran with an open hand, then brought her hand around to make the same gesture to each of her crew in turn. "This is Coronata. The tall one is Merewen. This is my brother, Ulric, and I am Ksara. Thank you for agreeing to see us."

"So you have an intriguing idea." Rhenn sat on the edge of the table and leaned back on her palms. "About restoring the Lux. Bringing Noksonon back to what it was before."

"It's the least we can do," Ulric said, appraising Rhenn very much the same way Coronata had appraised Khyven. He came forward and sat on the edge of the table next to her, mirroring her posture and putting his back to Vohn and Slayter.

Khyven moved quietly off the wall. He wasn't worried about Rhenn—she could handle herself and then some. He had assessed all of these people as physical fighters, and none of them were in Rhenn's class.

Also, Ksara wouldn't have been aware that Rhenn was immune to sunlight for short stretches of time because of Slayter's sword, which hung at her hip.

"You all took the bastard out," Ulric continued. "Saved us the trouble, kept the world from being enslaved. Let us help undo this little thing with the Lux."

"Little thing?" Rhenn raised an eyebrow.

"We destroy worldbreakers as a matter of course, Your Majesty." He inclined his head with a charming grin. "We have a plan."

A small smile drew Rhenn's lips wider. She appeared to enjoy the man's flirtation. "Do tell."

"What Ulric is saying is that we may have a way to undo it. A simple way. Harkandos created something called Lighteaters—"

"We know about the Lighteaters," Rhenn said.

"Oh …" Ksara seemed surprised by this.

"Paralos told me," Vohn said.

"Oh, of course. And you know about Xos."

"We know about Xos."

"Then you practically know the plan."

"Pretend we don't," Rhenn said.

"Well, Paralos and Xos have been fighting each other for centuries. Xos wanted exactly what Harkandos delivered. Paralos wanted to keep the world the way it was. They were evenly matched, and so the world stayed the way it was until Harkandos changed the game. Paralos and Xos are still evenly matched, except he now has the upper hand. Xos is protecting the Lighteaters, and she can't move him aside."

"So we just need to charge in there and kill the Lighteaters," Khyven said.

"Well…" Ksara began.

"Don't mind him. He's like that," Slayter interjected. "Everything can be whacked with a sword."

Coronata sighed contentedly.

"I don't think you can just charge in and kill the

Lighteaters," Ksara said. "Xos has mastery of the Dark. Even though they're right there on the spot where the Lux used to be, you'd never find them. Once you came close enough, he'd bend you into a labyrinth of darkness, turning you this way and that, and you'd never find your way to the Lux—or out of the general area—again."

"So what is the solution?" Rhenn asked.

"I am," Ksara said. "Xos has lived inside me for a good long span of my life. I recently broke free of his influence, but I'm betting that whatever deceptions he could craft from the Dark, I could uncraft. At the very least, I could see through them. I could lead you through the maze. Once I've led you to the Lighteaters, you … Well, you know … Knock 'em down. Knock 'em over. Whack them with a sword."

"That simple?" Vohn asked.

"I really do think so," Ksara answered. "The difficulty will come in getting past Xos. With Paralos's help in pulling most of his attention away, I can do the rest, perhaps even without him knowing it. There is only one problem. It will take us a month to sail down there, perhaps another couple of weeks to hike inland."

"It will take considerably less time than that," Slayter said.

"We have resources that can take us there tonight, if we wished," Rhenn said.

Ksara looked stunned. "Tonight? Really? Is it… Through Vohn and his talent?"

"No, that kills people," Slayter said. "There's a physical-to-ethereal conversion that must happen. Even most Shadowvars cannot do it. Apparently Rauvelos—he's the steward of Castle Noktos—was instrumental in creating this aspect of Shadowvars. Well, some Shadowvars. Like Vohn. But it isn't something everyone can do. Even Avektos discovered that if you take a ride with a banshee and you don't—"

"We have a noktum cloak," Rhenn interrupted. "We can take everyone there in a few trips."

"We did have two, except first we'd have to find—"

Vohn smacked the mage on the arm.

"Oh!" Slayter glanced at Khyven. "Apologies, Khyven."

Khyven paused, his lips pressed in a line. But finally, he nodded and looked back at Ksara.

"Then we go tomorrow," Rhenn said.

"What about the people?" Khyven asked.

"We leave Lord Harpinjur and Zaith in charge."

"Zaith?"

"Yes." Rhenn met his gaze unflinchingly. Khyven didn't think leaving a Nox in charge of anything was a good idea at all, but apparently Rhenn had come to some decision about Zaith. Something had transpired between the undead Nox and Rhenn when she'd killed N'ssag. She didn't see them as the enemy anymore. At least she didn't see Zaith that way.

"You're the queen," he said tightly.

"Yes."

"Then that's what we do," Khyven said.

Rhenn turned to Ksara. "We'll make you comfortable in the meantime. Rest up."

"How does anyone know when tomorrow is anymore?" Ulric joked.

"Well," Slayter began. "It has to do with the rhythms of—"

"He's joking," Ksara interrupted. She glared at Ulric, who beamed back at her.

Rhenn summoned Aldon, and he escorted them from the meeting room.

"You all, too. Rest. We'll leave soon."

"Hmmm," Slayter said, cocking his head.

"You especially," Rhenn said to him.

"Hmmm?"

"You especially. Rest. Vohn, make sure he does."

"But I have to—"

"Come on." Vohn took Slayter's arm. Slayter looked at his disks, then quickly scooped them into his cylinder. He and Vohn left together.

Khyven and Rhenn exchanged glances.

"One more battle?" Khyven asked.

"You have it in you?"

"To the end," he said.

Rhenn put a hand on his shoulder. "She'll come back," she whispered.

"Let's give her some daylight to return to," he replied.

Rhenn smiled, and she left.

Khyven returned to his room, the one he'd shared with Lorelle, and lay awake for a long hour thinking about her before he finally drifted off to sleep.

CHAPTER FIFTY-FOUR

KHYVEN

T he darkness pressed close, and Khyven's flesh prickled. He'd never felt the … presence of the Dark like this. It was almost as though they were underwater. The thickness of it slid across them as they moved toward Jai'ketakos's cave, toward where the Lux should have been.

Ksara led. Rhenn trailed right behind her, Vohn came next, then Slayter, then Ulric. Khyven came after, with Coronata and Merewen behind. Atlas came last, insisting on rear guard.

Ksara kept her hand up to indicate that all was well. She told them that if she dropped her hand, they were to all stop and hold on to the person in front and behind themselves. She was, apparently, creating some kind of serpentine tunnel through the Dark, hiding them as they went.

Khyven couldn't see any tunnel. It all looked like the same noktum to him, gray and austere, except for the new thickness of the air and for the fact that he couldn't see more than twenty feet in front of him. Typically, the Amulets of Noksonon allowed him to see the horizons. Not here. Not in this thick place.

Still, everything seemed to be going to plan. Surely that couldn't last. Khyven couldn't remember a time when they'd planned a mission in Rhenn's meeting room, then went out into the world and had it go as they'd envisioned. So he was certain there would be mayhem soon. The Sword practically vibrated in its sheath. It longed to be unleashed again. It hadn't stopped calling him Slayer of Giants since he'd killed Harkandos, of course. Even Khyven found himself eager to fight. He wanted to rest, of course. He longed for another day like he'd had with Lorelle before the battle, carefree in a sunlit meadow.

But they needed sunlight for that. And the people of Noksonon had been terrorized enough for a whole lifetime. They had to restore the daylight, restore the Lux.

Before they left for the Great Noktum, Vohn and Ksara had spoken with Paralos, Xos's opposite number in the Dark. Now, she was attacking Xos, coming at him as though she intended to break through him to assail the Lighteaters.

Well, supposedly she was. Khyven couldn't feel a thing.

The group continued, and Ksara's hand stayed up. Apparently all was well.

They wound their way forward, up a ridge, and then down the back side. Ksara stopped then, and they all stopped with her. She seemed about to drop her hand, then didn't. She continued forward. They wound their way, more slowly, down the back side of the ridge.

Khyven still couldn't see any further in front him—if anything, the visibility had dropped from twenty feet to fifteen feet or so ...

But the blue wind flickered and swirled ahead, deep into the dark, further than his eyes could see. It flowed low across the ground, curling against something invisible, something that could be the shape of a person. A threat.

The Lighteaters.

Ksara stopped, dropped her hand. Khyven touched Ulric's

shoulder, as Ksara had bid them all do whenever they stopped. He felt Coronata caress his side, then tuck two fingers snugly inside his belt.

Ksara doubled back, made a gesture that they should gather together, huddle close. Once they did, she spoke.

"They're here."

"Where?" Slayter asked.

"Twenty-five feet that way," Khyven answered. Ksara looked at him, surprised.

"You can see them?"

"They're a threat," Vohn answered.

Ksara looked puzzled.

"If they're dangerous, Khyven doesn't need his eyes to feel them," Vohn explained.

"I have a question," Khyven said. "Are we using diplomacy?"

"Diplomacy?" Ksara asked.

"He wants to know if we're killing them," Vohn clarified.

"Yes," Ksara said without hesitation.

"We can't just capture them?" Slayter asked and, to his credit, he kept his voice low.

"They will not be tamed," Ksara said. "I ... feel them through the Dark. They are ravenous. Even the Lux, which still fights on, will not last forever. When they're done with it, I suspect they'll move on."

"To what?" Slayter asked.

"I don't know. But I know I don't want to find out," Ksara said. "They feel ... abominable. A twisting of the fabric of nature."

"We should capture one," Slayter said.

Ksara looked at Rhenn, her glance seeming to beseech her to convince the mage.

"Khyven," Rhenn said. "You and Ulric get close. See if there is the opportunity to capture one. The rest of us will fan out. If they aren't going to back down, and it comes to a fight, I want us ready. Go." She nodded at Khyven.

He and Ulric slipped forward, and Ksara paced them. He glanced back at Rhenn, who hesitated, eyes narrowed at Ksara.

"I am holding the Dark around us," Ksara said. "I stop that, and Xos is going to stop fighting Paralos."

Rhenn paused, then nodded.

They continued forward.

Ksara led the way, though Khyven could see the blue wind swirling, larger and larger as they drew near. He could make out the shapes of the things between the blue wind swirls. There were three of them close enough for him to make out. The silhouettes were all standing, backs rounded, shoulders hunched, heads tilted upward toward the sky like turtles looking for the moon.

Ksara slowed, and the darkness felt the thickest it ever had.

"We are upon them," Ksara said in a quiet breath. "I will break the cocoon I have wrapped us in, and you will see them. But then, they will see you."

"I'll go first," Khyven whispered. "I'll take the one in the middle, give him a good clonk, and we'll see if we can get Slayter his pet."

Ksara opened the veil.

Three of the Lighteaters sat before them, but they all shivered as they became visible. One of them turned. A grayish mist flowed down from the sky and into its flat face, obscuring whatever features might have been there.

It straightened, focusing on them, and took a step forward.

Khyven felt a pull at himself, like something had grabbed ethereal threads within his body and tugged.

"Oh, Slayer of Giants," the Sword said in his mind. *"A worthy adversary indeed ..."*

Yellow light flared to Khyven's left. He turned and saw, with surprise, that Ulric's fingers had ignited like someone had touched them with a torch.

"Ulric!" Khyven whispered harshly.

"It's not me. I didn't do it ..." He let out a breath and fell to one knee. Yellow mist now floated from his head, swirled into the air, and flowed over to the Lighteater. The thing walked toward them—toward Ulric—its hideous faceless face pointed directly at him.

"It's pulling him," Ksara said. "It's pulling the light from him. It's ... Oh!"

Ksara wobbled, then collapsed to her hands and knees. The thick darkness around them thinned, and whatever tunnel Ksara had put around them began to fade. Khyven could see fifty feet in any direction. He could see more Lighteaters, all of them sitting in a line, looking up into the sky.

"I have you, Slayer of Giants," the Sword said. *"I've sheared their insidious claws. They shan't take hold of you."*

"Ksara!" Ulric murmured, and fell onto his face, body limp, his fingers still burning bright.

The Lighteaters turned, now more than a dozen of them moving toward them, seemingly drawn to their group's very life force.

Khyven drew the Sword.

"Oohhhh, yes..." it said.

"Diplomacy's over," Khyven growled.

He leapt at the Lighteaters.

CHAPTER FIFTY-FIVE
ALSENDA / DAVI / MAI'VEK / ELORA

People would later call it the Killing Night, that weeks-long horror of the noktum swallowing Noksonon. It had come like a curse from the gods, bringing death and destruction, hailing a fear that embedded itself in every person on the continent and wouldn't go away for a generation.

Alsenda Baire had been thirteen, picking berries half a mile from her home when the Killing Night descended. She and her family lived in a small village over ten miles from the crown city of Demaijos. Her parents had just heard the local whispers that everyone in the country was being called in, some crazy idea of the king's. Supposedly something bad was happening. Alsenda's parents ignored the warning, as did most people in the village. The king had always been eccentric, and information that finally filtered down to the country was often wrong.

So Alsenda had been picking berries when the Killing Night fell. It took her what seemed like a hellish forever to make her way back to her home, as blind as a mole rat.

She'd arrived crying, scared, and hungry, only to find nothing but bloody corpses in the village, which she only knew because she touched the cold bodies with her hands, felt the gaping wounds, the bones where the flesh had been picked clean. Her delay in getting home was, she knew, the only reason she survived. The monsters had come. They'd killed everyone, and they'd left.

After, when she'd been asked how she managed to walk the ten miles to the crown city completely blind, she could never say. Sometimes, when sleeping, she would dream about that harrowing walk. Only in those dreams, she could see a curvy woman in brown leathers holding her hand, leading her forward. But when she would awake, she could remember nothing of the woman.

But she'd made it to the city, and they gave her an amulet so she could see. There was much to do, and Alsenda was eager to help. She swept rooms. She emptied chamber pots. She stacked firewood and helped light fires, loving the natural light they gave off within the noktum. It brought the monsters, of course, but somehow the city had been prepared for this. Someone had warned them.

Her parents had thought the king crazy, but clearly he'd been right, so Alsenda was going to do whatever she could to serve him for the rest of her life. It was the only thing that made sense. So she worked as hard as she could at whatever task the stewards gave to her. She handed out blankets and amulets to the stragglers that came in after her. She even went on dangerous missions outside the walls of the city when groups were put together, searching for supplies that the forest could give them that the inside of the city could not. Those who worked with her said she worked harder than anyone else, and that she had no fear.

Alsenda was on just such a mission when the blessed light of the Lux broke through the noktum again. It was as though someone had shot a fiery bolt of sunlight into the sky. It burst the darkness, throwing it in every direction. It blinded her at first, almost as completely as the coming of the Killing Night had done.

But the blindness faded, and true colors had returned. The rich green of the trees around her. The gorgeous blue of the sky.

Much later, when the world had been remade in the wake of the exploding noktum, when Alsenda had just begun following her calling to research the history of the world—traveling from nuraghi to nuraghi and unearthing tales of the times gone by, learning how the Eldroi built the world long before Humans inherited it—she took her first lover. He was another researcher, and their love affair lasted more than a month while they both investigated a noktum that had been revealed during the Return of the Sun.

On that first, passionate night in the midst of the act when Alsenda cried out in pleasure, the memory of the woman returned to her. The woman who had walked with her, held her hand through the dark, the woman who Alsenda had all but forgotten except when she dreamed. In that moment, with stark clarity, Alsenda recalled every detail of her savior, and she knew without any doubt it had been Grina, goddess of creativity, passion, and lovemaking, of thieves and rogues, artists and prostitutes.

From that moment on, whenever Alsenda traveled to a new place, she followed any stories about interactions with the Pentat of Gods who served Noksonon. Everyone knew their names, or at least the name of the god or goddess who served their particular people.

Senji was the warrior goddess, who served the northern kingdoms of Imprevar, Usara, and Triada. Her icon was a two-handed sword. She was the goddess of courage, strength, and making war.

Lotura was god of the Luminents in Laria. His icon was a golden marriage ring. He was the god of integrity and union, of fathers and mothers, of friendship, of rules and nobility.

Libur was patron deity of all mages, with white robes and white eyes. He appeared as a man to some and a woman to others, and sometimes as both—or neither—at the same time.

His icon was an opening door.

Asper was god of the Taur-Els on the isle of Taur. His icon was a golden coin with a stalk of wheat behind it. He was the god of physical health, good harvests, and prosperity.

And of course, there was Grina, whose icon was a quill poised over an ink pot. She was the patron goddess of the Shadowvar, Demaijos, and Nox.

With every story Alsenda unearthed, with every new city she visited, she found an undeniable truth.

The gods had returned to Noksonon during the Killing Night. Every city she went to had tales of mysterious—and sometimes powerful—people arriving to lead others to safety, to give them tools to survive the dark, or to show them pockets of food or weapons.

But those stories were often secrets that Alsenda had had to pull from their owners; those stories ran as an undercurrent to the Killing Night. Another story—which was the same no matter which city or village she visited—ran like wildfire over the kingdoms of Noksonon. It was the story of the one who had killed the Eldroi who had made the Killing Night. It was the story of the one who had saved the world, saved them all. Not a god, but a hero.

Khyven the Unkillable's name became synonymous with hope. Within a month after the Return of the Sun, his name became a chant to bolster courage, to spur people to push forward when all seemed hopeless.

Just as Alsenda saw flashes of Grina in her dreams after her harrowing flight through the noktum, she'd also seen a flash of a man in that glorious moment when the sun had returned, when the Lux had burst free of the eternal night.

She'd had her bow raised to take a deer when the light exploded and the colors returned. In that instant, between her and the deer, a man appeared. He was tall, over six feet, with mismatched armor and scars on his face. She saw his sword, like a sharpened piece of the night, cutting through a creature that was swallowing the light.

She saw that flash, and then it was gone.

It would only be later when she had heard descriptions of Khyven the Unkillable, and even later than that when paintings and banners were made of the man in every kingdom on Noksonon, that she would know it was him she'd seen in that instant when the daylight returned.

In her middle age, she would recount all the stories she had unearthed from days gone by, wisdoms that had been forgotten under the heavy weight of time, arcana she had unearthed from a hundred nuraghis in a dozen different lands.

But her favorite story to tell was how she had seen Khyven the Unkillable in that one instant, through some prophetic vision or magical whiplash. She never tired of telling how he had been at the heart of returning the light to the world.

* * *

Davi survived the Killing Night, as the whole world later called it. His straggling group of refugees had been saved by Khyven the Unkillable, Queen Rhenn, and their friends. They'd been brought to Castle Noktos. He'd even survived the time after, when the Giants and the bloodsuckers killed almost everyone.

Margery, the woman who had cared for him when they had all fled through the dark to Castle Noktos, had been taken as food for the bloodsuckers. He'd never seen her again after that. Davi had been kept with the rest of the Usarans in the room with the sunlight.

He'd been there when the mage, Slayter, had knocked the totems down, and the only light in the room had been staggered shafts piercing the darkness up to the ceiling. He'd seen— barely—the image of Khyven fighting the Giant who had killed so many. He'd seen Khyven slay Harkandos.

Davi had wanted to be like Khyven. He loved Khyven for what he'd done. When Davi thought he might go insane thinking about the horrors that had happened—the terror of the absolute dark, the deaths of his parents, the loss of Margery—he always conjured a vision of Khyven overcoming them, and he felt safer somehow. It was his favorite thing to do whenever he was scared. His favorite thing until ...

Well, until the Return of the Sun.

Davi had been standing on a balcony in Castle Noktos when the sun burst across the lands once more. He'd been looking out over the dark forests and the enormous Cakistros moving far away, giant spidery legs lifting over the trees, looking for prey. The Cakistros never came to Castle Noktos, but one or two could always be seen far away, hovering over the treetops.

Davi had a short sword strapped across his back, just like Khyven wore his sword. There were plenty of weapons now in Castle Noktos after the war. So many had died, but their weapons remained. Davi spent most of his time burying those dead outside the castle with the crew he'd been assigned to, but whenever he had time, he practiced with his sword, imagined that he was Khyven the Unkillable, and that no one could stop him.

The Return of the Sun happened so suddenly. One moment, Davi had been thinking about the Cakistros, and how Khyven could probably have killed one of them with his sword, too, when the sky cracked. It was as though they'd all been kept inside a giant black egg, and the egg split open, revealing the blue sky beyond.

Sun shot down like arrows from above, and then the arrows became everything. Blue sky returned. The distant trees turned green, and the ground as well. The Cakistros shrieked, a sound that both terrified Davi and filled him with joy. The enormous creatures moved faster than he'd ever seen, chasing the fleeing darkness to get beneath it again.

In that instant, at the very moment the blue sky appeared and the Cakistros shrieked, Davi saw Khyven.

It was just a flash, just for a moment, but it burned into his memory for all time. His hero was superimposed over the vista that spread out before him, as though a giant Khyven stood on the air of that expanse. He wielded the Sword of Noksonon as he slew a creature that was sucking light into its face.

It happened so fast that Davi felt if he'd been looking somewhere else, he'd have missed it. His hero, not just saving them from Harkandos, but bringing the world back to the way it was supposed to be.

The noktum burst apart. For one moment, it seemed as though it would vanish entirely, that not only would they get back the places that had been in sunlight, but also all the places that had been noktums before the Killing Night. The night recoiled, but then it fought back, slinging tentacles of pure dark overhead. They fell and landed. For a moment, Davi thought they would crush him, crush the castle itself, because one of those horrible tentacles did fall on the castle, only twenty feet from Davi.

But there was no weight to them. They were only darkness, and when they fell they created entirely new noktums from what had existed before. The hundred-foot wall of dark cut straight through the middle of Castle Noktos, and it extended to the east as far as Davi could see. Beyond it, in the light, he saw the ocean, and against it as his light-starved eyes worked to adjust, he could see the crown city of Usara, its white palace gleaming in the sunshine like the very source of hope.

We're going home, Davi thought with an excitement that brought tears to his eyes. *Khyven has not only killed the Giant that brought the darkness, but he has killed the darkness itself.*

Davi felt to his knees and wept.

* * *

Mai'vek would never forget the day the sun returned. Because there weren't as many noktums on the isle of Taur, and because the Human Reader with the magical cloak had warned them of what was coming, the Taur-Els of Bol, as well as its surrounding farming communities, were ready.

They retreated to their strongholds of old and fended off the monsters that came. A few of their number died, but not nearly as many as the reports—which came flooding in after the Return of the Sun—from the mainland. So many of the races of Noksonon did not know how to work together efficiently, a trait the Taur-Els had always possessed. When they moved, they moved as one. When they fought, they fought as one. So when the fierce denizens of the noktums came looking for blood, they paid for it at a high price.

Due to the Reader's warning, they stockpiled goods and food to survive a very long time. They did not lack for sustenance. Only light.

Still, many of the crops died in the dark during the weeks of the Killing Night. And when the sun burst forth, Mai'vek marveled. They had expected the night to last a long time, possibly forever. It had been predicted by their shaman that the Eldroi had returned, and that meant hard times were upon them.

The Taur-Els had once been the warriors of the Eldroi. They had been created and bred for strength and speed. And so the shaman predicted that when the Eldroi came again, be it in a matter of days, months, or years, they would enslave the Taur-Els again, and possibly put them to the work of war once more.

There were some who argued they should pick up their yokes without complaint. To fight the Eldroi would be to sacrifice their lives. They argued that living under the lash of the Eldroi was what they had been created for in the first place, and that these past seventeen centuries were a temporary gift from Asper, a respite for their race before the inevitable work must be picked up again. Now it was time for this generation to pay for the previous generations of peace.

There were some who argued the opposite. They said that living under the lash was not life at all. If they were to be used for war for the Eldroi, they should make their own war first. If they had to take up arms like the ancestors had, they should fight for their freedom ... or die where they fell.

These were the conversations that occupied the eating halls in every section of the city. Mai'vek's life-partner believed that living under the command of the Eldroi was better than dying, and so far Mai'vek had not offered dissent.

But deep in his heart, something had awakened. He couldn't find his way clear to believe that his purpose was to give his allegiance to the Eldroi to pay for the free lives that his ancestors had lived.

More and more, he woke with rage in his heart, and the more he saw this grow within himself, the more he realized that the stories must be true. That once, instead of simple farmers who used their great muscles to work the earth and reap its bounty, the Taur-Els had been killers, the most powerful killers ever to walk Noksonon.

The more Mai'vek thought about bending the knee to the Eldroi, the more he wanted to kill. It grew every day, and he felt if his partner Kolei-fik told him once more that they should submit to the coming Eldroi, Mai'vek would explode.

He had a decision coming. He felt he was walking down a hallway that was narrowing more with every step, and soon there would be no direction to go except through a red door into bloody violence.

Was this what his ancestors of a bygone age had once felt? This slowly building, slowly kindling bonfire of rage? Was this how all of his people had been before the shamans of Asper brought the words of peace, farming, and prosperity?

Mai'vek had turned his great horned head toward the darkness above, and was flexing his hands into fists, then relaxing them, then flexing, then relaxing. He didn't know whether he was trying to calm himself down or whether he was working himself into a rage when the darkness opened.

It was as though blue roots suddenly plunged down from above, growing and snaking outward across the endless scope of black, digging deep, separating the noktum.

And then the noktum split and broke under the growing, demanding roots, and the roots became the blue sky. The darkness flew away like harvest ribbons in a strong wind, coiling and retreating, then lashing forth again like whips. The whips created entirely new noktums, splashing down like oil and making the tall, impenetrable fortresses of night.

But for an instant, right when the blue roots were shattering the noktum, Mai'vek saw a Human man. He wielded a dark sword and cut down a faceless, shambling creature that Mai'vek knew, somehow, was the one who had swallowed the light.

This image came and then vanished, and it would be weeks before Mai'vek would hear the name of the Human who had brought back the daylight.

The Human was from the far north of the mainland, and he was called Khyven the Unkillable. The legends about him were large, and it was said that he had not only brought back the daylight, but he'd saved the Taur-Els and everyone else on Noksonon from enslavement by the Eldroi. It was said he fought six of them, killed half, and sent the rest running.

A tall order for a Human, yet everyone seemed to believe it, and so Mai'vek chose also to believe it.

There was no more talk of submitting to the Eldroi once the sunlight returned. The shamans fell silent about their predictions, and Mai'vek felt grateful to this distant Khyven the Unkillable.

Mai'vek's rage eventually subsided, and in the subsequent decades of his life, he never felt that rage rise again. He and Kolei-fik lived long and prosperous lives, as the shamans recommended, as the god Asper commanded.

Mai'vek had never thought much of Humans. Violent little creatures who backstabbed those within their own race, a concept that was very difficult for a Taur-El to understand; they had purged those urges generations before Mai'vek was born.

So every year after the Return of the Sun, when he'd personally seen the face of the legendary Khyven the Unkillable, Mai'vek would make a pilgrimage from his modest village to the city of Bol. And there he would give an offering of his harvest at that spot where he had raged, seen the vision, and then cooled the fires of his hate. Mai'vek was renowned in his village and beyond for his three-horned pumpkins, and it was always his finest that he laid on that walkway in honor of Khyven the Unkillable, the Human who had saved them from slavery.

* * *

Ellora nearly took her own life on the day the Lux returned. The floating civilization that her people had been forced onto was slowly degenerating into violent tribalism.

The Brightlings of Luxo-Hallath were warned by the Human Reader with the cloak of death. And they had believed. To a person, they had believed. There were some among them who had long worried something like this would come. For decades they had worried.

The Brightlings lived south of the Lux, which wanted to break the darkness apart, and the Great Noktum that eternally tried to swallow it. That great war had been waged since the beginning of time.

The Brightlings had been designed by the Eldroi to weather the blinding brightness of the Lux and their bodies, of a necessity, fed upon the light. Oh, a Brightling could survive the night. They could even survive trips into the Great Noktum for days at a time. But it was known that if the Great Noktum ever won its battle against the Lux, the Brightlings wouldn't survive for more than half a year. Without any access to light, they would eventually wither and perish.

And so when the Reader came with her confirmation of their prophecies, the Brightlings had taken to the ocean. Their ancestors had prepared enormous rafts for them a century ago in preparation for it. And with those rafts, most of the Brightlings sailed out to sea to escape the reach of the noktum.

But the rafts were too few to bring every Brightling. Some were forced to stay behind while others escaped to where there would be light, at least, from the sun if not the Lux.

Those left on the mainland to fend for themselves were promised that every three days, the raft would return and swap out part of its population. A third of each raft would disembark, and an equal amount of those who had stayed behind could embark and sail back out into the sunlight.

The leaders failed to keep that promise. Rising factions within the floating cities seized power, killed those who had made the promise and then decided that it was too dangerous to return.

It was madness. She watched her two best friends, Mara and Vuelle, take up sides with different factions. The two had argued bitterly, and then retreated to the factions' fortified edges of the raft.

When Ellora found Vuelle stabbed to death and simply left on the expansive deck behind a stack of wooden crates, she wept bitterly for her lost friend. She wept because she suspected that it was Mara who had done it.

And she wept because the entire world had gone crazy. They had left the mainland to ensure they survived, but this was worse than the dark that would slowly kill them. It was so much worse. Only their bodies would have died on the mainland, but here the very soul of her culture was dying.

She'd left the corpse of her friend and walked to the edge of the raft. More and more, it was not safe to walk around in the open at night, outside of a fortified faction's area.

But she didn't care. She went to the edge, fully intending to dive into the sea and let it have her. There were monsters beneath the water. Not as many as in the noktum, but they were still there. She wouldn't survive for more than an hour, she figured. Even less if she dove deep and took a deep lungful of seawater.

That was when the shell of dark on the distant mainland cracked.

Ellora's heart beat faster as she saw the Lux break through, saw it swell like a creature that had been buried beneath a dozen enemies, but had somehow fought free and thrown off its tormentors. The noktum flung thick ropes of darkness left and right as the Lux swelled back to her original grandeur.

Ellora cried out, and at that moment as the night was split

asunder, she saw a Human flash before her eyes.

It was as though he was as tall as the Lux itself. He stood on the waves of the sea, arm cocked back as he delivered a blow with his death-black sword. He smote a creature, a beast that Ellora somehow knew, without knowing how, was responsible for swallowing the Lux. The image was gone in the next second, but the light of the Lux remained.

In the days and years that followed, the factions continued fighting. The Brightling civilization collapsed with the coming of the dark, but Ellora survived. Two of the rafts had already gone to war by the time the light returned. More than half the people on those rafts were slain.

But on four of the other rafts, including the one upon which Ellora stood, the factions eased their vitriol long enough to work together, long enough to guide the rafts back to the shore.

Nearly all of their fellows left behind on the mainland were dead. Some had been torn apart by beasts, some had died from overexposure to the dark. A handful had found ways to feed themselves sunlight, but they did not come rushing back to join those who had abandoned them. They scattered and disappeared from Brightling society.

Ellora spent her remaining days searching for those who'd been left behind. She never joined any of the factions and became a wanderer, a medicine woman who found those in need and tended to them.

But once every year, she would go to the very edge of the Lux. She would thank the light for being so courageous. And she would thank the nameless Human who had brought the world back to itself.

Chapter Fifty-Six

RHENN

With her hand on her red-jeweled sword, Rhenn stood in the newly-won sunlight Ksara and her crew had helped them achieve. It had gone exactly as she had hoped: With Paralos, both teams, and even Rauvelos—who had returned after a prolonged battle with Mentos just before they'd left for the Lux—Xos had been fooled. The Lighteaters had been overwhelmed.

The Lighteaters had hurt Ulric, and Khyven had gone into a frenzy. The Sword of Noksonon had cut through the Lighteaters like paper. It was as though they were completely comprised of magic, and nothing cut through magic like the Sword of Noksonon.

As soon as half a dozen of the Lighteaters fell, the Lux began to reassemble itself, shards of light flying up like pieces of glass from the ground, smashing together, creating a small glow, then a powerful glow, then a blinding ball of white that swirled and burst and blew apart the noktum like an explosion of heat-less fire.

They'd tried to end Xos at the same time, but the ancient Giant had slithered into the scattered noktum. To Xos, the noktum was like the ocean, and he was a current. They would always have to keep an eye out for him when traveling the noktum now.

It was a lost opportunity, but she couldn't lament it. She'd brought her people back to safety. After weeks of terror, heartbreak, and loss, they could return home, back to Usara.

The crown city had been half-returned to the sunlight, with a newly placed noktum covering half of it. Rhenn figured that about the same amount of noktums remained as before the Killing Night, but they were all in different places.

It was appropriate that the city was half in light and half in dark, in this new age. Light and Dark had to coexist, and she was determined that her people would navigate both. Living only in the light during these last seventeen centuries had made her people staggeringly vulnerable. Her kingdom would have education about the Amulets of Noksonon, about the creatures who lived within the borders of the noktum, how to handle them or—if necessary—to slay them.

Should the noktum ever return in its entirety, Rhenn was determined her people would be ready.

In their previous culture of noktum avoidance, the noktums had been as much a part of any map created in the last two millennia as the mountain ranges, the oceans, and the deserts. The maps may as well have had the words "Here There Be Dragons" written upon every noktum. No one had visited them. To go into the noktum was to die, and that was how people had seen them.

Rhenn didn't yet know what this looked like on the rest of the continent, but one third of Usara was still swallowed by the Dark, including that portion of the palace and the crown city. Not only that, but half of Castle Noktos was now in the sunlight, almost as though it had been an intentional exchange.

The sudden sunlight had, no doubt, slain a number of denizens of the Dark who could not stand the light, burning them as they tried to find shelter in the rearranged noktums. Some of Zaith's people were lost in just such a way, suddenly standing in stark sunlight with the nearest noktum too far away for them to reach before they burned.

But many had remained, and rather than making this event a stark division between their peoples, Rhenn had encouraged Zaith to stay, to live in the noktums in Usara, even inside the crown city. To build this new Usara together.

She didn't know if it would work, but she knew she wanted to try. Rhenn herself now straddled the line between the light and the dark, between Human and Nox, between living and dead. She was uniquely situated to attempt to integrate these disparate worlds.

She would do her best.

But for now, she was simply grateful to see the line of her people moving back into the city. She saw many shedding tears of joy as they hauled their meager possessions on their backs—or walked with no possessions at all—toward the walls of the city.

They wanted food. They wanted shelter. They wanted a scrap of the familiar.

They wanted to go home.

But the truth was that there was no home anymore, no real safety. The horrors they'd endured would mark them all forever. Whatever sanctuary there was left in the world, they were going to have to make it inside themselves first. They were going to have to fight for it.

Rhenn planned to help by putting her people to work immediately. Cleaning the streets. Burying the dead in the city, cleansing a way for a new future.

It was going to be unbelievably difficult, but she would see it done.

She knew if there was one thing that could allay the despondency that threatened her people, it was sun-up-to-sundown work. Work them to exhaustion. Give them no time to think about the horrors that preyed upon their minds.

And then, perhaps, one day not far from now, the city would be cleansed, and there would be room for other thoughts. Room to hope. If she could simply push them past the obstacles in their way, she thought she could give them hope.

So many of their resources had been stripped from them, along with so many of their citizens, but there were new resources that now existed. The Dark offered so many things they'd never considered before, and Rhenn planned to leverage it.

But perhaps the most significant resource in the fight for public morale was how everyone was now looking at, and looking to, Khyven. Rhenn, Slayter, and even Vohn had all been there when the Lighteaters were slain, but something had happened during the battle, and it had only happened to Khyven. Rhenn—none of them, in fact—had known about this singularly odd bit of magic until they returned to Castle Noktos.

Apparently an image of Khyven slaying the final Lighteater had been … projected somehow. Some unknown magic or act of the gods had taken that final triumphant moment as the Lux returned, cracking through the noktum, and had imprinted it in the minds of anyone who had been looking outside at the time, looking up at the sky. In Usara, several dozen people had seen it. Not all, but many. And Rhenn began to suspect that perhaps other people in Noksonon had seen it as well.

Khyven had been a celebrity before. Now he was … revered. People looked to him as something more than Human, like he was a disciple of Senji come to walk the lands.

Shortly after returning, Rhenn had announced they were moving back to the crown city. She had brought them here in the dark to protect them. Instead they'd been decimated by Harkandos's attack. She wanted to leave that memory behind.

She'd expected this announcement to be met with cheers, but it was met with silence. They had actually hesitated, then all looked to Khyven instead of her. He had been standing off to the side some ten feet away. When all eyes went to him, his eyebrows had raised and he'd glanced at her. It was as though the people weren't going to leave Castle Noktos unless Khyven was.

Rhenn should have been jealous, but she wasn't. Instead, she felt overspilling pride and a crazy love for the man. She knew exactly what the people felt when they looked at him. She felt it, too. When she'd been held down by N'ssag's primes in the Thuros room in Daemanon, when she'd felt all hope was gone, Khyven had appeared. He'd told N'ssag to let her go, and in that moment she had known everything was going to be all right.

Her people felt that if he was with them, they could get through this. If he wasn't leaving Castle Noktos, neither were they. To them, wherever Khyven was, there was safety.

She used it to the advantage of the kingdom. She set Khyven in front of her subjects and started him walking. They followed right behind him, and the pilgrimage back to the crown city began.

Now, the last few stragglers were almost inside. She had likewise told Zaith and his people that they could move into the corners of the city now covered in darkness, and he had agreed that, at least for a while, they would.

Days later, the clean-up in the city was, miraculously, nearly done. Temporary quarters had been made in the first day, and now, with the dead bodies cleared out and being buried, Rhenn had been assigning permanent houses and living quarters to everyone. It was a testament to her subjects' resilience that they'd come together so quickly, cleaned the city and readied it for the next step.

The Nox had moved into the darkened part of the city as well, and during the nighttime hours, they had been the driving force for clearing and burying bodies. It had surprised her how well they were integrating. She had thought their blood-hungry nature would overcome some of them; that they'd want to hunt Humans, but not a single Nox had fed upon a Human since Zaith had taken charge. The Nox not only deferred to him, but they deferred to her as well.

That had taken her by surprise, but she had discovered

something about the Nox over the last few days. Just as Khyven had become a symbol of worship for her people, *she* had become that to the Nox. Zaith was their leader, but she was the one who had broken the hold of their enslaver. She had undergone the same transformation they had undergone, and she had not only recaptured some semblance of a normal life, she had retained the reins of her kingdom. Rhenn was a symbol of hope to the undead Nox, that their lives weren't over, that they might rise again as a viable culture.

That was when she knew this crazy experiment of hers might just work. Humans and Nox, the living and the undead, coexisting in peace and cooperation. An experiment that perhaps other kingdoms in Noksonon might emulate.

Now, Rhenn stood on the balcony of the darkened side of the palace where her apartments had been moved. She could be in the sunlight, but only for short periods of time. It was easier for her to reside in a place that would not immediately destroy her if she didn't have her sword.

As the sun rose over the lighted part of Usara, she found her thoughts shifting from the welfare of her people, and now of the Nox, to the welfare of those who had held this kingdom up.

Slayter, Vohn, and of course Khyven had been instrumental in shepherding everyone to this place, and some semblance of security and normalcy had been returned. Now it was time to pay debts.

She had summoned Khyven only ten minutes ago, and already his knock sounded on her door.

"Come in," Rhenn said.

He entered quietly, closed the door behind him. The Sword of Noksonon rode his back. He didn't go anywhere without it, and based on the short conversations she'd had with him about it, he wasn't likely to. The Sword and Khyven had made a promise to each other, and the Sword didn't like being separated from him. It made her apprehensive. The Sword of Noksonon was beyond their knowledge—even Slayer's knowledge. It was like an alien sentience among them, unquantifiable and unknowable. But along with that, it had saved them. As much as Khyven, the Sword was the reason they were all still alive.

The Sword was not at its normal immense size. When Rhenn had first seen the thing, it was six feet long with a handle that a Giant could comfortably wield. Now it was barely three feet long, and the hilt was much smaller. It fit easily across Khyven's back.

Unquantifiable. Unknowable.

"You wanted to see me," he said.

"Yes, but not for long." She left the balcony and sat down at the small table in the center of the room. She indicated he should do the same.

Deftly managing The Diplomat at his hip, he sat opposite her. He paid no attention to the Mavric iron sword on his back, and Rhenn guessed that was because it would shrink or grow to accommodate his sitting.

"Not for long?" he echoed.

"How are Vohn and Slayter?"

"Settling in. Vohn finally drugged him, I think."

"And Slayter didn't notice?" Rhenn asked. Slayter had been running himself into the ground every day. The mage still hadn't recovered from the fight with Harkandos, and that had been weeks ago.

"I think maybe he noticed, but perhaps he had no more arguments to stand up to Vohn's harangue." Khyven shrugged. "I think more it's that the people are settled in. Before we went to the Lux, he mentioned some percentage about the likelihood of Usara continuing as a kingdom, as a culture, without us."

"Us?"

"You, me, Vohn, Slayter. The group of us."

"I take it the percentage of success was low."

"I think we may have crossed a threshold and the odds are much better now. Therefore, he can rest."

"Has he been messing around with Lore Magic?"

"I don't think Slayter needs Lore Magic," Khyven said. "He ... naturally sees more than others do."

"In certain ways," Rhenn said.

Khyven chuckled. "Yes. In certain ways."

"So, he and Vohn are living in the same apartments?"

"When I was there, they were each sitting in cushioned chairs, reading books. With tea."

"How domestic. They're adorable."

"Insane. I think you meant insane."

"Our insanity—each of us in our own ways—was what led us here. Insanity of a certain stripe isn't bad."

Khyven cracked another smile. "That's one way of looking at it."

"We've stabilized for the moment, Khyven. We're safe."

"I suppose."

"As safe as anyone can expect to be in this world."

"Mmmm."

"My point," Rhenn said. "Is that it's time."

"Time?"

"Lorelle hasn't returned. I know you've wanted to search for her every day that has passed."

He didn't say anything.

"It's time for that," she said. "We need you, yes. The people need you. I need you. But you've done your part for now. The citizens of Usara can do without their hero for a few weeks. Go. Find her. Find her and bring her back."

He stood up. "Are you certain? Everything seems so ... fragile right now. I mean, if a horde of noktum beasts came hunting ... And we aren't sure the Giants are going to leave us alone. Just because Harkandos is gone doesn't mean one of those others, like Orios, won't try to take what they feels belongs to them."

"I don't know if you noticed this, but Giants take a long time to decide on any kind of action. Goodness, we beat them more than seventeen hundred years ago, and it took this long for them to come together and challenge us. It took Harkandos's return to give them the spine—or instill them with the fear—to make them do it. And look what happened? Most of them got killed, including Harkandos." She shook her head. "No, I don't think Orios is coming anytime soon."

He took a step toward the door. "Are you sure?"

"You need her. We need her. Go, my friend. Go get her back."

She had barely finished the sentence when he was out the door.

CHAPTER FIFTY-SEVEN

VOHN

T he steward delivered the pot of tea at six o'clock in the morning. The queen now lived in the part of the palace that was always in the noktum, high up on the fourth floor. Vohn and Slayter had taken up chambers near the line of the noktum, also on the fourth floor. It had been difficult to get the mage to sleep anywhere aside from that dungeon room right next to his laboratory, which was where he was going to spend a good deal of his nights anyway. But Vohn was slowly convincing him that civilized people didn't just work until they fell over, then climb into a dog pen until their body woke up again. Civilized people had rooms specifically to divide their work and their personal life.

Vohn wasn't sure Slayter grasped the concept of a personal life, but Vohn was patient. They could walk there one step at a time.

Slayter currently slept in the bed. He'd been sleeping more than ten hours a day for the last few weeks. Slayter had almost killed himself. It seemed he simply didn't know how to moderate his strength. He either didn't use it at all, or he used everything he had and collapsed. It was a wonder he hadn't died long before now.

Even as Vohn piled admonishments up in his mind, though, he knew that wasn't precisely true. If it had been, Slayter really would be dead. He was the most aware person—about the things he cared about—that Vohn had ever met. Perhaps it was fairer to say that Slayter knew his limitations better than anyone in the world. He just chose to go right to the line, to give everything he had for his friends, for his kingdom It was one of the many reasons, Vohn supposed, that he loved him.

Vohn took the tea service, piping hot, and set it on the nightstand. It was too hot to drink now, but in half an hour when Slayter awoke, it would be perfect.

Vohn would be gone by then. There were rounds to be made. Rhenn, Slayter, and Khyven had wrangled the kingdom into shape through sheer force of will. The streets were clean of bodies—the Nox had been amazingly helpful with that—the old city defenses had been restored, the new defenses were being constructed. The trauma of what they'd been through could never fully be healed, of course, but Vohn thought the people were beginning to feel safe again. There were many challenges ahead, but it was nothing short of a miracle that Rhenn had led them this far, this fast.

When Vohn had walked the streets these past few weeks, he didn't just see dead eyes in the people of Usara. He saw hope. He'd seen children, always more resilient than adults, actually playing with a stick and a ball in the street. They'd been *playing*.

He watched Slayter for one more moment, then left the room quietly, the door closing on silent hinges. Vohn had ensured it was well-oiled so he didn't risk waking Slayter during these early morning walks.

The walks were important. Someone had to pay attention to the details, after all. Rhenn was looking at the big picture. Slayter was looking at the bigger picture. And Khyven had recently found and brought Lorelle back to the palace. No one expected him to be looking at anything except her right now.

So yes, someone had to pay attention to the details.

Vohn had been working on the kingdom's finances and the city's logistics: in short, the absolutely essential components of living that Rhenn barely paid attention to, that Slayter *never* paid attention to, and that Khyven thought was boring. Vohn had joined forces with Lord Harpinjur. Against the odds, the old battle axe had actually survived everything that had happened to them. The man seemed indestructible.

Together, the two of them worked to ensure the crown city stayed fed, and that some form of commerce started up. Usara's tradesmen had barely begun to put their shaky hands back to work, so there weren't many goods to speak of, which was fine so far because the trade routes had completely collapsed during the Killing Night. No goods were coming into the city from other places. Nothing was going out.

So for the moment, what Usara produced was what Usara had.

Crops had been shoved into darkness for weeks, so the summer harvests were spotty at best. Strangely, certain crops had continued to grow in the dark, as though they'd been designed that way long ago, but some had withered. Those that hadn't had been nibbled by noktum denizens. It wasn't a total loss, but one thing that had been relatively unaffected by the noktum was the sea. There were still plenty of fish. Lord Harpinjur and Vohn had assigned crews to repair and man fishing boats. The population of the crown city was going to be eating a lot of fish for a while.

Vohn and Harpinjur had a meeting scheduled for mid-morning, and before that, Vohn would make his rounds. He went up the hallway to the line of darkness that marked the noktum that was now a part of their daily lives. Most of the population had their amulets, and Slayter had said he would soon make more so that every citizen could cross over into the darkness.

Vohn, of course, had Rauvelos's ring. He could actually see

colors now in the noktum, gorgeous purples and lavenders. He was told by Zaith that this was something like the sight the Nox had.

Vohn entered the noktum and went to Rhenn's royal apartments. Two Knights of the Dark stood post outside her door—one of them a Human male and one of them a Nox female. Vohn still wasn't entirely comfortable with the undead bloodsuckers serving as guards after they had feasted upon Humans in Castle Noktos, but Rhenn had insisted. The Nox hadn't killed a single Usaran since daylight had returned, but ...

He suppressed a shudder as he approached the guards.

"The queen is resting?" Vohn asked in a voice so low it was barely audible. Both guards nodded.

Good. With her new supernatural body, Rhenn didn't need the same kind of sleep as the living. She could stay awake for days at a time, but apparently there was a balance between good, honest rest, and how much blood she had to devour to keep herself animate. Rest actually was a factor, and the more Rhenn slept, the less she had to kill to keep herself alive.

Vohn continued on to an audience chamber at the end of the hall. It wasn't used for anything at the moment. Well, nothing except Vohn's own personal exercises. Slayter had reinforced it with a kind of cage spell to keep Vohn from flitting away against his own will.

He entered, closed the double doors behind himself and listened for the audible click. Slayter had told him this would activate the spell that would help corral him in his banshee state.

Vohn took off his ring.

The Dark rushed into him like a wind, and his body swirled away. When in his banshee form, it was as though the entire world was made of winds, not physical objects. Normal walls, floors, furniture, trees, mountains were no more an impediment to his banshee self than the blue of the sky was to an eagle. He could fly around them or through them. He had absolute freedom, but the problem with absolute freedom was an absolute lack of boundaries.

For Vohn, that was a nightmare, and it was his greatest problem with the banshee form. He constantly fought to form coherent enough thoughts to navigate where he wanted to go in the Dark.

In the past, every terrifying time Vohn had taken on his banshee form, he'd promptly gotten lost in the Dark and had a nearly impossible time trying to focus his desires, take himself back to where he ought to be. It was why Slayter had to come find him after Vohn had killed Avektos.

But Vohn was practicing. He was getting better.

He specifically forced his mind to stay on the mundane tasks he'd been thinking about, to keep the structure of his corporeal body's worries and interests while flying about. And it was working.

The first time he'd done this—at Slayter's urging—he'd bounced around this room like a fish flopping on a bank, running into the magically bounded walls and floors until Slayter pulled him back out. That had been weeks ago.

This time, Vohn concentrated on flying about the room, touching the walls, but not running into them. He was slowly learning control.

"Vohn ..." Paralos's voice rose from the Dark like the distant hammering of drums.

"Paralos."

She had been critical in the restoration of the sunlight. Vohn had been terrified of her when he'd first entered his banshee form. Even after she had helped him with Shalure, he'd been wary. But without her, Khyven would never have been able to slay the Lighteaters. She was a Giant, yes. But an ally.

By Lotura, if they could create a community with Nox bloodsuckers, perhaps they could also form a community with a Giant as well.

"I have scoured the noktums of Usara," Paralos said. "There is nothing."

"And the Lux?"

"Harkandos's Lighteaters were utterly destroyed. Khyven

and the Sword of Noksonon did a thorough job."

"And there's no way Xos could make more?"

"Xos is not the mage Harkandos was, despite what he would like to believe. Neither am I, for that matter. But from what I gather, Harkandos's success in creating the Lighteaters was as much an accident as intentional. Those wretched creatures had been twisted and warped by Harkandos's untended magic for seventeen hundred years. Even if Xos could duplicate it, I suspect he would need centuries to bring such a creature to fruition."

They had been looking for a counterattack from Xos ever since they'd broken his barrier around the Lux and killed the Lighteaters. They'd tried to kill the bastard outright, but killing a sentience inside a noktum was easier said than done.

Slayter was working on it.

In the meantime, they had accrued a debt with Paralos. They owed her, and there was something very specific she wanted.

She wanted out of the noktum.

Apparently, Nhevalos had promised her long ago that he would extract her from the noktum, that he would recreate her body and bring her back to life the way she had been before the Human-Giant War.

And Slayter thought he could do it.

"We've begun the search," Vohn said. They needed something of Paralos. Slayter said that one hair from her head would do the trick, but finding the hair of someone who had died almost two millennia ago was impossible. "Slayter thinks we may be able to use the mirror instead. There's a part of your essence in the mirror. That might be enough to reconstruct your physical body."

"I thank you," Paralos said.

"Lotura, Paralos." Vohn shook his head. "You've done your part and then some. It's the least we can do. Just give us some time. Slayter hasn't failed to do anything he's set his mind to before." He paused. "Well, that's not true. Slayter has failed a thousand times at what he's set his mind to, but he keeps going.

He keeps going until he succeeds. Just give him time."

"Time is what I have."

"He'll get you out."

"Again, I thank you. Your practice with your Dark state comes along."

If Vohn had had a face in his banshee state, he would have smiled. "Look at me, hovering here. Not flying every which way."

In his first few incarnations as the banshee, Vohn had thought Paralos was trying to trap him. Come to find out, she was just trying to corral him, much like Slayter's spell was doing right now. She wasn't a bad sort for a Giant.

"I'm going to go now," Vohn said.

"I will see you tomorrow," she said.

"You will."

Vohn concentrated. This was the hardest part. By all the gods, this was hard!

He imagined himself on the ground below, imagined pushing his body into that image like the noktum cloaks pushed a body through a straw. He had to literally recreate his entire body from his imagination, and then shove himself into it. It didn't make any sense, which was why it was so difficult. Slayter had tried to convince him that working magic was the art of skipping over the gaps of logic between what a mage wanted what was actually there.

Which also didn't make sense.

But step by step, Slayter had showed him how to prepare the mind to will the fictional into the concrete.

Bit by painstaking bit, Vohn shoved his body together, combining his imagination and the wind of his surreal banshee body.

It seemed to take forever.

Then he stood on the floor of the huge chamber, two fingers pinching the ring he had just shoved onto a finger on his other hand.

"I hate that ..." Vohn murmured, falling to one knee. He

felt like he'd run five miles. "I hate that every time."

"It will get easier the less you hate it," Paralos said in his mind.

"Now you sound like Slayter," he growled.

"I could do worse than sounding like Slayter."

That made Vohn chuckle. He stood up shakily and nodded to the Dark.

"Until tomorrow," she said.

"Until tomorrow."

He left the room, clicking the doors shut, and headed back into the sunlit part of the castle, heading toward Shalure's room. She wasn't in the palace's official infirmary for the population at large; that one was downstairs. Many had been injured during the war, and Rhenn insisted that all of them be brought into the palace first. The palace had been the most devoid of dead bodies—being as how Rhenn and most of the fighting knights of Usara had been in the palace when the noktum hit. She had decreed that until the city could be cleaned up, the wounded would stay in the royal infirmary where they would receive the best care, and where she could visit them.

Rhenn and Harpinjur had taken care of the wounded population, but Vohn had insisted on taking care of Shalure.

There were quite a few unused rooms in this part of the palace. These were the expansive royal apartments, and Vohn had taken one of the many rooms, an opulent homage to one of Rhenn's grandmothers. It had old style brocade curtains and bed covers, as well as a few priceless vases and a basin that might have been three hundred years old. When she'd come to the crown city, Shalure had wanted to be a woman of importance, of standing, a lady of the court. Vohn thought she would like it. When she awoke, she would like it.

He opened the door quietly, as though she was sleeping, but he could have thrown an armful of pots and pans on the cobblestone floor and she wouldn't have stirred.

And, of course, she didn't. But he closed the door silently, reverently.

She was unchanged. Her hair was still as white as snow, and her skin was almost as pale. Anyone else with that color of skin would look dead, but there was no gray cast to her, no rigor mortis that stiffened the face or the limbs. She didn't look dead. She looked like an exquisite marble statue, except she was warm to the touch. She breathed.

The fact that she was unchanged was remarkable on a number of levels. First, she hadn't eaten. It had been weeks since her transformation, since their flight from Jai'ketakos. She had not wasted away even a little. Breathing in, breathing out. Never eating. Never drinking. Never needing to use a chamber pot or do any of the things a Human body normally needed to do.

Secondly, at Castle Noktos, she had been in the infirmary with all the other wounded. She'd had her own bed in a line of beds, at the far end of the hall. And when Khyven had fallen, when the Trolls and the bloodsucking Nox invaded, the wounded had been devoured first. They were the first to go before Harkandos designated the feasting room for the Nox.

Shalure should have been devoured with them. Defenseless, alone, she should have died.

Neither the Nox nor the Trolls had touched her.

When Vohn finally had a moment to go looking for her, he'd found her in the blood-spattered infirmary, still laying in her bed, still breathing in, breathing out, eyes closed. He still didn't know if it was because they simply didn't see her because of some spell, or if the idea of sucking her blood was anathema to them.

He was, of course, utterly convinced of some kind of magical interference. Paralos hadn't understood what had happened to Shalure any more than Vohn did. There was no normal explanation for it. He would have put Slayter on the job, trying to sleuth it out, but the mage had enough to untangle without thinking about Shalure.

After all, if her unchanged state was perpetual, then she was no longer in any danger. Vohn would take care of her. This part of his daily routine had become ... sacred to him.

Shalure had saved them. She had sought her purpose within

the group for so long, and at the moment when Khyven was about to be slain by Harkandos, Shalure had helped Vohn stop that from happening. It was because of Shalure that they'd won the day.

Without her, Vohn shuddered to think what might have happened to him, to Khyven, to Usara ...

To all of Noksonon.

She was that key person at that key moment. That deserved reverence, and since he was the only one who really knew what had happened, he'd taken it upon himself

"Slayter is recovering," Vohn said to her as he pulled his stool up to the bed. He sat down and took her hand. "He likes to pretend that he's all right, but I can see how drawn he is. He looks almost as pale as you."

Vohn removed his satchel from around his neck, opened the pouch and withdrew the *Ovander Tales*. Vohn had found a copy in Castle Noktos before devastation had descended upon them. It was a collection of short stories written by a young writer who'd lived during the reign of Hestus Laochodon III, one of Rhenn's distant ancestors.

That period had been a dark chapter of Usaran history, though not quite so dark as this one. Theos Ovander had, perhaps as a literary counterpoint, written a series of lighthearted, optimistic short stories. There was one about a group of young nobles riding about the countryside for a picnic. There was one of young squires who went into a noktum and returned with a magical sword, unharmed. There was one of a young girl whose silver ball fell into a lake. She dove after it and found an entire fantasy world, upside down, on the bottom of the lake. She lived there with the lake's upside-down denizens until she decided to return home, leaving the silver ball with them to remember her by.

They were all like that, hopeful little tales in a time of sadness. Ovander had done what he could to lift people's spirits, and Vohn had selected it specifically to read to Shalure. He could only guess what hell she might be in, trapped inside her own head. If his voice might somehow light her way back, he was going to try. Every day. For the rest of his life. Until she returned.

He withdrew his spectacles from his vest pocket, worked the wire ends around his ears and adjusted them on his nose. He found his bookmark, thumbed the book open to the spot.

"If I'm not mistaken, Fygeri had just found the cave." He licked his thumb and turned to the previous page to reorient himself, then turned it back. "Yes. The cave. I can only imagine what he might find there. Let's see ... Yes. He followed the trail in the wood, it came to the cave, and he saw, engraved in gold, a stylized door in the process of being opened right over the archway. An icon of an opening door."

He glanced up at her as though she was actually hearing him. "The mark of Libur, you know. What would you like to bet that magic is involved somehow?" He grinned at his own joke, then settled in.

"Vohn," Shalure said from behind him.

He jumped so high the book flew into the air and he nearly toppled over backward in his chair. Vohn staggered to his feet as the chair clacked onto its back. The book bounced off the edge of Shalure's sickbed and tumbled open onto the floor, pages down.

Shalure stood behind him, shining white. She wore that same white enameled armor from the battle at Castle Noktos, and that same winged horse stood with her. He wasn't sure there was actually enough space for the horse to be in this room, and it rather bent the mind to see it standing there.

This time, though, Shalure wasn't wearing her helm, and he could see her face. Her green eyes, that slightly upturned nose, the gentle slope of her jaw. Everything about her face was the same.

Nothing else was.

Her shoulders seemed wider, more muscled, as though she'd been fighting in the Night Ring for a decade. Her hair was just as white as the marble statue in the bed, her skin just as fair, but she was alive and vibrant.

The Shalure he'd known before this transformation had been afraid of just about everything and, before Vamreth had cut her tongue out, had covered that fear with a flirtatious bravado.

Not this woman. She stood with the open, equal-legged stance of a warrior. This woman knew exactly who she was, and what her place was.

For a moment, he couldn't think of what to say.

"Do you plan to come here every day?" she asked.

"O-Of course. Until I get you back," he stammered.

She smiled warmly. "You really are the sweetest."

"So I didn't dream it. You really did … You know …" He made a wave-like motion with his hand.

"Help you in your time of need?"

"Fly me up and drop me on a Giant."

She chuckled. "What an interesting way of describing it."

"It's an entirely accurate way of describing it."

"I suppose it is. Yes. I did."

"I … What happened to you?"

"I will tell you, if you wish, but I'll warn you that I cannot stay long. It takes a great deal of my vitality to simply be here. But you keep distracting me with your stories. I keep having to look down here to see if you're all right, and I do have other things to do now."

"My reading is distracting you? You can hear me?"

"I will always be able to hear you, and I will always come when you call, but as I said, there is a limited amount of me. If I use too much of what is left of my vitality, then I will … Well, I suppose I'll simply cease to be."

"Then you should go! Don't spend time talking to me!" He made a shoo-ing motion with his hands.

"I am all right for the moment, dear Vohn. And I need to explain my situation to you so that your heart can rest easy. So you can know that I'm not in some horrible place."

"But if this is hurting you—"

"I promise I won't overextend myself." She smiled warmly

again.

"Well ... All right."

"When you ... tried to help me, tried to save me by taking me into your banshee state, it nearly killed my body. It would have, but Senji took my spirit. She took it up to be with her, and she cast a spell upon my body. A preservation spell."

"Senji ... the goddess?"

"She gave me a choice. I chose this." She gestured at herself. "That body..." She gestured at her body laying on the bed. "Will stay in state. You will need do nothing with it."

"So you ... You live with Senji now?" Vohn rubbed the curly hair between his horns. She was living with the *goddess*?

Shalure paused, and for the first time looked a little sad. "I ... did. Now I ... Well, the equivalent for you would be to imagine me living in Senji's house. Saving me was within Senji's powers. Resurrecting Khyven was not. Or at least not without a terrible cost. Senji is ... gone. She gave her immortality to bring Khyven back."

Vohn opened his mouth and found he couldn't close it for a moment. "She what?"

"She's gone now, but I find ... Well, she wouldn't want us to mourn her. Or rather, she didn't see her sacrifice as a sadness. She saw it as the culmination of her purpose. Senji never ran from problems. She ran at them. It is why she was the goddess of courage and war. She knew as well as anyone what was at stake in this war with Harkandos. She wanted, more than anything else, to help the Humans of Usara. Throughout the centuries since she became a goddess, she called her shots, every time. Gods are not all-powerful, like many believe, but they *are* powerful. Senji used her magic and her influence to guide Humanity when she thought it would do the most good. She would have been proud to see what her sacrifice wrought, what Khyven did—what you all did—with her gift. If she were here, she would tell you there wasn't a better use for her life."

Despite Shalure's assurances, tears came to Vohn's eyes. "We killed a goddess," he whispered.

Shalure shook her head. "No Vohn. You gave purpose to a goddess."

He blinked away the blurriness. "Such high costs. Such high costs everywhere …" He glanced back at her sleeping form.

"Don't mourn for me, dear Vohn."

He turned, and now she stood close, right in front him. She seemed taller than before. Before, they'd almost been of a height, but she seemed to tower over him now. She touched his chin.

"Thank you for your kindness," she whispered. "For picking me up when I needed you. Don't ever forget that your sacrifices also changed the world."

"Shalure …"

"I have to go now. I've spent my time here. Tell the others … Well, you'll know what to tell them."

He reached up to put his hand over hers. It was warm and solid, not the ghostly thing he'd expected.

They lingered like that for a moment, then Shalure withdrew her hand. She went to her winged horse and mounted with graceful ease.

"Will we ever see you again?" he asked.

"Oh, for certain." She pulled her helm down on her head. She looked so … right with it. So perfect. He didn't know why he'd never seen this warrior woman within Shalure before.

Perhaps she had wondered the same thing.

Her winged horse danced in a neat little circle, and then she reined it still. "Perhaps, if you like, you could still read to me."

"Yes! Of course I will."

"But maybe just once a month." She winked. "Once a month will be a lot where I am."

Vohn had a dozen questions, but he simply stood there. He held up his hand in farewell.

"Goodbye, Vohn," she said.

She wheeled her horse around and this time, the creature launched into the sky. Of course, there was no sky, but for a moment in that small room, it seemed like there was. A deep blue sky with unbelievably white clouds, light shining down between them.

Then she was gone, and the room was just a room.

"Goodbye, Shalure," Vohn murmured.

CHAPTER FIFTY-EIGHT

KHYVEN

Khyven sat on the bed, tipping the nearly empty glass over the edge of the nightstand just so. He balanced it with the tip of his finger on the rim. The glass was a ridiculous, bulbous Triadan thing. Apparently Triadans made an art out of blowing glass into odd shapes, and this was part of a set. The base was wide; it slimmed in the middle, then widened even more at the top.

Nobles and their finery. What was wrong with a mug? If Khyven was going to drink, just a good old mug would do. Banded oak, like a miniature keg. That was workable. Pewter was better, of course. He'd even once drunk from a pewter mug with a thick glass bottom so you could look at your fellows as you drained it. That was approaching too fancy for Khyven. And really, just a deep wooden cup that had been hollowed out of a thick tree branch worked just fine. Khyven had drunk from one of those for years in the Night Ring.

But a glass shaped like a—well, like a woman's figure, he supposed—just seemed silly. But Rhenn liked them, so that was what had been delivered to the royal beds of the infirmary.

It was glorious to be back in the Usaran Palace, with the sun shining outside, with its warmth once again in the crown city. Nothing, of course, was back to normal, but there was hope again. Hope that it could be normal someday. Maybe it wouldn't be for this entire generation, but it could for the one after that.

With a flick of his finger, he spun the glass and watched it wobble and settle a quarter of an inch from the edge of the nightstand. He was getting better at that. He kept trying to spin it like that closer and closer to the edge. The first two times the glass had fallen and he'd caught it. This was his tenth time, and he thought he pretty much had the balance of the thing now. Everything had its balancing point. You just had to find it.

He looked over at the sleeping Lorelle. Washed and clothed in the softest, warmest night clothes, she was tucked into the thin blankets of her bed. Their bed. Well, what had once been their bed.

Khyven had not listened to Zaith.

Or rather, he'd listened for a few weeks while he helped Rhenn bring back the light, bring everyone they could find back to the crown city.

Then things had settled down. The people began to feel more secure that another disaster wasn't going to crash down on their heads. They could go a day without seeing him.

The word had gone around after the war, that somehow Khyven was at the center of the victory. It wasn't true, of course. If anyone was at the center, it was Rhenn. But people tended to choose their own heroes and believe what they wanted to believe.

The most important thing—and Rhenn agreed—was that people needed someone to look to, someone to hang their hopes upon. Hopes for the future of the kingdom. Hopes in themselves, that they might measure their courage against their chosen hero's courage.

Khyven had been thrust into that place in the tale, and Rhenn encouraged him to accept it. The name Khyven the

Unkillable was now known from Usara to the rocky western seacoasts of Imprevar all the way south to the blinding lands of the Demaijos and over to the verdant islands of the Taur-El.

The people of Usara looked to Khyven and felt safer. So he did what Rhenn had bid him do. He made appearances. He walked through the city. He stopped at new building sites and talked to the people who toiled in the newly-returned sunshine.

When things settled down though, Rhenn had finally let him off the leash, and bid him to go in search of Lorelle. Two weeks was long enough.

He had prepared for a month-long hunt, a journey where he would have to learn the tricky art of woodland tracking, looking for prints in the dirt and grass, finding a trail and following it, asking local denizens for word of a Luminent who looked like a Nox except for the single golden lock at her brow.

He had prepared for it, but in the end he hadn't needed it.

He'd found her at the first place he looked: their green meadow. He'd found her sleeping in the now permanently sun-drenched meadow where they'd made love, where they'd had their last wonderful day before the horrible battle that had changed everything. He'd found her asleep, and he'd laid down next to her. He laid there until a normal, natural night had fallen. He'd fallen asleep near her.

When he'd awakened the next morning, she was gone. He didn't give pursuit. He just waited. That evening, she returned, and he pretended to be asleep. He didn't say anything, didn't try to engage with her. That first night, she just circled him, and then left.

She returned the next night, circled him again, and again he pretended to be asleep. This time, she laid down ten feet from him and slept again just where she'd been when he'd first found her.

The next night, she slept five feet closer. The next, she laid down by his side.

They never spoke. Four nights, it went like that. Khyven ate the food he'd prepared. Every night, he offered her some. Every night she refused, until finally she took a roll from him on the fifth night and ate it next to him. Two more nights it went that way, until the food bag was empty.

On that seventh day, he took her hand, and she let him. They went on a walk. When the walk ended, they were back in the palace. He brought her to their room, and laid her down in their bed. She slept.

Now he sat by her bed, playing with the woman-shaped glass. She'd been asleep for three days, and he waited. He didn't feel anxious. He didn't try to rush anything. It seemed destined, as though there wasn't any other way to do it. She would emerge in her time.

He brought her food every day. He ate with her. They never spoke. He toyed with the glass, practiced with the long daggers he'd taken off his doppelgänger—he was coming to like them— or practiced with The Diplomat, which had miraculously survived the entire war.

And so it was, three weeks after the fall of the great Harkandos and the breaking of the Giant army, when Usara and perhaps even the entire continent of Noksonon had nearly been destroyed, Lorelle Miere, Luminent and last of her line, awoke and for the first time since Khyven's death, spoke to him.

"Khyven?" she said sleepily.

"Yes," he said calmly. Joy and excitement thrummed through him, but he spoke as though her words were the most normal thing in the world.

"I've had horrible dreams."

He nodded.

"I'm sorry," she said.

"You found your way back. I knew you'd find your way back."

She sat up and hugged him, her warm, lithe body against his, and he squeezed her tightly in his arms.

"You came after me," she said.

"I did."

"I ... thought you wouldn't."

"Well, you're silly then."

"I couldn't hear you. I couldn't … see you."

"I know."

"I was lost."

"That's why I went looking for you."

She pressed her face into his neck desperately. "Thank you."

"That's what we do," he whispered. "We find each other when we're lost."

She inhaled a long breath of him, then kissed him on the neck. "You died."

"Yeah."

"It … broke me."

"I'm back."

"How is that?"

"It's a story. Want to have some breakfast and I'll tell you?"

"Yes?"

"It's a good one. I met a goddess."

"Is that a euphemism for flirting with pretty Humans?"

He chuckled. "No. An actual goddess."

"Then yes, I want to hear it."

"Very well then. Let's sneak down to the kitchens. We'll have to go the back way," Khyven said. "If Rhenn sees you, she's going to want you all to herself for at least a few hours."

He pulled her to her feet.

"I should go like this?" she asked, looking down at her nightgown.

"You should go however you like."

She dressed, and they scampered down to the kitchens like children.

He thought about the soul bond, and if it was something they could recreate.

But as they smiled at each other, eating pastries that the new head cook had baked fresh barely half an hour ago, dripping with drizzled sugar and cinnamon, Khyven knew it didn't matter.

Luminent soul bond or no, he belonged to her; she belonged to him.

They ate the pastries with gusto. She seemed ravenous, and he realized he was also ridiculously hungry. He watched her, just watched her. The elegance of her neck. The glitter in her eyes as she watched him over bites. He grinned.

"You've got something on your ..." He reached out and caught a drip of warm sugar frosting that had run down her chin. He brought it to his lips and licked his finger.

"I beg your pardon. Steal your own sugar!" she said.

"Come get it back." He smiled.

She kissed him, and he wrapped her up.

"Don't get your sticky fingers in my hair," she murmured with her lips to his.

"I'll do as I like, I think." He entwined his fingers in her luxuriant dark hair, and she squeaked, going rigid and trying to wriggle away.

"See how I am? Now you'll have to take a bath. And I'll have to help you."

She went soft in his embrace. "Oh. Well, in that case."

She pushed her sticky fingers into his hair, and they both laughed.

CHAPTER FIFTY-NINE

NHEVALOS

Nhevalos stepped out of the noktum cloak into Castle Noktos, right where the battle had been weeks ago. The great hall was bathed in sunlight through the glass skylights overhead, and he could see the blood stains. The Humans had removed the bodies, Nox, Troll, Human, and Eldroi alike, but the stains remained on the walls and the floor.

He had spent the past weeks traveling all over Noksonon, casting the *kairoi*. He had offered a place at his side to Elegathe, to go with him and witness what they had wrought. She had declined. Apparently, she wished to return to her lover in Imprevar.

It mattered little. He had no need of her anymore. For her service, he had gifted her with his last spare noktum cloak. She had left immediately.

It was for the best, really. She had been, quite frankly, tedious since she had lost faith in him. But despite Khyven's death, Nhevalos's plan had, in the end, prevailed.

Nhevalos still wasn't exactly sure what had happened there,

though he was almost certain it had to do with the properties of the Sword of Noksonon. Not even he knew the extent of what the Sword could do. Perhaps even the Sword did not know. Noktos had imbued the weapon with a substantial part of his life force, plus the entire life-forces of four other Eldroi. The *kairoi* were silent on the matter, but Nhevalos suspected the Sword had used one of those life forces to bring Khyven back from the brink of death.

Of course, Elegathe's abandonment and Khyven's return were all academic matters now, to be studied at leisure. The crux had arrived and gone, and what Nhevalos had hoped for had come to pass. He had won. He had completed his master project.

Oh, there were other Eldroi still lurking in Noksonon, but those that remained had gone back into hiding. Raos had returned to her deep, dark forest with her beloved Cakistros. Orios had vanished as completely as she had seventeen hundred years ago. Even Nhevalos would not be able to find her now, and he had no inclination to do so. Orios was powerful, so there was no need to poke at her. But she was no Harkandos. She did not have his sheer strength and, moreover, she did not have his drive. She might contemplate overtaking Noksonon in the years and centuries to come, but she would never act upon it.

Tovos had vanished before the fighting started. Nhevalos suspected once he had been freed from N'ssag's control, he'd fled from pure shame. He couldn't be left to plot his revenge, so Nhevalos would have to hunt him down. Tovos wasn't in Orio's class in any way. Finding him wouldn't be hard.

As to most of the mortal kingdoms, they were recovering. Some faster than others. A few had been utterly destroyed, but he was prepared to accept those losses. He, Nhevalos, had done the job. He, a Noksonoi who had been disregarded by his fellows as irrelevant, had rearranged the entire world. He had saved the mortals. Every creature on this continent owed its life to him.

For the first time, he wondered what he would do now. He

thought of throwing the *kairoi* to see what the future had in store, but for the first time in two millennia, he found that ...

He really didn't want to know.

A smile came to his face, and he laughed. Perhaps he would ... rest. He had been working so long, putting every possible resource into blunting the return of the Eldroi that the idea of rest was alien to him. But yes, perhaps a few mortal lifetimes worth of decadence would suit him. One should celebrate a victory of this magnitude.

He again looked around at the blood splatters on the wall and suddenly saw them as the art that they were. The blood was a painting, really. An abstract representation of centuries of work. It was his signature, a flourish at the culmination of a master work.

Perhaps I will move back here, he thought.

Though this had been his home before he'd embarked on his project, though Noktos himself had given Nhevalos this castle, he had not thought of it as his home for centuries. Perhaps it was time to return. Perhaps he would begin his new life next to the mortals of Usara.

There was an appeal to that. There was—

Nhevalos felt the unmistakable sensation of magic being used, that peculiar feeling of cold that was not so much cold as an ever-so-slight expanding of the arteries of the body. An unnatural twisting of the fabric of reality. Most Humans only experienced this sensation as a "chill" of foreboding, but Nhevalos knew exactly what was happening.

He spun, and to his astonishment, the mortal primaries of his plan materialized before his eyes.

Rhenn, Slayter, Vohn, Lorelle, and Khyven all stood there, but there were more. Elegathe was also with them in her low-cut dark robes and the noktum cloak he had given her. Behind them all loomed Rauvelos. He looked, as ever, like the steward that he was.

None of them had been there a moment before, and Nhevalos was certain they hadn't used the noktum cloak. He had not felt the movement in the Dark, only a slight usage of magic. *Slight* usage. Where had they come from?

"Well, that worked a treat," Slayter said, and Nhevalos caught the fading glow of orange from his hand.

"The Lore Magic blunting?" Rhenn asked in a completely humorless voice.

"No, no." Slayter shook his head, then paused. "Except, well, yes. That worked as well. I'm ninety-seven percent certain that is how Harkandos fooled him about the duplicate Khyven."

"What is this?" Nhevalos demanded. "What are you ...?"

Nhevalos couldn't say why he suddenly felt the need to look to his right, but he did.

Another figure emerge from the deep shadows cut from the room by the bright light.

Paralos!

She stepped into the sunlight. Her straight black hair hung to her waist, just as it had centuries ago when they had begun this project. She wore a black gown, except this time it was not created to tantalize him. It had a tall neck that ended in a subtle ruffle beneath her chin and sleeves that extended all the way to her wrists, again with that understated ruffle. Only the black tips of her shoes showed beneath the floor-length hem as she stopped and fixed her dark gaze upon him.

They had freed her! How had they freed her?

He looked at Paralos, then at Slayter. That mortal mage had somehow pulled Paralos from the noktum! Such magic should have been beyond him, not to mention he had just orchestrated a spell that Nhevalos hadn't seen and still didn't understand.

Nhevalos had seen none of this in the *kairoi*, though he'd thrown it three times to keep tabs on this very group.

A swift chill ran through him. He realized he was in very real danger here, but checked the urge to flee. Rauvelos was, after all, right there, and Rauvelos was his loyal servant.

All of this flashed through Nhevalos's mind in an instant. Slayter was still talking.

"No, I meant the illusion spell. I only had a second to see

what Harkandos did, so it took far longer than normal to recreate it, but I think I got it."

"That's enough, Slayter," Rhenn said, moving to the front of the group. She had her sword in hand, the one that made her impervious to sunlight. She stepped into the bright light without flinching.

Khyven paced her, the Sword of Noksonon sheathed on his back, his hands open and empty, but the Ringer was smiling his casual, deadly smile. Nhevalos knew how fast Khyven could draw his weapons. That the Sword was on his back meant virtually nothing. Normally, Nhevalos would not have worried about Khyven's prowess. He knew how the blue wind worked; he knew how to evade it.

But the Sword was another matter altogether. That Sword was made to kill Eldroi, and in Khyven's hands, it could be devastating.

Nhevalos cleared his throat, deciding that a firm and commanding tone was the route to take.

"You have done well," Nhevalos said. "I congratulate you."

"He congratulates us," Rhenn said. "Do you feel congratulated, Khyven?"

"You set us up to die," Khyven said, still smiling.

"Nhevalos, I acknowledge that this castle once belonged to you," Rhenn said. "But I have claimed it for the people of Usara. We won it in combat, a combat for which we paid dearly. Castle Noktos belongs to us now."

"Of course we did," Nhevalos said. "That was the plan all along. We are victorious—"

"*We* are," Vohn said. "*You* are not a part of *we*."

"We want you to go," Rhenn said.

"Go?" Nhevalos narrowed his eyes. "This is *my* castle—"

"Not anymore." Rhenn shook her head.

"I am master here," Nhevalos said. "It was given to me by Noktos himself."

"The laws of the Eldroi no longer apply," Paralos said softly. "You saw to that. So what Noktos might have wanted, or not wanted, is no longer relevant."

"Paralos—"

"They have won it from you, *beloved*," Paralos said softly.

Nhevalos turned to Rauvelos. "I think its steward will have something to say about that. He serves the master of this castle. That master is me."

Rauvelos inclined his head. "I did promise to serve you in life and in death, Nhevalos. I have done so. Out of respect for you, I even served you, or at least your plan, with part of my new life."

Nhevalos blinked as he remembered the oath the noktum phoenix had made so long ago. In life, and in death. His fight with Jai'ketakos had incinerated the noktum phoenix, as it had been designed to. But the moment the noktum phoenix had perished and been reborn, he had served out his oath.

"I bear you no ill will, Nhevalos," Rauvelos said. "I am keen to witness what will transpire here."

Nhevalos swallowed. So he would get no help from Rauvelos.

"This victory belongs to me, more than any of you," Nhevalos said. "I put together the impossible sequence of events that allowed you to win. I gave you the tools to face Harkandos. I *guided* you to this place."

"Yes," Khyven said. "And then you sacrificed all of us."

"To save Humanity!"

"Are you trying to tell us you love Humanity?" Rhenn asked. "Paralos told us about your project. You have no love for Humanity or anyone else. You treat us like pebbles on your game board, to be used or sacrificed when you see fit."

"I never claimed to love Humanity," Nhevalos said. "Only to save it. Which I have done. None of you would have been prepared without me. I brought you to victory."

"You brought them to defeat," Elegathe said. "They fought their way to victory."

"Khyven would be dead without the Sword of Noksonon," Nhevalos said. "I gave that to you!"

"It wasn't the Sword," Khyven said.

Nhevalos blinked. Not the Sword? Then what ...? "I prepared you. I gave you gifts you could never have found without me. I made this victory possible!"

"That's why we're not going to kill you," Khyven said. "That's why we're giving you a choice."

"You're ... giving me a *choice?*" Nhevalos spluttered. His face grew hot with rage.

"Exactly. Go." Khyven reached up and deliberately pulled the Sword of Noksonon from its sheath. Nhevalos could feel the power of the thing even at this distance. "Or don't go."

His predatory smile showed teeth now.

Nhevalos's gaze flicked to the looming noktum phoenix. "And Rauvelos?"

"He can stay." Khyven smiled. "We like him."

Nhevalos clenched his teeth. "I am the architect of your victory."

Rhenn swung her sword back and forth in front of herself like she was warming up. "You're the architect of Khyven's death, my death, my resurrection, my enslavement, Lorelle's insanity, Vohn's torture, and Shalure's half-life. Normally, somebody does even one of those things, we kill him, but we acknowledge your higher plan. You ... had your part to play. So take your life and be grateful."

"Grateful?"

"But go," Rhenn continued. "And don't ever come back."

"If you return," Khyven added. "If you carve any more of your spells into us, if you try to manipulate us in any way, we will consider it an act of war. We'll respond in kind."

"Khyven ..." Nhevalos said through his teeth. "You cannot conceive of the sacrifices I have made. Your sacrifices pale in comparison. This is far more my victory than yours."

"Then take your victory and celebrate it with your friends," Vohn said.

"That isn't us," Rhenn clarified.

"It doesn't have to be this way," Nhevalos growled. "The

threat is over. The war is over."

"And this is how we choose to celebrate," Khyven said.

Nhevalos looked from face to face, and he grew grim. He saw no room to move this conversation, not at present.

"Goodbye, *beloved*." Paralos waved, a subtle and dismissive gesture.

"As you desire," he said through his teeth. "But know this: I find you collectively ungrateful. This is the thanks of mortals, I suppose."

"You don't have to suppose," Rhenn said. "This *is* our thanks, make no mistake."

Nhevalos triggered his noktum cloak and vanished.

CHAPTER SIXTY

RHENN

It was the longest summer Rhenn had ever seen. They were easily a month into fall, but the gentle temperatures lingered. Even the leaves on the seasonal trees seemed confused. Only a few of them had started to turn, throwing polka dots of yellow into the green.

The renovations of Usara were coming along so well that she had extended their projects to Castle Noktos. Rauvelos had decided to stay on as castle steward and assist the Humans, Nox, and other mortals in remaking it to house people smaller than Eldroi. Rhenn planned to create a stone road between the castle and Usara, something that would stand the test of time. The castle and the city were too far apart to join them—at least at this point—but she wanted the connection cemented.

Things were going so smoothly that, for the first time in months, she had found some time for herself, and she stood at the edge of the noktum that paralleled the stone road that, as yet, only existed in her imagination. But she had already brought enough of her imaginary projects into reality these past months.

The stone road was coming.

She had arrived at this halfway point between Castle Noktos and Usara, this halfway point between light and darkness. Straddling the two worlds was where she lived now.

In the past months, Slayter had perfected her sword. She could now stand in the daylight—as long as she had the sword on her person—for hours. But the Dark was her home now. It cooled her when she stepped into the noktum. She could feel her body relax. The sword protected her from the sunlight, yes, but it still felt unnatural. The very fibers of her body could sense that they were a hair's breadth away from obliteration. When beneath the sun, she was like a woman with lead weights on her ankles, standing on a raft in the middle of the ocean. Always a little bit on alert. Never fully relaxed. Always waiting for the raft to tip.

She slid her hands down to her belly, now a pronounced swell with her unborn child. E'maz's child. She had wondered so many times whether it would perish, but it had seemed to thrive through the horrible traumas Rhenn herself had endured. A survivor. The baby would have to be, she supposed.

Rhenn entered the noktum, felt its cool darkness flow over her, and breathed a sigh of relief. She walked for a time, wending this way and that through the dark trees. In the distance, she saw a Cakistro ponderously working its way deeper into the dark. The giant spiders were such a frightening sight, but they never bothered her. They didn't seem to bother anyone, except to frighten them from a distance.

After a few minutes, she found the place she sought, a beautiful little glade, a purely noktum glade. Purple trees ringed this place and in its center, a natural stone pillar jutted up at an angle. It looked like a holy place, something almost intentional. It felt like nature herself had built this glade in homage to something that Rhenn, as a sentient creature, could never fully understand.

She stopped a few feet from the angled monolith, descended to her knees, and withdrew N'ssag's ruby-topped rod. It was the weapon he'd killed E'maz with. It was the artifact he'd used to inject Rhenn with the life-force of the Mouth Dog.

She took a deep breath, then lifted her tunic to expose her side and a little part of her distended belly. She ran a loving hand over the baby again, then carefully put the sharp tip of the rod at her ribcage, just at the point where N'ssag had placed it shortly before she'd killed him.

With a wince, she jammed it between her ribs and upward, carefully avoiding the baby. She gasped as the point shoved up, inward, following that old path and nearly touching her heart. The baby kicked fiercely, frightened.

Blood trickled down her side, one thin streak.

Tears welled in her eyes at the pain, at the baby's distress, but she had to do this. She had to know.

She closed her eyes, imagining the wooden room where she had defeated N'ssag, where she had seen E'maz's ghost.

She had told Lorelle about the visitation, how E'maz had arrived with her daughter in his arms when Rhenn had nearly lost her soul to N'ssag, how E'maz had seemed so real. So very real ...

Lorelle had suggested it was only her projection of E'maz, that Rhenn had needed strength, and her mind—her heart—had found that strength in the image of E'maz and her baby.

For these past months, Rhenn had been content to leave it at that. After all, she'd been busy. She'd pushed the notion to the back of her mind: that it had actually been E'maz, some residue of him left in the spike's ruby, some part of his life force still there, still trapped. A ghost of her lover.

But as the kingdom began to right itself, she thought more about it, and the idea plagued her.

The wooden room in her mind, where she had fought and defeated N'ssag, appeared startlingly fast, like it had never left, like it had simply been waiting for her to return.

This time, there was no chair with its thick, unbreakable ropes. There was no beastly and enormous N'ssag. In place of the chair stood a wicker basinet. It rocked slowly, and Rhenn covered her mouth with her hand.

Cautiously, she approached, fearing what she might see in that basinet. Not for the first time, Rhenn considered that the baby inside her might be some kind of abomination. How could the undead create life, after all?

She peeked over the edge of the basinet.

The baby was swaddled in clean white cloths, nothing of her visible except that same cheek Rhenn had seen before. She reached out a shaky hand to touch the baby, but froze halfway. She felt a foreboding and withdrew her arm.

"Rhenn ..."

She whirled around. There was no one in the room. But she knew that voice. That had been E'maz.

She kept turning, glancing everywhere, then made a second inspection, slower, studying every grain of wood in the walls, ever possible wisp of dust in the air, searching for his figure.

"Rhenn ..." the voice came again. It wasn't coming from the wooden room. It was distant, heard by her real ears, heard in the glade where she was kneeling.

"Open your eyes," E'maz's voice said again, and Rhenn retreated from the wooden room.

Her eyes snapped open. At first, she saw the angled stone before her, but then she focused past it, just beyond the leaning stone.

E'maz, transparent and ghostly, stood in the glade.

"What are you doing, my love?" he asked gently.

"I knew it," she whispered, and the tears from the pain, from the fear, finally spilled over. "I knew it."

"Take that thing out of your side," he said.

"No."

"Rhenn, it's dangerous."

"I know. But if I pull it out, you'll vanish."

He didn't answer.

"You'll vanish, won't you?"

"It's hurting you," he said.

"I've been hurt before," she said. "It's worth it to see you."

He shook his head. "I can't stay here with you."

"You're in the gem. A part of you is there, isn't it? That's how you came to me when I needed you."

He hesitated, then said, "No."

Except E'maz was a horrible liar.

"E'maz, you don't know what we can do now. Slayter, he … He has become ridiculously powerful with all of these Giant artifacts he's unearthed. If your life is in the gem, he could bring you back. He brought Paralos back from the noktum."

E'maz shook his head. "Don't, Rhenn. I don't want you to do that. This … It isn't me. It's an echo of me."

"He could put you into a new body."

"No!" E'maz darkened, clenching his fists. "No. You will not do that."

"Why not?"

"Who's body, Rhenn? Some innocent?"

"Of course not!"

"A corpse, then? How would you bring me back?"

"I …"

"No. I am … I don't want you to do that."

"I want you back," she whispered, and the tears started again.

He came to her then, his ethereal body appearing to walk, though his feet did not depress the grass. He touched her chin, and she thought she felt the barest wisp of warmth.

"I can't be here with you," he said.

"Then what is this?"

"A ghost," he said.

"Then I want the ghost."

"You are going to hurt the baby," he said. "Is that what you want?"

"Of course not."

"Then you have to let me go."

"E'maz—"

"Remove the rod. Let me go. You will have our daughter, and that must be enough."

"I'll take it out, and I won't do this again."

"Good."

"Until she's born. Then I am coming back here. If all I can have of you is a ghost, then that is what I will have."

His lips pressed together in a firm line, and he shook his head.

"I love you, E'maz. If all that remains of you is an echo, I will love the echo."

"I'll never be more than this. You don't want that in your life—"

"I'll decide what I want and don't want in my life," she said.

"This isn't a good idea."

"Is anything ever really a good idea?" she echoed what he'd told her when he'd first taken her to his bed after her transformation.

He shook his head ruefully. "I'm not going to sway you, am I?"

"What do you think?"

"Crazy foreigner," he muttered.

"You hold on," she whispered. "You understand? You hold on for me."

"I should have fallen in love with a milkmaid," he muttered.

She half laughed, half sobbed again.

"I'm coming back for you," she said. "I'm coming back."

He closed his eyes, resigned, and he whispered, "I love you."

She yanked the rod from her side. He vanished.

She clenched her teeth against the pain, pressed a hand to her side. The baby kicked. Rhenn cradled her belly with both hands, one clean and one bloody. The baby's distress faded.

"I will see you soon, E'maz," she whispered. "I will see you soon …"

CHAPTER SIXTY-ONE

SHALURE

halure rode across the white fields, and the blue sky seemed more blue than it had the previous day, more so than the day before.

Her mount ran so fast her hooves sounded like thunder. Shalure could have encouraged the horse to take to the skies, but the truth was she enjoyed the feel of riding on the ground, the impact of the hooves, the powerful churn of the horse's muscles.

For one fleeting instant, she thought of naming her steed. She'd had the same thought a thousand times before, but somehow that thought always fluttered away.

After all, what need did she have for a name when steed and rider were always together? When there were no commands or obeisance between them? When their communication was instantaneous and always aligned?

Shalure would think something, and her steed would work to achieve that something. She could feel the beat of the horse's heart, the flick of her emotions, the sounds that caught her ears, and the sights that called her gaze. They moved as one. Perhaps that was why there was no need for names between them.

Shalure rode until they crested a rise over a great valley. The white grass had given way to green, the white trees to green, and below stood a small azure lake.

She had never seen this lake before, but that wasn't surprising. Senji's land seemed endless and constantly changing, especially of late.

To the left of the lake grew a single silver poplar, enormous, larger than any poplar Shalure ever seen. Its thick, low branches twisted out over waters so blue they rivaled the sky.

Shalure slowed, and both she and her mount felt the call of that water, the thirst in their bodies. They dropped to a walk and descended the slope.

Shalure fell to thinking about her friends. Whenever Vohn read to her, she could hear his voice in her mind, distant, like the buzz of a hive of bees somewhere behind her, and when she focused on it, she could hear the words.

Sometimes, when she was occupied with something else, she would miss the buzzing and Vohn's words would seem like her own thoughts before she realized it was actually him.

But this time, it wasn't him. She was simply ... recalling upon some of the things that were happening elsewhere, in the world where her former body lay, in the world Humans thought of as the "real" world.

It made her smile.

Khyven had become a legend. He was on the lips of every person who had survived the Killing Night. Some made offerings to him at holy places. Some people used his name to punctuate their stronger emotions in curses or blessings. Some used it as a prayer to protect them.

She could feel their homage in this place. She felt it, perhaps, even more strongly than Khyven himself felt it.

Although he *did* feel it. She knew because, though she did not do it often, she would sometimes return to that other world to check on her friends. It was difficult, as time ran differently here. One hour there could be as much as a year here, which was why Vohn's habit of reading to her every day had been an incessant and distracting buzz in the back of her mind.

When she would return, she would always check on Khyven first. She still loved him. He was her first and only love. Oh, she had known the affections of a few men during her life in the other world, but she hadn't understood love until Khyven had risked himself to save her. Until this man whom she had betrayed, whom she had tried to use for her own selfish desires, had treated her humanely, had taken her in when he'd had no earthly reason to do so.

He had many new responsibilities in his new life, but he balanced them deftly on those broad shoulders. From selfish Ringer to protector of his family to hero of the people, Khyven had grown nicely into the icon his worshippers imagined.

And he had done something amazing with that worship. In the past months, he had rekindled the temples of Senji. Not only had he led the refurbishing of the mostly forgotten temple in the crown city and revitalized its ancient grandeur, but he had traveled to five of the closest cities and done the same.

He passed the worship that came to him on to Senji's memory, a tribute to her sacrifice.

It was lovely, and Shalure thought it was part of why this world, this once predominantly white and misty world, was growing in color and scope. Once only white grass and white sky, it was now filled with colors.

She and her mount clopped down to the water's edge. Shalure dropped off and felt the glorious impact of her own feet on the verdant ground. She pulled off her helmet and set it on a small hummock, then dropped to her belly and put her lips to the cool, clear water.

Her mount drank similarly a couple feet to her right.

"What's your name?"

Shalure started upright, water splashing her face. She blinked past the droplets as she rose to her feet.

A girl sat on the lowest limb of the tree. She couldn't have been more than six years old, and her skin was tanned from long exposure to the sun. She had ice blue eyes and long white hair tied back in a lopsided braid.

She hopped down from the branch and walked toward Shalure. She wore a strip of wolf's fur over her flat chest and a wolf's fur loincloth.

"You're the first person I've seen here. What's your name?" the girl asked.

"I'm Shalure. How ... How did you get here?"

The girl looked over at the tree, then down at the water, then back to Shalure. "I don't know. I think I was ... Well, I was just here. I can't remember what came before, except ..."

"Except what?"

"There were swords. I remember swords. But I can't seem to find one here. I looked in the tree, but there aren't any swords in the tree."

Shalure's heart beat faster. The temples. Khyven and the temples. The worship of thousands, directed back to the temples.

"Here." Shalure drew one of her short swords, flipped it around, and handed it to the girl hilt-first. "Try this."

The girl's face brightened. She took the hilt and swung it left and right like it was a missing part of her hand, finally returned.

"Yes!" She said joyfully.

"Is this where you live?" Shalure asked.

"Yes," the girl said. "I think, though, that maybe I live everywhere."

"I think maybe you do, too," Shalure said.

"Would you like to see my tree?" The girl asked, holding out her hand.

"I would like that very much."

The girl took her hand and led her toward the tree.

"You'll like it. It's a good tree. And it has silver leaves. I like silver leaves."

"So do I."

"Oh, I forgot to tell you. I'm Senji."

Shalure grinned, and tears filled her eyes as she walked

toward the tree. "What a beautiful name ..."

CHAPTER SIXTY-TWO

KHYVEN

The first chill wind of winter swirled through the crown city of Usara. The smell of it, the sharpness of it, invigorated Khyven. He had always enjoyed winter, the challenge of the severe weather, the falling snows. He was looking forward to the warm hearth, a crackling fire with friends close at hand.

Of course, the leaves hadn't even fallen from the seasonal trees yet. Golds and reds filled the greenswards of the city and dotted the mostly evergreen forests beyond the walls. Until today, summer had seemed endless. Slayter had commented on it twice already, that it was unseasonably warm for an unusually long time. The warmth had extended halfway into fall. It was as though there had been enough hardship in this place that the gods had decreed the growing season extended, that the easy days of summer should last until the people of Usara got back on their feet.

And they had. The crown city thrived. Surrounding hamlets and villages had rebuilt at a quick pace, and even the distant duchies and baronies had begun rebuilding.

The crown city could never have come so far so fast if not for the influx of new people. It seemed that anyone with even a hint of wanderlust—or religious fervor—was making a pilgrimage to Usara to see Khyven the Unkillable, the man who'd brought back the sun.

The unending stream of visitors brought trade, new ideas, and an infusion of exotic people from far flung kingdoms. Demaijos, Shadowvar, even Taur-Els and Brightlings, not to mention Sandrunners, Triadans, and Imprevarans. Rhenn's open-door policy invited people of all races and creeds, and there was a surprisingly low amount of conflict, as though the people of Noksonon had had enough of war.

Of course, there were those who entered the city with chips on their shoulders, or were more interested in violence than putting in a hard day's work, but Rhenn's masterful policing of the city, as well as the population's intolerance for such nonsense, ensured that these anomalies remained small.

By and large, the city flowed with a wealth of goods and extra hands. Looking around at the new shops, the shining paint jobs on the old shops, and the public works going up, it was hard to believe that only a few months ago, this city had been an abandoned slaughterhouse with half her population decimated. It simply wasn't the same place.

Khyven stood in the center of the Night Ring which, soon enough, wouldn't be recognizable as the arena of blood and death it had once been. The black sands had not seen a fight since the days of Vamreth, and they never would again. Rhenn had ordered a statue built in its center. It was going to be five stories tall, a figure rising above the pentagonal walls, inviting others from all walks of life and distant kingdoms to this place where the Second Human-Giant War had begun and ended. Rhenn had intended that figure to be Khyven, welcoming all visitors to the city.

He had staged an open rebellion.

She told him that the pilgrims came to Usara because of him.

He told her: If you build that gaudy thing, I'm leaving.

He liked the idea of a statue; he just didn't want it to be him. In the end, they'd agreed that the statue ought to be the goddess Senji, who Khyven knew was the real hero.

Khyven paused in his reverie, raised his head, and then smiled.

Lorelle had found him. He knew she would. He had snuck away from the palace to watch the sunrise in the center of the arena where all of this nonsense had begun a year ago.

Senji's Braid, had it only been a year?

Khyven felt her approach; he didn't hear her. Her light Luminent feet were silent. No, it wasn't sound that had alerted him. He imagined it was because he could feel her smile through his back.

Their connection was a warm and joyous thing. When she was within thirty feet of him, he could always feel her. Sometimes, he imagined their soul-bond had grown back, but sometimes he thought it was because he ... expected her to be near. Because that was the way the world was supposed to be. Because he loved her.

They could have asked Slayter if their soul-bond was regrowing, the tendrils of their souls slowly healing. The mage would have taken on the project with fervor—like he did everything else.

But Khyven hadn't asked him to. The truth was, Khyven didn't want to know. He already knew everything he needed to know about Lorelle, about himself, about the two of them together.

"The statue, eh?" she said. "I thought you had already hashed this out with Rhenn."

"I did. It's going to be Senji."

"I don't remember you being this religious before Senji kissed you and sent you back into the world. Should I be jealous?" She swept around him and fell into his arms, the back of her hand languidly pressed against her forehead as she draped herself artfully over him.

"She didn't kiss me."

"So you're not in a kissing mood, is what you're saying?"

He laughed and kissed her.

When they stopped, she righted herself and breathed, "Well, that was answer enough for me. I didn't taste a bit of infidelity in that kiss."

"Is that something Luminents can taste?"

"We can do all kinds of things."

He chuckled.

Lorelle winked and stood on her own feet, looked up at where the top of the statue would be. "It's going to be good, I think."

"Oh, this statue is just what the city needs now." He nodded at the base of the enormous project, which had barely begun. "Rhenn is something of a genius."

"She is."

The statue's construction was being led by an extremely talented Taur-El stone smith. Khyven liked the bull-headed people from the south. They were soft-spoken, intelligent, hardworking, and didn't seem to have a violent bone in their bodies. It was a nice counterpoint to the people he had grown up with. The stone smith's name was Cenquil, and Khyven thought he and the Taur-El were becoming friends.

"Although I do like the idea of my Human being five stories tall," Lorelle said. "Are you sure Rhenn and I can't convince you?"

"You do *not* like that idea."

"You're the master of my mind now, are you?"

"Heart."

"What?"

"The master of your mind *and* heart. I know you meant to say that. I just thought I'd remind you."

"Oh really?"

"And body. My apologies. Master of your mind, your heart, and your body. I want it all."

"I think maybe you'll get none of it. Ever again."

"Just try and stay away." He winked.

She purposely stepped a pace away from him and crossed her arms over her chest. She stayed that way for the briefest of moments, then flung herself into his arms again. He caught her, laughing.

"I tried," she said. "I tried my best to stay away. How did I do?"

He picked her up and started toward the arched exit that would most quickly lead to the palace.

"You're just going to carry me home?" she asked.

"Well, that was a dicey moment back there. I'm frightened you'll try to stay away again. I'm not taking that chance. In fact, I'm having a collar fashioned. With a leash. That way I can—"

She pinched the tender underside of his arm.

"Ow! Careful, I'll drop you," he said.

"That's the idea."

"Oh. Well then I'll hold you forever."

"That's a better idea."

He laughed and continued up the archway, toward the palace.

Toward the future.

ABOUT THE AUTHOR

Todd Fahnestock is an award-winning, #1 bestselling author of fantasy for all ages and winner of the New York Public Library's Books for the Teen Age Award. *Threadweavers* and *The Whisper Prince Trilogy* are two of his bestselling epic fantasy series. He is a founder of *Eldros Legacy*—a multi-author,  shared-world mega-epic fantasy series—three-time winner of the Colorado Authors League Award for Writing Excellence, and two-time finalist for the Colorado Book Award for *Tower of the Four: The Champions Academy* (2021) and *Khyven the Unkillable* (2022). His passions are great stories and his quirky, fun-loving family. When he's not writing, he travels the country meeting fans, gets inundated with befuddling TikTok videos by his son, plays board games with his wife, plots future stories with his daughter, and plays vigorously with Galahad the Weimaraner. Visit Todd at toddfahnestock.com.

AUTHOR'S NOTE

This is the final installment of *Eldros Legacy: Legacy of Shadows*, and I'm getting a little misty-eyed. What an epic adventure this has been. What a Herculean task! From the beginning brainstorming of the joint world building to coordinating the various authors who participated to just keeping my own roster of characters on track. There was no end of hard work, but it was a labor of love.

These characters, starting with Khyven, spoke to me from the start. And they did more than talk. They wrenched the story from my grasp, often saying:

"Take a back seat, keyboard monkey. We know where this is going."

(I'm glad *somebody* did.)

And it just got worse as the volumes progressed. By the time we reached *Slayter and the Dragon*, I just threw my hands up (or more accurately, kept them avidly on the keyboard).

I feel that *Slayter and the Dragon* and *Bane of Giants* are actually one huge book. The story slithers from one volume to the other without stopping. As I finished *Slayter*, I dove right into *Bane* without skipping a beat. Everything was pointing to the end, and in that way the writing was actually a little easier.

Writers train themselves exhaustively to create characters, weave plot threads, and birth worldbuilding pieces. Hours and hours, years and years. But *ending* character arcs? *Tying off* plot threads? *Closing down* worldbuilding pieces? Not as much.

I know that I, personally, have only a fraction of the experience ending stories that I do beginning them. But with *Bane of Giants*, it came fairly naturally. I had so many things I'd been wanting to do from the beginning. Hero moments for Khyven and Rhenn. Brilliant moments for Slayter. Moments of wisdom for Vohn. And most importantly, since this series started specifically as a story for the fans, I wanted to give the readers what *they* wanted, as much as I could determine it and as much as I could fit in the book.

To that end, there is more falling action in this story than any story I've ever written. No less than twelve chapters. Thirty thousand words of this novel is just falling action, scenes that take place after the big climax.

I wrote those thirty thousand words while landscaping.

Books are sometimes forged in unusual places. Crammed into a tiny laundry room. Backed into the wall at a crowded cafe. Sneaking in chapters at the family dinner table after everyone has gone to sleep. Capturing moments while sitting in a plastic chair at the airport.

In that tradition, the last half of *Bane of Giants* was forged among the weeds of Pueblo West. Okay... So I was not actually sitting in weeds while I was writing. But I was down there doing some landscaping.

The job was a week-long adventure.

I would not have chosen this situation. This necessary landscaping popped up at the most inconvenient time, but it had to be done. The last thing I wanted to do was drive an hour and a half away and pull weeds. I wanted to stay on the final leg of the *Bane of Giants* journey.

So I married them up. Galahad, my Weimaraner, and I drove down to the house, and for a week I landscaped and wrote. He had the time of his life.

Strangely, so did I...

The physical exertion sparked my creativity. Spending intense hours inside my head crafting story and typing it down sparked a compulsion to move my body.

And any time I am productive, it lends me inspiration.

So, this unwanted happenstance created the perfect storm. I wrote until I had 2,000 words, fell asleep, got up, worked in the sun for eight hours, then wrote 2,000 more words, then fell asleep, got up, worked in the sun for eight hours... and so on. The surge of utter productivity lent me some strange kind of invincibility.

And every one of the final twelve chapters was written during that surge. I can still feel the grit of the dirt and the smell of the weeds. I can feel the cuts on my forearms from all of the prickly branches.

It was interestingly appropriate, though. I was shaping up the house and yard just as I was shaping up the final bits of *Bane of Giants*.

After all the jungle I hacked through in this epic story, it seemed appropriate that the final bit of it should be punctuated by whacking through actual weeds.

I hope this adventure was as exciting for you as it was for me, and I thank you for taking the path all the way to its end.

See you in Noksonon...

-Todd

IF YOU LIKED...

Eldros Legacy (Legacy of Shadows)

Khyven the Unkillable

Lorelle of the Dark

Rhenn the Traveler

Slayter and the Dragon

Bane of Giants (forthcoming)

Tower of the Four

Episode 1 – The Quad

Episode 2 – The Tower

Episode 3 – The Test

The Champions Academy (Episodes 1-3 compilation)

Episode 4 – The Nightmare

Episode 5 – The Resurrection

Episode 6 – The Reunion

The Dragon's War (Episodes 4-6 compilation)

Threadweavers

Wildmane

The GodSpill

Threads of Amarion

God of Dragons

The Whisper Prince Series

Fairmist
The Undying Man
The Slate Wizards

Standalone Novels

Charlie Fiction
Summer of the Fetch

Non-fiction

Ordinary Magic

Tower of the Four Short Stories

"Urchin"
"Royal"
"Princess"

Other Short Stories

Parallel Worlds Anthology — "Threshold"
Dragonlance: The Cataclysm — "Seekers"
Dragonlance: Heroes & Fools — "Songsayer"
Dragonlance: The History of Krynn —
"The Letters of Trayn Minaas"

Other Eldros Legacy Novels